GORKY

GORKY

Michael Nilsen

Matador
9 Priory Business Park,
Wistow Road, Kibworth Beauchamp,
Leicestershire. LE8 0RX
Tel: 0116 279 2299
Email: books@troubador.co.uk
Web: www.troubador.co.uk/matador
Twitter: @matadorbooks

ISBN 978 1788033 688

British Library Cataloguing in Publication Data.
A catalogue record for this book is available from the British Library.

Printed and bound in the UK by TJ International, Padstow, Cornwall
Typeset in 11pt Minion Pro by Troubador Publishing Ltd, Leicester, UK

Matador is an imprint of Troubador Publishing Ltd

To my grandma, nana, and two grandads,
unfortunately no longer with us...

PART 1
TERRA INCOGNITA

1.

The Disease

*'If thou art not for thyself, who will be for thee?
But if thou art for thyself alone, wherefore art
thou?'*

Hillel Hagadol

A long time ago, so far in the past that it could easily be the future, was a village not unlike one that existed in your Iron Age, apart from the odd difference, of course. Life was fairly idyllic there until a virulent disease brought in by a mysterious source took hold of the community. The disease initially spread in the recipient insidiously, and once it had established itself, tufts of body hair would fall out; fingernails would drop out; gums would rot and teeth would drop out; then skin would excoriate, until the sufferer would bleed to death.

When the disease had really taken hold of the community, the elders decided it would be a good idea to hold a meeting. Some of the young ones wanted to be included in the parley, but the elders deemed they were not old enough. Some of the elders were worried that if the elders with the disease were included in the meeting, the elders who were clear would contract the malady, and without elders to guide the tribe, extinction would be certain. So, those elders who believed they had not yet caught it stood on one side of a large Perspex partition, and those who obviously had, stood the other side. There were one or two unprincipled elders who claimed they had not caught it, claiming they were naturally bald, until someone checked under their armpits. One made the outlandish claim he had begun shaving under his arms, then someone called him a woman: he countered by saying why should it be only women who shave under their armpits; another, fairly forward thinking elder said, but why should women have to shave under their armpits: and it was finally agreed to convene an important meeting concerning armpits.

So there they were, the gathering of the elders, trying to look noble, but knew the situation was well out of hand. Boswald, the leader of the Hookookoo tribe began, 'People of Firkin Forest, villagers, comrades, we have reached an unprecedented point in our history: we face the horrid possibility of extinction. Who knows how many now have this dreaded disease. Who knows how long before complete annihilation of all the tribes. All I know is, we must do something before it is too late'.

There was a silence; a silence that seemed to penetrate time; a silence that was the underlying existence of eternity; a silence which was always there, waiting: a silence which would not go away until it had the final say.

'Yes, but what?' said Gavin of the Geekeekee section of the village, a man who had once wrestled a rhinoceros type creature and killed it with his bare hands: but who now stood there trying to stop a large strip of flesh from falling off his forearm.

'Yes, what?' said mighty Argon, who had once dared to venture twenty miles, the furthest anyone had journeyed from the village, but had not been permitted to tell the full truth of his exploits. However, a man who was feted for his indomitable bravery, but who was now petrified because he had woken to find a large clump of hair on his pillow, but had not told anyone.

Now, while all this was going on, I was hiding behind a hedge, watching. It was obvious to me that the elders were at a loss, but I should not have been surreptitiously listening: so I kept quiet. Who am I? Well, I often wonder myself, but as I am telling the story, I suppose it is only courtesy that I introduce myself: they call me Gorky. I am nobody exceptional: in fact, I am able to walk around the village fairly anonymously: but, I watch, and, I listen. If there is a story being told by the fire, I am there, assimilating. I have secretly attended many of the elders' meetings. Whenever there is any kind of discussion by anyone of note, I try to be there, somewhere. I have accrued much of the knowledge of our people. My function in the village is to carry pails of water from the river to the water tanks. I am known by most as the waterboy. Over the past few years, as I have grown into a young man, my toleration for being called 'boy' has diminished. I am growing impatient at being ignored, and as I listened to the elders' procrastinations, something welled up inside me, something strong, something undeniable. The future of our people depended on this indecisive bunch: and all they could do was peer at each other through the Perspex and say, 'What?'

I had to speak before my head exploded: but I had to present myself in an appropriate manner. My opening gambit could not be, 'Hi, I'm Gorky, a mumbling fool who cannot construct a coherent sentence.' I instinctively leaped from the bush. 'It is true, gentlemen, that we have reached a critical time in our village's history. It is also true that if we do not take action forthwith, it could prove irrevocably cataclysmic. The extermination of our race looms, and it is now, while there is still a vestige of strength in our bones, that one of us must venture forth inorder to discover a panacea. I have heard told that beyond the Dead Forest that circumscribes Firkin Forest, there is a vast desert; and beyond that vast desert is a mysterious Forest of Life; and beyond this forest is a great mountain range; and beyond this, there is a lake, a sacred lake known as Sacradia: and this lake possesses extraordinary healing powers. It is said that who ever drinks from this lake will be cured of all ailment, no matter what it is. I propose, gentlemen, that I venture forth on a quest to find this lake and retrieve some of its magical water.'

The elders looked at each other dumbstruck, looked at me, then looked at each other again, then looked at me. 'Well?' I imperiously asked. Where I got this unprecedented confidence from I do not know, but the situation was dire and I had now broken the ice, so I shed all insecurity.

'Who are you? How dare you interrupt the village council with your inane stories of fabled lakes. You are not an elder, and you have certainly not been invited here. Explain yourself.'

'I am Gorky.'

'Gorky?' said Olaf Oohaha.

'Yes, Gorky. I'm the waterb…er,carrier.'

'The waterboy, ha!' said Ronald, the village shaman and doctor. 'The boy who's great responsibility is to carry buckets of water from the river to the water tanks intervenes our gathering to talk of a lake that has only ever existed in the collective imagination of our people. You, boy, are in trouble. We do not take kindly to interruptions from menials. Now, run along, and we will deal with you later.'

'But I have a right to hear what the elders are proposing to do to save our tribes. These are no ordinary times. The people are dying, gradually, horribly, one by one. What are you going to do?'

'That is why we are here, boy, to decide what we are going to do: but we cannot convene our meeting while any Tom, Dick or Harry interrupts our deliberating. Now, do as the shaman asks, or he will put a curse on you that will cause incredible suffering. Go!' said the mighty Argon, who had developed an inveterate habit of feeling under his arm.

'I do not fear Ronald,' I said. 'If he is so powerful, why doesn't he save us with his *magic*? It is apparent that no one in the village can save us. You must allow me to travel the unchartered lands and find the much needed cure. It is our only hope.'

'You have no authority. You cannot make demands. If you have a suggestion it must be processed through the appropriate channels. You are displaying disrespect and subversiveness. If you do not leave now, we will implement force. Go!' said Gavin, thrusting his index finger into the direction of the village, which caused his fingernail to shoot off and hit Olaf in the eye. Witnessing such absurd obstinacy, the total lack of vision, I felt irresistible ire bubble in my veins.

'It's because of your backwardness that these tribes have ossified!' I yelled with unbridled passion.

'Ossified! BACKWARDNESS!' Gavin screamed, more than matching my indignation. 'This is inciting insurrection! You have now found yourself in deep water! We will deal with your insubordination shortly. Security! March him back to his hut!' With that, four identical burly security guards, all brandishing spears, manhandled me away.

And so I brooded in my hut. Curiously, and propitiously, no guards were posted at my door: I can only assume because of the elders preoccupied with the disease that protocol was slacking and orders were forgotten to be issued. Now my quest took on new urgency: despite their apparent lax, the elders, it was expedient to assume, *would* 'deal' with me 'shortly' and indict me for some trumped up charge tantamount to instigating anarchy. Because of my outspokenness, I had to leave soon or face dire consequences; I must hasten my departure for fear of reprisals, at the very least, excommunication. Whilst Gavin had been belabouring me, I was already formulating a plan. With or without permission from the elders, I must go to Sacradia to seek the purifying waters of the lake. Was I not the waterboy?

7

Would it not be appropriate for me to bring the life saving water to the village? I felt it was my divine right, a calling I could not deny, my raison d'être: besides, for many years I had possessed an irresistible wanderlust. I walked to my hut inorder to prepare for the long and arduous journey. I knew the undertaking was not to be taken lightly. I needed to gather the correct provisions. The next few days I went covertly about my business. I procured packets of dried fruit, warm clothes, and other things I deemed useful. The blacksmith, an old friend, was one of the few people who knew what I was planning. He had advised me, before I departed, to pay him a visit.

'Gorky, what you are about to attempt is unprecedented. Only Argon has ventured from the village, and he is now a living legend. He is considered great by virtue of his intrepidness. I am sure you have heard the subsequent rumours regarding his exploits, although maybe apocryphal, are still chilling. As he progressed further into the woods, it grew increasingly darker, and hostile noises emanated ubiquitous. He ardently believes he had reached the edge of the liveable world, and beyond was darkness and death. He was honoured for his bravery, commended for his adventure: and it was decreed there after that no one should attempt such a futile journey again. Gorky, our people are dying. We cannot sit here like rats in a trap waiting for the inevitable. The elders have declared another meeting next week inorder to discuss the meeting they had this week. Somebody has to do something. I have known you since childhood. I remember it was forbidden to practice martial arts: but you would hector me to practice conspicuously. You said it was a person's inalienable right to learn how to defend oneself, and that vulnerability leads to being an aggressor's target. Much of what you do goes unnoticed in this village. You have trained your mind and body discreetly. You are more than just a waterboy. You are, for a young man, wise and strong. You do have much to learn: but, if anyone can succeed in this quest to Sacradia, it is you, Gorky...'

'Thank you in believing in me, Barney. You are one of the few who do. You have always been a great friend,' I smiled.

'I have something for you, for your journey. I was going to present it to you on your birthday, but now seems as good a time as any. The metal has been folded a thousand times. It is resilient and can cut through iron with its razor sharp edge. I am sure that this sword is enchanted. When you walked into my workshop, the blade took on an unusual lustre. I subliminally felt it vibrate and pervade the surrounding air with energy as if it was aware that its owner was now present. This sword shall protect you from evil. Take it my friend, and may you succeed in your quest.'

Barney handed me the sword: I brandished it through the air, effortlessly swishing, and the sparkling sword began to mystically sing: for an instant I felt a strange calm come over me, as if everything was going to be okay.

'Barney, you have worked tirelessly at your trade. You have wrought metal into shapes that no one else could have even envisaged. People from all over the village come to you and request your skills. You are one of the lynchpins of our society. You are a strong and honest man. I thank you for your kind words and this most excellent sword. And, as you have always taken pride in *your* work, so, rest assured, *I* will try my best. I hope the next time we meet will be in more auspicious circumstances. I ardently hope I can bring back the sacred water to cure our people of the virulent malady. Farewell my friend. I will gain strength knowing you support my endeavours. Valedictions comrade!'

'Valedictions, Gorky, may the strength of the blacksmith be with you.'

I left Barney's workshop more resolved than ever. I admit, after the rebuke from the elders, my spirits were a little low. Ideally, I needed the support of the people if I was going to risk my life in order to save them, but I did not want public clamour, or to raise false hopes: that is why my departure must be as covert as possible: besides, if I had raised awareness at what I was about to attempt, the elders would have indefinitely detained me. Nevertheless, I had to bid my farewells to one more person.

Helena was tending her beautiful flower and herb garden. When she saw me her face bloomed like one of her roses. She had been in the grip of the awful disease for some time, but such was her propensity to love life, that an intense light shone in her eyes belying the illness that was seeping through her veins. 'Gorky!' she exclaimed, and rushed to embrace me, but then checked herself because she hoped I did not have it yet, and she feared passing it on. I went to her and held her tightly: for if I could not hug her, I was as good as dead. 'Helena, my beautiful Helena,' I whispered near her ear as her hair lay gently over my cheek. I held her, not wanting to let go, reluctant to relinquish my embrace. I did not want to leave her. Every fibre of my being cried out to stay by her side: but I knew I must soon be gone: the survival of my people depended on it. 'Helena, I am to go soon.'

'Soon, Gorky?'

'Yes, it must be soon. I am ready. There is no profit in procrastination.'

'Gorky, you will be careful. You will return, no matter what, won't you?'

'Helena, my home is by your side. I could never stay away for too long, but necessity compels me to venture forth into the unknown and find the cure our village so desperately hankers for. Helena, I must go, every moment here increases the difficulty to tear myself away. Know this, I love you, I always will my darling. You are more precious than my own life. You will be with me every moment of my journey. I must go now my love.' I kissed her quickly, turned round, did not look back, and rapidly made my way from the garden to my hut so I could collect my provisions and depart.

2.

The Dead Forest

'The bright sun was extinguished... rayless... and
the icy earth swung blind'
George Gordon Byron.

I decided to leave on Argon day, the day when Argon stood in the village square and waved at everyone while they cheered and waved back: that way I could leave unnoticed. I made my way to the river where I had, on so many occasions, collected water, a route I had taken every morning, the furthest point I had ever been away from the village. Once there, I filled my canteen, and without further ado, commenced forward into the great unknown. It felt strange moving away from the river, like I had breached a forbidden threshold. Behind me was the village, and each step meant that the village was further behind. I was leaving the familiar for the unfamiliar. Something in my heart cried out for me to go back, go back to what I knew, spend the remainder of my days with my loved one, and tread the path between the river and village like I had done so many times before: but something also dared me to venture forth, a yearning for adventure, a need to find out what lay beyond my wonted existence. I would be lying if I said I did not feel fear: there was a continual pang in my stomach. I was alerted to my new surroundings: my perceptions seemed to sharpen as I encroached upon unaccustomed territory.

Then I saw the perimeter fence with the ominous sign 'KEEP OUT!' in bold red letters. 'This is for real,' I whispered to myself. I heard a crack of dry twigs. Footsteps! It was the guards! I hastily leapt over the fence and began to run, run with all my heart. I did not look back but ran towards The Dead Forest. As I ran I felt a creeping malaise enter my soul, like life was being siphoned from my heart. Were the woods watching me? The trees felt like a complete organism, breathing, whispering, discussing the strange traveller that had dared to come this far. As I moved onwards, the foliage overhead became denser, until the sky was completely blotted out. The respiration of the trees suddenly ceased. I found myself in pitch darkness. I lit a torch. There was an eerie silence other than the crackling flame. A crazy dancing orange flame heated my face. The darkness in front of me almost had substance and seemed to warn me to go no further. The hairs on my nape prickled. I felt at any moment a great claw would swipe and cleft me in two. I was the quarry of a mighty predator and death was its name. It waited, hiding in the shadows, stalking me. It was only a matter of time before I would come to a horrible and bloody death. Each moment was charged with pure energy. My instincts compelled me to hide, cower, turn and run, but a rational urge impelled me onwards, ever onwards into the bleak black lifeless dark.

I thought about my lovely Helena. The insidious disease was eating her life away. It was only a matter of time before she would be a grey lifeless bloody corpse. I remember her in the spring of her youth. She would sing. She would laugh. She smiled and looked at me. She felt warm. She gave her love uncompromisingly to me. I had always felt undeserving to have such a divine being as a mate. She was heaven on planet Zugra, the most precious thing to me, pure light, so sweet. I could not relinquish my task. If I returned prematurely, I could never look her in the eyes again. I would be disgusted at my cowardice. I would blame myself for her demise. Her suffering was already my suffering: I did not want to compound it with timorousness. I had to go into the dark, for, beyond it, out there, must be the magical life enhancing waters of the lake, Sacradia. The lake, yes, the lake, for the villagers' sake, I must go to the lake. I walked into the darkness. I followed the glowing flame that I held out in front of me. Almost hypnotised by its bright effervescent lustre, I walked forwards, or was it backwards? I did not know, all I knew was that I must keep putting one foot in front of the other. Do not stop. No, do not stop, keep moving, yes, keep moving, one foot in front of the other, moving, moving, into the darkness, the darkness, the all encompassing deadly still darkness. Darkness pervades me. Darkness weighs down on me. Every where, every where, is darkness, darkness, darkness. Oh tenebrous! The flame, the flame, the bright orange flame, how beautiful the flame. It dances, dances, swirls, crackles, energy, pure energy, the light of the flame, the essence of life, the flame, the flame, the flame. I have been walking all my life. All my life I have been walking in this oppressive darkness. This darkness, this darkness, dark, dark, darkness. I must rest. I must sleep. Weary am I. I must lay. Sleep, sleep, sleep...

Helena's beautiful flower and herb garden, wind, soft wind, sounds, buzzing golden bees, singing multi-coloured birds, verdant leaves flutter, scarlet butterflies, flowers, colours myriad, purples, oranges, yellows, pinks, reds, green, so much green, and a beautiful big bright blue sky, a blue-blue sky, and a bright warm yellow sun. Helena, your delicious smile, your pretty turned up mouth, your inviting lips, your kissable lips, your pearly teeth, your smile, your friendly smile, your friendly shining eyes, eyes, eyes, eyes, your eyes Helena, your eyes. Your smile. Your eyes. Your laugh Helena. Your happy joyous life enhancing laugh. I live in your laugh. I am your laugh. Your laugh Helena. You laugh...

When I awoke, the drear darkness stared in my face like an intense hatred, like a hatred of all things, like hatred for hatred's sake. It confronted me. It challenged me. How much did I want to live? How much effort would I apply to hold onto sanity. How much would I fight? How much did I believe in love? Come, stay in the darkness. Lose yourself in chaos. Go mad. Be free in pure unadulterated lunacy. Come, live in the liberating darkness forever. Be the king of darkness. Rule in this dark demesne. Just you, you in the massive stillness of dark. You can have full reign to run riot in the dark. No repentance. No regret. No responsibility. Cackle, scream, shout what you like, it does not matter, no one can hear you. No one can judge you. Lose yourself in the dark. Be at one with the dark. Be the dark…Some strand of sanity induced me to light the torch. It thankfully crackled into instant life. The flame was life. It was my friend. It drew me to it and I cared not what else it may draw towards it, what attention this intense moving light in the still darkness would create. I must see the glowing flame, my own body, my own hand. I must know I take human form. I must be human. I want to be human. I am human. I must strive like a human. I must move onwards. There must be an end to this dreadful darkness, somewhere. Eat. Eat you fool. Stop and eat. With my free hand I fed. I ate some bread. I felt the masticated bread slide down my stomach and digest. I gradually felt my blood become fuller, imbuing me with vitality. I must hold myself together if I want to get out of here alive. I did not want to die in this merciless darkness lonely and forgotten. The gloom had tried to tempt me into its ostensibly safe womb. I must resist. I have an important mission. I am determined. I will overcome. Onwards, onwards, I must march onwards, deeper into the darkness, or towards the light, I know not which. All I know is I must move forwards, or is it backwards? Whatever, I must travel there, there where the tantalizing unknown resides. I had to walk, walk, walk. As I walked, I began to feel an increasing anxiety. I was utterly disorientated. I knew not if it was night or day beyond the crown of trees. Indeed, it felt like infinite darkness lay heavy on my head. The trees were so wide, so smooth, so giant in stature, the lowest branches had seemed to elevate themselves rendering it impossible to climb. I so longed to be out of the stifling darkness. I began to panic. Blind terror took over me. I dropped the torch and drew my faithful sword from its sheath. I thrashed the dark still air with it. 'Come on! Come on!' I shouted, wielding the deadly blade around my head. 'Come on! I know you're there! Fight! Fight! I'm sick of waiting. I'm sick of being observed. I'm sick of you hiding! Come on! Why don't you fight?' The razor sword swished the moribund air, this way, that. I battled the imaginary foe, but no matter how powerful I thrust, no matter how quick or how clever I moved, the adversary evaded me, watching and mocking. I thrust and parried, until, exhausted, I fell on the floor weeping...

My sword began to melt and transmogrify into a young woman. She wore a flowing silver dress. Hair was silver, her skin silver. Her eyes shone silver and she spoke in silver tones. 'Stand up, Gorky, keep going. If you lose sanity now you will be lost for eternity. Only in a state of equilibrium can you leave the darkness. It is within your means to find the edge of The Dead Forest. There you will encounter a moat that circumscribes this awful place. There lies the threshold of The Desert of No Night, vast, barren, and inhospitable. When you reach the moat you must make a parasol from fallen leaves and fill your canteen with fresh water. You must then rest, for the ensuing journey is treacherous and will take all your strength and vigour. You must use a fallen log to cross the moat. The next stage of your journey will begin. The mighty desert will be before you. You have so far been starved of the sun, and this has tempted you into madness: but in the desert the sun will challenge your sanity again. You have far to travel. Be strong and believe.'

In a flash she was gone and the sword lay by my side. I felt calm and purposeful. I moved onwards with great resolve, into the pitch darkness, into the maws of night perpetual. For hours I walked. If any creature chose to ambush me, I was completely vulnerable: I would not be able to thrust my sword in time. I intuitively felt that these creatures could see with acuity in the dark and could strike from anywhere; I was walking blind, groping dense night. I was at the mercy of the tenebrous forest. I was a fly waiting to be squatted, an ant about to be trampled, but still I walked on, into the steel teeth of night, into the noose of hell, into the core of darkness, deeper-deeper, darker-darker, exposing my raw psyche, my fears, my worst horrors. I could be here forever, lost forever, never seeing another human face, never seeing another day, lost in perpetual night, aimlessly wandering in the immense blackness of eternal night, gone, forgotten, losing my self identity, losing everything, gone, gone, ha-ha-ha, gone. I'm gone. I'm gone. Ha-ha-ha! I'm gone! I'm gone! I'M GONE!!! Na-na-na-ha-ha-ha-la-la-la! Ha-ha-ha. I began to spin round and round, faster and faster, losing track of my direction, abandoning all concern. I did not care if I escaped. I did not care about anything. I was free, free in the dark. I was lost, lost forever. I knew all the time but I just did not admit to it. Now I could be truthful to myself a great burden extricated from me. I no longer feared. I no longer cared. I was free. FREE! FREE! I began running around dancing. I threw the torch. I threw the sword. I took off my clothes, and I danced, danced, danced. I embraced the night. I embraced the dark. I was at one with dark. The dark was me. I felt whole, complete… and…suddenly…very…very…calm.

I felt a welcoming warm wind on my face: the first time I had felt the air move for a long time. I followed to where it was blowing from. The air began to smell sweet and fresh. I began to see silhouettes of trees. As I moved towards them, suddenly, the light hit me, filled my soul, bathed me. The great bright white light of day assailed my eyes. A pain shot into my eyes, my sensitive eyes that had so long been searching in the dark: squinting, they gradually opened. In the vistas I saw refulgent yellow sand stretching to the deep blue sky, the luminous and vastness of that beautiful big blue sky. The wind kissed my ears, the wind, the noise of the wind, a stroking zephyr, a friend, the wind. Then, trickling water, gargling water, the silvery delightful tones of clear cool water. My starved senses were replete. I was in touch and in tune with the elements. I could hear the clouds swirling, leaves fluttering, grass growing, worms crawling underground. A plethora of sense impressions exalted my spirit. My eyes with laser like intensity distinguished between each molecule of the composite whole.

I began to integrate with myself. I recalled my quest. I must compose myself and prepare for the next phase of the journey. I reached for the canteen on my belt. I had to fill it from the moat. My canteen, it was not there! I desperately looked down. I was naked. All my equipment, everything, had been thrown into the darkness. It would be suicide venturing forth into the blazing desert naked without water; and the thought of re-entering the hostile Dead Forest without my sword filled me with dread. How could I continue? I must go back into the darkness to retrieve it all, for if I was to succeed in going forward, I had to make a reconnoitre of my previous whereabouts, to step once more into the heart of darkness.

I tried to step back into the awful gloom, but I baulked. I took a large intake of breath, and with great resolve, I tentatively moved. With the wind at my back the light gradually diminished, until I was surrounded again by the oppressive stillness of darkness. I stopped for a second. A stark fear invaded me. What if I was to get lost again, this time never escaping? I could make my way to the sunlight now, but further on…? The chances of finding all my accoutrements were slim, but without them my journey was futile. I shrugged my shoulders, oh hell, get moving Gorky. I took a tentative forward step and felt a heavy metallic object hit my foot. It was the canteen! I placed it against a tree and used it as a central point of reference. I walked in a straight line away from it carefully counting my steps, then, about turned, and made my way back. I walked 90 degrees to where I had just been, and took several steps until my foot heavily hit the razor sword. I felt it slice into my instep, and blood oozed from the cut: for a moment panic swept over me, but I had to remain calm. My clothes should be nearby. I could staunch the flow with a strip of cloth. Sure enough, I stumbled across my clothes. I tore a strip and bound my foot. I fastidiously combed the area and managed to retrieve most my belongings: but I began to grow concerned about my injury: it felt like a significant laceration: I urgently needed light to assess the trauma. I calmly made my way back to the margin of that dreadful forest of perpetual darkness: although, at one anxious point, I began to think I had lost my way because it seemed such a long time before I felt the delightful wind on my face again.

The first thing I did in the glorious light was unwrap my injured foot, but, strangely, there was no sign of any wound, although the cloth was drenched in fresh blood. I checked again. I examined closely. There was nothing. I had not time to ponder this peculiar occurrence, my mind pre-occupied with the ensuing journey. I sat under a tree at the edge of the forest dipping my feet in the clear cool purling waters of the moat. I felt a sense of intense relief that I could put the dark foreboding Dead Forest behind me. I felt a sense of anticipatory excitement that I could walk onwards knowing I was verily making headway. Already I had ventured further than anyone in the history of our tribes. It was said that Argon had only managed to encroach upon the darkness for a short period of time before retreating. I do not know how long I had been in the Dead Forest, for in its unrelenting heart time becomes abstract, but I had made it to the other side. Here, stretched before me, I was looking in wonder at the shimmering desert, a desert that only existed in the myths of our people, a desert much debated over midnight fires, a desert I was about to cross. I sat there thinking, wow, I've actually traversed through the Dead Forest, the forest that contained and restrained our people, but could not contain or restrain me.

Now, I was going to cross the desert, to the Forest of Life, a fabled forest which contained strange fruits, animals, and many weird and wonderful tribes of people. My people spoke of the splendid hues of green, how the glorious sun shone through the canopies, how the congenial forest contained effulgent sunlight, and how strange and inexplicable sounds could be heard. I, Gorky the waterboy, had already travelled further than anyone in our tribe. 'MEEE!!!' I shouted in the air.

An old woman rose up from the purling moat and hovered on the surface of the water. 'Gorky, you must contain yourself, for if you develop a boastful and arrogant propensity, you will invariably fail. You must remain humble. You must remember what effort it took to get you here. You have indubitably endured, but this journey, remember, is not about you: this journey is about your people. Do you want to die an ignoble death? Do not compare yourself to others. Argon was a brave man, and should be honoured thus. His intentions were magnanimous. He paved the way for your journey. You learnt from the tales of his endeavours. Do not undermine him or anyone else. The circumstances for your journey are beyond your control. For a blade of grass to grow it needs soil, light and water: you need that which you cannot comprehend for your success. Remember, be humble. You are mortal, not omnipotent.'

With that, she slid descending into the moat. Nothing suggested she had appeared other than transitory effervescence. I was so relieved to have the amiable sun shining on my face. I began to surmise the difficulties of traversing across the hot desert sands. All I needed to do was rest...I am exhausted...I am safe...I have fresh water...I have to...sleep...yes...sleep...I must sleep...Helena, your efflorescent garden is beautiful, how I adore the times we have spent in its arbour wiling away pleasant hours...

3.

Desert of No-Night

'Have thy soft piteous eyes beheld
The weary wanderer thro' the desert rove?'
William Blake.

Wonderful it was to awake to a welcoming cerulean sky. I ate
the last of the bread, drank from the purling moat, cleaved a
log with my razor sword, put it a float, and paddled to the other
side. I scrambled up the bank and espied the vast terrain ahead:
a long level plain of golden sand as far as the horizon. I braced
myself and walked onto the sand. Immediately, I felt the heat
on my soles; and the extra exertion, required, to push, my body
weight, along this, yielding surface. I eradicated any thoughts of
turning back. I utterly committed myself to the idea of success.
Failure was not an option. Every now and again I turned
around to see The Dead Forest waning in the distance: until
it completely disappeared behind the expanse of golden sand.
The sun ferociously beat down like some angry torturer. As I
walked I began to feel terribly exposed to the stifling heat. It was
then that I remembered that I should have made a parasol from
the desiccated leaves. I yearned for shade from the incessant
heat. I stopped. Should I turn back? I had already been walking
for some time. No, I had not the patience to continually keep
going backward inorder to proceed. I decided it was too late
to turn back. I convinced myself it would have been a waste of
time and energy. It would take too long to return to the forest's

edge. On I trudged, drinking warm water, sparingly. I began to miss the coolness of the forest. The sun was like a giant set of teeth gnashing at my skin. I began to feel nauseous. There was nowhere to seek refuge from the great ball of flame which concentrated its burning rays on me. Please stop burning. Hide behind a cloud. Go away. Leave me alone. Please go, I exhorted: but the sun steadily gazed, blazing such amazing heat. I fastened the tunic around my tortured brow, which meant exposing my midriff: and, so, my tunic moved in rota, a stint protecting my head, a stint protecting my torso. The water was a miracle, so clear: how could a liquid be so perfectly constructed? The last drops fell from the canteen onto my out-stretched parched tongue. I held the canteen aloft upside down over my head shaking the very last of the precious contents. I looked to the burning quivering horizon and all I could see was sand. Be determined. I would be a hero when I completed the intrepid journey. Would I not be celebrated way beyond the magnitude of Argon day? People would worship me. I will bring back the waters of Lake Sacradia. I would marry Helena. We would live in abundant wealth. I would transcend the reputation of the elders, more listened to, more respected, regularly sought after for advice on weighty matters. What was a desert to me? I would easily conquer a desert. My profound volition would make nature diminutive in comparison. All I had to do was keep on doing what I had been doing all my life: walk. Keep walking, Gorky, or you are going to die. If you lay down and sleep you are going to fry. Keep trying, Gorky. Keep trying. Please! Please! You must keep moving.

'You're never gonna make it.'

'What?' I say, stopping in my tracks and urgently searching around for where the voice came from. I could see no one.

'I said, deafy, you're never gonna make it.'

'Are you a talking cactus?'

'Full marks. How observant.'

'What do you mean I'm not going to make it?'

'Look at the vastness of the desert and how puny you are.'

'That's not very encouraging.'

'I'm a cactus. I'm supposed to be prickly.'

'That's a bad joke.'

'No, you're a bad joke.'

'Could you tell me if I'm going in the right direction?'

'Where are you *trying* to go?'

'The Forest of Life.'

'I wouldn't tell you if I knew.'

'You're right, you are prickly.'

'I told you!'

Move on, Gorky, move on, pointless sojourning with the indifferent.

'Well, goodbye.'

'And good riddance!'

On I walked, relentless sun beating down: with every step it felt like the hot yellow globe in the sky was getting closer. My mouth and tongue became unbearably parched. I sucked the blood from my cracked lips, the metallic tasting liquid partially lubricated my arid tongue. When I spoke, I croaked like a frog. What is that small cloud of dust in the distance? What is it? It's coming towards me, getting larger. It's a…it's a…a horse, a white horse. A horse. A horse. I'm saved. The gleaming white horse galloped towards me. Its hooves made no noise. It glided effortlessly over the shimmering sand. I tried to cajole it towards me. If I could mount it, I could ride away in double quick time to the Forest of Life, the forest that bore so much exotic food. My resolve strengthened. I tried to speak, but a meagre croak emanated. I tried to say, here horsey-horsey, but as I did, I heard a voice in my head distinct from my own.

'Do not waste your time, boy.'

'What was that?' I thought, startled at the cerebral interloper.

'It's me,"horsey-horsey".'

'But, but, how…'

'I am a unicorn, boy. You have completely overlooked the fact that I have a spiral horn protruding from my head. Tut, typical human, put blinkers on horses, but wear blinkers right over their own eyes, seeing only what their feeble brains will allow. I am magic, boy: I can communicate telepathically.'

'Unicorn. Yes, I have heard stories of such creatures. So, you do exist!'

'Yes, boy, apparently so, but why waste my time here I do not know: you have ignored specific instructions from the preternatural beings assigned to assist you: you were told to construct a sun shield before you entered the desert: what is the use of apparitions conveying good advice if it is to be eschewed?

'But I…'

'Silence, boy! My time is limited. The forces of good can grow impatient too. You have put yourself in a dire predicament. You are, in fact, on the verge of death. Why the fates chose you for this journey is beyond me: I will have a word with them about this. You are arrogant and presumptuous; you think that covetousness is all it takes to procure. Look at your feeble self; look at the great desert you find yourself in: is there a comparison? No. This place would swallow you without even noticing. You must be more respectful of nature. She existed long before you. Are you listening to me?'

'Yes, I…'

'Shut up, boy, for I must leave soon. Listen carefully. You must, in future, be more diligent in constructing contingency plans. Spontaneity is all very well, but unforeseen circumstances will arise if you are not prepared. Diminish your dependency on chance. Your luck will soon leave you if you carry on in this reckless manner. Do I make myself clear?'

'Yes, but…'

'No buts! Now touch your canteen against my ivory.'

I did what I was told. Suddenly, the canteen began to gurgle, became heavier and cool: it had miraculously filled with water.

'Thank you, I...'

'Silence, impetuous youth! Now, tie one of your hairs around my ivory.'

Again, I felt compelled to obey.

'Now, think of a wide-brimmed straw hat,' the unicorn admonished. Without a second thought, a clear picture of a hat came into mind: with that, a hat materialized onto my head.

'Thanks, I...'

'Right, my work is done. Do not take this succour for granted, boy. You have not made it yet: all I have done is rendered you with an outside chance. If I had not appeared, you would certainly have died, you foolish boy.'

With that the unicorn flew across the sand and was soon out of sight...

I took a greedy quaff of water and instantly spewed it back up. I sat on my haunches looking at wet sand. I then took a few measured drops, enough to moisten my cracked lips and parched tongue. I then took a few more. Gradually, I began to feel my body again. Uggh! The nigh on intolerable pain! My dissipated thoughts began to focus. I took a few more drops, and poured a little water over my head. The cool fresh water enlivened my brain and brought me into the present. I drank a little more water: and this time I could feel the cool liquid pour into the depths of my being. I stood. My face was cooler in the shade of the straw hat. I looked to the horizon. Had I really seen a unicorn? Had I always possessed the luxurious straw hat? How was the canteen so suddenly full of water? My spirit cried onwards: so I began to tentatively propel myself forward to the horizon, the tantalizing horizon that never seemed to change. As I walked, I came to be more vigilant in the distribution of water. I walked more steadily; I paced myself so as to maintain maximum efficiency. I saw a vivid image of beautiful Helena. She was smiling at me. I reciprocated the smile and embraced her. I held her close to me and buried my face in her sweet smelling long dark shining hair. I desperately grasped the air. I was surrounded by desert. The scene was the same wherever I looked. I span around. Where had my gorgeous Helena gone? Helena! Helena! Please do not leave me! The hot oppressive sky swallowed my voice. I fell into the scolding sand sprawling and weeping. Helena! Helena! Please do not leave me. I am nothing without you. I have nothing. I am empty when you are gone. Something inside told me to pick myself up, induce mobility, or I would be buried into the sand, an unvisited grave, forgotten in the wilderness. I had to put my anguish aside. If I languished in sorrow, I would disintegrate. Walk. Walk or die. When you walk there is a chance. Take a little water and walk…

The body is capable of incredible endurance. When it is faced with the prospect of death it can bestow on itself great powers: it has an instinct all on its own for survival, to claim the soul for its own in order to live. The soul, also, if not ready, is reluctant to leave corporeality. It would prefer to live in that which is familiar. Although the after-life is a perennial fascination to it, it would prefer not to transgress the limits of the flesh. If body and soul are threatened, they are capable of great feats of strength. Indeed, the body may want to relinquish the struggle, but the soul cries no; the soul may want to leave, but the body holds on. How I managed to keep walking did not seem plausible. The voracious sand swallowed each step. Like a little boy who holds a magnifying glass over an unsuspecting insect, concentrating the sun's energy to frazzle the wretched tiny body, the sun's incessant heat seemed to be focused only on me. I pictured the Forest of Life. I tried to envisage how it would be. I wanted so much to be there. I envisaged the cool verdant forest and pushed hard with my legs.

As I moved on, I noticed something glittering ahead. The closer I got the more I had to shield my eyes. As I approached the source I could espy a...a...diamond! Yes, a huge diamond. It was embedded in the sand, like an iceberg. The light from the sun refracted from its surface spreading large beams across the sand. In our village, only the elders were permitted to own diamonds: they were the ultimate status symbol. A lustful acquisitiveness began to consume me: if I could own this diamond I would truly be at the top of the hierarchy. As I stood before it my body quivered with excitement: but as I began to dig around it, I realized it was bigger than I anticipated. I expelled valuable energy manically attempting to exhume this impressive stone. Sand flew everywhere as I dug and dug and dug. I finally managed to disinter its bulk. I could hardly put my arms around it. I lovingly caressed it. It was beautiful. I kissed its cold surface. I threw my canteen aside, and strangely began to feel the weight of my sword upon my back. I heaved the diamond onto my shoulders: my spine creaked. I moved slowly and my feet sank deeper into the sand, sometimes up to my knees. I thought of the admiration this prize would bring me, and it drove me on. The pain was excruciating. My body threw down the rock, rejecting any more part in this cruelty. I cried 'No!', and dragged the diamond, rolled it, pushed it. I had to take it with me. I could not wait to see the elders' faces when I marched into the village with such a humongous precious stone glittering by my side. Their haughtiness would quickly change to deference. It took every ounce of effort to push the diamond: but I was now the richest man in the world. I became utterly exhausted, unable to continue, the sun baking me. I was severely dehydrated, but I hugged the diamond, whispering sweet nothings into its glassy surface.

I fell into a profound unconsciousness, spiralling into the dark. It was sweet letting go, disavowing the strain to survive.

However, I was soon falling out of control: I was falling into a deep lonely existence, a place, in the deep dark void, where only I would be. I began to make a concerted effort to clamber back to consciousness. I wanted to be awake. I wanted to be back in my body. I wanted to live. I DO NOT WANT TO DIE! LET ME LIVE! As I fell, I realised I was tenaciously clinging hold of the diamond: in disgust, I slung it away from me: this slowed my descent. Suddenly, my eyes opened. I gasped. The sun glared down: but I was so glad to see that splendid yellow orb. My eyes closed, and I slipped a little. I fought. I battled. My eyes opened again. Every effort went into keeping my eyes open. Above me stood the Silverwoman.

'Gorky wake up. You must wake up.'

'I love you!' I shouted. 'I love you!'

'Gorky, hold on. Wake up. Take some water.'

I desperately poured water over my face. My senses came flooding back. I stabilized. I drank some cool refreshing water. The Silverwoman, where was she? I looked around: I was surrounded by hot baking desert. I stood up. I picked up the sword: it felt lighter now. I looked at the diamond and felt repulsed at the cupidity it had engendered in me: I still appreciated its beauty, but in a more measured way. I could not let this gleaming chunk of crystal detain me any longer: I must go further into the blazing desert. I moved over the sand unburdened. I purposefully strode on as the rising heat shimmered.

I continued to walk. I walked with determination and purpose…

What is that? A small black dot on the horizon. As I quizzically moved closer, I began to make out the silhouettes of three large figures sitting behind an imposing table: I was saved! On approaching, I realised they were not humans, but three dishevelled vultures.

'Arr, the accused,' one announced.

'Yes, Gorky, the water...b-o-y,' another continued.

'That's me,' I naively confirmed.

'Yes, we know, boy. Stop interrupting,' said a second. 'You are accused of rash presumption, gross negligence, unbearable arrogance, vile jealousy, dirty greed, manic recklessness, and a over bloated ego: how do you plead?' said a great slobbering vulture sternly looking me directly in the eye.

'Wh...what are the charges again?' I stuttered, bewildered.

'Let's add ignorance to that...Okay, let's make it more simple for you,' the vulture grimaced, as if talking to me was a thoroughly painful experience. 'Let's start with rash presumption. Is it not true that you presume that everybody is stupid and wicked before you have even spoken to them?'

'What makes you say that?' I retorted, indignant at such an accusation. I was now beginning to compose myself. These scruffy old birds were not going to outwit me.

'Did you know,' said the third vulture, smiling innocently at me, but every time he thought I was not looking, would sneer, 'we have been perched on your shoulder and reading your mind from birth.'

'Oh,' I sighed, slightly deflated at such an epiphany. 'From birth?' I inquired for confirmation.

'Yes,' said the first vulture. 'Now, let me see...' He looked down at his notes, which interminably unravelled across the desert.

'Mmm, as a baby, did you not scream and cry expecting to be fed at a whim?'

'All babies do that,' I scoffed.

'All babies are not on trial,' said the one on the left, 'and you have already been advised about comparing yourself with others.'

'But...'

'No buts, it is an offence to use too many buts,' said the centre vulture who would bang down his gavel at any opportunity.

'But, I cannot remember,' I pleaded.

'Ha, selective memory loss, a typical criminal trait,' said the right hand vulture, who was promptly congratulated by pats on the back and handshakes by the other two.

'I am not the same person I was then,' I grumbled, interrupting their celebrations.

'What was your name then?' the centre vulture replied, leaning forward, as if waiting to pounce on a quarry.

'Gorky.'

'And what is your name now?' said the left vulture, holding the centre vulture back.

'Gorky.'

'I would say that is conclusive proof, wouldn't you?' said the vulture on the right, who was beginning to find it a chore to speak to me.

'But...'

'Any more buts and we will hold you in contempt of court,' they all sang in chorus.

'But this is absurd: how can you indict me for something I did as a baby?'

'We are merely trying to present a character profile of you as a child, so as to make it clear what type of person you were, and how you went from bad to worse,' the middle vulture said, wincing when he spoke.

'Yes, we will move on now,' said the left vulture, looking along the gargantuan notes with a sly grin. 'When you were five years old,' he continued, 'you collected some caterpillars in a jar. Did they survive?'

'Mmm.'

'No mmming in court,' the right one said.

'No mmming in court,' the left one said.

'Answer the question,' the middle one said.

'I, I cannot remember,' I wailed.

'You plucked seven perfectly healthy caterpillars from a

bush, dropped them into a jar, and tightly screwed down the lid. You gave them no air, no food, and you even shook the jar. You left them to suffocate! Is that not the epitome of callousness?' he pointed his ragged wing at me while the other two gleefully glared with evil intent.

'And is it not true, at the age of ten, you made a sword out of wood, and played at fighting with a friend, specifically against the laws of your people?'

'Er...'

'And when you were caught and ordered to stop the simulated violence, you went on in private, displaying gross intransigence.'

'Yes, I remember that,' I said, 'but I wanted to learn how to defend myself.'

'You mean you were looking to commit violence on the innocent... Why do you carry a sword now?'

'I am on a quest. I do not know what dangers I will encounter,' I retorted.

'Quest?! QUEST?! Fiddlesticks! This futile venture is to satisfy your own inferiority complex. You have always resented being a water carrier. You have always envied anyone of higher rank. You have grown bitter, had ideas above your station, and, heedless of any advice, recklessly gone forward into the unknown. Why are you carrying a sword?' the left one vehemently reiterated.

'I told you, to defend myself.'

'That sword is a lethal weapon: it can decapitate, slice flesh, chop limbs, split someone down the middle, shed blood, blood, BLOOD!' said the middle vulture, as they all began to salivate and become quite animated. 'You carry a weapon of destruction: you are an evil man. How do you plead?' the middle vulture screamed hoarsely, flapping its ragged wings, feathers flying everywhere.

'You are aware that "he who lives by the sword dies by the

sword"?' said the vulture on the right, as they all opened draws in the table and drew out knives and forks.

'I am risking my life to save my people,' I shouted.

'For fame and renown. You hanker after Gorky Day. You selfish petty piffling little man: you make us sick. You left your girlfriend ill and vulnerable while you go gadding about. She died calling your name in vain, "Gorky, how could you leave me?"' With that, the vultures became still, and, smirking, scrutinized me for a reaction. My energy sank into the sand. 'You wanted to be renowned but you have been renounced by the villagers of Firkin Forest. You are vilified. Your name is dirt. The rumour is you were scared of the disease and ran away. You abandoned your people in their time of need. Gossip is now fact: Gorky the pusillanimous!' All three then placed shiny dinner plates on the dusty table.

'There is nothing left in your village but disease and hatred for you, you traitor.' The middle one said glaring at me in glee.

'Coward,' the left one said.

'Megalomaniac,' the right one said.

'You have no one, Gorky. You are truly alone,' said the middle vulture, rising from its seat.

'The common sense thing to do is lay down and die,' the left one said, leaping onto the table.

'Yes, die, fall in to d-e-l-i-c-i-o-u-s oblivion,' the right one said, who was now circling above drooling like a waterfall.

'Yes, d-e-l-i-c-i-o-u-s,' the other two said, flapping dishevelled feathery wings to join their fellow accuser, swirling around in tight circles through the arid air.

All three gradually swooped in closer, rapturous eyes ablaze, glaring, intense and ravenous. I could not reach for my sword, for that was gratuitous violence. In fact, I did not have the will to fight at all: I was an evil man. My motivations had always been selfish. I only loved Helena to receive her love. I deserved to die. I closed my eyes waiting for the *coup de grace*. I waited, and waited, each moment my eyes closed tighter, completely defenceless, hoping it would be quick and painless; please, get it over with. The waiting was unbearable. The tension grew too great.

I opened my eyes, but all I could see was desert. A heat haze ascended from the sand. The air danced in an undulating motion. The vultures had gone! There was no sign they had ever been there. My instinct was to move on without any deliberation. I had to leave that awful experience and put it far behind me. I longed to see people, a kind face. My resolve returned. I had to retrieve the alchemical water from Lake Sacradia and return to the village. I could surreptitiously put the water in the tanks: that way, the life preserving liquid could be disseminated amongst the people, they would begin to recover, and no one would ever know how or why. I did not want fame. I just wanted my people to live. I wanted to grow old with Helena, have children, and be happy. I began to appreciate the life I had in the village: I had always been well fed and sheltered. My heart yearned for Helena. I felt wretched being surrounded by nothing but barren desert. The weight of the universe pushed down on my soul, oppressing me with isolation. I *had* to move on. I wanted to be loved, to feel her company. I sought security in her smile. If I lost my sanity, I would never see her again; if I gave up, I would be forever lost. Walk on, Gorky. Do not give up the fight. Think of the good people you left behind. I began to chide myself at the ready capitulation to the austere judgemental vultures. Walk on, Gorky. Never relinquish the struggle: at least die on your feet; do not die laying down.

The desert heat was intense. The blazing sun increased in size. Through all my vacillating thoughts, one thing remained constant: my love for Helena. She was sacred, a light in my heart, my reason for being, my motivation for pushing forward.

The only thing I held with certitude was my profound love for Helena: I would not lay down and let the hot desert sand swallow me into oblivion. The pain and torment was nothing compared to the anticipated pleasure of meeting my beloved again. I drank some revitalizing water, and boldly marched forward towards the shimmering horizon, defiantly confronting the fierce desert: I strode forward knowing I had to conquer its vastness: I walked and walked, sometimes in a trance, sometimes tenaciously hanging onto consciousness, often gibbering to myself, crying, laughing, but always walking forward…

On the horizon I discerned a large cloud of dust and sand. It was rapidly approaching towards me and thought this huge mass may be a dust storm I had heard villagers speak of whilst attending the soirees around fires at night. As it approached I saw scintillating scarlet within the cloud. Fear began to permeate my body as I tried to prepare for a head on collision. The dust then dispersed to the left and right and suddenly I was surrounded by a heaving sandy dust cloud. As the sand began to settle, there, before me, were scarlet lizard people, choking on the fine particles and dusting each other down. They then turned their attention on me. I felt threatened by this imposing sight. Their scarlet scales shone bright in the desert sun. They were all wearing t-shirts, which I later learned were tie-dye. I drew my sword and held it before me. 'No need for that, man,' a lizard said.

'Yeah, we're unarmed, look,' another said, holding her reptilian hands up to show me they were empty. Then, all in unison, the rest showed me they were unarmed.

'We come in peace,' one said.

'Yeah, good one,' another said, patting the previous speaker on the back and congratulating her.

'What do you want?' I nervously asked, still desperately clinging to my sword.

'Dude, chill,' one said.

'We're the Lacertilia, and we're searching for our Lizard King,' another said.

'Yeah, he can do anything,' another added.

'Have you seen him on your travels?' another asked.

'Lizard King?' I repeated.

'Yeah, he can do...'

'Do anything, yes, I got it,' I interjected. 'No, I've seen the Silver Woman, a unicorn, some vultures and a rather fractious cactus, but not, erm, the Lizard King.'

'He can...'

'Yes, yes, but I haven't seen him,' I confirmed.

'Well, if you see him, tell him his tribe are looking for him,' one said.

'Yeah, he's probably tripping out in the desert somewhere,' another said.

'Tripping?' I asked.

'Yeah, he goes off on his own "to find himself",' one said, using his hands to indicate, as I later understood, inverted commas.

'Right, Ill bear that in mind,' I replied, using my hands to indicate inverted commas to be polite believing this was a reptilian gesture of friendliness, but having no idea what the Lacertilia were talking about.

'Great, nice one, man,' one said.

'Yeah, cool,' another said.

'What you actually doing in the desert anyway?' one asked.

'I'm on a quest, to find Lake Sacardia,' I asseverated.

'Lake...? You ain't going to find any water in the desert,' one said.

'I mean to travel beyond the desert, over many lands to find it,' I determinedly declared, feeling rather important.

'Good look with that,' one sarcastically laughed.

'Yeah, you look so bedraggled you ain't going much further,' one joked. This comment caused a quiet chuckling amongst the scarlet reptiles.

Well, that is what I am doing, and I *will* make it,' I defiantly said, feeling slightly hurt and my self-importance wounded. 'Er, do you know if I'm going in the right direction,' I sheepishly asked.

'The desert is all we know,' one said, 'Though there is a forest in that direction,' he pointed.

'Yeah, but we stay away from that, and with good reason,' another added.

'Why is that?' I inquired, joyful to hear of the forest, but concerned it was something to keep away from.

'It was nice to meet you, man,' one said, holding her hand out for me to shake, which I cordially did. With that they zipped away disappearing into a cloud of sandy dust. What could they have meant about the forest? It sounded ominous, but I had come this far: I would not be deterred.

On I walked through the baking heat. I followed the directions given to me by the tie-dye reptiles. There was some solace in the fact that The Forest of Life was more than just myth. Suddenly, I heard a faint singing: 'Break on through to the other side,' I believe the lyrics were. I walked towards the intriguing sound, and there, sat on top of a dune, in the hot desert sun, was a huge lizard creature, gold scales sparkling in the sun, with a golden crown casually tilted upon his regal head. 'Hi, d-o-o-o-d,' he smiled.

'Hi,' I replied, shielding my eyes from the bright glow of his golden scales.

'Are you The Lizard King?' I asked.

'Yeah, and I can do anything,' he proclaimed, braking into deep jovial laughter which was so infectious I had to smile. 'Bow before august royalty!' he smirked. I was in such awe of this golden creature glittering in the desert sun that I made obeisance and respectfully lowered my head: this induced him to break into a fit of laughter. 'Only messin' with you, man. Take a pew,' he said, waving his arm inviting me to sit. I cautiously sat beside this imposing creature. He gently patted me on the back, 'G-o-o-o-d,' he said.

'Your tribe are looking for you,' I informed.

'They're always looking for me,' he grinned.

'They told me you're trying to "find yourself",' I said.

'Yeah, man, I am,' he laughed.

'And have you?' I asked.

'S-u-r-e, he grinned, 'many times, each time I find a new me.'

'Oh, and how do you do it, this, erm, "finding yourself"?' I inquired.

'Take this,' he held out his hand, which contained some kind of dried up plant.

'What is that?' I asked.

'It's p-e-y-o-t-e,' he enunciated, 'taken from the good old cactus, L-o-ph-o-ph-ora.'

'Lopho...?'

'Take it,' he urged.

'What will happen?' I asked, fairly concerned at what I could be getting myself into.

'You'll break on through to the other side,' he sang.

'What's at "the other side"?' I inquired.

'Immaculate perception, perfect reality, waltzing with the other-worldly,' he grinned. I thought for a while. I was not sure if I wanted to *waltz with the other-worldly*. This golden reptilian creature, though a magnificent sight, looked so spaced out, and possessed such an inveterate dissolution of concentration, I was loath to give *peyote* a try, although admittedly curious.

'I think I'll give it a miss,' I eventually said.

'Okay, it's your loss,' he grinned. I could sense The Lizard King was disappointed that I declined the offer to *trip* with him, so I sensed it was best to be on my way.

'Well, it was nice meeting you,' I said, feeling a little shame I did not have the courage to *get to the other side.*

'Yeah, whatever,' the Lizard King shrugged, appearing like he was on the threshold of transcending corporeality. As I walked away, I heard him shout, 'If you ever want a trip... I'll be in the desert somewhere... I could recite to you some of my poetry... It's insightful! I am The Lizard King. I can do anything!' I had to smile at the eccentric Lizard King, his profound and wistful gaze evinced a sublime poetic heart. As I trudged towards the shimmering horizon I tried to imagine the visions his expansive mind had witnessed.

My amusement soon turned to earnestness as I was reminded of the harsh desert environment. How long I struggled with the unforgiving desert is not easy to say. Time may have concertinaed, or stretched, for is invariably relative to the particular experience: sometimes in semi-trance, sometimes acutely aware of the desert, I intransigently strode onwards...

I heard something in the distance. I was not sure if I could trust my heat infested brain. It sounded like a cawing. The vultures! They had come back to finish me off. No, it was a beautiful big black shining crow: it flew overhead, cawing, as if to say, welcome. I then received a delightful whiff of tangy citrus: the appetizing smell stimulated my juices, and I began to salivate at the prospect of delicious fruit. I lengthened my stride and the arduous preceding journey seemed to slough away. I peered at the horizon and saw a line of lush vegetation, flowers innumerable, fruits of every colour scintillating in the sun hung from verdant trees: up ahead, within my ken, was the glorious Forest of Life! I began to almost run along the yielding sand. I started to manically laugh and feel delivered from the unforgiving desert. I could not wait to taste the delicious fruits and meet the tribes that legend said inhabited these magnificent forests.

4.

The Forest of Life

On approaching this most welcome sight, myriad colours and heady smells danced with my satisfied senses. I was sensitive to the rhythms of the forest's primeval energy. The noble forest possessed exotic fruits of all description. After the dire struggle in the hostile desert, the trees seemed to be a congenial host. I joyfully plucked a large purple berry as big as my stomach from a nearby branch. I dug my thumbs into the thin soft skin and peeled away the rind. The sweet smelling flesh was ripe, juicy and luscious. I greedily bit into the flesh, juices dribbling down my chin. I eagerly devoured this mysterious fruit and felt gloriously satisfied: my arid mouth was alive again. I slumped my weary body down onto the grassy margin of The Forest of Life looking out to the desert contemplating my long and arduous journey so far. At least the journey back would not be such a mystery: I would be more experienced, hardened for the return.

Now, I needed to rest: my body began to feel heavy. It felt comforting to lay in the shade of a benign rustling tree. My thoughts projected out to my beloved Helena. How I wished to learn of her condition, and to tell her I was safe. I dismissed what the implacable vultures said as lies: besides, I was unsure if I had really seen them. Although there was a restlessness in my spirit to go on, I knew I urgently needed rest: I had to regain my strength. I drifted into deep slumber…

The Silverwoman manifested before me. 'Gorky, what do you know of The Forest of Life?'

'That it provides sustenance, and that I am now safe from any hazard.'

'It is true that there is much food here, but with food there are food chains.'

With that, she disappeared.

I suddenly awoke. I was so relieved that I could put the tortuous desert behind me. I sprang up knowing there would be food strewn all along this part of my journey. I was pleased to see there was an inviting pathway: traversing was quicker. I walked into the forest with vigour, refreshed after food and rest. The noise at first was faint, but became more distinct as I travelled to its source. 'Pooh-pooh, pooh-pooh,' then suddenly, 'POOH-POOH!' People, it must be people! I quickened my step. The noise grew louder, until there, in a glade, was a group of around twenty men sat in a circle. I did not want to intrude at this stage: they seemed to be in the process of performing a very important religious ceremony. As time passed, nothing changed, nobody moved. The same chant continued. I began to grow irritated waiting for the inane spectacle to cease. The noise began to grate on my nerves. (I suppose it is akin to when you have perfect peace on Sunday afternoon. You are just beginning to fall into slumber after a lovely meal, when, suddenly, your neighbour lets out the miniature dog into the garden. It begins incessantly barking and rudely snaps you from your reverie. It furiously barks in the same tone and rhythm interminably and obviously signifies nothing but noise for noise sake.) Eventually I could not tolerate it any more: I decided to confront these peculiar men. 'Excuse me,' I said, 'I hope I am not interrupting, but…'

'Pooh-pooh, pooh-pooh, POOH-POOH!' the men continued, oblivious to my presence.

'Excuse me,' I said, a little louder, 'I hope I am not interrupting, but…'

'You hope you are not interrupting?' one suddenly replied.

'Yes, I…'

'You interrupt us to tell us you hope you are not interrupting?' another said.

'How two faced,' another one said.

'I'm sorry,' I apologised, 'it's just that…'

'You're sorry?' said another.

'If you were going to be sorry, why did you do it in the first place?' said some one else.

'Yes, why?' said one more.

'Look, all I want to know is if I am going in the right direction to Lake Sacradia.'

'Lake what?' said one.

'Lake Sacradia. I'm on a quest, and…' with that they all began chanting 'Pooh-pooh, pooh-pooh.'

Undeterred, I tried to negotiate. 'Look, if you want, I'll go away, and come back when you've finished.'

'Come back when we've finished?' said one.

'It's a bit too late for that,' said another.

'You've completely spoilt our meeting,' said one more.

'Yes, completely spoilt it,' said another.

'Meeting?' I scoffed.

'You barge in here expressing great sorrow at your interruption, and as you interrupt, mock our proceedings, while showing no sign of stopping your interrupting.'

With that they all bellowed, 'POOH-POOH!' as if ratifying what had just been said.

'I just want to make sure I have not lost my way,' I futilely pleaded.

'I'll say you've lost your way,' said one.

'No manners,' said another.

'No manners at all,' said one more.

'Well I can see you are going to be no help,' I exasperatingly exclaimed.

'Don't raise your voice at us,' said one.

'What a vile temper,' said another.

'Terrible,' another concurred.

'Quite horrendous,' another rejoined.

'Quite,' said another.

'Are you going to help me?' I implored.

'What a demanding individual,' said one.

'Yes, quite unreasonable,' said another.

'Very rude,' said one more.

'Incredibly rude,' said another.

I shook my head in disbelief: I just could not elicit a sensible reply. I decided to try one more time: these were, after all, the first people I had seen in a long time, and maybe for some time yet.

'Look, I am really sorry for interrupting, I will soon be gone, but could you please tell me if you have heard of Lake Sacradia?'

There was a pause, and in that silence I began to be optimistic that I may receive a sensible response, but, suddenly, and in unison, they let out a loud, 'POOH-POOH!'

It was time to leave. I walked into the forest disappointed but hoping to see another tribe: this, after all, was the Forest of Life.

I walked on trying to focus on making progress: I had to guard against enervating maudlin. I walked with a determined stride. The lush forest cheered me: there was light, water, food and shelter. As I walked, I began to have an uncomfortable feeling of being watched. I seemed to be surrounded by eyes. The feeling of safety abated. I shuddered. The forest's atmosphere became perceptibly hostile. Smog ominously clung to the floor. I felt nervous. Then, there before me, nailed to a tree, was a creepy human skull. I gazed, startled at such disrespect to the deceased.

I froze. I had only ever seen skulls in drawings. The skull grinned at me as if to take glee at my disconcertment. Then the word 'food chain' flashed into my head. Suddenly I felt vulnerable and exposed. I hastily unsheathed my sword. I grasped it tightly for security. At least I could die fighting. There was no question of turning around. I defiantly walked past the deathly blank stare of the skull. I was now on hostile ground. I felt acutely alert, senses tuned, ready for any sudden attack. My ears strained for the slightest noise. I must reach Lake Sacradia. I must save Helena. I walked on ready for anything. I felt a calm fury that could explode at an instance upon any assailant: I would not be stopped. As I walked, the smog slowly crept up my legs, to my waist, then, to my shoulders: finally, my neck stretched to maintain my head above the miasma. I carried on walking, slowly, cautiously...

Suddenly, I was helplessly swinging upside down, my head choking in the smog! My sword went flying. I could not see anything. I tried to extricate from the bond around my ankles. It was useless: I was fastened tight. I hung there, vulnerable. I tried to grope for my trusty sword: but I could not reach the ground. Then, I felt my self being further bound, cut loose, and unceremoniously bundled into a hessian sack. I heard a pole being slid into the top of the sack. It was all done silently and efficiently. I heard no voices as I bumped along. I was unarmed and scrunched up like a foetus wondering what was to become of me. The feeling of powerlessness and exposed to hostile people is quite alarming. Usually we have means of protecting ourselves: we can run; we can hide; we can fight: but waiting unarmed and defenceless for a violent attack leaves one feeling like a worthless piece of meat. I wanted to live and protect my self, but had no physical means.

I was then callously dumped on the floor: the sack was opened. I had thoughts of rushing them and escaping: but I had to assess the situation first, which I soon could: I was surrounded by seven foot women clad in shiny rubber, all beautiful and perfectly formed: but all armed with menacing spears. A dozen or so pointed their formidable weapons at various parts of my defenceless body. I was malevolently prodded to a pole, then, bound tight again. A stunning woman approached with a glinting knife. I thought I was going to be violently gutted. She ran the tip seductively around my pulsating body, gently stroking my exposed flesh. She then curmudgeonly removed my garments until I stood naked. A dance was then performed in front of me, a dance so erotic in nature that I began to feel aroused. I then noticed a line of women. For ages I stood bound to the pole, while each came up in turn, clamped their legs around me, and took my seed. After a while I became utterly drained and exhausted: but they had a way of getting maximum performance from me, waiting till I had just recovered, then, another a beauty stood before me, teased me, and took me. I cannot recall how many women took advantage of my helpless state: all I know is, each was like a greedy animal with manic lust in their eyes; and with frenzied passion they kept me awake, extracting my life precipitating juices. They fed on me as if their lives depended on it. I was thoroughly spent. I began to doze. My head dropped: but I was rudely awakened.

'Who are you?' said a gorgeous young woman who towered above me. Her sable hair fell in squirls around her shoulders: but I was so debilitated, that I could not speak. 'What tribe are you from?' she demanded, gripping my hair and holding my head up, her lips nearly touching mine: I could feel the heat of her breath.

'I come from beyond the Forest of Life,' I eventually managed to say.

'The Forest of what?' she said, gritting her teeth in a savage fashion.

'I have travelled the Desert of No-Night, beyond the Dead Forest, I am from Firkin Forest,' I murmured.

'It is not possible you have traversed the desert: it has no end: but, you are not from one of the tribes of this land: where did you get such a sword?' she demanded, taking the sword from one of the Dryads and holding it in front of my face.

'It was made for me by a friend,' I replied, staring at her long lithe frame.

'The men of this forest are not permitted weapons,' she snarled, gritting her teeth, her eyes mad with fury.

'No...I am not...'

'Men were irresponsible, quick to anger: their facile pride created war. We women, through eugenics, have rendered them harmless. Women rule this forest: men are just a means to procreate. We take their seed then roast and eat them. You are our next meal.'

'But I am not from this forest,' I implored, beginning to feel alarmed, and looking in her eyes, appealing to her humanity.

'You are a man, and must serve as men do: you are our food: you have no other purpose: be pleased you feed women.'

'Where I am from men and women have an equal partnership' (Yes, I tendentiously neglected to mention the intransigent patriarchy of the elders), 'for: they love and honour each other. They...'

'Love! We have heard of that ridiculous fable: utter folly. Love is a misconception causing nothing but anguish and irrational behaviour. We have evolved since then: we are practical, stronger. We line up, take the sperm, then kill and eat: what could be more efficient? Besides, we will give you a chance to survive: if you can go sun-moon-sun-moon without ejaculating, we will let you go.'

'You will let me go in two days if I do not come?'

'Yes, that is all you have to do.'

'Why, I can do that,' I said, thinking I would soon be free.

'We will see,' said the dusky woman, who was apparently chief.

With that, the Amazonian women departed, and I was left to ruminate about my predicament. Oh Helena, my heart has always been faithful to you. It is only you I love.

So there I stayed for two days and two nights, trying to gather my faculties for imminent manumission. The final night a full silver moon was shining overhead in the clear balmy star bedighted sky. The ominous miasma had lifted. My strength had returned. With alacrity I looked forward to being unbound. I must remember to ask them to give me my sword back.

Suddenly, the silence was disturbed by rhythmic beating drums. The rubber clad women appeared from the darkness of the forest. Maybe this was the emancipation ceremony. I eagerly waited. A tall lithe blond woman gracefully moved forward.

'You have been here sun-moon-sun-moon and not yet ejaculated,' she stated.

'Yes, can I go now?' I supplicated, smiling at her nervously, for she was an imposing sight.

She sauntered closer. She looked me up and down and licked her lips. I could not help noticing her pert breasts. One of her hands stroked my inner thigh and the other began to fondle her mound. I began to rise.

'I thought you were going to set me free?' I feebly whimpered.

'The moon still shines,' said a red head girl, who went down on me.

'But this is unfair,' I protested.

'Why? Control yourself and live, ejaculate and die,' she said, running her tongue around my bulb, 'though no man has ever escaped.'

The blond woman ran her moist tongue around my nipples, and then ran it over my stomach, and joined the red head in fellatio. Both took it in turns to put me practically whole into their succulent mouths. Oh God, if I come, I die. I tried to transcend the parameters of my body. Another young woman sidled up, crouched, and put my balls in her mouth. I had two women sucking at my testicles while the other eagerly sucked my end. I had never been so hard. Then, one stood up, and slid me into her. Her hips began swaying and pumping in rhythmic motion. The blond picked my sword up. I believe I was to be decapitated on ejaculation. 'Come on!' the red haired woman moaned as my penis disappeared into her moist love tube. The two other women crouched voraciously chewing my hanging testicles. Pump, pump, pump, I was about to spurt when she stopped and the blond woman mounted me. In I slipped: she had a different rhythm to the first woman, but equally as stimulating.

'Enough!' cried the dusky woman. 'I will finish him.' She sidled up to me, kissed me, and cooed, 'Give me a baby darling.' She raised her legs around my waist. She never took her eyes from mine as she eased herself on to me. I knew my life would soon be ended! She moaned and groaned…and I involuntarily did too! If this was the precursor to death, I wanted more. I *had* to come deep into this beautiful woman. She smelt of sex. Her odour was intoxicating. She ground her hips against me. I came more than I ever had in my life. It was a deep penetrating orgasm vibrating through my whole being: my body moved in spasms, like a great muscle. As I writhed my bonds loosened, just in time, for she had leaped from me, held the sword aloft, and was charging towards me screaming, 'Die!' I just managed to move in time as the sword hit the pole. I quickly took evasive action from the thrashing blade. Somehow I managed to wrestle the blade from her. I wasted no time in legging it: rubber clad irate women charged after me, screaming, 'Kill him!' I quickly grabbed my clothes and ran into the shadowy forest with the Amazonian women in hot pursuit. I now ran for my life as hundreds of maniac women pursued me. They had long legs and were very athletic: it was difficult to extricate from them but adrenaline flowed through my legs. I did not want to fight them: they were too beautiful to hurt. I ran fast. I ran straight. Utilizing my previous experience from the pitch black Dead Forest, I managed to escape them.

I ran and ran till my body cried for rest, but still I pushed myself. My hungry lungs gasped the cool night air of The Forest of Life. After a while, I began to feel I had eluded those savage women. However, I kept walking a pace, panting, and looking behind. Those women were deadly and I was in no mood to be roasted on a spit.

As I walked onwards, I espied up ahead, what looked like hundreds of candles flickering, strewn across the floor and branches of trees. I was drawn by the lambent and silently moved towards the glowing radiance. Then I saw small red lights dotted in the darkness, intensely glowing, then brightness mitigating. The forest air smelt peculiar, like a burning herb.

Suddenly, I heard, 'Aaarrgghh!' I had stood on a plump prostrate young man who was smoking something in a cone. There, scattered around the ground, were hundreds of pale corpulent men all smoking and barely moving. The rising smoke made me cough and my eyes watered. No one seemed to be unduly alarmed at my presence.

'Sit down maaan, have a toke,' said the man I had trodden on. 'Here, have this one. I'll roll another.'

'Yeah, c'mon, sit down, smoke, eat, reeelax,' said a flabby man who was eating a large chunk of chocolate, and then taking deep drags of a tube which seemed to be connected to a bubble device. The smoke began to make me feel light-headed. My quest's relevance seemed to melt away. The urgency I had always felt from leaving my village began to allay. To lay down and take it easy seemed a good idea. Shit! I was always rushing around. What did a silly old quest matter anyway? What did anything matter, ha! Chilling, yeah. Somebody passed me a smoke.

'What are y' all doin' layin' aran ere?' I asked.

'Maaaan, can y' think of anythin' better t' do?' said a large blubbery male who had just exhaled a large dense cloud of smoke.

'But aren't y' vulnerable to attack?' I asked.

'Who from man?' said another, who was in the process of rolling a great cylindrical object.

'Well, what about the Rubber Clad Dryads?' I said.

'Maaan, we live t' be caught by those beauties,' said another, who's eyes momentarily became animated, then relaxed back into a profound stupor.

'Yeah,' said another, 'can you think of anything better than being caught by those nymphomaniacs?' A couple chuckled in concurrence.

'But they kill you,' I said, as I found myself helplessly giggling along with them.

'Yeah, maaan, but what a way to die!' another one said, as he moved his groin up and down, the most movement I had seen from them.

'Yeah, man, we live for it. We wait here hoping we are next,' another said, who tried to sit up, but then changed his mind.

'You mean to tell me,' I said laughing, 'that you are all lounging around waiting to be carried away, decapitated, eaten, and you do nothing?'

'What can we do?' said one, with a gooey sugary substance dribbling from the lower half of his face. 'They're bigger than us…besides, we *want* to have sex with them. Our whole lives are centred around this.'

'And eating,' said another.

'And smoking,' another rejoined, and they all quietly chuckled in unison.

'If you wait here with us, you can get fucked,' said another. We all rolled around in hysterics. I laughed until tears streamed down my face.

'Yes,' I finally managed to choke out, 'it was good until she cried "Die!"'

'Die!' another one said, laughing uncontrollably. We all continued to laugh and I forgot all my cares.

The Silverwoman appeared in my head. 'Gorky! What are you doing? Look at these people. LOOK AT THEM!'

Still laughing, I looked around at them. They all lounged around, idle, eating, smoking. The food they were eating was stuck in their hair. Ash had fallen on everything. I suddenly stopped laughing. I began to feel revolted at them. I dragged my heavy body up, feeling dizzy, trying to hold steady. I negotiated myself around a sea of prostrate bodies. Illusions of rubber clad women cajoled me and tried to lure me to stay: they did all manner of erotic gestures. My pulse raced. My stomach ached. No, no, I must get out of this dead end. The blond woman said, 'You know you want to,' and blew me a kiss; the sable haired girl stood next to her and did a long lazy wink; 'Come on,' the red head said, and let her tongue slip down her chin. No, no, I must get out of here. I staggered forward. With all my determination, I dragged myself away. As I moved on, my head slowly began to clear. I started to think of Helena. I felt my ardent love rekindle. I staggered away, away from the stultifying torpor.

Nearby was a fast running stream: I tuned into the gurgling language of nature. I unbuckled my trusty sword and dived into the cold water, waking my dormant senses. I began to feel refreshed. The morning sunlight illuminated The Forest of Life into a beautiful vibrant green. I thought of the next phase of my journey. How far was it to Ice Mountain? Beyond there I would surely find Lake Sacradia. I stepped out of the stream, buckled my sword, and moved onwards. I stealthily moved through the trees. I regained my confidence and purpose: I began to feel in control. The ground flew past me...

'Halt, who goes there?'

I looked around, but could see nobody.

'Oy, down here.'

I looked down and saw a tribe of tiny men no taller than my knee.

'Oh, hello, who are you?' I politely asked.

'We are the Muldari, mighty and fearless. Identify yourself or we will shout at you and call you horrible names,' said a diminutive man who boldly stuck out his chest and stood on his toes.

'I am Gorky from Firkin Forest. I am on a quest to...'

'Silence you gibbering fool. You are Pooh-Pooh who have roamed into our territories with the Dryad's permission.'

'No, I am not Pooh-Pooh, I am...'

'Yes you are, you, you, smelly feet,' he shouted, looking round at one of his kinsmen for support.

'Yeah, and, and, smelly arms as well,' said the one next to him.

'Smelly arms,' they all said in chorus, waiting for the affect of their apparent vicious attack.

'Smelly arms? I am not from here. I am a traveller going to...'

'Silence, you, you, greasy haired person with very *very* smelly arms,' said their leader, as they all eagerly waited in expectation.

'If you don't mind, I will be on my way,' I said, deciding that asking them for assistance would be futile.

'This one is strong,' said the leader. 'He is able to resist our worst attack. I think he could easily overthrow us if he said anything nasty. We must offer him deference in order to pacify him and hope that he spares us.'

With that they all genuflected their knees and began to beg for forgiveness. Their demeanours suggested true remorse, for they wailed and blubbered and great tears rolled down their tiny cheeks.

'Please do not say anything nasty to us,' said the leader. 'We did not mean that your arms are smelly,' he continued, 'no, we meant your arms smell very nice. Yes you have nice smelling arms. We will call to day, in honour of your arrival, nice arm smell day. Please spare us.' He began to tug the bottom of my trousers. I felt an urgent need to leave. As I walked away I could hear them wailing in bitter remorse. I quickened my step. I wanted to be away from the forest. I longed to see Ice Mountain...

As I walked, the air became slightly cooler. Suddenly, between the vistas, in the distance, I saw great gleaming mountains, peaks obscured by clouds. I approached the periphery of the Forest of Life, which was still in healthy foliage, but there, beyond the forest, some distance in front, was the giant imposing stillness of mammoth protruding rocks and ice: Ice Mountain! I sat on the edge of the forest marvelling at this wonder of Zugra. I had only ever seen mountains painted in my mind's eye by the storytellers of my village. Nothing prepared me for the magnificent reality. I was awestruck at this phenomenon and excited at the prospect of climbing it. I fastidiously filled my bag with the fruits and vegetables of the forest's providence. I could roast or boil the vegetables: it would be important to eat hot food whilst scaling Ice Mountain. I remembered the skills of our village weavers and from the cotton plants I managed, with trial and error, to weave a heavy woollen coat with hood; I made wool trousers and wool coverings for my feet: for necessity is the mother of invention.

I then took a well earned nap. To recoup was paramount for the next ordeal. Helena, the success of my journey was now beginning to look realistic. I felt a surge of excitement at the prospect of returning to you. I had left you while you were fairly strong. The rosy hue of youth was still sitting on your cheeks. You were still in possession of your beauty: though your eyes, Helena, the door way to your soul, would always be beautiful. I dreamt of your sensuous hair and skin; I was wrapped in your hair and covered by your body; I could feel your breath against by body and hear your heart steadily beating: we lay entwined slumbering inseparable.

How disappointed I was to awake and find myself alone. The mountain stood daring me to scale its incredible heights. I could not wait to be on my way. I voraciously ate my fill on a variety of tasty nuts and bananas. I donned the woollen attire and gathered my provisions. A few steps from the shelter of the forest and the air instantly became chilled: I was pleased of my wool protection. Each step towards the mountain meant the temperature would drop.

5.

Ice Mountain

Soon I was treading on crunching snow, and icicles began to form on my eyebrows. I pertinaciously trudged forward: and, although, as I approached, the mountain's height rapidly increased, the base seemed to be no nearer. I began to realise it was presumptuous to believe that success was imminent. The mountain loomed overhead. The journey had just begun. The closer I got the more my doubt increased. The mountain towered ominously above me: and just when I thought I had nearly reached its foot, I walked further, and the mountain grew even more. I became intimidated. It sprang from the ground to blot out the sky. I started contemplating circumscribing the monster: but I looked to the left and right of me, and the mountain went on as far as the eye could see. So preoccupied with this organic mountain that I forgot how cold it was: for as the mountain increased in size so it grew colder. Ordinarily, I would not have had a second thought about turning back: but I could not go back and look Helena in the eyes. I had, by volition, willed myself to be so determined, so monomaniacal in my pursuit, that I was completely focused on the task. To any rational being, the scaling of the mountain was impossible: though I was profoundly nervous, my ardent love instilled in me the conviction that I could conquer this great obstacle and retrieve the magical waters of Lake Sacradia. The mountain grew gargantuan and dwarfed me to insignificance: I was an atom; it was a giant. It scorned my diminutiveness: like a bully, it threatened me to walk no further. I disregarded any notion of failure, and defiantly stepped onwards: for, though I was diminutive, the love inside me was infinite: this is how I would beat the mountain, with the power of love.

With much relief, I finally reached the base, the exhilaration of anticipating the climb abated. I slumped in exhaustion. I could hear nothing but my desperate attempts to inhale icy air. Soon, I regained my breath, and then all I could hear was deathly stillness. How could a mountain so huge be so quiet? I noticed that my apparel had become inundated with ice. I must have been carrying half my body weight in frozen water. I lay debilitated at the foot of a massive peaceful giant, the overseer of an ice terrain. I felt at one with Ice Mountain and at odds with it.

I fell into a deep delirious dream: I was sat cross legged on the summit of Ice Mountain opposite an elder I did not recognise who was chanting an old tribal song: his chant was in harmony with the mountain and my soul: all life rhythmically oscillated as one: the meaning of life manifested in the song...

I woke deeply grateful for the vivid dream: it strengthened my resolve; it bolstered my belief that there was something more than wonted consciousness: there is something wise and benevolent inextricably connected to our corporeal existence. I made a fire with some wood I had transported. I boiled some vegetables and made a hot broth. I became a tincture warmer: but my suit was penetrable to the biting cold. I had woken shivering: nevertheless, the hot food and crackling fire brought my flesh back to life again. All the time I was eating, I was mentally preparing for the climb: the mountain was a smooth wall of glassy ice: there were no anomalies, fissures, or salient points to get a good hand or foot-hold: the formidable façade presented itself as quite unassailable: I was perplexed as to how my ascent should commence. I decided to walk along the base in order to search for a more appropriate place to start my climb. During the scan I discerned that the mountain's surface was forbiddingly uniform, as if it had deliberately constructed itself to be insurmountable to any living creature.

'Having difficulty?' a voice suddenly broke the icy-silence. I span round, startled. There, standing on two legs, was a goat like creature. He looked rather ridiculous: his bottom half was human (wearing trousers); and the top half resembled a goat. My first instinct, after the shock, was to laugh: but I drew my sword, and held it before me anticipating an attack, either from him, or his comrades. 'Tut, tut, that's quite unnecessary,' he said. 'Can't you see I'm unarmed, and have no propensity for violence what so ever? Please, put that dreadful thing away: you're making me feel quite nervous.' I scrutinized him and the surroundings. Was it a trick, a ruse to put me off guard? I cautiously sheathed my sword: I decided it was expedient that I came in peace. 'There, that's better,' he said, sounding some what relieved. 'Now, if I may be so bold,' he continued, 'I assume by your demeanour that you intend to scale this here mountain, but are rather at a loss at how to do so: would I be correct in my assumption?'

'And if you were?' I countered.

'If I am,' he replied rather pleased, 'then I am the right person to help you in your endeavours.'

'I do not need any help,' I said, rather indignant that this scraggy creature had the knowledge to do something I obviously did not. 'I have come this far on my own,' I said rather bitterly. How and why he was there I had no curiosity to inquire. I began to be impatient for him to leave so I could continue deliberating how to find a way to start my ascent. 'Thank you for the offer,' I said, 'but I am not intending to climb the mountain just yet, but, when I do, I will not be needing any assistance. I bid you good day.' I boldly strode past him to continue my struggle in solving the riddle of the mountain.

'Do you have any climbing equipment?' he shouted after me. I ignored him and continued to walk purposefully forward as if I knew what I was doing. 'Well, when you have decided you are getting no where,' he shouted after me, 'just holla, and I'll be along.'

'Humph,' I said to myself, 'he's so sure that I do not know what I am doing: I will show him.' I suddenly turned to the mountain, for I was tired of walking along side of it, and began to scale the ice wall, or so I thought: but I could not even raise myself from the ground. I looked around, cringing, hoping he was not there to see my feeble efforts: luckily, he was gone. I sat down in deep despair. There must be a way to conquer this ice giant: I just needed a little more time to figure it out.

So, there I sat, stationary, pondering in the sheer cold: I remained in an icy-trance for some time. During my profound introversions, I became oblivious of my body's condition, which, slowly, but surely, became increasingly numb: I was rooted to the spot, incapacitated: my consciousness impelled me to break free from this moribund reverie: but, it was too late, I began spiralling into the darkness, dark-void, blank…

I awoke in a brightly illuminated cave of ice. The first thing I perceived was the effervescence of a brilliant orange incandescent dancing flame that crackled energy. Dotted around the cave were impressive sculptures of fantastical creatures carved from solid ice. Stood before the fire was the absurd looking creature I had tried to ignore. 'So, you're finally awake,' he said. I tried to talk, but could not. Every fibre ached, like I had been dropped from a great height. My instinct was to sit up: but when I tried, my head span: my body, quite simply, refused. The great fleece he had covered me with felt like the weight of the world. 'You were lucky that I checked how you were doing…Not too well,' he said, with a wry smile and waving his hoof in disapproval. 'You have obviously no idea what you are doing: but I wish not to rebuke you: the elements have seen to that. Here, drink some of this.' My initial response was revulsion: I did not want any thing from this monstrosity, and yet, the instant the potion settled on my palate, I began to feel vigour. The sand which had lay heavy in my veins, transformed into blood, a warm electric liquid energy. I began to feel vitality in my muscles, urging movement: I sat up, my eyes wide a wake. The toils of my journey sloughed from my body and I stood over the fire feeling stronger: restlessness grew inside me: I wanted action, physical exertion: I wanted to leap over the mountain in a single bound: I must be gone: I had a mountain to climb. I looked for my sword and equipment and hurriedly donned my gear, and made my way to the exit. Where was the exit? 'Where is the exit?' I commanded.

'There's a storm raging out there,' he said, 'and I must warn you that if you adopt the same strategy for climbing the mountain as previously, you will invariably fail: I use the term strategy loosely, for all I could witness was a lost fool blindly and stubbornly ambling around.' I was in no mood for this goat-boy to condescend to me. I was a mighty adventurer who had travelled over many lands. Who was he but a stupid looking creature that lived entombed in an ice cave: I drew my sword and held it at his hairy throat.

'Silence, Goat-Boy, I could behead you in a single stroke. How do I get out of here?' I commanded, angry that he did not look intimidated while I was doing my best to be menacing.

'Is that any way to talk to somebody who has saved your life?' he rejoined, gently placing his hand on the sword and slowly lowering it. 'Though I am beginning to wonder why I bothered: your arrogance, it seems, has no boundary. Also, *mountain-man,*' he smirked, 'if you kill me, you will never leave this cave.'

The initial surge of the potion wore off, and, suddenly, realising the gratitude I should owe to this, this, goat, I slumped on the floor.

'Okay, okay,' I concurred, 'I am in debt to you. I…I…a-p--o-l-o-g-i-s-e. It's just that, I am a great explorer, and I must be moving on: I have to conquer the mountain.'

'You have no idea what you are encountering: you must know how to negotiate this formidable phenomenon: brute strength alone is no use: you need finesse, skill, savvy. Comprehend?'

'Continue,' I frowned, reluctant to trust this weirdo.

'I', he said, whilst walking around the cave, gathering ropes, iron stakes, and other hoisting devices, 'was once like you, an arrogant adventurer: I too was on a mission: I was going to Lake Sacradia to retrieve the water to cure my people. A dreadful disease had taken hold: they were rapidly dying. I had been elected, with two others, to sally forth and retrieve the magical water. My two compatriots died in the forest of life: they were subjected to involuntary coitus, cut into pieces, and made into a casserole. I luckily escaped, but unfortunately I could do nothing to save them.' He looked very distressed and guilt ridden when he told me this. After collecting the equipment he sat by the fire and continued his story. 'Where I come from, there are many precipices, much rugged terrain: we are no strangers to snow and ice: we had anticipated that which we encountered on the trek. Ice Mountain, though, was far more hazardous than I imagined: I had to muster all my guile and strength to ascend this precipitous wall of ice. The going was tough: sometimes it felt I had made a mistake in attempting to tackle Ice Mountain. It seemed alive in its stubbornness and uncooperativeness: it shunned me, rejected my efforts: I was ground down by its hostile propensity: it was relentless in its refusal to comply with my ascension. Half way up, I began to feel forlorn. I had eaten all my food; my strength was ebbing; I was extremely low in morale: I sat dejected. I must have passed out, for, when I regained consciousness, I was in a wooden cabin. A fire joyously danced in the hearth. I then heard a woman's voice, "So, you are awake at last," she said. Her tones were convivial, like a heavenly aunt. She had prepared a table with all manner of delicacies. "Are you strong enough to sit at the table?" she inquired. "I think so," I replied. The smell of such delicious food quickly revived me. I ate heartily, and afterwards told her of my quest to find Sacradia. She listened intently, and spoke only when I had finished. "I could help you to get there," she said. "So it does really exist!" I exclaimed, because, although I had participated in the quest with gusto, part of me had always remained cynical. With the affirmation from this amiable woman, I began to feel new resolve. "Yes, it exists as sure as you are sat there," she said, "but there are many dangers to be had before arriving. I can alert you to them, and, also offer advice on the best course of action to take." I leapt up. "Well, tell me as I get ready to leave," I said, as I looked around for my heavy coat. "You must help me first," she said. "When you have done what I request, I will impart the knowledge for success." "Look, I do not wish to be rude," I said, "the meal was nice, and I appreciate you saving me, but I have already wasted time: I must crack on." "But it is not much I ask for," she remonstrated. "If it is not much, I am sure you can do it yourself," I retorted, finding my coat and equipment, but as I reached for them, they vanished. Yes, completely disappeared. "You selfish little boy," the woman said, her voice becoming more raucous. The room took on a darker aspect as the flames in the hearth changed to lurid green. Her mien seemed more malignant, and her eyes glared with evil intent. "You will never leave this mountain," she screeched. "You are destined to roam this barren ice mountain for the rest of your life: any attempt to leave, and you will surely perish; if you try and vacate this side of the mountain, you will die." She was quite excitable now. "Calm down old woman," I said, starting to feel alarmed, because she had become distinctly more shrivelled. "What is it you want me to do?" "Too late! Too late!" she yelled, and pointed her craggy finger at me: sparks leaped from her bony hand and swirled around me: my torso began to grow long grey hair, and I felt horns protrude from my cranium: it was quite painful as the structure of my skull transmogrified: my hands were next: the fingers shrank, then vanished: hard bony knobs developed: and before I could do anything, I had hooves that once were hands. "What have you done?" I bleated: my voice now had a sheepish quality about it. I stood bewildered waiting for the final transformation: my top half had become goat; but my lower half still remained human. "Leave!" she commanded. "Leave before I finish the spell." I needed no further prompting: I ran for all I was worth: I did not want to be a goat: I clung to the vestiges of human that were left. Of course, in retrospect, I may as well have waited for her to complete the odious spell, at least I would have been warm: my legs are always cold, but, from my waist upwards, I always feel warm.' He looked at the fire in sad reverie, imbued with a lamentable regret.

'So, what is it she wanted you to do?'

'I never did find out,' he replied.

'Have you tried escaping from Ice Mountain?' I continued.

'No, if she has the power to vanish my equipment and turn me into this dreadful creature, I can only presume that she has it within her means to kill me if I leave.'

'What do you have to lose in trying? Look at your life, living in this inhospitable place. You may as well take a chance.'

'Where there's life there's hope,' he said. 'Do you think I'm going to assist you to the summit for nothing? I want you to return with some of Lake Sacradia. The water is a panacea; it can cure anything: I am certain that if I drink some, the spell will be broken. If I help you, will you help me?' he pleaded.

'It just so happens I'm going there anyway. But what about the enchantress, will she intervene?'

'Don't worry about her: I am hoping she is unaware of your presence here'

'Hoping?!' I thought for a few seconds: this creature had been so accommodating. If it was not for him, I would have been an ice statue at the foot of the mountain. 'Okay, I'll do it. Can I ask you one more thing?'

'Sure.'

'What was in the drink I took?'

'Oh, that, it is a tonic provided by the old woman so I do not become too low-spirited: spending aeons on this desolate mountain induces profound despair, which, at times, can be quite overwhelming: she had seen me a number of times in a depressed stupor, and took a little pity on me: you see, I'm in limbo: I cannot die: and yet, I have no life.'

'How do you pass the time?'

'I climb to the peak of the mountain: I have had much time and much practice to climb it: then, I look longingly down the forbidden side, imagine my descent, and the discovery of Sacradia. Sometimes, I carve ice figures with my hooves; other times, I spend in long dialogues with myself. She has seen to it that I do not need to eat or sleep…That's my life really.'

'You spend your life trapped on this mountain with no company. You do not eat. You do not sleep. You have no purpose other than to wait.'

'I wait for somebody like you to assist in my emancipation. I can help you to the summit. I can take evasive action to avoid the enchantress and her spells. You can pass down the side of the mountain that is forbidden to me and retrieve the water that will break the spell. Without me, I can assure you, you will not climb this mountain. With out you, I may remain interminably trapped. But enough of this talking: I have waited a long time for some foolish, er, for a mountaineer to appear. I have a sense of purpose again: although I fear it will be too late to save my people. Here, take this rope, Ice Ax and crampons, and put these climbing boots on.' Before we embarked, Goat-Boy explained the triangle technique, body weight transfer and general movement pattern of ascent. He became quite animated in his explanation, and I could tell that climbing a mountain was serious business. 'Let's go!' he finally yelled.

I was now laden with climbing equipment which was quite impressively light to carry, although I could not say the same for my own provisions. He ushered me to one of the ice walls of the cave and suddenly a portal appeared. We both exited the cave and I discerned we were already some considerable height from ground level. Ice and sleet relentlessly rained down like arrows: I pulled the woollen hood tightly around my head: but still my face was stung. 'The mountain consists of a series of escarpments and plateaux. Although the escarpments are precipitous and hazardous, we can camp and rest on each plateau. My hooves are able to gouge footings in the ice that enables me to raise my body. As I climb, I will attach additional pitons for you. You will always follow me and do what I say. I have climbed the mountain umpteen times, and you must remember it is now my home. Do as I say and you will be standing on the summit: ignore me, and you will fall to your death. Are there any questions?'

Goat-Boy had become quite authoritative, and at any other time I would have objected to his imperious tones: but I also had an urgency to move on: I wanted to reach Sacradia as bad as he did, and, like it or not, for now, we were a team.

'If there are any questions which arise I will not hesitate to ask,' I rejoined, 'but for now, let's get climbing.'

Goat-Boy scurried up the side of the ice wall in bewildering rapidity; my laboured movements, were, quite pedestrian, in comparison: but it was a great feeling to be ascending the mountain at last. The walls were steep, and it took every ounce of concentration and strength to haul myself up, even though the way had been meticulously prepared. I would certainly not have stood a chance in climbing the mountain alone: and, although part of me was still disappointed in needing aid, I realised the incontrovertible necessity. Goat-Boy was an extraordinary mountaineer who handled a vertical like a horizontal. After a time I began to hanker for a plateau. My body ached. Suddenly I slipped from the stake that had been driven into the ice. It seemed I fell for eternity. I did not stop falling. Then, BANG! The rope that was tied around my waist became taught and took my whole weight: it knocked the wind out of me and I emitted an involuntary yell. I was suspended in the air, hanging by a rope. It felt like my back had broken. I fought to stay conscious.

'Are you okay?' Goat-Boy shouted down to me. I could not answer; I tried to shout back, but a pathetic croak was all I could muster. 'Are you okay?' he shouted again. After the shock, I began to recover. The rope was uncomfortably tight around my waist. I managed to take a grip of the stake in the ice wall and support my weight: this relieved the tension of the rope and I began to breathe easier.

'I'm okay,' I shouted, as I swallowed blood. 'Just give me a moment to recover. How much longer is it?'

'Not much longer,' he replied. Goat-Boy had made a habit of saying this.

I began to laboriously haul myself upwards. How I desired a flat surface to rest my weary body…

Goat-Boy was tireless in his enthusiasm to keep on climbing. Whenever he sensed I was waning, he would issue encouragement. I was his only means of escape, and with that premise, I could be assured my life was in safe hands…er… hooves. Sometimes my body only felt half its usual weight, and I could only presume that it was because he was hauling me up, impatient to scale the mountain. 'Come on! Come on!' he would say when ever I began to lose momentum. With effort, I pulled my body upwards. 'Not long now to the first plateau,' he would say.

'How many plateaux to the top?' I gasped.

'Not many,' was the inevitable reply. So this was how it was: him above me encouraging me onwards; me, slowly, and methodically, raising myself piecemeal, yearning for a flat surface…

After much effort, I eventually slumped onto the first plateau: it was smaller than I imagined: but there was enough surface area to allow me to sprawl on the ground and realize the pain of my body. After the large physical effort, when volition and adrenalin finally subsided, the body suddenly indicated the sheer strain it had been under: I lay exhausted, almost in tears, bewildered at how much effort it had taken to get this far, and knowing it would take a lot more to reach the top. Goat-Boy lit a fire to boil a pot of water: in it he put carrots, suede and potatoes. Soon there was a delicious smell of vegetables stewing: this perked me up: the food was delicious: I greedily scoffed the lot. I noticed Goat-Boy did not partake in the vegetable stew.

'Did you want some?' I asked, after finishing.

'I do not eat, remember?' he replied.

'Do not eat?'

'I told you, the enchantress has denied me that pleasure.'

'And yet she gives you an elixir?'

'What can I say, she's a complex woman.'

'Food is one of the finest pleasures in life…Have you any of that elixir?' I queried.

'No, it's rationed,' he replied.

'Where is the enchantress's cabin situated?' I asked.

'Do not worry about that,' he said, 'we will steer clear of her habitat: if she knew you were here, she would certainly take measures to thwart your quest; she would not allow you to assist me in extricating from this spell.'

'Where does she live?' I reiterated.

'Some distance from here,' was all the reply.

'Could she not use magic to scour the mountain in order to locate us?'

'I presume she does not suspect any thing as yet; visitors to this region are so rare that she will not be vigilant in detecting anybody.'

'Why does she choose to live here in this cold and barren place far away from people?' I could see Goat-Boy was becoming irritated at my incessant questioning.

'She came from over the sea in order to become a recluse.'

'Why is she a recluse? What is *the sea*?'

'Call yourself a great adventurer?' Goat-Boy laughed. 'You will find out what the sea is soon enough. As for why she chooses to isolate herself, a man she once loved abandoned her: full of anger and bitterness, she fled her native land so she could forget. Sadly, she has developed into a cynical old woman; she is mostly misanthropic: her heart is frozen as ice.'

'But what of *the sea*?' I asked, feeling piqued that my great sense of achievement had been undermined.

'The sea?'

'Yes, the sea,' I said, eager to know.

'Oh, you'll know soon enough,' he said, as if there was something momentous afoot, warming his hooves by the fire.

'Why soon enough?' I urged.

'Do you think your journey is over when you reach the other side of the mountain?'

'Well, I was hoping it would be, though I never really gave it much thought.'

'No, you never: in fact, your whole quest has been dependent entirely on chance, has it not?' he snapped.

'It is not my fault you are in this predicament,' I exclaimed.

'You have no map; no appropriate equipment; you're ill prepared: it is a wonder you are not dead. You think you were

going to dance over this mountain and dive into Lake Sacradia?'
he sat scowling at me, and allowed the silence to oppress me.

'Okay, what is beyond the mountain?' I said.

'The great Sea of Leviathans: you thought the desert was big;
you think the mountain is high: wait till you set sail on the sea.'
His eyes widened becoming suffused with intense earnest.

'What is *a sea*? What does *set sail* mean?' I began to feel
concerned: the sea sounded formidable: I did not relish the
prospect of *setting sail*.

'The sea is a great salty expanse of water,' he said.

'Is that all?' I replied with relief. 'I am Gorky the waterboy. I
have collected water from the river since a child. The sea will be
no match for me,' I proclaimed triumphantly.

'The sea is like no water you can imagine; it cannot be drunk;
it is not still; it does not trickle; large waves buffet any floating
thing; the sea roars and foams: it has giant crests and troughs, up
and down, up and down, higher, lower.' Goat-Boy became quite
animated, waving his hooves around in violent gestures, which
I supposed emulated the sea: I started to feel a little afraid. 'The
sea contains monsters, large carnivorous creatures, with teeth
like swords, savage and merciless. The sea is to be respected.'

'The, the sea,' I repeated, trying to envisage what it would be
like, my courage sinking and despair taking over: for, just when
I thought I was making headway, something greater, something
larger, stepped in my way to thwart my ambitions.

'How am I to traverse the sea?' I inquired, forgetting
about the treacherous and rugged climb ahead: Goat-Boy then
produced a folded paper from his pocket.

'Here is a plan for a making sailing boat,' he said. 'When
you reach the coastline, you will discern along the shore all
types of tree. Here are the instructions to construct a boat from
those trees. With your sword you can make tools. You need to
be patient, skilful and determined, but it is within your means.
He gave me the diagram. I read a part of it: 'There is a forest

that lays before the Sea of Leviathans which can supply the raw materials needed for constructing a sailing ship which will be capable under the correct supervision to conquer the sea.' Goat-Boy then took out another piece of paper. 'Here,' he said, 'is a map with directions that will lead to Lake Sacradia.' I looked at the diagram, there, beyond the mountain, an image of the sea, a sea with horrific creatures depicted in green swirling waves: and, beyond this, was a silver oval that represented… Lake Sacradia. 'Do not be fooled by the scale of the map,' he said, 'for the sea cannot be represented by a piece of paper.' I recalled the desert: the diagram belied its size and heat; and the picture of the mountain did not depict the real ice giant: but, there, on the map, the sea out scaled everything. I touched the picture of the lake: I had a small schematic diagram of Lake Sacradia at my fingertips. I began to daydream of the moment I would fill my canisters with the magical water, the feeling I would derive from drinking it… The sea presented an unknown peril: I tried to imagine what it would be like: it filled me with trepidation so I decided to blot it from my mind. I pictured the silver oval that was Lake Sacradia: I would not let the silver oval leave my mind: the silver oval was my destiny.

I fell asleep: I was a flea on the map: I crawled over the picture of the desert and the mountain and the sea to the lake: but it was only silver paint: the map folded around me: I was immersed in the various hazards of the quest: I was trapped in the paper unable to escape.

I woke with a start, gasping for air. The bright white ice flooded into my senses; great wads of snowflakes descended from the ice-grey sky. Goat-Boy was gone! I was stuck on a narrow plateau, no way up, no way down, and a great height from the ground.

'Goat-Boy!' I shouted, but my voice dissipated into the

hoary sky. I was trapped; at the mercy of the elements: the mountain victorious. I was to die after all, on a little ridge, with the snow as my tomb: my quest was over. 'Goat-Boy!' I shouted. He had deliberately left me to my doom. The instructions for the boat, the map, were part of his sick joke to raise my hopes before deflating me. I took one last look at the phoney map and threw it on the smouldering fire: the fire burnt a curious green. I was about to sling the instructions regarding construction of the boat, when Goat-Boy appeared.

'What are you doing?!' he exasperatingly shouted.

'Where were you?' I asked, unconvincingly trying to not sound panicked.

'Making a reconnoitre, and if you want to alert the enchantress to our whereabouts, I suggest you continue to yell,' he glared accusingly.

'How was I to know where you had gone?' I remonstrated, stuffing the boat plans deep into my woollen pocket. 'Let's go,' I ordered, knocking the settling snow from my coat. The flakes fell so fast the fire was soon covered: we had to keep moving, or be lost in snow and ice.

'I have prepared the next phase of the climb while you slept: but I warn you, the enchantress is sensitive to any anomalous disturbances in the air,' Goat-Boy advised. 'Let's hope she has not heard your big mouth. Follow me,' he frowned. Goat-Boy was soon climbing the wall of ice and disappearing into the snowy sky: I quickly followed determined not to be out done by this haughty goat. As for the enchantress, did I not wield a formidable sword that could slice through metal? She was only an old woman: her physical strength was incomparable to mine. The snow landed on my face making it difficult to see: it hindered my progress: I had to keep wiping it from my eyes. Goat-Boy's long hairy eyebrows shielded his eyes from the snow: and when the snow landed on them, he simply raised his eyebrows, and it fell away. We soon fell into the laborious routine of yore: me hauling myself up the stakes, the foot holes, the rope: and him impatiently cajoling me from above. To take my mind from the climb, I mentally built the boat: though I found it difficult because I had never actually seen a boat before: nothing in our legends had ever mentioned seas: we thought Zugra's mythical waterways were only streams, rivers, and, of course, Lake Sacradia. I was to set sail in a boat... a boat: it sounded so much grander than a log. A boat twenty times longer than me with a great sail and rudder: I would be at the tiller steering forth towards the beautiful alchemical lake. I must have began to mitigate my efforts, because Goat-Boy started ranting, 'Come on!' he said, 'do you want to reach the summit?'

'I'm pacing myself,' I growled. He sharply tugged on the rope attached to my waist inducing a visceral pain that made me feel nauseous. 'Arrrgghh! You idiot! Do not pull the rope like that!'

'Shut up!' he vehemently replied.

'You shut up!' I scowled. 'I'm going as fast I can. I am not a bloody goat. I have not spent aeons clambering up and down this mountain like a lunatic.' The anger I felt induced a surge of energy into my bones: I pushed forward with aggressive purpose. I could not tolerate Goat-Clown bossing me around: was he not in thrall by an old woman. I would beat him to Lake Sacradia. He needed me to save him. I made so much effort in climbing that I must have fainted: I regained consciousness on the second plateau. Goat-Boy had made a fire and constructed a shelter that protected us from the snow.

'That fall,' he said, 'must have done some internal damage: you began vomiting blood, then became unconscious. We will have to sojourn here longer than I would have liked for you to recuperate.' I sat dejected, staring at the fire, wondering just what injury I had incurred: I hoped it was not too serious... Goat-Boy had begun making an annoying habit of saving my life. I was utterly dependent on him during the climb. I disconsolately sighed and stared into the fire. The flames entranced me. Oh Helena, how abjectly cold I feel: your body, sweet lady, is so warm. Visions of her smiling in her garden tending the flowers flashed before my eyes: what paradise to be with her beautiful soul right now. Even my old job as waterboy seemed more attractive, people of my village taking on a more benign aspect. I remembered times when I was blithe and insouciant. I recalled the tinkling stream, singing birds, and rustling leaves: everything there was safe and relaxing: why had I felt so unsatisfied? I was startled from my reverie: a tuft of hair floated from my head onto the fire: it crackled and smelt of putrescent death: shocked, I gazed into the flames. Me! I had the dreaded disease! I never even considered the possibility: it happened to others, not me. A strong sense of mortality instantly pervaded me. I looked at the falling snow and saw nothing but beauty now: each individual flake was perfectly formed.

'How long are we going to stay here?' I asked Goat-Boy, who had been gazing into the flickering flames of the fire in a reverie of his own.

'Are you strong enough to move?' he asked.

'Yes,' I unconvincingly claimed. I began to gain the impression that my time for retrieving the alchemical healing water was becoming contracted. Goat-Boy had not noticed my hair melting in the fire: he was prone to a melancholy trance whenever he became inactive. I stood up and fastidiously gauged my energy levels. It was expedient to start making more progress. As Goat-Boy began to ascend, I grabbed him by his hairy shoulder. 'Let me go first,' I said: I was tired of having him above me leading the way: I would be expedition leader. Maybe it was a way of confronting death: for, if I could take control of the climb, I could take control of my life.

'Is that wise?' he queried, 'considering you have fallen twice, and passed out on a number of occasions too? Would it not be better if I led the way? I have had much more experience climbing the mountain than you.' He put his hoof up to stop me.

'Unhand me, I mean, unhoof me: you are not my boss,' I imperiously declared. I had to climb with exigency: I did not know how much time I had left or how far away Lake Sacradia was: all I knew was I simply had to retrieve its recuperating powers. I could smell the healing waters in the distance. 'And I won't need to be fastened to you!' I barked, hauling myself up the ice wall surface. Goat-Boy never said a word: he merely shrugged and followed me...

I started to feel more confidence in handling the cliff face: I became more adept: I felt less clumsy, less ponderous, more agile, more relaxed; I developed a discernible rhythm; there was a spring in my step: I was sure I could surpass Goat-Boy's climbing exploits: 'Just call me mountain man!' I yelled. Then I slipped. I fell through the air: but this time there was no safety rope. I landed on Goat-Boy with a thud: it was like hitting an immovable object. I managed to grab his ankles; there I was grovelling at his feet. I managed to transfer my weight onto the stirrups fastened into the mountain. Goat-Boy lowered me a rope, which, at first, I rejected: here he was coming to my rescue again. He steadily and reproachfully stared at me. I reluctantly attached the rope around my waist: once more I was following Goat-Boy. We carefully made our way to the third plateau...

I flopped onto the surface melting into the ice floor: I had propelled my reluctant body beyond its limitations. The relief of another stage washed over me. 'How much further?' I gasped.

'Not long now,' was the wonted reply.

'How long is not long?' was my rejoinder.

'Not long'.

'HOW LONG!' I desperately panted.

'Soon,' he calmly replied, belying his irritation.

'Your abstract distances leave me no wiser,' I said. Each plateau looked identical to the last: we could have been arriving at the same plateau and getting nowhere. I suspected Goat-Boy was an evil prankster: but I had no choice other than to trust him. However, I was rapidly developing the skills to ascend the interminable surface, and deemed it was less crucial to have his assistance. Goat-Boy kindled the fire and threw some turnips and potatoes in the cooking pot: I greedily ate the food, for there is nothing like exercise to stimulate the appetite. I soon grew impatient to get moving again. 'Come on,' I said, 'let's get climbing.'

'Not so hasty, we have just finished a long and arduous climb: it is necessary to rest.'

'Look, your people may be dead, but mine are not: I have to save them: dilatoriness will increase fatality.' Goat-Boy scowled at me: it incited my indignation. 'As a human being, I am officially taking over this expedition, you, you, moufflon-man! You are half-animal, and nowhere in the history of my people have animals controlled us: you must fall into rank, and serve, as your kind always has.' I stood up, towering above him, to let him know I was superior: I drew my sword for emphasis. His delineations conveyed perplexity and exasperation.

'You are perpetually attempting to take command: but you are perpetually ignoring your own blunders. It is true, I appear half-animal: I may have a goat's head, but I still possess my human mind, so, technically, I am *all* human: therefore, I warn you, if you persist in your inclinations for autocracy, I will leave you here to your own devices. I strongly desire freedom, and, unfortunately, you are the only means to attain it: but I still have my pride: I will not humiliate myself and defer to you. Now, you either let me rightfully take control of this climb, or you are on your own.' He looked at my sword in disgust: then fixedly stared at the fire.

'But then *you* will be on your own,' I declared. 'And as for autocracy, it is you who is fond of issuing irrevocable commands: that is over now: I do not need you: but, I will spare your life.' I sheathed my sword and continued to climb upwards, glad that I no longer had the responsibility of helping him. Besides, I was tired of his introverted self-sorry ruminations. I was independent again, the great lone voyager. Up I climbed. The mountain held no more surprises for me. In all likelihood, I was fast approaching the summit. I climbed upwards, up, up, up. Though I grew weary I did not stop. Soon my body grew heavy. I tried to push on, but I began to feel feint. I clung hold of the Ice Ax. I momentarily lost my footing, but managed to hold on for dear life, scrambling to acquire purchase with my crampons: there I clung, helpless, at the mercy of the unyielding mountain; I could neither rise nor descend. I belched a globule of blood...

When I regained consciousness, Goat-Boy said, 'I should have left you to die, you fool.' In a daze I looked around and found myself on the fourth plateau.

'What happened?' I inquired.

'I had decided to follow your progress: you were frozen to the mountainside: I had to release your frozen grip. Why do you continually rebuff my efforts to help you? Why are you so determined to deny that you cannot do this without me? Your obstinacy is going to get you killed.'

I felt deflated: I wanted to be the invincible saviour of my people, not just a paltry waterboy.

'Oh shut up, you are not helping me for philanthropic reasons, but to emancipate yourself: in me, you see your escape from the mountain,' I retorted.

'Yes, in you I see the possibility of extrication from this seemingly ineluctable place: but when I escape this wretchedness, I will be able to help others: and, I also assist you, because, although I was not able to help my own people, there is still a chance your people can be saved.'

'Shut up Goat-Boy, you have been forthcoming in your aid because I can save you. ME! Now, light a fire, or I will never return to this God forsaken place, and you will be destined to stay here for eternity, freezing and lonely.' Goat-Boy stared at me incredulously, then began to depart from the plateau. 'Wait, where are you going?' I feebly implored.

'I would rather freeze than be subjected to your peremptory attitude: I have had enough of being on a rope team with you: it's akin to suicide: I am going, goodbye... and, er, good luck, but I suppose you are too high and mighty for the whims of luck.' Seeing him making his departure filled me with horror.

'No! Er, wait, look, I'll make the fire. It would be a shame if, er, you were stuck here and I did not help you. Together we'll conquer this Ice Mountain, and I'll bring the magical waters of Sacradia to you... I promise.' Goat-Boy stopped his descent, thought for a second, and then returned to the plateau. So I made the fire and we sat in silence as I ate cooked vegetables. After the meal I took a nap...

I heard funeral rites and people cheering, celebrating: how strange to hear such a gleeful congregation at such a solemn event: I found myself lying prostrate in the darkness, in a small rectangular box: I pushed on the lid, but it would not yield: I called to the people outside: they were oblivious to me; there was soil being slung over the box; I felt worms crawl over my body, slithering over my face, and wriggling into my mouth: I woke screaming.

I sat up staring at the fire fully engaging in the dancing flames, glad to have regained consciousness. 'Let's move on,' I blurted.

'Are you ready?' Goat-Boy asked, looking at me a little bewildered.

'Yes, I'm ready, er, lead the way.'

'Lead the way? Are you sure, oh great one?' Goat-Boy looked at me with an irritating smirk. I decided it best to ignore his sarcasm.

'Yes, yes, get moving will you: I crave for movement: I cannot wait to get off this wretched mountain: come on, let's go.' In truth I was afraid: the dream had been so vivid. It is peculiar how we cannot detect the transition between waking and sleeping; and how gently we are lulled into the world of surrealism: for if the dream is not lucid, we are tricked into believing these products of the mind are actuality. I was also aware that if I allowed thoughts of the disease to preoccupy me, I may become despondent: I decided to force the thoughts of the malady deep into my unconsciousness: I had to remain focused in order to function effectively: if my mind wandered, I would fall: maybe if I stayed positive I could delay the spread of the disease: thoughts can determine feelings which can affect behaviour.

As we climbed, I began to develop a reluctant admiration for Goat-Boy: he was strong and reliable and had been reasonably patient with me. He had been trapped in this icy environment for ages, and never once had I heard him moan of his lot. I decided that I should change his nomenclature. I had deliberately chosen Goat-Boy because it was demeaning. I would now call him Mountain Monk, yes, it sounded so much more dignified. After an arduous climb... we eventually reached plateau number five.

'Mountain Monk!' Goat-Boy laughed. 'From a hairy oaf, to a holy-man, ha, that's some promotion!' He began to posture around the plateau, strutting, with his head held aloft, and waving his hoof in small circular motions: then he sat down and stared into the fire. 'I do not know if I can handle such a lofty position. Thanks all the same.'

'So what's your proper name?'

'Goat-Boy will suffice. I am a silly looking hairy half-man-half-goat, a mere tool for your success. Do not bother to ingratiate yourself: I have already said I will help you.'

'Okay, how much further? I asked, as I held a spoon of frothing vegetable stew with a backdrop of colossal brilliant white snow. My appreciation for food had refined. The whole process for preparing and eating it was integral to my success. Food equals energy, and it was the only real thing to occupy myself while we rested on each plateau. The food I had brought was nearly finished. I could now understand why Mountain Monk had not imparted distances to me: it would have been extremely daunting and demoralizing: but I felt it was now crucial for me to know. I looked over the edge, but everything was obscured by dense mist; I looked upwards, but the snow obscured my vision: I could only surmise how high we were now. The air was growing perceptibly thinner: I was breathing harder. It was becoming progressively colder. Mountain Monk was lost in his holy musings as the fire danced in his human eyes. 'How much further?' I asked, a little more forcefully and pulled him out of his reverie.

'What does the stew taste like?' he replied. 'It's been such a long time since I had the pleasure of eating.'

'Well, eat.'

'I have told you, I cannot: if I do, I am violently ill and vomit: her wicked spell ensured I could never eat until it is finally broken.' He looked at me, fascinated as I ate. 'Let me have the vicarious experience of eating: what does a carrot taste like?'

'Er, I do not think I can describe what a carrot taste like, erm, it taste like, like, like a carrot.' I began to feel decidedly guilty as I ate: I continued in a manner that suggested I was not enjoying it, while all the time thinking, what a privilege to eat such delicious food. After the meal, I slept...

'Helena, are you okay?' The efflorescent garden was vivid light:

the stark colours of flowers were too bright to look at directly: sunshine flooded onto lurid foliage: askance, my eyes squinted in pain: then, suddenly, everything became dull and grey. 'Helena, I would follow you into the darkness.' Each footstep heard insects scream. 'Helena, are you there?' Insects to my knees; sinking into a ground of scurrying beetles. A grey flower, being eaten by a slug, drooped in front of my face, with a decaying note tied to it, 'Ignis Chthonic.' I sank into the insects and heard roaring fire below me. I began to spiral downwards and as I did the temperature increased until the heat became unbearable… I woke with a start, screaming into the snow filled air.

Mountain Monk looked amused. He had grown accustomed to my dramatic awakenings. 'I used to love sleep,' he said, ignoring my wild staring eyes, 'I felt utterly deprived when the enchantress took it from me: but seeing you… Ha, ha, ha…'

'What does "Ignis Chthonic" mean' I nervously inquired.

'Ignis chthonic?'

'Yes.'

'Fire of the underworld, why?'

'Oh, nothing.' A wave of acute despair swept over me.

'You look extremely troubled. What's wrong?'

'She is not in the garden. The garden is dying. She's not there.'

'Who is she?'

'Helena, my lady, she's gone.'

'It's only a dream. Your mind can have dark imaginings, especially when you are unhappy; you are only anxious because you cannot be near her: think nothing of it. The seventh plateau is the peak, okay? We will soon be there.'

'Two more?'

'Yes, two more, and it's down hill from there: in fact, you will be descending a lot quicker than you ascended.'

'What do you mean!' I shouted, pulling at his hairy arm.

'Ouch! Get off. Pull yourself together. I have carved the

plateaux so they are equidistance apart: so now you know what it will take to reach the summit.'

'Right, let's get going.' The thought of the summit only two plateaux away lifted my flagging heart. We gathered our things and began to ascend. I blanked the dream from my mind: I would not tolerate any impediments to my success. Helena *was* alive and waiting for me: she was always my inspiration to strive. The air was thin. I was cold. My body ached. I gritted my teeth. Climb. Climb on. Climb. Grab. Push. Lift. Ascend…

On the sixth plateau the wind and snow raged. Mountain Monk shouted through the howling, 'We cannot light a fire up here. Huddle yourself in the corner. You will have to eat the remainder of the food raw.' I was in a stultifying daze. The effort of climbing, the thinness of the air, the pelting snow: it was manic up here. An ice mask formed on my face. I felt profoundly numb: it felt a relief. Was I alive? I floated outside my body and hovered above my shell: I was perfectly serene…

'Eat!' Mountain Monk shook me and I came crashing back into my flesh. Pain! I mechanically began to eat raw turnip: the vegetable juice stimulated my sense: but I felt drowsy, and my head began to nod…

'Eat!' Mountain Monk shook me again: I was startled from my trance: I realised I was dying and a nervous energy surged through my blood. Do not die on this forsaken mountain, Gorky… Why not? It's peaceful shedding clay… No, you are too young to die: you have things to do: live!

'Eat!'

Again I snapped from the reverie. Mountain Monk thrust a potato into my hands. I chewed the food as if it was the anchor to existence. I felt more secure inside my flesh. I voraciously ate all the food that was left. I felt weak, but this time not with soporific death but with balmy sleep. 'I need to sleep.'

'I do not think you should sleep just yet,' Mountain Monk advised.

'It's okay. Let me sleep...'

From the top of the mountain I see the world: refulgent sun; golden desert; green forests...what is that crystal blue shimmering, amazing cobalt blue expanse flecked with frothy veins, blue mass of movement, living, breathing, heaving, sighing? The sea!

'Wake up, Gorky!'

I woke to ice-pellets pinging on my face, the howling swirling wind, and vigorous dancing snowflakes in manic circles.

'How are you?' he concernedly inquired.

'You woke me from a wonderful dream: I was at the summit: I could see the world in all its splendour: extreme colours filled my senses: how serene it looked: Zugra was heavenly.'

'Are you ready for the final stage of the climb?'

'Yes, bring it on: I am enticed beyond reason: I have to be there again. Let's go.'

The final stage was horrifying: if I had not been so close to the summit, I would have gladly relinquished the struggle, and extricated from this excruciating misery. The snow fell like missiles, vertical, fast and hard. The wind taunted and screamed in my ear, 'You cannot do it. You cannot do it. Give up. Give up. You are beat. Spent. Useless. Weak. It is too difficult. Listen to the truth, Gorky. The truth is, you cannot do it!' Yes, the wind seemed to be speaking, incessantly howling in my ear to relinquish my efforts. It occasionally bit me. It nipped me. It tore at my face. 'You are dead! You are dead if you continue! Turn back! There is no summit! There is no peak! It just gets worse! It goes on forever!!!' I tried to look beyond Mountain Monk to see how much further I had to climb: but I could not see beyond my eyelashes. Mountain Monk had said that each plateau was equidistance apart: but this seemed to go on forever into the bowels of ice-hell. I did not think beyond each small laboured movement: for I was unsure if there would be another. I began to believe there *was* no end, that I would keep on climbing until I perished. Death was the only summit. Death, the unconquerable foe... Then I heard Helena's soothing voice: 'Do not be deterred from the fight. Fight to the last. Climb deeper into its realm. Defy. Never give in. Die fighting. Let it know you are for real. You are serious. Climb, Gorky. Climb.' But the implacable wind howled: 'You are a dead man. The further you go, the more trouble you are in.' Gusts snapped at my arteries. It tried to eat me, chew on each tingling nerve. Hot spikes embedded into my exposed skin. My flesh, bruised and bloody, screamed in dire agony. Climb. Climb higher into the violent sky. Climb Gorky. Do not stop climbing until you die...

'We are here!' Mountain Monk gleefully shouted from above. Suddenly, incredulously, I was actually standing on the top of Ice Mountain. I desperately inhaled large quaffs of ice cold oxygen depleted air. I could see nothing but swirling snow, thick squalls of ferocious ice pelting down; I was being bombarded by unrelenting ice and snow. It was murder! I could not stay. The pain was too great. Why did Mountain Monk bother making a habit of coming up here? Mountain Monk quickly uncovered a contraption. 'Strap yourself into this!' he barked. I did not think twice: I wanted this nightmare to stop. I instinctively clambered into the cockpit and eagerly awaited further instructions. 'This is a glider,' he calmly stated.

He then unceremoniously pushed me off the edge.' What the hell are you doing?!' I yelled at him as I disappeared over the side. Pushing me to my death! I tried to resist, but his sudden shove left me helpless. I fell like a stone and my stomach rose into my throat. I expected to plummet to a bloody demise. But as I fell the *glider's* nose suddenly rose and I was in shock to find myself suspended in the air and pushing through the mist at great speed: the snow bombarded my eyes and I was flying completely blind. I was entirely at the mercy of the reliability of the flying machine. I looked at the wings which had been constructed from a frame made of wooden poles and stretched hides. I glided through the air, gradually dropping in stages: every now and again my guts rose to my mouth. I felt the air whiz past me. Suddenly I was out of the mist: the warm air hit me but I had no time to enjoy the pleasantness. I saw the ground below me! I was incredibly high! I flew over a forest. My first concern was that it was the Forest of Life and Mountain Monk had sent me the wrong way: but, further ahead, I saw a great blue expanse, 'The Sea of Leviathans,' I whispered to myself in awe.

6.

The Sea of Leviathans

On thermals I zipped through clement sky. A flying-machine? I had never heard of it, and yet here I was hanging in the air fastened to wood and animal skin. My life was actually hanging by animal skin! How exhilarating! So much faster than feet. Over the land I flew, out of danger from that below, safe in the sky, speeding along, steadily descending by gradations. As the sea came closer a sense of urgency pervaded me: it was imperative I did not over-fly the mark: I wanted to land on the coastline. There, below, was a long stretch of sand that would make for a soft landing. I managed to point the nose towards the beach and went hurtling downwards. The ground was approaching too fast for comfort but I could not slow my descent. I never even had time to brace myself. BANG! My knees hit my chin as I went somersaulting along the ground. The glider smashed into smithereens. I came to a halt. There I lay, still… sprawled motionless for a while… waiting for blood or the pain of broken bones to suddenly manifest… No, I felt alright. I was safe.

'Shshshsh!' the sea said: a repeated shushing noise of waves pushed shingle up the shore entering into my psyche as if a mystical incantation; peace imbued my spirit as the great mass of heaving water gently said, 'Shshshsh!' I stared at the sea following it out to the horizon: the sea dominated the landscape. It was the last great obstacle. My mouth dropped at the sublime sight of so much water gathered in one place.

Here was the sea, boldly confronting me. The ice began to melt from my wool suit and steam started to rise. I doffed the protective layer that had partially insulated me from the extreme conditions of Ice Mountain. I looked to see if I could view the mountain: I could just descry its peak beyond the forest I had recently flown over. The climate here was temperate: I enjoyed the warm ambience. Nevertheless, I felt a restless duty to make preparations for the next phase of the journey: I removed the diagram from my pocket and unfolded it. The instructions represented systematic construction of a sea worthy boat gradually built in pragmatic stages. The first picture represented the raw materials needed; the final picture was of a magnificent sailing boat with sleek lines. Another piece of paper I had not been aware of dropped on my lap: it was a letter from Mountain Monk:

'If you are reading this letter I presume you are safe. I did not tell you how you were to descend the mountain in fear of you objecting: but I knew once on the summit you would follow instructions in order to abate the discomfort. Along the coast there are banana and coconut trees: stock up, for you will need them for the sea voyage. (For the sail use the skins from the wings of the glider.) The sea is an unforgiving entity: it is important the craft is securely built. For navigation, follow the geosynchronous Purple Star: it shines both day and night. Follow the Purple Star, for it is said it shines directly above Lake Sacradia. Lastly, I congratulate you on climbing Ice Mountain: you have demonstrated strength and courage: you will need these attributes to conquer the sea. Good luck. See you when you return.'

The Purple Star? I looked upwards scanning the ethereal world. Where was the Purple Star? I searched the sky, systematically scanning the whole region. There, in the distance, slightly obscured by the sun, was a tiny glimmering purple dot encrusted into the sky. The Purple Star, the way forward, the first visible evidence that Lake Sacradia did exist! Below the star was the lake. A warm welcoming feeling came over me. I drifted to sleep… I slept a dreamless slumber…

On wakening, I felt satisfyingly refreshed. The first thing I did was swim in the cool ocean: I washed away the night's sleep with cold sea foam. I felt bright, alive and sanguine. For breakfast, I ate roasted coconut. Then, I quickly set about my business: I gathered raw materials for the boat. With my sword I constructed tools like wooden mallets and measuring sticks. Hard wood was to be driven into soft wood. Different trees were for specific parts of the boat. It was not long before I had shaped components for the frame: then, I lay them out and fastened them together. Soon, the skeleton of the ship stood on the shore proud and sure. I sat back, eating mango, admiring my handy work, celebrating my newly discovered ability. In any other situation I would have said building this boat was impossible: but left with no option, once starting it, I had increasing faith I could complete the task. Building the boat was like a microcosm of my adventure: I had to methodically move forwards, stage by stage, until the glorious end. The ocean seemed to applaud my efforts, as if it was eager for a craft to sail upon it; the sea was a great benign friend encouraging me, for I was soon to be supported by its moving mass and dance amongst its waves. Why it was called the Sea of Leviathans? I did not know: it looked so calm and inviting. I could not wait to set sail towards the Purple Star.

After a hard day's work I began to feel a tincture drowsy, so I took a little nap. I could relax knowing I had spent a productive day: construction of the boat was becoming a reality. I felt confident of achieving my objectives. As I drifted away I ran through the process of laying down decking and fastening planks to the hull which would be shaped so the prow would effortlessly slice through the water... My sword turned into a pool of liquid silver on the sand, transformed into an obelisk, arms and legs grew, and, then, before me, was the Silver Woman. 'Oh, hello,' I said, 'long time no see.'

'Take the girl,' was all she said before metamorphosing back into the sword...

When I awoke, I leaped up eager to continue work on the boat. I had no immediate recollections of my dream, as is often the case. As I moved closer, scanning the craft with a critical eye, I discerned a note fastened to the mast: it read, 'I am nearby. Do not panic. I wish to talk. Holla, if it is okay.' I ran to my sword, unsheathed it, and swung round to the dense forest. 'Who's there?' I called.

'Me,' came the timid reply.

'Reveal yourself,' I demanded. The undergrowth rustled, and then appeared a young female. She had green skin and long purple hair. She was exotic in her loveliness. She cautiously and gracefully sidled up to me never taking her big black shining eyes from mine.

'Hi,' she said, then gave a nervous smile and seemed to cringe at her own greeting. I tore my eyes from her to look beyond her.

'Who are you with?' I peremptorily inquired.

'Nobody,' she said, frozen in her tracks, intimidated by my stern demeanour and the flashing blade.

'Nobody? Where are you from?' I interrogated.

'From a village deep in the forest. They will not follow; they never venture far,' she said.

'What do you want?' I said, lowering my sword.

'Are you going to sea?' she nodded at the boat.

'What is it to you?' I was still unsure if it was a trap.

'Where are you going?' she smiled, and I found it difficult to maintain aloofness.

'It's none of your business.' I could feel my heart pounding against my chest. After the ordeals of Ice Mountain, this adorable creature was a welcome sight.

'Are you going in that direction?' she pointed towards the Purple Star.

'My boat will not fly.' Stop looking at me in that way: you are disarming me: I will be vulnerable to attack.

'I know that, silly, but you can steer a path to what lays below the star, can't you?' She moved a little closer, her eyes sank into my soul: for the first time on my journey I did not feel alone. 'Are you going to the wonder water?' she further inquired.

'You mean Lake Sacradia?'

'Is that what you call it? Our people call it the wonder water. It is in our legends: a few drops have the power to reanimate the dead.'

'Reanimate the dead? Are you sure?' I knew the waters had restorative qualities, but had not realised to what extent. I felt even more alacrity to resume my journey.

'Is that where you are going?' Her eyes indicated a profound and benevolent spirit: I sheathed my sword. She moved even closer: I could feel her sweet vibes. 'My grandmother is dying, and I want to save her,' she said with ambivalence, for she was happy I was beginning to trust her, but saddened at the news she imparted. 'Also,' she continued, 'I have an irresistible curiosity to learn what lies beyond the sea.' She moved closer until she was standing before me. My mouth became dry and I could feel my stomach warming with excitement. 'I have often sat staring at the sea as it quietly calls me. "Nubile," it whispers, for that is my name, "Nubile, come sail over me and see what lies on the other side".'

'You are a lot safer here,' I stated. 'I have been told that the sea is fraught with danger.' Although I doubted this, for I had now seen the sea for myself: nevertheless, I was still slightly suspicious of this exotic beauty: what if she suddenly turned into a cannibalistic monster; or a tribe of blood-thirsty lunatics suddenly sprang from the thicket? Although my desire for this girl was growing more intense by the moment, caution was expedient, and I still had a duty to my people: but, I also felt the need to help her if I could. I did not like to see her frown at my evasion. 'Yes, you surmise correctly: I am going to the lake, for I also need its restorative powers: and, I promise, Nubile, that I will return to you with some of the water for your grandmother.' She could not suddenly turn into an assailant; she would not set me up: it was impossible.

'But I *have* to go: besides, I will be an extra pair of hands,' she implored. I became oblivious to everything around me: I drank her in.

'You will be an extra mouth to feed. You will be a burden,' I unconvincingly said.

'I eat and drink little, and, besides, I know how to fish.' Oh your eyes Nubile: how can I deny you?

'*Fish?*'

'Yes, fishing, something I invented while taking covert trips to the sea. I decided one day to run a net through the water to see what lay below the surface: I caught something I call *fish*: I cooked one, and tentatively ate some: it was delicious and highly nutritious. I often come here to…'

'Go back to your people,' I demanded, feeling miffed that I did not know what fishing was.

'You can have my body,' she desperately offered, protruding her ample breasts: oh my God, what beauty, such a delectable body. Nubile then pleaded with large shining eyes: I gazed, hypnotised by her heavenly loveliness: I had to take her with me; I would be glad of such gorgeous company: she was so wonderfully unobtrusive.

'Okay, you can come with me,' I shrugged, trying to sound

insouciant. She then gave me a large hug pressing herself against me: instinctively I put my arms around her slender waist and gently squeezed her to my body and buried my face in her long fragrant hair. The toils and rigours of my journey abated in a warm embrace. Simultaneously, we let go, and looked at each other reflecting gratified countenances.

'Will your people follow you here?' I asked, concerned that a search party may foil our plans.

'I will return back to my people to allay suspicion. I will continue to visit until the ship is built.' She stroked my hand, then quickly disappeared back into the forest.

With a daft grin on my face I gazed at my hand where her finger tips had been. I then surveyed the boat: it was now a craft for two. I had to make sure it was seaworthy. With added vigour, I continued to build the sailing boat. I am sure she would be in no danger during the crossing: the sea seemed so serene. The worst perils were surely behind me. Nubile would make such an agreeable travelling companion. I began to feel elation that the journey would be more salubrious from here on in. I could almost smell Lake Sacradia: all I had to do was cruise an ocean. The warm air and pleasant sea breeze filled me with optimism. I put flesh on the bones of the beautiful craft with alacrity. It was not easy: the planks took some shaping to the frame; some creaked and split: but, with trial and error, and perseverance, the boat became near completion: the rigging and sails were the only thing left to do.

'What a beautiful thing,' Nubile said, running her toe through the sand. 'How much longer?'

'Not long now,' I said. 'I would be grateful for some assistance: I need help with the sails, and to push her into the water: then we must put the ballast in and stock up with provisions.' So we worked together: we adapted what once were glider wings, reshaping them into sails; wooden darning needles I had carved stitched the sails and weaved vine to make the rigging. With some effort we heaved the boat into the water: there she sat, buoyant and bobbing on the waves. She was a little too high and slightly askew: but sand for ballast in the guts put her on an even keel. I proudly stood on deck and purposively looked to the horizon: my boat would soon be speeding there. Nubile looked at me from the shore grinning ear to ear. I jumped overboard and we cheerfully gathered victuals: the forest yielded myriad nuts and fruit; Nubile brought fresh water from her village's stream. Everything was ready…

So there we were, standing on deck. The boat gently swayed, creaking slightly: but I was sure she was well baulked and water tight. I weighed the anchor and set the sail: at first she sat motionless in the water: but then a zephyr gently pressed against the sails filling them like an inflated balloon propelling the craft steadily forward; the prow pushed through the foam: we were on our way…

I located the Purple Star and fixed the tiller: but I maintained vigilance to ensure the craft was heading in the right direction. We watched as the coast gradually disappeared from view. I felt a knot in my stomach as we eventually became surrounded by nothing but sea. As the boat moved into deeper waters, the boat began to rise higher and lower; each peak and trough more pronounced: but the craft rode the waves well and I was confident we would reach our destination safely. There I sat at the helm as the boat skimmed over the rhythmic waves. The sea intoxicated my senses: I felt peace: I suffused into the sky and sea: the mystery of cosmic sanctum was revealed to me. Nubile sat and gazed over the edge, every so often running her fingers in the water to feel the cool foamy invigorating sea. We sailed on…

The boat pushed through the waves like a veteran craft. I derived a sense of prodigious progress as I watched the sighing sea rush passed. 'I will cast the nets soon,' Nubile said.

'What for?'

'For fishing, I told you.' She walked up the centre of the boat and placed herself beside me: I put my arm around her, which invited her to snuggle closer.

'Are fish fruit or vegetable?' I asked.

'They are the fruit of the sea,' she smiled, gently placing her hand on my thigh.

'What do they look like?' I further inquired, trying not to become too stimulated.

'Silver, with scales, and fins, and they go...' to which she widened her eyes and opened and closed her mouth in a rather comic fashion: this flummoxed me even more...

After a while, Nubile walked over to the nets and cast them into the sea: they splashed as they hit the water then sank into the depths. She cheerfully set about her work: she placed some slates on deck and built a cone of branches on top of it then lit a fire. Although fish were a fruit, she said cooking made them far more edible. We pushed on through the sea and I was actually beginning to enjoy our ocean adventure. Soon Nubile was heaving the nets up. I was most impressed with her physical strength. Much to my surprise, the net was filled with strange silver creatures with large vacant staring eyes, no arms or legs, but flapping and thrashing around trying to extricate themselves from their tethers. 'This is terrible,' I stated. 'It's barbaric. This is not fruit. They are alive. You are going to kill and eat them. Let them go back into the sea where they belong.'

'This is wholesome food: it will keep us strong,' she claimed, looking bewildered at my paroxysm.

'I cannot permit the eating of flesh,' I imperiously proclaimed. 'We have sufficient food on board. Let them go, now!'

'I will not!' she boldly retorted. 'My people have always eaten the flesh of animals for sustenance: although, I admit, they know nothing of fish: but fish are obtuse creatures and seem to have less feelings than any animal we slaughter: there is nothing wrong in eating fish.'

'They *seem* to have less feelings. How do you know? They are animate, are they not? Or are you saying they are no more aware of their surroundings than a banana?'

'They display less intelligence than a pig: and we eat pig,' she said, intransigently.

'Oh, I see, your people eat things according to how intelligent they are. Can't you see these fish are in distress: put them back where they belong: or I will throw *you* overboard.'

'You would kill me to save a fish?' Nubile was becoming increasingly angry. 'You carry a sword, which never leaves your side, and you dare moralize to me?'

'My sword is for protection.'

'To kill!' she screamed. With that, a great wave came crashing over the side extinguishing the fire and nearly sweeping me away: Nubile lunged for me, grabbing my hand just in time. I was saturated... In a daze... I looked at Nubile: fury lit her eyes. The sea began to roar in anger. The boat buffeted about, tossing this way and that.

'Go below. Stay there,' I beseeched. Nubile glared at me and stormed below deck. The boat rocked violently back and forth. Strong gusts of wind crashed into the sails. Ferocious waves mast high crashed down onto the deck knocking me off my feet. With effort, I pulled myself up, and lowered the sails. I untied the tiller and tried to steer from danger: it was futile: there was no haven: all I could do was hold on and hope the storm would abate; I felt helpless, clinging on for dear life. We rose; we plummeted: up-up-up-down-down-down-up-up-up-down-down-down: we were going to drown! A great wave hit me knocking out my breath: I reeled about the deck like a rag doll. If I was going to die it would be in the arms of Nubile. I staggered below deck. Nubile was huddled in the corner trying to suppress her fear. I sat next to her, put myself around her, and tried my best to comfort her. 'It's okay. It will soon be over. It was very clever of you discovering how to catch fish. I am sure they are very delicious.' I said, stroking her hair. Her trembling mitigated and she melted into my body. I felt an overwhelming urge to protect her. Our souls heated. My emotions were inextricably linked to hers: her well-being was my well-being: an irresistible force came over me to always care for her. I caressed and kissed her: she began to respond to my caresses and reciprocate my kiss. As I entered into her the storm gradually abated. The sea became a millpond. And, after, when we finished, we lay together, and slept a long calm sleep…

Me and Nubile walked hand in hand in a heady perfumed field of flowers: the day was sultry as we carelessly chattered: never had I felt such peace…

We woke at the same time. Her eyes looked longingly into mine. 'We were in a field of flowers,' she smiled.

'Yes, but…' Helena suddenly flashed into my mind: I drew myself away from Nubile: she looked at me with alarm and sadness.

'What is it?' I felt the dejection emanate from her, impulsively I held her, kissing her forehead, kissing her cheek, then kissing her sweet mouth. She drew away from me. 'No. Stop. This is not right. Something is on your mind. Do not be nice to me because you feel sorry for me.' She pushed me away. It was not because I pitied her: I wanted to feed on her deliciousness. Her smell in the after glow of sex, her warmth, her smooth skin, I could not deny it: I wanted her. Yet, I loved Helena no less.

'Nubile, I have to go on deck to assess the situation: we have been drifting aimlessly for I know not how long.'

'Go on,' she replied, staring into the darkness. I rose and climbed outside. I scanned the boat. The ship was intact: the sail was torn but it could be repaired; the slates for the fire were strewn across deck; the fish had gone. I looked for the Purple Star: there it was, no bigger than before, but I was glad to view it all the same. The sail was fixed and off we set: I sat by the helm happy to be resuming our journey...

Although sailing the boat occupied much of our time, there were still lull periods: and so I practiced some drills with my sword; the blade flashed through the air at lightning speed; I shadow boxed; I skipped with twine; I did press ups, sit ups and pull ups on the door frame; and then relaxed with some yoga. Nubile looked on amused: soon she was joining in. Everyday we would regimentally exercise together: I would gently spar with her; she developed aptitude in the martial arts: soon she was kicking, punching, parrying and wrestling with confidence (I particularly enjoyed the wrestling!). These rigorous workouts helped pass the time. She grabbed me in a headlock, laughing and scrubbing my hair: a great tuft of it came out: she screamed and let go. It lay there on deck, a mnemonic of my malady. We both stared as it blew out to sea. 'Why did that happen?' she exclaimed, looking at me with intense concern. Suddenly, a wretched notion entered my mind, in my selfish lust I may have passed the infernal disease on to lovely Nubile: more reason to reach the lake now. 'What is it?' she shouted, for she must have noted my lineaments.

'Er, nothing,' I stammered. 'It's, er, it's a trait of my people: our hair, erm, our hair easily falls out.'

'Your countenance has become decidedly pallid; when you saw your hair on deck, you looked ghastly...like death itself. I do not even know your name! What is this about?'

'Nubile, my name is Gorky. The hair, Nubile, it's nothing, really; it's only hair falling out: do not worry.'

'Why do you need the restorative powers of the water, Gorky? Tell me.'

I could not be dilatory any longer: I did not enjoy deceiving her: but how could I tell her our village was dying of a virulent disease, and I was showing incipient symptoms? I could be the instrument of her future death.

'Nubile, my people are dying of an insidious disease. How it manifested, nobody knows: but it has spread like wild fire through out the village. The extinction of my people is imminent if I do not return with the alchemical waters of the lake.' Nubile looked at me with disgust: she was fully aware of the implications of what I was saying.

'Why did you not tell me before?'

'I just forgot...'

'You just forgot?' She looked at me for a short while with an accusatory glare: her mouth dropped: then, like a living cadaver, she absently turned round, and, slowly, walked into the darkness of the hold.

'Nubile! We will be at the lake soon,' I cried after her: but a chilling silence was the reply. I walked to the entrance of the hold, 'Nubile! I am sorry!'

'Keep away!' she cried from below. I walked to the side of the ship and looked out to sea. Such was the virulence of the contagion, that one only needed to be in the vicinity and breath the same air: I starkly realised I could be culpable for spreading the disease to all the people I had encountered on my journey. My heart sank. I slumped on deck. I wept a bitter lamentation. I was the harbinger of death for all who came into contact with me. The sky turned dark and the sea incarnadine: I became gripped in a vile vision: warts, worms, oozing puss, bursting boils, rotting blistering maggot infested skin: my despair grew cocooning me in desolation: alone, alone, forever alone: I lay for eternity, painfully and acutely aware of my wrong doings: alone, alone, and forever in isolation: oh wretched bleak and deep dark solitude! Into the abyss I deeper fell...

'Do not cry love,' a heavenly voice carried me from the darkness: I broke from my reverie: as dawn spread her roseate fingers, Nubile smiled above me. She knelt beside me and kissed me with her perfect lips.

'The disease!' I warned.

'I have probably already caught it… I assume in the heat of passion you forgot your malady. You are not intentionally evil. You are on a perilous journey to save your people. If you become too disheartened, we will never escape from the maws of the sea. Stand up, we steer askance of the Purple Star: reset the rudder; re-trim the sail: let us derive maximum propulsion from this craft.' She gently coaxed me up and I set about as was advised. She cooked vegetables and prepared fruit. Team spirit was aroused. Nevertheless, a heavy weight of contrition bore upon my frame. If Nubile was life itself; I was death incarnate. I felt incredibly humble she had forgiven me so easily: she remained cheerful and positive and always responded to my attempts at conversation. Shame pervaded me: I felt uneasy looking upon her divine countenance. My incentive increased: I must bring Nubile to the silver lake: I had to preserve this beautiful life force.

We voyaged for time interminable… The sea was constant, regular rhythms: almost as if we were stationary: and yet the prow cleft the water and the boat glided like *a fish*. 'I wonder how long now,' I audibly mused.

'We have travelled a long way,' she replied, 'longer than I anticipated. Stores are running low: we are going to have to ration it.'

'You can have what food is left,' I said, feeling strong self-revile.

'We both need sustenance,' she admonished.

'But, Nubile, I did not mean to…'

'Shshsh. You must put you remorse aside and focus on the journey. Let's eat the last of the food together.'

She gave me an apple: how pleasantly congruous it looked on a backdrop of blue sea and sky: the shining green sphere engaged my senses: its tangy juices enlivened my palate. 'Apple,' I wistfully said aloud. She looked at me with a wry smile. Eating delicious food in the company of a beautiful woman makes a man oblivious to time and place.

'What will your people be thinking?' I eventually asked.

'Thinking?'

'Yes, will they not miss you?'

'They will probably be angry,' she shrugged.

'And worried?'

'I left a message: I told them I was feeling restless and yearned for adventure. I informed them that I had gone to sea on a craft made by a stranger who had fallen from the sky. I said we were to seek the wonder water.'

'Will they do anything?'

'What can they do? They will not leave the parameters of the village. They will probably have a meeting and wait for my return so they can reject me.'

'Can you face rejection?'

'If I bring back the water I'm hoping all will be forgiven.'

'As anyone left before?'

'No, there are tales of evil that lurks beyond the village, bloodthirsty creatures that live in pits of fire, nothing but darkness and death: it is generally accepted that it is inhospitable outside: but even if anyone wished to venture forth, there is an official edict that anyone who sets outside will be immediately ostracized: intrepidness is forbidden.'

'"Blood thirsty creatures that live in pits of fire," and knowing this, you departed?'

'Yes, but there were secret tales of amazing lands, great seas, and, the wonder water, of course. My unmitigated curiosity enticed and tantalized: I just had to find out for myself, so I ventured from the village: I was both afraid and excited. The light gradually dwindled to nothing until I was in pitch darkness. I denied my instinct to turn back. I walked for some time in the blackness and acute anxiety imbued me: all manner of fear taunted: horrifying imaginings vexed me. Until, eventually, I smelt the soft salt air of the windy sea. The sea was shushing a welcome. I ran onto the beach and the sky and sea hugged me. I ate strange fruits from trees strewn along the coast. I went back to the village and told my terminally ill grandmother: at first she was horrified, but at my persistence, she eventually smiled and held my hand. I told her I would one day return with the wonder water. She became my greatest advocate. Each time I made the journey to the sea it was easier to negotiate the dark forest: for it was only dense foliage that blotted out the sky, the rest was psychological...One day, while sat fishing, gazing at the Purple Star, I saw a strange bird rapidly falling from the sky making a raucous yelling noise. I hid behind a tree and watched it hit the sand with such ferocity I thought that it was dead: for on landing it smashed to pieces. But, then, a man stood up from the wreckage, covered in sand, and looking quite shocked. I watched you, Gorky, building your boat: and soon realized you had been sent to me. I was slightly intimidated, for you wielded your sword with such deadly precision: you worked with such obsessive application that I thought you maybe demented: your eyes were fierce and intense: so it was some time before I dare confront you. I left a message while you slept as way of introduction: I watched in nervous anticipation as you woke and found it there: I felt fear as you unsheathed that sword and your wild eyes scanned the area. When you said, "Who's there?" you sounded belligerent and angry. But I was desperate to find a cure for my grandmother, I knew it lay over the sea, and you were the only means to make that journey: so I abandoned all caution. When I approached you my anxiety eschewed: I could see beyond your semblance of truculence: you looked afraid and lonely. Now, thanks to you, I have a chance to save her. It means

I may have to live in exile: but it was imperative that I departed.'

I listened rapt at Nubile's story: it very much paralleled my own. I was impressed at her courage. I held my hand out for her to take: but she recoiled.

'You are a strong and brave woman,' I said. 'It is sad that your people do not recognise this and honour you accordingly. You have risked your life to save your grandmother.'

'I think I would have gone anyway,' she shrugged.

'I admire you,' I rejoined, eager to touch her, and finding it difficult to refrain.

'Save your admiration: it will not feed our stomachs.' She turned from me, looked out to sea, and I saw the universe in her eyes: I was purged by her beauty...

And so onwards we sailed: the prow slicing effortlessly through the foamy brine. As time passed, hunger grew: we became enervated with the lack of sustenance. My principles regarding the ingesting of fish began to wane; and, also, annoyingly, Nubile refused to eat any without me: I knew my stubbornness was killing us both: eventually, I could not tolerate this beautiful woman starving before my eyes. 'Cast out your nets,' I eventually implored.

'I do not want to disgust you with the eating of that which was once animate,' she replied.

'Hunger is more disgusting: we are too weak to let my personal principles intrude. Please, cast them out,' I supplicated, holding out the net to her.

'I want no reprisals later on,' she remarked, taking it from me.

'Of course not. Fish, or we will die.' She cast out the net: it spread onto the ocean's surface and sunk below the depths. The boat sped along dragging the net through the water. Soon we were hauling it up: four silver fish frantically flapped in the net. Nubile expertly gutted and grilled them on the fire.

'Eat,' she commanded, handing me a plate of fine white fillets: I tentatively ate a piece: my face contorted at the expected vileness: as I ate, my face relaxed: it was delicious; they were so agreeable to my palette, that I was soon forgetting these creatures had been innocently swimming in the sea without a care: I voraciously ate the fish: it was the most filling and satisfying meal that I had ever had: it was not long before my blood felt vital again; I felt energy surge through my veins. Nubile looked more desirable than ever. She must have sensed what my eyes indicated. 'Now you have some strength back,' she frowned, 'there is work to do: the sails and nets need repairing.' I gave a disappointed smirk, then climbed the mast, and with darning needle and twine, fixed the sail, while, every now and again, watched Nubile glide over the deck...

Dear reader, despite short respite periods, I do not want to relay the impression that voyaging over the sea was easy. Indeed, it took all our application and fortitude. Neither I nor Nubile got much sleep. The boat needed continual monitoring and tending to. We worked in shifts, but sometimes it took both of us in attendance. At one point we were only grabbing twenty minutes sleep intermittently over a period of days. Traversing the sea was a severe test of our resolve...

We sped along, skimming over the water, sails full of strong wind, as we moved towards the Purple Star. My desire for Nubile steadily grew over the days. She drifted by me like an unobtainable ghost. My eyes burned with desire: but she coolly went about her duties unperturbed. She confidently cast the nets out... The sky and sea were saturated with her presence. The nets sank deep into the ocean. We determinedly sped along. With relish I looked forward to our next meal. The boat flew like an arrow over the sea dragging the nets with it: but, then, slowly, but surely, lost its momentum. It slowly ground to a halt. It tacked and veered round. It propelled onwards against the strong breeze. The speed rapidly increased. The prow of the boat pushed deeper into the water until great gushes of water came over onto the deck. I was knocked over by the force of an incoming wave. We were taking on water fast... too fast! Nubile rushed over to me, took my sword, leaped to the net, and chopped the ropes free: all traces of the net quickly disappeared into the ocean's depth. We stared at each other. The deck was knee deep in water. All was eerily calm. The boat quietly creaked and bobbed about on the waves. Without a word we began to bail the water out; we manically went about jettisoning the cold seawater. THUD! We reeled across the deck. We stared at each other: this time with an intensity that suggested our lives were in danger: the powerful jolt seemed a portent for future woe. 'It sounds as if we have hit something,' I asseverated, 'I'll go below and check the hull.' She earnestly nodded in concurrence. I hastily descended inside the craft. I heard the hissing of water. My stomach twisted. There, in the boat's side, was a rift allowing a powerful jet of spraying water onboard. The sea was already to my ankles. I waded to the aperture, put cloth into it, and nailed a plank over: this was difficult as the force of the water was strong and unrelenting. The water still came in and I did my best to staunch the flow. The surrounding area was also damaged: but as yet holding out. Suddenly, I heard a horrifying guttural scream that made the hairs on my nape tingle. Nubile! I rushed up top...

She was gone! There was no sign of her! I ran to the side of the craft and looked out to sea: nothing! Frantic, I ran round the edge, eyes popping, trying to find where she might be. I searched every part of the boat: nothing! Over and over my eyes scoured everything in view: NOTHING!

I dived into the sea and submerged. I manically searched below the surface. I swam as deep as I dare. Instinct told me not to dive too deep without having enough air to surface. I re-surfaced, gasped for air, lungs replete with sky, then dived over and over again. I saw nothing but sea... NOTHING! NUBILE! Where are you?! NUBILE! N-O-O-O-O!

Even when one is utterly desperate and driven on by a super-human effort, energy is still frustratingly finite. Against all my inclinations, exhausted, I had to relinquish my search...

I clambered back on board, whimpering and sobbing. Precipitated by shock, I slumped in a trance: profound introversion rendered oblivion; transcending to timeless void: spinning, falling, spinning, falling... then... tranquil world of numbness...

The boat became inundated with deathly cold seawater. As the boat sank into the dark depths, I was sucked after it: I was dragged deep down and the cold salt seawater jolted me back into reality. My body had an urgent need to breathe: my arms and legs thrashed against the water. I kicked like fury lifting up through the sea. I was on the verge of succumbing to the relentless might of the sea, disavowing my struggle and taking a sharp intake of breath so that sea water could rush into my lungs and kill me: but then, not a moment too soon, I broke the surface into the life giving air of our benign planet: I greedily gasped the air, inhaling great volumes of it. Around me was flotsam, the remainders of the wreckage from the boat. The mast floated near me: I took hold.

So I kicked day and night,
Threat of being swallowed by a leviathan any time,
But now a machine without thought or feeling,
I stopped contemplating any meaning.

Kick, splash, kick, splash,
Onward to The Purple Star,

Numb and cold and in a trance,
I must travel far.

Onward, onward, kicking, hold,
Floating on the gallows' pole,
I must reach my destination,
Morbid mind in isolation.

Kick, splash, kick, splash,
Passing through days and nights,
Like an automaton,
Too mechanised for fright.

What became of my wits,
What became of my soul,
I cannot recall,
Or will ever know.

Onward I went, weak and spent,
Mind and body surely rent,
Kicking though I knew not why,
Caring not if I lived or died.

Day and night, night and day,
Kicking, Kicking, come what may,
Focused on the Purple Star,
Kicking-kicking very far.

The sea, the sea,
Surrounding me,
Circumscribed by inanimate brine,
Losing sense of what is mine,
Losing sense of place and time,
Towards The Purple Star that shines.

An Angel!
White wings gliding overhead,
Have you come to take me,
For was I at last now dead?

Seagulls with your sea-blue cry,
Am I living? Have I died?
How beautiful you are up there,
Angels flying in the air.

Seagulls, seagulls, with your cry,
Miracles flying in the sky,
Beautiful sounds fill my eyes,
Angels take me. Have I died?

Seagulls, seagulls, everywhere,
Angels of the sky-blue air,
Am I passing on
To the next world where I belong?

Seagulls, seagulls, guard the gate,
To the Heavenly realm where God awaits,
And there I will meet sweet Nubile,
And melt into her lovely smile…

As I was kicking, there I found,
My feet kick against solid ground:
My ankle sharply hit a rock
And made me leap from out my shock.

I looked ahead, was it a dream?
A line of froth hissed on the beach.
A golden shoreline, swaying palms:
I must now be safe from harm.

I stood and staggered, and took steps,
I walked from out the water's depths,
My feet kissed the sandy beach:
I then slumped down and fell to sleep...

7.

The Masked Tribe

I want to make it patently clear, this chapter has nothing to do with mocking indigenous tribes. I have upmost respect for tribal culture and traditions. They have a profound connection with nature which the so called 'developed world' has sadly lost. I am fascinated by so called 'primitive'art, more aptly called 'Traditional Art', which is actually quite sophisticated, and has profoundly influenced Western art. Frank Willett says, 'African art... is one of the highest expressions of human culture.'

'The trouble with a mask is it never changes'
Charles Bukowski.

I slumped on the golden sands and gasped for air. I had been on automatic pilot for time immeasurable. My bereavement for Nubile had rendered me numb. To avoid the intense emotional pain I had immersed in extreme physical activity, and it had probably saved my life. Now the effort had caught up with me. My moribund body felt like lead and sank into the sand. As I began to drift away my sword melted into the Silverwoman. Her previous advice came instantly to mind and I felt a strong urge to accuse her. 'You asked me to bring Nubile along on the voyage. Now she is dead. Why?' I furiously inquired. From behind the Silverwoman stepped Nubile.

'Hello, Gorky,' she said. 'Do not worry about me: I'm fine.

My passing was quick and painless. I hovered above the boat. I watched you erratically run about searching for me. I called your name: but you could not hear me. Then my grandmother appeared, though she was in the bloom of youth, and told me there were many kind people waiting to greet me. I did not want to leave you, Gorky, for I knew you were in danger: but she insisted I must go. Can you remember the flower field in our dream? It is here. I have met someone who knows you. I have spent much time with him. We are married, Gorky.' With that a man I did not recognise stepped from behind the Silverwoman.

'Hello, Gorky,' he said. The voice was strangely familiar. 'My name is King Reginald Harvey, or so I was known before my incarceration on Ice Mountain.'

'Mountain Monk!' I exclaimed, 'what's happened to you?'

'The glider had always been a source of amusement for the Enchantress: she called it my false hope: but when it went missing, her suspicion grew. She put a truth spell on me and became livid that I had assisted in helping someone conquer her Ice Mountain: with one zap of her finger, she killed me. My goat exterior fell away: my soul rose as I transformed into my former self. The Silverwoman was waiting for me and said there was some one I should meet: she introduced me to a beautiful young woman: we walked for eternity in a field of flowers. We fell deeply in love. Nubile is gorgeous, is she not?' With that, he put his arm round her, and they looked at each other, smiling: a violent envious pang welled up inside.

'You looked better as a goat,' I grimaced. The Silverwoman intervened.

'Gorky, you should be pleased for their happiness: their lives are now complete.'

As I woke, I tried to move my arms and legs, but they were bound tight. I raised my head, and a creature wearing an angry looking mask was shaking a spear. The mask had fangs and two large penetrating eyes that had been painted on with some aplomb. My sword was lying next to me, undetected, but utterly useless.

'Get up,' he ordered. I made a half-hearted attempt to rise.

'I cannot: I am tied up,' I stated.

'Get up,' he said, and thrust the spear into my arm making a deep incision. I winced, tried again, but helplessly rolled over, not raising in the slightest.

'I cannot!' I yelled, glaring up to the eyeholes in the mask.

'Get up,' he said, staring down at me, about to stab me with the spear once more.

'Enough!' a tribe's creature commanded, who was wearing a mask with a haughty expression, and pushed my assailant from me. Behind him was a tribe who were also wearing identical ferocious masks as my original attacker. 'What is the problem here?' queried the haughty masked man, who I assumed was the leader.

'He won't stand up.'

'You fool!' yelled the leader, and gave him a backhander that knocked his mask off to reveal his physiognomy: he had a furry face; large bucked teeth that completely filled his mouth; and a single small peering eye in his forehead: he twitched his nose and looked quite docile: he hurriedly put his mask back on. 'Forgive my subject,' he said, 'he has been incarcerated in the, ha, ha, small egg shape cell for too long. He has lost all his faculties of reasoning. He is quite mad…quite quite mad. You will be going there too. Ha, ha, to the small egg shaped cell carved deep into the rock. No light. No sound. You will be quite quite mad when we eventually let you out. Oh yes, quite mad, ha, ha, quite malleable, and quite mad, oh yes, ha, ha, quite mad. Take him to the cell, the little egg shaped cell that is carved deep into the rock.' His cohorts stood there, looking at each other through their masks, waiting for someone to make the first move. 'Take him away!' he bellowed. Eventually, after much shuffling and nudging, a volunteer stepped forward.

'Er, noble one,' a tribe's creature nervously ventured.

'What is it?' he impatiently replied.

'Er, We've just had a thought,' the tribe's creature said, humble and cringing, which looked quite incongruous to his fierce war like mask.

'A thought? How dare you!'

'Er, I'm sorry, oh noble one, it won't happen again.'

'A thought indeed…What was it?'

'Er, I can't remember.' He turned to his comrades, 'Anyone remember?' They all shrugged and furiously shook their heads.

'Can't remember?! Now, take him to the little egg shaped cell carved deep into the rock, quick, quick, run along.' And so masked tribe's creatures carted me to a small but thick iron door hewn into a large rock. The door swung open: they thrust me inside: and the door ominously slammed behind me.

I could hardly move. I was immersed in pitch darkness. I ran my palms along the cold stone walls: and, sure enough, the mini-dungeon was carved in the shape of an egg: its length a little smaller than me; its height, half the size. I could hear no noise other than my amplified heartbeat and breathing. 'How long am I to stay here?' I shouted: but my voice absorbed into the thick rock. No one could hear me; I could hear no one. I placed my feet against the door and tried to push it open: solid. I pushed against the rock: unyielding. 'Why are you doing this?' I hollered: but my voice rebounded back to me. 'Are you there?' My tones, distinct, vibrated into my brain: a voice heard only by its creator. 'What have I done to deserve this?' I screamed, as the incipience of panic taunted. My voice seemed alien to me, a separate entity from myself. 'I have a sword: it has special powers: I will give it to you if you let me go. I can take you to it. Please! Are you there!' How weird my voice was. I desperately ran my hands over the prison walls: all I could feel was finely hewn stone; the small iron door that had a smaller door within it; and directly below me, a tiny wooden trap door, no bigger than my hand: I opened it to feel a thin shaft: air blew upwards from it: I put my arm down it but could feel no end.

After a while, the door within the door opened, and a plate of dry bread and water was passed through: this happened on occasion, and was the only means to measure time. I softened the bread with the water: it was not very appetizing: but I had to stay as strong as I could. I tried to stay relaxed: for I knew if I became anxious, it would precipitate disequilibrium…

Over time, to compensate for sensory deprivation, my imagination became palpable and uncontrolled. My first preoccupation was with Nubile: I had forever lost her. I chided myself for going below deck and leaving her. I recalled the vision with her and Goat-Boy: I became irked with acute jealousy. If my dream was real, an ex-goat was now enjoying my delightful beloved. I tried not to imagine them together, it filled me with bitterness.

I slipped into deeper reverie: I was in a field of flowers: every colour conceivable nodded and danced on the temperate air: harp music swirled in delicate zephyrs: harmonies enticed me to recline as I sedately gazed at ponderous flocculent clouds imperceptibly changing from purple to red to orange to yellow to green to blue and back to purple again: I began to discern the sound of a couple chatting: as their voices grew louder I understood them to be laughing and joking: I began to perceive adumbration: it was the outline of a man and woman: as they approached I comprehended features. 'He would continually look at me lasciviously,' she said.

'I was trying to assist him but all I received was scorn,' he said.

As they came closer, it was obvious who they were. I tried to raise myself to defend against their accusations: but I was unable to move: they walked towards me, oblivious to my presence: they walked over me, treading me into the mud: the mud slowly sealed over me. I screamed.

The womb-tomb egg was small and dark.

I awoke to find myself in a familiar double bed: it was late evening and the sun was descending: the birds merry chirping suddenly ceased: I turned around to see the back of Helena's head: she was sleeping beside me: I stroked her hair: she slowly turned around: a manically grinning skull. I screamed.

The womb-tomb egg was small and dark.

I was carrying buckets of water. 'Waterboy, why are the tanks not yet full?'

'But, sir, I have been working all day.'

'You are not working hard enough: look at the results of your meagre effort.'

The tank's sluices opened and a gush of maggot-infested blood drenched me: the maggots covered my skin and fed: they buried deep into my flesh and ate my internal organs. I screamed.

The womb-tomb egg was small and dark.

As I walked through the cemetery, bodies began to rise from the graves: bedraggled and grey they circled me pointing: it was the people of my village. 'Why did you desert us, Gorky?' said a corpse, barely recognizable as a human.

'Why did you run away, Gorky?' intoned a haunted child.

'I was dying, Gorky, while you were fornicating with other women,' said a woman, who resembled Helena, but surely it could not have been her. The rotting bodies began to close in on me, stench over whelmed, teeth chattering, bony fingers pointing, piercing into my flesh, eating me alive. I screamed.

The womb-tomb egg was small and dark.

I stood in a brilliant white marble cube room: it was three times the length, breadth and width of me: it was infused with a refulgent light: on one of the walls was a equilateral triangular shaped mirror: as I approached it, it moved away twice as much: the more I moved towards it the further away it got: until it was a tiny silver spec in the distance, like a faraway star in the night. Everything went black. I screamed.

The womb-tomb egg was small and dark.

How long I had been in the infernal oval prison, I could not say: and what dark and horrific imaginings it engendered were too numerous to mention. I do not want to trouble you, dear reader, with the dark recesses of my mind: but after I had been on this journey, I felt a resolute tranquillity pervade me. I had tapped into all my fears, all my innate anxieties, and extirpated them; I had cried an acute lamentation of woe and sorrow from deep within the core of my being that abated my sadness.

The main door of the cell finally flung open. My mind was calm, lucid and stalwart. 'Out!' came a voice from outside. I crawled from the cell into daylight. Light burnt my eyes: but the air, alive and fresh, and the sky, large and bright, made me marvel at the intelligence that allowed this alchemy to happen. 'We are to burn your balls,' said a masked tribe's creature.

'Pardon?' I incredulously queried.

'We are to douse you testicles in flammable liquid and set them alight: you are a non-believer, and so you must not have babies.'

'You are going to ensure I cannot propagate?'

'What did he say?' a masked tribe's creature said to his neighbour who just shrugged.

'A non-believer? How do you know I am a non-believer?' They looked at each other through their masks: I guessed their expressions indicated perplexity.

'For it is said that non-believers do not believe, and it is the duty of believers to burn their balls.'

'Here, here,' said another.

'What constitutes a non-believer?' I said.

'What con…constipates a non-believer?'

'What is it I am supposed to not believe in?' I said.

'Er, I don't believe I know. Do you?' he turned to his neighbour.

'Are we going to burn his balls?' he replied.

'What is going on here?' the haughty one inquired as he approached.

'We are about to carry out the ball-burning, as you ordered, oh noble one.'

'Then get on with it, you imbeciles,' he commanded.

'I have a sword,' I said.

'A sword?' he replied.

'Yes, a special sword, you can have it if you set me free.'

'A sword! I have heard of such a thing: this would give me great power. Where is it?' the haughty one joyfully exclaimed.

'I will show you,' I said, for I would do anything to avoid conflagration of the genitalia and get on with my quest.

We walked to the beach, tribe's creatures intermittently gratuitously prodding me with spears. I scoured the area where I had been washed ashore. The marvellous sword could not be found anywhere. The whole tribe systematically searched, frequently bumping into each other as they wandered around concentrating on the ground. We searched until the sun began to lower in the sky and I was beginning to lose heart .The haughty one was growing impatient: then, I kicked something in the sand: the sword! Four spears instantly pointed at my head. 'The sword?!' the haughty one cried, and tried to pick it up: but it was too heavy for him. He became angry, and grunted, and groaned: and the masked tribe began to snigger around him. 'Silence imbeciles!' he raged, 'I have another idea: bring the bracelet.' The tribe's creatures were still suppressing small chuckles. 'Bring the bracelet, you incompetent fools!' There was a little commotion and then a tribe's creature walked forward with a wooden bracelet. It was then clamped around my wrist. The haughty one was handed a little box with a button on it. 'This bracelet,' he said, 'may look harmless, but it is an incendiary device, which I can detonate, ha, ha, at any time. Do not try to remove it or I will not hesitate to blow you in pieces.'

'I thought you were going to let me go if I gave you the sword.'

'Do you see up there?' he pointed up to a craggy mountain ridge. I nodded. 'Up there is a cave, and in that cave is a ferocious dragon. Such is the violence of that beast that we live in constant fear. It attacks indiscriminately, at any time, with such anger and malice, ha, ha, that we must destroy it before it destroys us. If you can return with its head, I will set you free.'

'And if I refuse?'

'We burn your balls.'

'Can I take my sword? I will need it to fight such a creature.' A little snigger emanated from a masked tribe's creature to which the haughty one turned round to silence him.

'What is wrong with you for crying out loud?!' he demanded.

'Er, nothing, oh excellent one.'

'Then shut it!' the haughty one peremptorily demanded and the masked tribe's creature in question crossed his legs and started shaking in silence. 'Do not try anything, intrusive stranger, or I will blow you up,' the haughty one continued, pointing to the button on the box.

I thought about his proposal: have my balls burnt or face a ferocious dragon. At least if I faced the dragon I stood a chance. My sword had magical powers and I was sure all I had to do was hold on to it in order to vanquish such a beast. 'Okay, it's a deal: I will slay the dragon if I am allowed to go free,' I declared.

'Untie him.' The tribe's creatures stood there, motionless, looking at each other through the masks. 'Untie him!' the haughty one reiterated. And so, after much debate from the tribe how to untie me, I was set free. I picked up the sword and they nervously moved away. 'Do not try anything, and, remember, if you do not return, I will, ha, ha, blow you up.' He held out the box in front of him with his index finger poised over the button for emphasis.

And so I marched into the forest towards the craggy mountain where the dragon's lair awaited. The prospect of leaving behind those buffoons was a blessed relief. As I walked, I noticed a high wire fence with a long festoon of small slabs of red rotting meat tied to it. I stopped in curiosity. Beyond the fence were women, wearing masks of smiling faces, automatically going about their chores, cooking and washing clothes in silence. 'Move on!' a sentinel commanded.

'I am Gorky. I am to save your people from the dragon.'

'I know who you are. Move on and do it then.'

'Who are they?' I asked.

'They are our women. Move on!'

'What are these slices of meat?'

'Move on!' He prodded me with his spear. I was in no mood to argue: the sooner I killed the dragon the sooner I could resume my journey to Lake Sacradia: and so I walked deeper into the forest onward to the lair.

8.

The Dragon

On leaving the masked tribe behind I began pondering the prospect of meeting the dragon. There had been fire side stories of such creatures in our village. I surmised dragons were huge, redoubtable, and unrelentingly ferocious. I began to have reservations concerning my welfare in encountering such a beast: but then I thought of my magical sword: its powers were implacable, could slice through anything; the sword would guarantee my safety. I became excited at the idea of being a bold dragon slayer: I am sure Helena would be proud of me. I unsheathed my sword and swished it around chopping branches as I walked, warming up for the kill: I pictured the dragon in front of me: take that! And that! It would be no match for me.

I reached the base of the rocky mountain: it was nothing like the formidable Ice Mountain: it consisted of jagged rock that stretched before me like steps: I was soon bounding up with considerable ease. However, the further I climbed, the more hazardous it became: and I had to use all the strength and skill I had acquired on Ice Mountain. I climbed in stages, sitting on small ledges to rest. I looked over the Masked Tribe's forest to the interminable sea: beyond that was my Helena waiting for me: I gave a wistful sigh.

As I was peering out to sea, I felt a powerful draught of air: it was emanating from a hollow recess in the rock. Around the entrance were shiny green scales that led into the maw of the mountain. This is it! There, like a portal to the netherworld, was the entrance to the dragon's lair. I instantaneously unsheathed my sword and gripped it with my aching hands. A fingernail dropped to the ground. I payed little heed for beyond this giant fissure dwelt a massive fire-breathing dragon. I took a deep breath, psychologically bolstered myself, and, entered the lair.

As I walked further in, the air became still. Water dripped from stalactites of mauve crystal that shone lambent and lit the cave with a glorious light. Drawn on the walls with coloured pigments were beautiful impressions of the natural world: trees with branches like fingers ramifying across the rocky surface, and strange creatures with horns and manic eyes. I shuddered, for hoped I would not have to encounter such bizarre beasts. However, I was impressed with the dexterity of application, such deep feeling: I assumed that someone had lived here before the dragon. Maybe the Masked Tribe had evolved from here... or regressed! I stealthily walked deeper into the mountain. I tried to make no noise but the cave amplified the sound of my slightest movement: echo, echo. Carefully I crept. My senses were alert. I anticipated a sudden ambush from the fire breathing dragon.

Then, I could hear an intermittent hissing noise, like the pressurised hissing of steam. Was that it?! It could be the dragon! Cautiously, I moved onwards, holding the shaking sword in front of me. I must admit, the glint of the sword gave me some comfort, but my resolve was beginning to wane. As I moved forward the air became warmer and the hissing noise became louder.

Until, there, in front of me, was the dragon, sleeping. I froze. It was a giant! I looked at it, and looked at my tiny sword. The huge beast lazily lolled itself out, stretching its great length across the rocky cave. Its tail was protectively wrapped around three smaller dragons that were huddled together. Small hissing sounds emitted from the baby dragons' nostrils. Their perfectly formed scales were shining green and red; wings of green leather stretched over a jointed bone frame; teeth, white cones of ivory that tapered into needle points; claws, curved, razor sharp. As the dragon slept, it sighed, and seemed to have a slight grin on its face. Every now and again its front claws would gather the babies into its belly. Each breath was a warm gust of air: I began to sweat profusely; beads of saline ran down my face. I slowly drew nearer, raising the sword above my head. I had to be swift. I did not bank on killing four dragons: but I thought it would only increase my reputation. I would kill the biggest threat first: then the others would be easy. One swift chop of the neck, no, gulp, maybe quite a lot of chops. Here goes!

The dragon casually opened its eyes; bright yellow orbs blinked at me. I froze. It slowly lifted its head, put its claw over its mouth, and let out a great yawn. I stared aghast, dumbfounded, petrified to the spot. 'Oh dear,' it said, 'I think itsss lossst all power of movement.' The dragon examined me closely. The babies stirred: then, one by one, woke up.

'Whatsss up mammy?' one said.

'Oh nothing, darling. We have a guest: a ooman hasss come to sssay hello.'

'Another one?' the baby said.

'Well, ooman, what are you waiting for?' Its eyes were like two suns, golden, shining, penetrating. Three pairs of big round eyes looked from mother to me. 'What a lovely looking sword, ooman: I bet you could easily kill us with that.' She insouciantly smiled at me, defying me to move closer. I lowered my sword in resignation: I derived a sense of her power, and could feel her contempt and anger simmering underneath.

'I don't think the ooman can talk,' said one of the babies.

'Can you talk, ooman?' the mother said.

'Cough, I am sorry for the intrusion, cough, I did not mean to disturb your sleep, cough,' I finally managed to say.

'I wasss not asssleep ooman. Do you think you got thisss far by ssstealth? I sssaw you long before you even began to climb my mountain: did you not sssee me sssoaring above you?

'Above me? Er, no,' I stammered.

You are not from around here, are you?'

'Cough, no, cough.'

'No, I thought not…'

'I have been sent to, er, cough, cough, sent to, cough…'

'Ssspit it out ooman, you have been sssent to kill usss.'

'I had to, it was the only way I could gain my freedom.' All the time she lay perfectly still, almost as if to not make me any more afraid. But I sensed she could have struck like a cobra at any instant. The babies kept looking from her to me, blinking in curiosity, examining me from head to toe. 'They told me I must, er, cough, kill you, or they would burn my, er, burn me: and if I did not return, this bracelet would explode.' I very slowly held my arm out to show her.

'Arrggh!' the mother cowered in mock fear, then began to laugh.

'I take it the explosion would not be big enough to harm you?' I said.

'No ooman,' she smiled, 'nor you.' She then slung at my feet a collection of wooden bracelets identical to the one I was wearing. 'Those, ooman, are what I have colleted from others, like you, who were coerced into killing me, and my family, by that masssked fool. Unlike you, they did not hesssitate: and, unlike you, they are now dead. They have tricked you ooman, and now you are in a predicament…aren't you?'

'Cough… I… er… I thought you were more primitive. Cough… I did not know you could speak. They said you wreaked havoc amongst the tribes' people, killing at random:

I thought I would be doing them a favour by getting... er... mmm... getting rid of you.'

'Isss that what you thought? And what do you think now?'

'Er... I do not think it is such a good idea...In fact, mmm, I think it is a very silly idea.'

'Do you know ooman, that we have never been left in peeesss. When our home is impinged upon, I am forced to kill to protect my babies: I do not enjoy this: I loathe it: but what choice do I have? It'sss me or them.'

'Well...why don't you move away?' I asked, sheathing my sword.

'Move? We were here firssst: we have lived in thisss cave for thousandsss of yearsss.'

'Have you tried speaking to them?' I queried.

'Yesss, many timesss, but they will not lisssten: besidesss, what happened reeesssently meansss, I will never try again.'

'What happened?'

'I cannot sssay,' suddenly, great globules of tears welled in her eyes, and she looked quite sorrowful: it took me aback, for I did not expect to see a dragon cry.

'Don't cry mummy,' a baby said.

'Yesss, do not cry,' another said.

'Tell him, mummy, tell him what the Masssked Tribe did,' said the third.

'Yesss, tell him, maybe the Massked Tribe will lisssten to him,' a baby said, wiping a tear from mother. She looked at her children, mused a while, then turned to me.

'Oh, okay, what isss there to lose? Not long ago, me, my husssband, and four babiesss, were flying to a secret peach orchard (for, dessspite what they sssay, we do not feed on meat, we are strict vegetariansss), when, sssuddenly, a hail of arrowsss and ssspearsss flew up from the ground: my husssband and baby were hit: they plummeted to the ground: I tried to pursssue: but the missilesss flew thick and fasssst: me, and my three babiesss that remained, could do nothing but essscape. Later, we returned to the place where we had been attacked, but my husssband and baby were not there: they have been carried away sssomewhere.' The dragon fought back tears as the brood consoled her.

'I am sorry,' I sincerely consoled, 'now I am free of the bracelet, I have no need to try hurt you.' I could not stand her crying and began to feel emotional myself. 'Look, when I first saw you, I was in awe: your beauty astounded me: you are magnificent: how anyone could kill you, I simply do not know.'

These poor creatures had been persecuted for aeons: I could not let the opportunity for seminal rapprochement go wasted. As we spoke, I learnt that these creatures had lived long before humans even existed: the wisdom they had accrued far exceeded ours. I learnt dragon lore. It transpired that the dragons had painted the wonderful murals: they taught me how to paint. I became immersed in their arts and philosophies: I grew to love these amiable reptiles. I became so absorbed with being enlightened, that I thoroughly forgot my quest.

Then, one night, I had a vivid dream of Helena. She looked sad: but she told me not to worry. She told me that she missed me, and asked how much longer would I be away. I answered by saying I did not think I was far from the lake, and that I would be home as soon as I could…

That morning, I informed the mother dragon the purpose of my journey, and that I had to move on. I thanked her for the hospitality. I sorrowfully kissed the babies heads one by one. As I made my way to the entrance of the cave, I heard her voice echo behind, 'It's Lake SSSacradia you are going to, isss it?'

'Yes, below the Purple Star lays the water,' I pointed to the star, for by now I could locate it with ease.

'I know where it isss,' she smiled.

'I must go now. My people will be waiting,' I retorted.

'Have you any idea how far the lake isss?' she inquired.

'It can't be far now,' I shrugged, 'looking at the star with renewed intention.'

'Gorky, it isss very far,' she exhorted.

'Oh, how far?' I said, slightly deflated at the odious news.

'You will ssssee sssssoon enough… I have decided…asss you have been acceptable company, and you have changed my viewsss on oomanssss, I am willing to fly you to Lake SSSacradia.'

'Fly to the lake? On your back?'

'Yesss, on my back.'

'I do not wish to inconvenience you. It is a very tempting offer, but I have made it this far.'

'I can guarantee you will not make it without my help.'

'Really, why?'

'You *will* ssssee ssssoon enough.'

So I gave it a cursory thought. I trusted this dragon's wisdom. I would *not* make it without her help? Well, how could I fail with a dragon on my side! 'Okay. Thank you. Your assistance would be most helpful. I accept your offer.' I gave her a great hug: though trying to put my arms around her large neck was quite futile.

'Now, now, that'sss quite enough of that. I've been meaning to go to Lake SSSSacradia anyway. If I could find out where my husssband and baby are buried, I could reanimate them with the magical water. I ssstill live in hope that I will one day dissscover their whereabouts.'

'When will you be ready? I am really eager to go,' I impatiently inquired.

'I can go now,' she grinned with her enormous fangs, 'I will inform my children what we intend to do.'

9.

Lake Sacradia

So, I sat by the entrance of the lair waiting for the dragons. How could I fail now? I had reptile power on my side! I looked to the cynosure Purple Star, underneath its scintillating presence was the incredible restorative powers of Lake Sacradia. My hopes and aspirations were becoming a reality. My village was to be saved. My beautiful Helena would live.

The three babies eventually appeared first. They were carrying large earthenware pots chattering and excited at the prospect of an adventure. Then mother dragon appeared. She seemed to be more animated than usual. Her large scaly body breathed hard at the prospect of the journey. My quest seemed to have expedited her own needs. Why she had not gone to Lake Sacradia before I mentioned it, I do not know: maybe she was in stultifying mourning; or she felt it was pointless possessing the alchemical water without knowing her husband's whereabouts: all I know is my quest had sparked her into action, and we were now on our way. 'Climb onboard, Gorky,' implored the mother. The huge dragon then fastidiously lay down and gently helped me up: I proudly sat astride her long scaly neck. 'Hold on,' she advised, wiggling her ears, indicating where I should grab for stability. The babies were already excitedly whizzing around in the air.

'Come on!' they enthusiastically called. The mother dragon spread her massive green leathery wings, and with one mighty flap, we thrust into the air: the jolt took me by surprise: and I nearly fell off as she ascended high into the air at great speed: the air zoomed past me and I held on with all my strength. Her power was incredible! Each downward thrust of her wings propelled her higher and higher. As we sped along, the babies were swooping, circling, diving and playing. The mother rebuked them and told them to settle down for there was a long way to go. We flew higher and higher and the land below began to shrink into the distance. We hurtled through the clouds in a steep upward motion. I could not help discerning we were moving more vertical than horizontal. 'Why are we flying so high?' I shouted, for, I had to shout, because of the noise of the air as we blasted through it.

'Gorky,' the mother said, 'Lake SSSacradia is not *below* the Purple SSStar.'

'Where is it then?'

'Lake SSSacradia isss *on* the Purple SSStar.'

'*On* the Purple Star?'

'Yesss, Purple SSStar is a long held misnomer. It is actually a Purple Planet. Hold on!' I looked downwards at the land I had left behind: it gradually shrank: I tried to combat vertigo as the land rapidly fell below us...

Soon Zugra was a beautiful sphere, like a jewel encrusted in space. How novel to see my whole world, everything I ever knew, all the people I had ever met, as a mere pin prick in the enormity of space.

I looked upwards: the Purple Star was approaching: it rapidly grew before my astounded eyes. I could now identify swirling purple clouds: then we burst into them: my vision was obscured by a dense purple mist.

'Weee!' the babies cried.

'Are you alright, Gorky?' the mother earnestly asked.

'Yes, fine,' I rejoined, though my hands were numb with

holding on so tight. Then we broke through the clouds, to the other side, and a strange new world unfolded before me. We skimmed through the air at a vast rate, purple sea, purple trees. 'Everything's purple,' I yelled.

'Yessss,' the dragon replied, 'not long to go now.'

I felt a sense of unmitigated excitement: I had finally made it! It was going to be great to see the magical lake that generations of our people had only spoken about: the much vaunted Lake Sacradia! It made me feel humble, that I, a mere waterboy, would be the first of my people to see its consecrated water. We began to lower, and the same sensation as the glider imbued me: my stomach rose to my head. We flew just above the surface of the ground: then, suddenly came to a halt. I catapulted through the air and unceremoniously rolled across the ground. 'SSSorry, Gorky, I'm not usssed to passssssengersssss. Anything broken?' the mother dragon solicitously inquired.

'No, I'm fine,' I rejoined, quickly assessing my body for damage. I stood up and slapped the purple dust from my raiment. We had landed next to a large crater. The babies' happy expressions changed to bewilderment: they looked questioningly at their mother.

'I don't know,' she shrugged.

'What's wrong?' I asked.

'The water hasss gone,' she frowned.

'Gone?!' I bewilderingly exclaimed.

'Yesss. You sssee here, this large concave in the ground? Thisss isss where the water should be: thisss iss the sssight of Lake SSSacradia, but it'sss completely dried up.'

I stood there in abject astonishment. I incessantly stared at the large crater, possibly in the belief that the longer I gazed circumstances would change. A myriad of emotions swirled through my head. My stomach churned as the realization gradually hit me.

'A drought?' I finally inquired.

'No, Gorky, Lake SSSacradia could never dry up.'

'So, where has the water gone?!' I shouted, no longer able to contain my bitter disappointment.

'Keep calm, Gorky. Anger never solved anything.' She then held her nose aloft, diligently sniffing the air. 'I think we should go to itsss sssource...to the Purple Mountain... Climb onboard, Gorky... I'll be more careful.' Mother dragon's determined mien instilled in me hope. I could tell she had far from given up on locating the magical water. I eagerly climbed on board: we took off, and followed a ravine where a tributary once ran. We ardently followed it, zig zagging up the mountain side. Mother dragon flew with dexterity, gently changing course as the fissure dictated.

Up ahead we saw something that made us both incredulously gasp: a massive purple man-made wall built into the mountain side. Mother dragon exigently landed on the wall. I instantly alighted her back, and eagerly peered over the side: there, at last, was the effervescent gurgling source of the magic lake: a beautiful bright bubbling liquid, swirling and hissing, emitting a pleasant aroma that induced the body to tingle! Instantly my spirits lifted. 'It's beautiful,' I murmured in awe and deference. The dragon, eyes aflame, gazed at me, smiled and revealed a line of white pearly fangs.

A hail of arrows and spears sped through the air at an unusual velocity: one zipped through the dragon's throat; another through her eye; and three arrows buried deep into her soft under belly. She instantly slumped: and with the force of the projectiles, she was pushed over the wall, and went toppling down the mountainside. The babies yelled in anguish and followed their mother to where she lay, and there lamented her broken state. They cried, 'Don't die, mummy!' But she had died before she hit the ground. I looked down to her, stunned, shouted, 'N-O!' as a spear hit me through the mouth and exited at my armpit.

I tottered in shock, and fell into the gurgling waters of the lake. I submerged deep into the heart of the water: my body convulsed as I became embalmed in electric energy: my brain contained the universe: dust and gas coalesced and metamorphosed into myriad stars; I was the heart of a raging sun; I saw spiral galaxies rotating: I witnessed a Big Bang and felt the sole occupant at the beginning of time...

The spear disintegrated; my wounds healed; and I rose to the surface of the miraculous waters, floating and feeling tremendously alive and healthy. I scanned the area to determine the position of the assailants. I seemed to have incredible acuity of vision.

There, by the margin of the lake, was an angry tribe wielding spears and shaking them with ferocity: they were purple leathery creatures that glistened. One threw a spear at my head: it flew through the air in a flash: as soon as the tip touched my temple, the spear disintegrated. Two arrows flew towards me, submerged into the water, and vanished with out a trace. I assumed whilst I was floating in the magical purple water I was impervious to attack. 'This is no use,' said the purple plumed tribe's creature. 'Get out of our water!' he commanded.
'Why, so you can kill me?' I rejoined.
'We won't kill you,' his angry mien suddenly turned to an ingratiating grin. I swam in the water, feeling unprecedented zest, noticing the tribe were gathering along the shoreline. There was many stood by the margin now, all trying unsuccessfully to curb their anger. 'Come on, please get out of our water, you'll be unharmed,' he unconvincingly claimed.

'I'm sorry,' I retorted, 'I really do not think that would be a good idea.'

The leader's face then seemed to light up in garish mauve. 'Oh…after him!' he bellowed.

Four of his creatures dived into the water: I swam away with all my might: I zipped through the water with unwonted ease; even though my sword was strapped to my back I glided through the water like a fish. Nevertheless, the purple creatures were faster: the daily diet of Lake Sacradia meant they had evolved into super beings. I tried with all my might to evade them, but it was futile: soon, my arms, and legs, were held fast by powerful purple tribe's creatures: and I felt myself manhandled and roughly dragged to the margin of the lake.

I was curiously dry the moment I was hauled from the water. I tried to struggle free but their grips were like vices. I was surrounded by mean looking purple leathery beings. 'Another thief comes to steal our water,' the purple plumed one announced.

'I only wanted a little,' I defiantly claimed.

'That's all anyone wants,' he sneered, 'and we have grown annoyed at aliens coming to our planet uninvited and plundering our land: that is why we have dammed the source of the lake…What is that?' he pointed to my sword. 'Let me see it.'

'Can I have some of your water?' I tried to bargain.

'You are in no position to negotiate. Let me examine the blade.' He commanded. Of course, the last thing I wanted was to be disarmed. Whilst I had the sword securely sat in its sheath by my side I had at least a fighting chance. A purple creature unsheathed my sword and I suddenly felt even more vulnerable. He passed it to the purple plumed one. The purple plumed one closely scrutinised it. A purple smile spread over his leathery face. 'It is said, in our legends, that when a certain sword arrives to our planet, a very special sword, a sword named Corky...'

'C-o-r-k-y!' the tribe wistfully chanted in deep reverence.

'Mmm,' he said, swishing it around, 'so light': then decapitated one of his tribe with a lazy single stroke, 'so sharp,' he casually said. 'Alien weapons cannot usually penetrate our leathery skin.' Somebody then kicked the head into the water: a couple of others heaved the torso in too: there was a gurgling and crackling of electric: then the head and body fused together: up the purple creature got, out of the water, checking to see if his head was firmly fixed on, completely unscathed, other than a look of annoyance towards his leader. 'It is chronicled in our legends,' the plumed one continued, 'that when Corky arrives, we would no longer need to feed daily on the holy water: but we could pass away, to the serenity of the Promised Land.' He examined the handle, which the blacksmith had inscribed, 'Good luck, Gorky.' 'Yes!' he exclaimed in triumph. 'It is the great sword, Corky. Look! Look!' The tribe gathered round to look at the inscription.

'Doesn't that say, Gorky?' one said. The purple plumed leader vehemently glared at him. 'No, I'm mistaken, it says Corky,' the creature shrugged and corrected himself. They all gazed goggle eyed at the glinting sword. A slow chanting began, barely audible at first, but became louder and louder.

'C-o-r-k-y! C-o-r-k-y! C-o-r-k-y! C-O-R-K-Y! C-O-R-K-Y! C-O-R-K-Y!'

They all chanted in unison, taking turns in touching the sword. The purple plumed one took a step back, and began to address the ecstatic crowd, 'Purple brethren of the purple planet, this is the greatest day in our history: the legends proclaimed that when Corky came, we would no longer have to observe the diurnal ritual of holy water quaffing. We can now retire to the catacombs in the nether-regions of our beloved purple planet, and there live how it is prophesised we should. People! We are now free to expire and pass on to purple heaven where we can dissipate into the purple haze and be at one for always. Let's inform our women of this miraculous arrival.'

They all ambled away, a procession of ecstatic purple leathery creatures, holding my sword aloft, chanting, 'C-o-r-k-y! C-O-R-K-Y!' Leaving me stood there on my own.

'So, it is okay to take some of your water?' I shouted after them: but they were soon gone out of sight. I walked to the edge of the cliff: there, at the foot, were three tiny figures huddled around the sprawled mass of their dead mother. I could hear faint sobbing carried by the air. 'Children!' I yelled, but they did not hear me. 'CHILDREN!' I bellowed. One small face looked up. 'Up here! Bring the pots! Quick!' One by one they reluctantly left their mother and flew up to meet me. 'Come on, fill the pots, and take some to your mother.' They looked around, fearful of another attack. 'They have gone. Don't worry. Go on, take some to her.' With that they set about filling the pots: then descended to where their mother was lying. They sprinkled some water on her wounds and poured some into her mouth. There was a momentary pause: then the ground began to rumble: and mother dragon's body glowed a refulgent orange: she gave a gasp: and then was suddenly on her feet. The babies cheered with joy and hugged their mother: she protectively encased them in her wings while carefully scanning the area. 'Are you okay?' she solicitously asked them.

'We're okay, mammy. We thought we losssst you for good: we're so pleasssed to sssee you alive!' they gleefully said.

'Now, now, children, everything isss okay. Where'sss Gorky?'

'Up there,' one of them pointed.

'Now, you be careful, while I go retrieve him.' The mother dragon was soon ascending to where I was. 'Are you okay?' she earnestly inquired.

'Yes, and you?' I replied with utter relief, for I wanted to hug this beautiful huge dragon.

'I feel great, never better,' she flapped her great wings and breathed a small stream of fire into the air to demonstrate her well-being. She then suspiciously looked around, 'Where did the attack come from?' she concernedly asked.

'From the purple leather creatures of the planet,' I informed, 'but it's okay, they have gone away to celebrate "Corky day."'

'Corky day?'

'I'll tell you on the way back: let's fill the pots and get out of here.' So we filled the pots with the magical purple water, and prepared to leave. I looked disapprovingly at the dam. 'It's a shame that wall is stopping the natural flow of the water, isn't it? No more Lake Sacradia because of it.'

'Yesss,' mother dragon concurred.

'It's a pity we should leave it like this,' I hinted.

Mother dragon knew what to do, with that, she spewed out a continual jet of flame against the dam wall: even though the water made the wall cool, it soon began to intensely glow a fierce orange-white. I had to back away such was the ferocity of the heat. It made me a little nervous for I was unaware how severe a dragon's flame could be once unleashed. Mother dragon could have burnt me to a cinder at any time. The dam wall eventually began to crack with the brutal heat: then the weight of the water pushed through the wall as bricks exploded and a torrent of water rushed and tumbled down the mountain.

I quickly mounted mother dragon and we flew, following the flow of the gurgling purple water to the great crater afore mentioned. We watched as the massive hollow filled with frothing magical water. The sound of the babbling water was melodic, almost as if it was singing joyously of its rightful return.

'Lake Sacradia,' I whispered in awe.

'Thisss isss how it shshshould be,' mother dragon solemnly

declared. We gazed at the mystical lake one last time: the air was charged with intense tranquil energy: I will never forget its timelessness and hallowed air…

Soon we were leaving the purple planet with our precious treasure: the waters of Lake Sacradia! We burst through the purple clouds. Our planet was a tiny spec in the cosmos. Quickly we shot through the air. The babies more in earnest now: seeing their mother die had engendered thoughtful countenances. Our home planet grew. There, on that globe, hanging in space, lived my darling Helena. I now had the means to heal her. The planet continued to grow. I have done it, Helena: I am coming home with the precious cargo. I will see you again, my love. I will be near you once again. My heart warmed at the exciting prospect at seeing my comely lady. The planet grew. Every one I knew was there. All my life, my existence, my experiences, had been on that revolving sphere: and I was returning to that dear beautiful world from whence I came.

We entered the atmosphere and soon white clouds were blowing through my hair. Never had I regarded the planet with such reverent love: my senses were alive with planet Zugra: home. My soul burst forth into a living breathing entity; all things connected in a wondrous matrix: holy environment.

We flew towards the dragon's lair. Below, I saw the Masked Tribe's demesne and the concentration camp of the women. My heart gave a thud as I remembered the women's wretched state. Then I recalled the powers of Lake Sacradia: if I could pour some water on them, maybe they would have the confidence to break from their servitude. 'Dragon.'
    'Yessss?'
    'See below?'
    'Where?'
    'Those women. Hover above them, please.' The dragon took

me over the confinement area undetected. 'Sprinkle some water upon them, babies,' I asked. A baby dragon spilt magical purple water from one of the urns. Sparkling drops of Lake Sacradia descended from the pots on the unsuspecting women below: they paid no heed, as they were lost in their laborious work. The fence began to crackle with an intense blue electric energy: the slices of meat began to waggle and work free. As the water landed on the women they felt inexplicably salubrious. The tongues that had been attached to the fences worked loose and bounded over the floor and leaped into the mouths of their respective owners: each woman looked on in shock as a tongue filled their mouth and fused itself onto the stump that remained.

'Arrgghh!' one cried.

'I can talk!' another delightfully claimed.

'Me too!' another concurred.

'Let's stop this slavery!' one yelled with unwonted vigour.

'Yes!' another agreed, throwing down the pots and pans she had been scrubbing.

'Come on girls!' another shouted 'Let's form a group.' They all gathered together, threw off their silly smiling masks, and began shouting, 'No more slavery! No more slavery!' There they stood, defiant: while the guards peered through their fierce looking masks, bewildered, not knowing what to do.

The superfluous water from the poured urns seeped through the ground, sinking lower into the earth, inducing roots and insects to buzz with energy: deeper and deeper it spread slowly dampening the subsoil: there, buried beneath the concentration camp, concealed by a mountain of earth, was a prostrate mass of tarnished scales and claws: the water finally reached the rotting flesh and suffused into its putrid pores: the body enveloped in a golden glow: the ground began to tremor: the rotting carcass began to grow new flesh: the scales shone: he opened his eyes, as did the baby sleeping next to him: he gave a great R-O-A-R!

the baby emitted a smaller r-o-a-r!: the great dragon flexed his limbs and the earth began to crack and buckle: suddenly father dragon and baby dragon broke through the earth ripping up the fence as they hurtled into the sky.

Such was his frenetic ascension father dragon collided with mother dragon, knocking me off her. I plummeted through the air and hit the ground with such velocity that I received multiple fractures: my neck broke instantly: and I lay there, in a heap, twisted and contorted. Every one looked in dumb amazement. The damp soil infused into me: I was soon dusting myself down.

Up above, the dragons were hugging in a tearful reunion: and the women of the camp cheered at such a sentimental scene. I looked up in glee: but was distracted when a couple of angry guards started running towards me: I quickly made for my sword: it was gone! The mother dragon, seeing my plight, swooped down and gently picked me up with her great talons just as the guards were upon me. We rapidly ascended followed by a couple of spears.

'Let'sss get out of here!' she yelled to her family. With that we quickly flew away.

We eventually arrived back at the lair. Father and baby were very mistrustful of the 'ooman' intrusion: they eyed me with intense suspicion. They could not understand how mother and the three other babies responded to me affably. At first, he castigated her for this unwanted presence: but, eventually, reluctantly acknowledged that the babies did seem relaxed. 'Gorky, are you going to sssstay with ussss?' one of the babies pleaded.

'I would like to,' I replied, 'but I have a yearning to return to my people with the water.'

'When do you intend to go?' earnestly asked another baby.

'Now,' I shrugged.

'Then, I guessss it'sss goodbye,' mother reluctantly murmured, her valedictions tinged with sadness.

'Yes, thank you for everything,' I said, trying to sound positive. I did not want a prolonged farewell. I hastily walked to the pots, and tried to lift one up: it would not budge. Undaunted, I pushed and pulled. 'Maybe I should take smaller containers,' I sheepishly remarked.

'Yesss, maybe,' the father concurred. So I filled my canteen from the pots.

'Gorky,' the mother said.

'Yes,' I replied.

'Will there be enough water in the canteen?'

'I hope so.'

'Father,' she said.

'Yesss, darling?' he smiled, still exuberant to be re-united.

'Gorky hasss travelled far to sssave his people: it will take a long time before he can return if he walks: I think he needsss sssome help.'

'Are you sssuggesssting we help a ooman?! That'sss preposssterousss!' father dragon bellowed, for though he had reluctantly acknowledged I was not like the Masked Tribe, he was still, after many years of persecution, unwilling to fully embrace the idea I was trustworthy. However, mother dragon had always hoped and believed in the potential goodness of people, so when we initially met she was more amenable.

'Ssspeak to him: give him a chance: sssee if he can change your mind,' she urged her husband.

At first father dragon frowned and appeared most intractable, in fact, most intimidating. (I remembered the fierce flame that could effortlessly burst from the nostrils and mouth of a dragon in an instant. I tried not to show fear before this huge formidable beast.) But mother was persistent: she would have her way. And whilst she persuaded him, I cowered behind her leg. In the end he reluctantly acquiesced. So, me, and father dragon, spoke incessantly through the night. At first, speaking to a scowling frowning beast was most unnerving, but I knew the success of my quest depended on it. I conveyed my adventures in the most modest fashion I could. I told him what I had learnt of dragon lore: to which he made fastidious amendments. I told him of my life in Firkin Forest. And, although he was initially impatient and agitated to find himself conversing with a 'ooman': he gradually became more attentive. I even managed to raise a smile from his great fanged mouth: which he quickly checked and tried to look stern. He told me more stories of his ancestry: it was interesting to hear old dragon stories from a dragon's perspective.

'Well, Gorky,' he eventually said, 'you better get some sssleep: for you have a long flight back to your people tomorrow: I will give my consssent for my darling to fly you back to your village: but do not try any tricksss: for if shshshe isss hurt, I *will* hunt you down.' His eyes momentarily raged: his nostrils flared: and white hot sparks sprayed in the air. Gulp, I thought!

'Goodnight,' he eventually said.

'Goodnight,' I replied, trying to stifle trembling.

I crawled off to sleep in the corner of the cavern. I lay there watching the shadows on the craggy cave walls. Silhouettes of my previous adventures played on the rocks: the forging of the most excellent sword; my farewells to my precious Helena; my venturing into the overwhelming tenebrous darkness of The Dead Forest; the bright glow of the sun and the fearful heat of the Desert of No Night; the bizarre Forest of Life; the majesty of Ice Mountain; the awesome presence of the turquoise Sea of Leviathans; incarceration in the womb-tomb egg; the flight to the purple lodestar; the acquisition of the magical purple water... 'Yes!' I whispered to myself, 'I've practically done it. My quest is almost complete.' I drifted away into a deep satisfying sleep.

10.

Homeward Bound

I woke up to one of the babies playfully tickling my nose with its claw. I sat up, rubbed my eyes, and felt a pang of excitement: I was finally going home. 'Do you have to go today?' the baby dragon queried: then all four babies huddled around me with imploring but smiling countenances. I was engulfed in dragon love!

'I would like to stay,' I replied, 'but I really have to go. I have been away from my village for some time now, as much as I have enjoyed your company, I miss my people.'

'Come on children,' mother urged, 'let Gorky get ready.' The babies sighed and reluctantly went away. Mother solicitously gave me a beverage and some food. I greedily munched the food and quaffed the fruit juice. Food had never tasted so good. It was a triumphal repast. 'Ssso, today'sss the day, Gorky. I bet you are looking forward to it,' mother dragon said.

'Yes, I am. I just hope everything will be okay,' I stated, smiling through bread crumbs.

'You have the water: it will be okay,' mother dragon assured. So I finished my breakfast and said goodbye to the family of dragons. I made a promise that I would see them again without thinking how. I hugged each baby in turn and shook the father dragon's great front claw. As I held his talon I felt the tremendous power emanating from the reptilian body. He had never fully accepted me, but I sensed he was gradually changing his attitude.

'Good luck,' he nonchalantly said.

'Have a safe journey,' the rest sang in chorus.

'Do not be too long,' father earnestly petitioned to mother, 'We have some catching up to do.'

'I won't,' she smiled, and rested her paw on his huge scaly shoulder. I climbed on board mother dragon. She held four large water urns, one in each talon. With a thrust of her large leather wings we were soon soaring high into the sky: the air blasted past and I had to hold on tight lest I slipped off. I felt the urgency in the beating of her wings. She wanted to return to her family and spend quality time with her husband.

The land rapidly sped past. Suddenly, the coast appeared and it was not long before we were flying over the Sea of Leviathans. A great expanse of blue lay before us and we flew along at an alarming speed. I saw large dark silhouettes gliding below the water's surface and shuddered to think I had been swimming in that sea. On we flew and the foaming frothing sea zipped past. To see nothing but ocean stretching to the horizon clinging to a dragon in the sky made me feel humble. I was a mere speck in the grand scheme of things. Suddenly we passed a crow holding a branch in its beak. Land ahead! I was surprised to see the coast come into view so soon. We flew over the forest that the beautiful and sultry Nubile had inhabited: but my head was filled with Helena. In the distance, I could see the grey mist of Ice Mountain. It was not long before we were enveloped by the ice vapours that clung there. The bitter chill brought back terrible memories of the extreme conditions I had endured while climbing the icy precipices. We flew over the summit and I wondered how I had managed to surmount such an incredible obstacle. On we flew, hurtling through the icy air. I vehemently shivered and could not wait to leave that inhospitable snowy terrain behind. Thankfully, we were soon descending and flying towards the Forest of Life. I could smell the verdure on the air that was carried by the temperate climate of the forest. We zoomed over the forest and I could hear the heaving mass of bustling leaves below. The Forest of Life whispered: the soughing seemed to say, 'Gorky is on the way!' The mass of leaves danced and swayed as if in celebration. The desert lay ahead, and the searing heat suddenly rose from the baking sand. Hot air rushed past as the sun belted down on my unprotected head. I felt my skin roasting in the unbearable heat. I began profusely perspiring and began to feel faint. The perils of the desert came flooding back to me. I began to lose grip of mother dragon's ears. She must have sensed the impending danger for flicked some drops of Sacradia on my forehead and suddenly I was revitalized. Up ahead, I saw the Dead Forest, and before long, we were flying over it. The dark stillness below tapped into the core of my mind. It seemed there was an immeasurable black abyss below. I began to feel profound despair: anxiety pumped through my veins. All was lost! Life was pointless! My quest had been meaningless! Helena does not love me! As we continued to fly the leaves gradually turned green and began to dance on a light breeze. My mood lifted. I felt sanguine. A broad smile appeared on my face. Home was near! Soon we were near the clearing of Firkin Forest village. 'Down there,' I eagerly pointed. The dragon rapidly descended past the crown of trees and gently landed on the ground.

'Getting the hang of passengersss now,' she attested. I alighted and walked around to her benevolent face.

'Thank you so much,' I gratefully intoned. 'Without you, my journey would never have been possible.'

'Think nothing of it… Thank you for ressssstoring my faith in humanity… Well…I mussst be going now,' she said, holding out an amiable claw for me to shake.

'Do you want to stay for a while? Recuperate after such an arduous journey. I am sure the villagers would be thrilled to see you,' I enthused.

'No, Gorky, I want to get back to my family. I do not feel tired. Our journey wassss not much. Besssidesss, dragonsss can fly forever,' she smiled.

'Thank you again,' I reiterated, feeling mere words were not enough to convey my gratitude to this magnificent beast.

'Goodbye Gorky... Now take a step back, there may be a significant back draught when I flap my wings.' I took a cautious step back as her giant wings down beat and disturbed the dust on the ground all around. She rapidly soared in the air and was soon out of sight...

I waved a last goodbye to the noble dragon, then, looked at the outskirts of my village. My stomach began to churn. After leaving without permission from the elders how would I be received? I was soon in the vicinity of the village by the babbling stream that I had so often borne water from. I decided I would introduce the magical water by stealth. It was quite possible the superstitious and overly wary villagers would reject my overtures. I rolled each jug in turn to the water tanks: they were heavy and cumbersome, but excitement ensured my ability to move them. Whilst manoeuvring the urns I heard a shuffling coming towards me: a human figure with large lumps of flesh hanging from his body- each movement seemed to be excruciating- slowly ambled, feet dragging over the ground. He systematically wiped trickling blood from his brow that perpetually hindered his jaundiced eyes. 'Boy, where have you been?' he ordered. Was that... was that my boss?!

'I...' but I could not get the words out, such was the dramatic change in his appearance. Also, I expected a more welcoming greeting after my arduous quest: evidently I had not been missed as anticipated.

'The tanks are low. Get that water into the tanks before you are fired. Now!' He stormed away leaving a trail of bodily debris. I shrugged, and began filling the tanks with the water of

Lake Sacradia: I felt the tanks vibrate with energy. When I had emptied the last of the water, the knot in my stomach tightened.

I walked into the village with some trepidation. The village smelt of death. What few people there were sombrely sauntered around by rote: they were in such a putrescent state that I could barely recognise them.

I made my way to Helena's house: the windows had a film of dust over them; the door hung from its hinges; the garden was overgrown: everything was in a state of disrepair. Heart pounding, I walked past the threshold of the front door. 'Helena... I'm back,' I yelled. I keenly waited for a reply... The deathly stillness awed me. 'Helena!' I cried, 'are you there!' I waited... listened, but oppressive silence chilled me. I rushed from room to room: large cobwebs hung from the ceiling: a film of dust had settled on everything. 'Helena!' I searched the house over and over until I slumped to my knees sobbing in bewilderment. 'Helena, where are you?'

'She's dead, Gorky.' I spun round: it was Argon, barely recognisable. 'I am sorry, Gorky...please forgive me... I just didn't know.' Bloody tears rolled down his face. He looked so much more humble now, such a change from the vain strutting hero of yore. 'I didn't know. I just didn't know,' he kept repeating.

'Know what?' I impatiently said, for my mind was occupied with my dearest.

'It was me, Gorky: I brought the disease to the village: when I ventured into the Dead Forest, I fell into a thorn bush: the thorns contained a virulent disease: I did not realise until later, when it was too late.'

'Drink this,' I supplicated, offering him the canteen.

'I am sorry, Gorky. I didn't know, I just...'

'Drink this!' I forced the canteen into his hands: he absently drank: he began to glow; his skin changed from cadaverous grey to a healthy hue; his hair and nails rapidly grew; the puss and blood dried up; he began to put on weight; the haggard look was replaced by his old self: but still he continued with his remorse. 'I am sorry, so sorry, I never knew.'

'Where is Helena buried?' But such was his lamentation, that he was oblivious to me: so I stepped outside.

I asked a passer by if they knew where Helena was: but they were so absorbed in misery that they walked by without acknowledging me; I asked another: he vacantly stared at me. 'Helena!' I yelled in his face. He, slowly, pointed to a great mound on the outskirts where two people were being interred.

Suddenly someone ran past shouting, 'I'm cured, it's a miracle!' Then, another, then another, until the word spread that the water was curing people. Soon people were queuing at the tank to feed on Lake Sacradia. People hugged each other and celebrated their quick return to health. It was not long before all survivors of the village were restored. There was a lively bustle of people congratulating each other, sobs of relief and ecstatic laughter.

I had one thing on my mind. I filled a pot from the tank: I walked to the burial mound and climbed on top: I poured the water into the soil: the ground vibrated, shook, rumbled; a fragrant purple smoke emanated from fissures in the ground; a golden glow shimmered on the surface of the soil; the ground began to break open: a hand thrust itself up grasping at the air. Soon, people were climbing from the mound, brushing themselves down, and greeting each other. The whole village had woken from its deathly slumber. I searched among the throng for my beautiful Helena… 'Gorky!' I swung round. There, before me, a divine sight, Helena, in the bloom of youth, never looking so lovely, smiling, large eyes shining, her arms stretched out to me: I ran to her and we embraced: a heat generated from our loving souls, entwined, as one, perfect.

PART 2

HUMANITARIAN MISSION

1.

Compunction

Life soon returned to relative normality in the village: dilapidation was repaired with alacrity. It was a relief to see the wonted infra-structure functioning again. I resumed my occupation as water carrier and was diligent in my work. The boss's rebukes seemed innocuous compared to yore. I was just glad to be surrounded once again by the familiar.

I spent most my evenings with Helena, with friends, or both. We would often sit in the garden listening to village musicians: people would bring food, and we would dance and chat, and appear to be bonding as a community.

In time, though, memories of the disease began to haunt me. As I watched people frolicking in the garden, their antithetical ghostly miens, emaciated and shrivelled with misery, would stand next to them and cast their jaundiced eyes upon me. I then recalled the different tribes I had previously encountered: 'Is this what you do, party whilst we suffer?' said a smoker, as he pulled his cheek from off his face.

'Come here,' said a dryad, as she opened her legs, and they kept opening, until both broke off.

'Oy, down here,' I looked down: a Muldari jumped up and poked me in the eye.

'Aaargghh!' I screamed. The village continued to party as if nothing was happening. No sign of The Forest of Life's tribes could be seen.

A lead mantle of shame hung over me: I imagined the outside world to be dying because of me: everyone I ever met on my journey could now be diseased. I felt powerless to assist them, and so vexation and worry increased.

I wanted to speak of my quest, but was reluctant to remind everyone of the disease. It was as if it had never happened, like everyone had wilfully self-induced amnesia: I began to feel incongruous to our garden soirees. I sat on the edge of the garden ruminating as everyone congregated. Maybe it was better they forgot: but I expected at least someone would be curious to know how the village was suddenly cured.

Helena sidled up to me, and I clung to her and buried my head in her belly: I wanted to purge the horrific memories from me, so I grasped her with inordinate passion. 'What's wrong, Gorky? You've been acting strange of late.'

'So you have noticed?'

'Yes, of course: how could I not?'

'What are your re-collections of dying, Helena?' This startled her, and she gently pushed me away.

'Shush, Gorky, you must never talk of that.'

'So you *do* remember the disease...'

'Gorky, you may have noticed that the village has come to a tacit agreement to never mention it. You must not. It is done. We must be thankful that it is over and carry on with our lives.'

'Helena, I cannot. I am plagued with concern: the people I met on my journey, I fear for their well-being.'

'There is nothing you can do. We are alive, make do with it.' She looked at me with earnest and such persuasive eyes: but contrition burnt deep inside: I could never be at peace with myself until I took measures to aid the possibly stricken. 'Helena.'

'Yes, Gorky.' She held my hand tightly, as if she knew what I was about to say, and she would not let me go again.

'There is a pot of Sacradia...I hid it in the bushes...I want to go forth and administer it to those who may be of need.'

'You are not leaving me again...and, besides, how do you propose to transport it? You know the dangers and difficulties you had before.'

'Dangers and difficulties? I never spoke of...'

'Gorky, I can read your eyes: do you think I have not noticed how you have changed on your return? I wish for you not to go.'

'Helena, my contentment has gradually turned to morbid isolation: the people around me seem so superficial, like they deny reality. This immobility, it's driving me...'

'Gorky, your candour will lead ultimately to your ostracism. Can you not see? No one wants to know the truth of what happened: they are merely content to continue as they were. Leave it be, Gorky, please, you will raise suspicion from the elders.'

'Helena, I wish to show you something.'

'What is it? I hope it is not trouble.'

'Come to my hut.'

'When?'

'Now! Come on.'

'Everyone will notice we have gone.'

'Hello, Gorky. Hello, Helena.' Gavin had strolled up, and was now standing before us. He placed his hands on his hips and spied me suspiciously. 'Everything alright, Gorky?' he inquired, but his voice less indicated concern, and more of, I hope you are behaving yourself.

'Yes, everything is okay, Gavin.'

'I am not Gavin to you... I am Geekeekee elder... I remember your dissent in the past... Are you okay, Helena?'

'Yes, Geekeekee elder, we are fine, thank you,' she dutifully replied. Gavin looked at me for a little while longer, squinting his eyes at me as if trying to find something out, then slowly walked away.

'Gorky, you are drawing attention to yourself; the elders regard you with suspicion: you are not behaving in your accustomed fashion. You look as if you have much on your mind; and, well, you are too aloof.' Helena regarded me with acute solicitousness, and it deeply moved me, for I did not enjoy her worrying.

'I'm not aloof with you, Helena.'

'I am not the only one here... and, well... yes... I have found you increasingly strange.'

'But Helena, I have just told you why. Come to my hut: I have the incipience of a plan.'

'A plan! No, Gorky, I will hear none of it. Now, I am to mingle... I suggest, to allay monitoring, you do the same.' With that she let go of my hand and whisked herself away. I visually followed her until she disappeared into the throng of revellers. My impulse was to follow her, but I wished not to impose myself or stifle her space: so I sat there, drinking in the remnants of her aura left on the seat.

'A plan, Gorky?' The seat was soon filled with Argon. He expanded his chest and felt comfortable with the space he filled with muscle. He looked fixedly into my eyes with a wry smile, and, with a hint of amicability, said, 'What of this plan, Gorky?'

'Plan?'

'Yes, plan...' Argon, as you may recall, was an elder who had unwittingly introduced the disease to Firkin village: and it was the elders that established an intractable reticence concerning the disease and its supposed cure. They would walk around the village, watching and listening, ensuring the status quo was maintained. I could not help notice that an elder, or their menacing security, was never too far away from me: though this was the first time one had approached me in such a candid manner.

'Er, we plan to, er, picnic on the outskirts of the village.'

'The outskirts?'

'Yes, the, the outskirts.' I nervously smiled at him and looked around to see if any of the other elders were watching. I could only presume as Argon was sat next to me, the others were full aware of what he was doing. 'Not to go in The Dead Forest though, not in there,' I tried to assure.

'Kind of an empty feeling, don't you think?' He casually folded his arms to reveal huge biceps: I began to shrink in his presence.

'Er, an empty feeling, what is?'

'To be surrounded by nothing but emptiness and darkness... The Dead Forest...'

'Oh, that, well, at least we have Firkin.'

'Did you tell anyone what I told you?'

'What?'

'About me inadvertently bringing the disease in.'

'You have not told the elders?'

'I have told no one but you. What was it you gave me to drink?'

'Drink?'

'Yes, Gorky, drink, that sweet incredible water, it cured me... it cured the village... didn't it? You've been to... You've been to Sacradia... haven't you?' I looked at him dumbfounded. Old sanctions still applied: there was nothing beyond Firkin Forest; we were the only people that existed. 'Haven't you, Gorky? Tell me!' Argon became animated with a furious urge to know.

'Argon, if I say, what will become of me? You will report me to the elders. I will be imprisoned, or exiled, banished into The Dead Forest. I can't say.'

'You just have! What is your plan?!' Argon grabbed me by the lapels: for an old man he possessed the strength of an ox: I felt myself choking as his eyes raged. I could not defend myself, for there would have been reprisals: even speaking to an elder without permission was a violation. The people around us merrily danced and spoke, seemingly oblivious to the scene. 'You've been to Sacradia, haven't you! What is your plan!' he reiterated with venom.

'Okay, okay, let me go.' In a way, I was glad to tell someone. Whenever I tried overtures with Helena concerning my journey, she issued reproaches in her eyes. 'Yes, I've been to Sacradia.'

'I knew it!' I expected him to strike me, or call the other elders: but he beamed with excitement. 'Good show!' he patted me on the back and nearly knocked me off my chair. I was utterly surprised at how reasonable he was to the news. 'Good show!' he repeated, and patted me on the back again, but this time I recoiled to absorb the impact. 'You plan to go again? Is that it?'

'Argon, when I ventured from the village, unbeknown to me, I carried the disease. I met other tribes on my journey: I fear I may have passed it onto them. I am consumed with worry concerning their well-being. I cannot be at peace until I have sought to aid them.'

'And how do you propose to do this? Can they not traverse to Sacradia themselves? Surely they are closer to the lake.'

'The lake is inaccessible to terrestrials... and... the people I encountered... are rather ensconced... that is to say, they have no initiative to travel: I imagine they will stay put ... and slowly... die.'

'If the lake is inaccessible to terrestrials, how did you acquire the water?'

'Yes, how, Gorky?' I looked up, and there was the grim countenance of Gavin, and next to him a host of other elders. They glared at me; I reciprocated with a disrespectful stare. In an instant my hands were bound and I was marched away to the incarceration unit: I was bundled into one of the stone cells, to await trial.

The cell was quite commodious in comparison to my previous detainment by the Masked Tribe. There was even a portal from which I could have easily made an egression: but escape was futile; there was nowhere to run to other than The Dead Forest: so I sat solemn and considered my fate...

In marched the elders, filling the cell with their presence, sternly staring with lineaments of revile. 'Your name?' Gavin asked, circling the stool I was sat upon.

'Gorky,' I sighed, for he knew my name.

'Do not take on that tone with us,' barked Gavin, slamming the door behind him, leaving me to face thirty hostile elders. 'Do you know, boy, that we could arrange for your disappearance... without trace,' he continued.

'Exile?' I said.

'No...' he said, raising his eyebrows.

'Dea...death?' I murmured incredulously. He slowly nodded his head in concurrence. 'But the death penalty has long been abolished... and besides... it was only rarely meted out after a public trial... What have I done?'

'We will tell you what you have *not* done,' said Olaf, who's tone evinced less severity.

'What I have *not* done?' I carefully enunciated. Never had I seen the elders so earnest: I could feel the tension in the cell. I felt intrepidity, for Gavin's death threat was unequivocal.

'You have not,' Olaf peremptorily intoned as he towered above me, 'ventured from Firkin Forest... have you?'

'Er... no... I never left... if that's what you want to hear,' I shrugged.

'Shut it with the "if that's what you want to hear" boy. We are serious: if people gain any inkling that there is life beyond

Firkin there may be a mass exodus: our society would crumble: our tribe would be irrevocably enfeebled,' stated Gavin with acute concern. 'We cannot allow this to happen.'

'Well,' I said, feeling my devil may care propensity swell, 'if they were happy here, they would not want to leave, would they?' With that, fury blazed in Gavin's eyes: he swiftly drew out a dagger and held it to my throat. The other elders took a step back in horror. 'We know it was you who saved us all,' he growled, 'and because of it, we might just have to kill you.' I steadily looked him in the eyes fortified by the ridiculous statement he had just made; also, I could sense that the other elders were not advocating Gavin's actions. Yes, I looked straight into his eyes as if to say, kill me, then, you fool: be it on your head: see how long you will last in your position. He was taken aback with my boldness and slowly drew the knife away. 'You must not say anything,' he reaffirmed.

'I have not said anything, so far,' I replied.

'So far? You will maintain diffidence. Do you… understand?' he scoured me, as if to say, next time, the blade will not leave your throat without tasting blood. I could not refrain: I had the full council of the elders as witness: if I did not express myself now, I may never have the opportunity to venture from the village with sanction.

'I want to leave again.'

'Leave again? But you never left before,' said Gavin.

'Oh be quiet,' said Argon, who strode forward and pushed Gavin aside. Gavin made attempts to strike him, but Boswald and Ronald held him back.

'What is the meaning of this?' screamed Gavin. 'Unhand me! I am your unacknowledged leader.'

'Unacknowledged?' challenged Argon, 'If no one has acknowledged it, how do you know?'

'But you all continually followed my suggestions,' Gavin unconvincingly sulked.

'Shut it,' demanded Boswald, 'we were waiting for you to go too far... You just did... You had the audacity to re-introduce the death penalty without consultation... or trial! We stood aghast! We cannot stand by and watch this debacle.' Boswald took the knife from a mortified Gavin and cut me loose. 'We surmised it was you, Gorky, that brought the cure. We have been monitoring you. We are concerned that if the people knew, the mass change of consciousness may be too disruptive.'

'I understand,' I nodded, 'but can the truth be shunned? I find it disconcerting how they have blanked it from their minds.'

'Be assured, it *is* on the people's minds, but, enough of that: why do you want to leave again?' asked Ronald.

'Because he fears he has spread the disease further afield,' announced Argon.

'What do you intend to do?' Ronald continued.

'I have hidden an urn full of the magic water...'

'Order a search for the water,' cried Gavin. Nobody moved.

'Continue,' coaxed Argon.

'I have been designing a flying machine...'

'A what?!' blurted Gavin. 'Are you going to listen to that fool?'

'This fool has saved our lives,' scowled Argon. 'A flying machine, Gorky? A machine that can fly?'

'Yes. If I may show you the diagrams: I believe we have the means to construct it.'

2.

Engineering Feats

So I led the elders to my hut. It felt a little strange to have the officials of my village on my side: but it felt good, and I derived great strength from the notion they were beginning to believe in me. I made a conscious effort not to exude too much certitude, for I was unsure if this machine could ever take off. As I entered my humble abode, I was joyous to see Helena: she was tidying the room, then, looked mortified to see me march in with officialdom. 'Gorky, you're in trouble!' she exclaimed.

'No, Helena, I don't believe I am... at least not yet!' I scanned the elders: they smiled amiably, for Helena could make the sternest man soften.

'Would you like a drink?' she asked. They eagerly nodded in approbation, and I went to reveal my plans. I had closely examined the skeletal details of the dragon's wings, and how they moved in relation to the air; I also recalled the glider I had been strapped to: I had devised a machine, that by pushing in circular motions with the feet, transmitting to a series of cogs, levers and pulleys, the kinetic energy would be then transmuted to a flapping motion of wings.

'The machine seats six, gentlemen,' I proudly proclaimed whilst masking my uncertainty, then waited for guffaws of derision, but gladly there was none... 'There is adequate cargo space for the urn. The journey is too long and arduous on foot, but, with this contraption, it is feasibly within our parameters: I could then rectify that which I fear I have done.'

'You fear you may have infected the outside world on your quest to save our village?' Olaf confirmed.

'Yes,' I stated, 'I am racked with guilt beyond imagination.'

The elders perused over the plans; they studied them closely. Too my surprise, they were actually taking my proposal seriously. Gavin was first to speak, without ever looking at the plans.

'It will never work. It's...it's too heavy...The wings will just vibrate the thing to pieces...You will never gather enough power from pedalling... It... it... are we going to risk our people's lives? Are we? Besides... there is nothing beyond Firkin.'

'Mmm,' said Ronald, 'I think the struts maybe too weak.'

'Yes,' said Boswald, 'and this pulley, here, probably too small.'

'And here,' said Olaf, 'the wing's cross section, could be more aerodynamic.'

'Aero what?' I asked.

'Er, I don't know, I just thought of it,' Olaf shrugged, 'but I know what it means.'

'So it is a waste of time?' I mumbled, feeling terribly disappointed. I mournfully gazed at Helena, who sympathized with my mood, but was relieved all the same.

'See, told you!' Gavin triumphantly declared.

'We never said it was a waste of time,' retorted Ronald. 'We merely pointed out some possible flaws in the design: but they can be easily amended.' They examined the papers further, ruminated, deliberated and debated. Argon eventually addressed me.

'Gorky, if you do not mind, we will retire to the forum to discuss this further and take a vote on your proposal... As for myself, I certainly think it is worth a try': then whispered, 'I do not want to be responsible for all those lives outside our village,' then announced, 'but, you must understand, our people's lives are at risk: it has profound ramifications for the future of our village… some good… and… maybe… some not so good. If we decide to go ahead, rest assured, you will have the full cooperation of the elders… okay?'

'Yes, er, yes,' I said, trying to assimilate that I was actually consulting with the elders, who were supposed to represent the collective wisdom of the village, but had been intractable for generations. And so, with that, they, the elders, the subject of much past indignation from me, left my humble abode.

'Gorky! If they agree, you will leave me again!' Helena remonstrated.

'Helena…'

'Do you know what it was like waiting for you the last time? Slowly dying, holding on with all my might. It was torture, Gorky. I was living in hell! Oh Gorky!' She began to weep a lamentable and profound paroxysm as she recalled her lone ordeal. I had no idea she was harbouring such anguish: I had been more concerned with my own. The epiphany induced me to rush to her side and hold her into my aching body. I absorbed her pain, soothed her distress. I felt it flow through me and dissipate into the air.

'Helena, I have no desire to leave: indeed, I cannot ever leave you again.'

'So what are you going to tell the elders if they agree?'

'Helena, the flying machine seats six… Do you want to come? We will thoroughly test the machine first: I will ensure it is safe before… Will you come with us?'

'To leave Firkin? To fly to other lands? To… to *fly*?'

'Yes, Helena. I cannot be without you again. Please, will you?'

'You will be interminably sad if you do not go on this wretched expedition?'

'I will not leave without you,' I earnestly whispered. Helena stared at me, rapt in contemplation. 'I feel I have been the harbinger of death to the outside world: I can't live with myself anymore.' A surge of emotion welled up from my stomach. I felt myself begin to cry, but quickly checked it.

'I know, Gorky.' She momentarily held my arm. Her mind raced through the idea, weighing the pros and cons. She moved to the door, opened it, and gazed up to the sky. She looked around the village, then back up to the sky. She turned round, and slowly walked to me, and held my hands. She gave a sigh, and looked deep into my eyes: 'Okay, if the contraption flies, I will go with you.' I was about to be overcome with joy and give her a huge hug, but the earnestness of her expression brought it home to me our undertaking. She let go of my hands and closed the door, then sat at the table, and urged me to do likewise. 'I have often wondered what lay beyond your tortured eyes: tell me of you travels,' she said. At last, I could tell my beloved of my adventures. And so I relayed the events, not mentioning the, mmm, indiscretions! I wanted to tell her, believe me, I was racked with guilt regarding my encounter with the Dryads and Nubile, but I did not want to hurt my darling lady. We were back together, and I had no intention of jeopardizing it in anyway...

Eventually, there was a knock on the door, and then it swung open: it was Barney the blacksmith, and his wife, Jenny. 'Are you okay, Gorky?' Barney inquired.

'Yes, why should I not be?' I nonchalantly retorted.

'I have heard that you have been interrogated by the elders.' Barney took his and Jenny's coat, threw them over a chair, made us all a hot drink, and sat at the table. 'So what happened?'

'I have told them of my quest,' I stated.

'Oh, and how was it received?' Jenny asked, so I assumed Barney had told her.

'There was a little internal wrangling...but now they have gone to discuss plans of a future expedition,' I informed.

'They have acknowledged there is life beyond Firkin! They plan to venture out?' Barney incredulously exclaimed.

'It has not been finalized yet, but indications suggest they are revising their ideology,' Helena replied.

'Revising their…? You, in cahoots with the elders? I can't… I just can't…'

'Believe it, Barney. I think it was only a single individual that was coercing them to behave in such a myopic fashion… Gavin. They grew intolerant of minority pressure. I believe we are on the verge of some major changes for this village,' I asseverated.

'Yes, Gavin… trouble that one,' Jenny mused.

'It was only a matter of time before they grew wise to his oppressiveness,' Helena replied.

'An expedition? Sanctioned? Is it possible?' Barney was still having difficulty assimilating the apparent change in the elders' attitude. He had lived all his life, as all of us, under a strict regime of prohibition concerning what lay beyond the parameters of our demesne. For them to now be discussing the possibility of travel, could, potentially, if they concur to the proposal, affect our whole way of life, our whole consciousness.

'Yes, Barney, and I believe I will have a say regarding who comes along,' I hoped.

'Should you not wait for the elders to return before you start making plans, Gorky?' Helena advised.

'Helena, I am going whatever happens,' I replied.

'On foot if necessary?' Helena queried.

'How else were you planning on going, Gorky?' Jenny asked.

'In this.' I slung the plans for the aircraft on the table.

'What is this?' Barney inquired.

'It is the diagrams for a *flying machine*,' I proudly declared.

'A *flying machine*? A machine that can fly?' Barney spoke with disbelief, 'Gorky, have you gone mad?' I stared at him fixedly to convey this was no joke.

'There are six seats... Do you want to be a part of the venture?' I inquired in a cavalier fashion. Barney stared at me, then studiously began examining the plans. His index finger fastidiously traced all the outlines whilst muttering to himself.

'Did you draw these?' he finally asked.

'Yes.'

He re-immersed himself in the diagrams, becoming quite absorbed. At one point he looked in a trance as he meticulously perused. It was good to see my dear friend privy to my hard work. I waited for him to finish.

'Well?' I eventually said. He looked up with a large grin on his face. He put his large blacksmith's arm round the chair of Jenny's.

'A flying machine?' he eventually said. He took a large quaff of his coffee. 'To distant lands?'

'Yes... Will you be on board?' I persisted.

Jenny glared at him, then balefully stared at me: she could contain herself no longer. 'The only way he is going is if I accompany him,' she intransigently stated. Barney gave Jenny a long loving look.

'Then it is settled,' Barney laughed, 'you have two new crew members: if that's okay with the captain.' He held his huge blacksmith's hand out for me to shake and I was at the mercy of a hammer and anvil grip!

There was a knock on the door. 'Enter!' I shouted. I had now thrown caution to the wind: there was no longer the need for secrecy with the elders on board. In marched Argon, beaming. He espied the diagrams on the table and stared transfixed at them.

'Seats six?' he smiled.

'Yes,' I said.

'Count me in!' he enthusiastically announced.

'They've sanctioned it?' Helena asked.

'Yes. We start building tomorrow,' Argon the adventurer announced. 'Barney, old boy, you will be consulting with the engineers of the tribes. Anyone who can make a useful contribution will be invited. Just think, whooshing through the air!' He made his hand into a wing and zipped it through the room. His intense enthusiastic mien evinced there would be nothing to stop us. I had never seen an elder so forthcoming in his geniality. It felt rather agreeable to have Argon's support as opposed to conflict.

'Argon, I would like Helena, Barney and Jenny, to be crew of the craft,' I declared.

'Yes, yes, Gorky, and me, of course, don't forget me,' he supplicated in a child like manner, but that was due to his boundless relish at the prospect and made him overlook the fact two women were now on board. 'A journey of a life time, what?' Argon laughed suddenly slapping Barney on the back: both were equally as powerful as each other, so Barney was unyielding to the overly exuberant blow, but took it in good spirits.

'That leaves one more seat,' Jenny informed. Argon looked at us all, two couples. Helena returned the look implying, how far will you amend your ideology: for the elders were quintessentially patriarchal. Events had been moving at such a pace that we thought Argon, the elders, would have sudden reservations and revert back to old ways. The adventures, in all our fables, had only ever been taken by males. I had been given considerable autonomy regarding the planning of the expedition. I had essentially been calling the shots. The trust the elders had shown in me could suddenly stop. But I sensed a significant change in the air. 'You have a wife, don't you, Argon?' Jenny continued.

'Er, yes, I do,' he said with uncertainty.

'Kelly... remember her?' Helena asked, smiling.

'Now, wait a moment!' Argon blurted, 'are you suggesting

Kelly come with us?' Jenny and Helena stared with ambivalence at Argon: seriousness and happiness.

'But women are for cooking, making babies, cleaning the huts,' he unconvincingly uttered.

'We don't intend to be doing much of that on our journey,' Jenny smiled.

'You've agreed to travel with two women,' Helena added. Up until now Argon had been so taken with the adventure and plans had been moving so quickly he had not considered the dramatic changes taken place. He thought for a little.

'By Jove,' Argon proclaimed, 'I know just the person to fill that final seat.'

'You do?' Jenny mockingly inquired.

'Yes, Why don't I ask my wife?'

'Good idea,' Helena said.

'Mmmm, flying machine,' Barney mused, lost in the papers again. 'What material are you intending to use for the frame and skin?'

'Er, I thought wood,' I hesitatingly said.

'Not robust enough,' Barney rejoined.

'Iron?' I asked.

'Iron? Not feasible,' said Barney.

'Too heavy?' I inquired, worried that the plan would not get started.

'Way too heavy,' he nodded. Barney then suspiciously scrutinized Argon, and I could see he was deep in thought, pondering a dilemma: then he shrugged, and said, 'I have invented an alloy... a special metal... light but strong: I call it aluminium... I, er, I've never dare mentioned it to anybody before. I was wondering what it could be used for: I think it would be perfect for the craft.'

'Excellent!' proclaimed Argon. 'This is great! Look, I'm going to make a... a public announcement: we need all the expertise we can muster. Must dash. Do you mind if I take the papers? Must get the artists to re-produce them so they can be disseminated.'

'Go ahead,' I shrugged, smiling.

'Splendid! Right, toodle pip. See you soon.' With that Argon darted towards the door, then disappeared, only to re-appear, poking his head round the door, 'Oh, I forgot, there's a meeting with the elders tomorrow at high sun. We have to arrange the labour details…amongst other things. I want this machine assembled forthwith. Bye for now.' And he was gone, leaving a sanguine air of anticipation.

'I will meet you at your workshop in the morning, Barney, if that's convenient?' I asked.

'Abandoning your water duties?' Barney smirked.

'No, I will do that first,' I said, for I had not forgotten that life depends on water.

'Okay. I am eager to get to work on this unprecedented project,' Barney mused, beginning to be infected by Argon's enthusiasm. Then he and Jenny bid farewell until the morrow. Helena was about to leave for her own home.

'Are you not staying the night?' I asked, deliberately pushing the boundaries of the elders' malleability: for only with ceremony was such a thing usually allowed.

'Gorky, you opportunist! I need a little time to think. This journey, well…' I looked at her with beseeching eyes. I did not want to be without her, particularly tonight: to be in her vicinity was comfort immeasurable. My eyes burnt into hers: I understood the perils of the journey: and hence, the present became so much more precious. She understood; her eyes lit. She never said a word, took my hand, and led me to bed…

The next morning I awoke at first light. I had to check myself to assure the previous day's events had not been an incredible dream. There, laid next to me, soundly asleep, was my beloved lady. I had no desire to disturb her sacred slumber. I rose and dressed in eager anticipation. I looked at the table: the plans had gone and was littered with tea cups. Yes, the village, the elders, had had a sweeping change of ideology, more open-minded, more progressive.

As I made my way towards Barney's workshop, the accustomed sleepiness of the village had been transmuted into a bustle; for the first time people were alive. In the commotion, I could hear people talking freely about the proposed journey to unknown lands. People acknowledged me, their eyes bright and animated. Entering Barney's workshop, his kiln was blazing, and men were working with zeal. Diagrams of the flying machine were strewn on tables and pinned to the walls. 'Arr, Gorky, catch this.' Barney threw a polished metallic lump at me: I expected my arms to be torn from their sockets: but I was surprised to feel the lightness.

'Alu... ?'

'Aluminium,' he affirmed. His work shop was a hive of activity. The village's finest engineers and craftsmen were fervently engaged in the task of building the flying machine. Already casts were being made for components: the sense of purpose and enthusiasm was infectious. 'I visited the elders this morning,' Barney said, 'I asked them for the blue prints, and permission to get the project under way post haste: they acquiesced, most cooperative. I've recruited our best engineers. We've had to make some adjustments to the drawings, but on the whole they were pretty good. I reckon if we successfully adhere to schedule, we can complete the project in fourteen suns,' he claimed, as he hammered out a piece of metal plate.

'What can I do?' I implored, for I was eager to be a part of the busy team. The sooner the flying machine was made, the sooner we could engage in the humanitarian mission.

'Well, you can stoke the fire for starters, then, you see here?' He pointed to one of the cogs on the drawing. 'See this compass? See that mould?' Barney issued me terse instructions for my day's work. I felt a little intimidated, not sure I was of any use, for I was only a mere waterboy. I was surrounded by the most able and best who went about their business with aplomb. But often imagination is worse than reality and I was soon immersed in the job of building an *aeroplane*, sometimes stopping to assist other engineers and other impromptu tasks: I pleasantly surprised myself at new found skills. Time passed quickly as we worked late into the evening...

At the crack of dawn, every morning, I turned up eager for work, involved in tasks such as constructing connecting rods, cope sawing intricate plates for the cross sections of wings, and debating about the best designs for certain parts of the machine. We cooperated as a team and had great sense of purpose. Some of the engineers invented what they called a peddle lathe: as time went on, tools were more precision made, which meant the product was more exact. After much assiduousness, the components were gradually assembled: the flying machine organically took shape...

Fourteen suns soon passed...We felt a great sense of achievement, for there, in the workshop, proudly stood a gleaming aluminium flying machine. It looked like some proud bird of prey, posing with its nose in the air. We reverently gazed at the product of our endeavours. There was an air of palpable excitement. We, the village people, who had generally never been beyond the confines of the outer parameters of the village, had built a beautiful sleek machine that was to take us over vast tracts of land and sea. We made last minute fine adjustments, lubricating all moving parts, tinkering with drive shafts and flaps etc. The atmosphere was imbued with energy around the symbol of our ingenuity and industriousness.

Word circulated that the machine was completed. Outside a throng of people were eagerly gathering, waiting to view it. The elders congregated around the door. We sat on benches listening to the tumult outside. We could hear Argon begin to address the audience: 'People of Firkin, this is a great day in our history: we have, in this workshop, the means to leave the confines of our wonted purlieu and intrepidly go forward to strange new lands. The opportunities are immense, the possibilities infinite, the, the, well, we could trade with other tribes, acquire new materials, exchange cultural knowledge, and, and...' The elders nervously shuffled as Argon's zeal began to boil, and so he quickly checked himself. 'That's, of course, if there *is* anyone out there.' (For, although it was now common knowledge I had travelled afar, the official line was more reticent.) 'Anyway, 'he continued, 'our lives will be profoundly altered, and should be improved: we will need to adapt with change, yes, change with change.' The crowd looked at each other and mumbled: this was news indeed, now officially publicized, it was really true. I heard one of the elders exaggeratingly clear his throat, as if a prompt. 'Er, also,' said Argon, 'there may be nothing out there but hostility: it could be, er, catastrophic for our insulated but protected society: and, believe me,' he stared at the people in their eyes (he felt confident in benevolently reaching out to the people now Gavin had been subdued), ' I would hate anything to happen to you fine and dear people. But, I have been speaking to some of you over the past few days, and, the consensus is, it is our immutable duty to push forward and explore: for not knowing has always been a question that has irked many of you; you have felt stifled being circumscribed by darkness: the darkness, people, is about to be illuminated!' He proclaimed it as if he was expecting applause, but diffident sceptical faces stared back. Sure, they had had a little time to assimilate the possibilities, but this was momentous, unprecedented; how could they possibly prepare for such a development. Argon wasted no time, for he could see the disconcertment in people's eyes: he urgently banged on the doors which meant to signify that the engineers should swing them open: but we were engrossed, arguing about the feasibility of the thing actually flying. Of course I was advocating absolute success: it was ultimately my design after all: but I was being met with stiff opposition from the more cynical engineers. Argon banged on the door more violently, and it distracted us from our intense debate.

'Go on, Gorky,' encouraged Barney, so I stepped outside, closing the door behind me.

'Argon, hello!' I cordially shook his hand.

'Er, hello, Gorky. The machine is ready?' he inquired.

'Er, yes, it is ready, for test runs… Could I say a few words to the people, if I may?' I asked. Argon looked at the elders: they muttered between themselves, then, much to my glee, nodded their approval. So, I began, 'People, before we start becoming too impetuous, we are not sure if the craft will even take off the ground… but… if it does… and that is a big *if*… if it does… I want to tell you, that the prime motivator for this expedition, is not to acquire new and exotic food etcetera, but to ply humanitarian aid to the tribes that may be stricken by the…' I hesitated, for the disease had not been openly spoken about during the aftermath of the outbreak. I was still trying to get accustomed to this unprecedented transparency. I was naturally cautious. I said no more, for the implications of what I had said was already been absorbed by the perspicacious crowd: it just confirmed what they already knew: of course they were aware there had been a virulent disease (by not being allowed to speak about it did not mean it had not happened); of course they were aware of a sudden miraculous cure; and of course they speculated that it was *somebody* who must have left Firkin to find it. There followed an awkward silence. I thought I was going to be mobbed, or the elders were going to cart me away again: but, unbeknown to me, everyone had come to realize it was me that had gone on the quest and retrieved the alchemical water. No matter how autocratic a regime, the truth cannot be denied. As individuals there was *apparent* diffidence, but news promulgated: and the relative safety in the anonymity of a crowd they could no longer contain themselves. They started cheering me, yes, I am pretty sure it was me they cheered, a belated token of their gratitude, and I fought back the tears: I looked at the elders for revile: they frowned as accustomed: but, then, their solemnity turned to smiles, they nodded, and applauded, making it even more difficult for me to contain my emotion. I rushed into the workshop, 'I hope this bloody thing is going to fly,' I said, feeling a tincture embarrassed.

The doors of the workshop swung open and the villagers stared in awed silence at the metallic bird: there she stood, grand and defiant. With relative ease, the engineers pushed the craft outside. People reverently followed as the machine was pushed into the public square: and there it proudly posed, the metal gleaming in the midday sun. Argon and Barney exchanged a few words, then, Barney addressed the villagers. 'Tomorrow,' he announced, 'tomorrow we test this, er, thing. We are, mmm, hopeful it will , er, fly. All the expertise of the tribes has contributed. The spirit of the people is, er, is undeniable… but…let's be realistic… well… let's hope it flies.' Barney walked towards where Jenny was, put his arm round her, and walked to his hut for a well earned rest. The machine was left in the square for people to view at their leisure, a symbol of hope, unity, and possible freedom.

I went to Helena's and became very tactile: I was to be one of the test pilots, and a strong sense of my mortality once more pervaded me: feeling so close to dicing with death meant I had to hold on to the epitome of life, my beautiful lady. She knew and understood, and tenderly reciprocated my nuzzling. At the

169

same time we diligently ran through everything we knew about the flying machine, for it would not be long, all being well, that Helena would be joining me as a pilot.

The next morning, I walked to the test site. A runway had already been cordoned off and a line of expectant people were waiting. Argon, Barney, and three other engineers stood there with grim determination etched on their countenances: the time for talking was over. The theory was, by a system I named *pedalling*, the energy, by a series of pulleys, would be transmuted to the wings, which would flap like the dragons. We had given them a gentle dry run in the workshop, and, so far, all was going to plan; all the mechanisms were working, and it was just a matter of now testing to see if the machine would actually fly. I met the test pilots by the aircraft: then, one by one, we all clambered up the steps into the cockpit and sat in our designated seats. The crowd became still and silent as we looked along the runway which headed towards Firkin Forest. We calculated there would be enough room to gain a fair head of speed before we met the trees. We busied ourselves with minor adjustments to accommodate our comfort. There we sat, staring ahead, nervous energy coursing through our veins. Argon shouted, 'Ready?' and we all responded in the affirmative. 'Go!' With adrenalin pumping, we pushed down hard on the pedals: the machine lurched forward and the crowd looked on stunned. We began to gain momentum and the aluminium wings flapped like the great dragon's wings. I was surprised and slightly dismayed at the effort it took, and we were pedalling flat out with the trees fast approaching. I was about to abort the first test and shout stop for I feared our work would be destroyed: but then, the wheels lifted from the ground. The crowd cheered.

'We're flying!' Barney cried.

'Yes, one inch off the ground,' I disappointingly said... But then the craft suddenly lifted higher... and higher... and we flew over the tree tops as the under carriage ripped away some leaves. I was concerned with the ergonomics: the effort to propel the machine could not be maintained for any substantial period of time: my calves burned and I dearly wanted to stop pedalling. Everyone in the cockpit must have felt the same, for we began to lower and skim over the crowns of the trees... Then, WHALLOP! We became ensnared in the branches, flipped over, came to a sudden halt, and we hung, clinging to our seats. I had not time to regain my senses, and I instinctively held on with numb horror.

'What a buzz!' Argon screamed, hanging by his finger tips swinging from the wing, utterly jubilant at our achievement. The ground was some way below us, and we would have surely been hurt if we fell. I managed to grasp a tree trunk with my legs and pull myself onto a tree. I helped the others, and the villagers appeared with a ladder to facilitate a safe descent. The aircraft was hoisted from the trees and taken back to the workshop for repairs. A heated debate ensued concerning the effectiveness of the maiden voyage, and how matters could be improved. A system of gears was introduced: other adjustments were made. It was agreed that once altitude had been reached, effort could be allayed: but the issue of sustaining propulsion was still a major concern. We continued to test the craft, and discovered although all six pilots were needed for take-off: two teams of three in rota, after physical training, could maintain altitude. We were soon flying over the outer regions of Firkin...

Mean time, Helena, Jenny and Kelly were instructed that they had to embark on a rigorous training program. After a while, when we had established that the craft was fairly reliable, they replaced the three engineers who had been test pilots. The allotted expedition team was soon flying over the village with consummate ease. People went about their daily business, occasionally glancing up to espy the massive metallic wings beating against the air carrying the excited passengers. I began to feel confident that the journey was finally becoming a reality. After further preparations, it was at last time for us to set forth into 'uncharted lands'... although I had them vividly chartered in my head.

I was summoned to the forum to parley with the elders. I assumed it would just be a matter of protocol, issuing good lucks and so on: but, as I entered, I met a series of grave faces, which made my stomach sink.

'Gorky,' Olaf said, in a most solemn fashion.

'Y-e-s,' I suspiciously replied.

'Gorky,' he earnestly repeated, and came and put his hand on my shoulder, and ushered me before the council. 'This mission *is* to establish trade links,' he confirmed.

'Not just for that,' I reminded him.

'Er, yes, the water... where is it, Gorky?' he matter-of-factly said.

'It is safe...mmm... nearby,' I carefully enunciated.

'We would appreciate it if you reveal the location,' Ronald said.

'Well, yes, I was going to, I mean, we have to load it on board the plane... don't we?' I innocently stated.

'How much are you intending on taking?' Ronald inquired, standing up to confront me. He took over with the ushering and led me to a seat before the elders, and gently pushed on my shoulders so I would sit down. I wanted to resist, but I did not want to risk putting the mission in jeopardy, so I acquiesced. 'Were you planning on taking it all?' he continued.

'We no longer need it,' I shrugged.

'Not yet, but we feel it is in the interest of the village to keep at least three quarters of it here,' he declared.

'Three quarters? But I may have to attend to many people,' I reminded.

'They are not *our* people, Gorky: our people must come first. If there is another outbreak of the disease...' Ronald carefully scrutinized me in attempt to induce shame. I looked at Argon: but he stared beyond me, not wanting to become involved.

'I will need at least half,' I compromised.

'Half!' Gavin suddenly stood up. 'You are lucky we have sanctioned this hare-brain scheme at all: and now you want to deprive the good people of this village the sacred remedy!'

'Half is a fair quantity: you would have sufficient to heal in the direst situation: it is a potent cure,' I yelled, twitching on the seat.

'This smacks of perfidy!' Gavin screeched. Argon vigorously raised himself from his seat, mien suggesting preparation for verbal combat.

'It *was* Gorky that retrieved the water!' he bellowed. 'Half is fair. Anyone with a vestige of perception can see his troubled visage gradually increases as his conscience plagues him: he means to save those tribes: I say, let him, and don't get in his way! Half is fair measure.' Gavin sneered at Argon.

'Are you going to allow a waterboy dictate terms to us?' Gavin turned to the other elders, 'What is this...this fiasco?'

'Argon's right,' affirmed Ronald, 'half is fair measure: we would still have enough of the panacea in our village for any emergency which may arise: for him to travel to distant lands with only a quarter, and then find he had insufficient supplies, would be defeating the object, for the disease would not be eradicated: and, may I add, as our community is on the verge of becoming less isolated, while the contagion is circulating, we are *all* at risk.'

'Is that not good reason to remain isolated?' Gavin responded. 'We run the risk of contracting the disease again.'

'We cannot baulk progress any longer. We have the resources to travel and explore: curiosity compels us; intellectual restlessness cannot be eschewed: nature dictates that we must evolve: besides, for Firkin to be renowned as humanitarians is good for relations with the outside world, and would oil the wheels of commerce. And, so I say again, half is fair measure,' declared Ronald.

'But what if they bring the disease back with them?' Gavin remonstrated.

'We will drink Sacradia when coming in contact with the stricken. I feel it is my irrevocable duty to go forth and make amends for my inadvertent blunder. I will need half the urn to do so,' I determinedly urged.

'Raise your hands if concur,' Ronald demanded. The elders looked around at each other, then, slowly, one by one, without exception, they voted that I would be permitted to transport half of the water of Sacradia from the village to use as I saw fit. Gavin silently fumed. I looked at him whilst putting on a semblance of blamelessness: to which he stormed from the forum.

'Right, that's settled,' declared Argon. 'Let's get the water loaded on board. We have a journey to embark upon.'

3.

Chocks Away

The next day, me and Helena sat at the table, eating a large breakfast of fried potatoes, mushrooms, onions and tomatoes, thick slices of bread and butter, biscuits, washed down with mugs of hot tea: it was imperative we were well fed: we would be expelling inordinate amounts of energy. We ate in silence. The air was tense. I could sense Helena was not taking this venture lightly: her eyes shone with deep introspection: the unwonted intensity on her face made me nervous and excited. She stared at me with such incredible concentration, that I felt her essence touch my core; I reciprocated with a silent nod, as if to say, soon.

We quietly collected our provisions, which were carefully chosen, for we did not want to over laden the craft: the plane had to be kept as light as possible: even essentials like food supplies were rationed: and as water is heavy in any significant quantity, how much to take on board was heatedly debated: we needed enough to cross the hot desert plains, so as not to have to dip into Sacradia.

We stepped outside, and the air, though charged with an irresistible energy, was fairly still, perfect for flying. We began solemnly walking towards the beginning of the runway. When I caught a glimpse of the plane gleaming in the warm morning air, my stomach turned: what we were about to attempt became most apparent. A group of people had already gathered, and there was an air of excited expectation. We stood by the plane in nervous alacrity. The entire village was festooned along the margin of the runway. The elders were nearby, looking on, dignified. I was anxious to climb on board: I had *selectively* briefed everyone what to expect on our travels, for I was loath to emphasise too much the intrepid undertaking: and it had augmented my relish for the journey. The tension and eagerness to depart had gradually increased in all the crew as the tests progressed. Argon stepped forward to address the crowd one more time, 'Fear not tribes of Firkin. We will return with many tales to tell. This, no doubt, is the seminary of developing avenues beyond our wonted purlieu. As we become more dexterous at flight, our knowledge of the world will increase, until it will become, I expect, one big village where we all gain from interaction.... Goodbye, and see you soon.' Argon looked at his companions to see if we had anything to add, but we waved at the people to concur with what had just been proclaimed: and we tentatively climbed on board. The crowd stared transfixed, physiognomies indicating a sympathetic understanding of our challenge. Someone must have thought the silence was akin to a funeral, and started to cheer encouragement: others quickly followed: instantaneously we were absorbing the energy of the crowd and derived great encouragement. We stared with fixed intensity ahead, facing a mild wind, which, we hoped, would assist in our ascent. 'Ready?' Argon asked, and we all confirmed: he counted to three, then said, 'Go!' We simultaneously pushed down on the pedals: the craft thrust forward a lot quicker than the initial test runs, and Argon changed gear at the apt moment. We sped along, bouncing over the prepared ground, then suddenly we lurched into the sky. The wings pushed down against the air in great bursts. The crowds cheering gradually diminished as they shrunk below. We were confronted by the immense sky. We attained a travelling altitude and Argon trimmed the flaps: we levelled off. Me, Barney and Kelly, ceased to pedal as the craft held steady. We swiftly moved along, parallel to the ground, smoothly and efficiently. Below us was Firkin Forest, the myriad of green hues swirled and fluttered, a carpet of verdure that was the crown of the trees: above us, the firmament, vast cobalt ether, eternal space...

We flew on, leaving our village and accustomed life behind us; unknown adventure ahead. Firkin Forest began to gradually fade as we started to fly over the Dead Forest. My mood became sullen as the inexorable influence of the emanating powerful darkness suffused into the marrow of my soul: my compatriots skin became wan and listless. I felt myself being sucked into the abyss below. We were rapidly losing altitude: my spirits waned. Argon desperately shouted, 'I think we all better start pedalling!' We all pedalled hard against the despondency and despair: the air seemed as thick as molasses: energy levels mitigated. I had not realized the effort it must have taken the dragon to fly over The Dead Forest, unless her scaly armour protected her from the psychological malaise below. The Dead Forest was like an open and starving mouth, enticing us to descend into the ostensible comfort of its pitch darkness. Helena turned to me and nodded: for I had forewarned her about the effects of it. Her eyes penetrated into mine, satiate with the cosmic energy of love and induced my heart to defy the deathly maws below. We pedalled with grim determination, against thoughts of the oppressive lifeless realm gaping underneath us. We became acutely aware of each other's life forces, acquiring solace and comfort. Below us, the emptiness of void; around us, people, alive, electric, warm, replete with many coloured emotions and thoughts. We pedalled on for each other's sake: all the time, death tried to draw us in. We defied darkness with our love: it hated us, envied us, and screamed for us to accrete with it: but the nobility of our nature could not permit such a thing. We fed the flame of life, rallied, pedalled on with all our might, and gradually regained height...

Gradually, the air became easier to flow through: the craft surged forward quicker: suddenly the sun burst down upon us and the vast gold of The Dessert of No Night assailed our eyes. Warm thermals suspended the craft with little effort; heat danced and rose and held us steady: and we pedalled and glided, pedalled and glided, drifting into the dessert. Argon, Jenny and Helena ceased to pedal as we became enveloped by the sandy expanse: it now only required me, Barney and Kelly after the toil of flying over the tenebrous forest. As we flew we erected a canopy above our heads and ate and drank. The ground darted past below us: each second of flight meant I would have been left long behind if I had been on foot: but here I was flying rapidly and with little effort through the air in good company.

I could now begin to ease my perturbed mind to seek the tribes and succour their welfare. I hoped the Rubber Clad Dryads would receive us more favourably than I had previously been, for we were relatively unarmed and had no proclivity for conflict. I had cursorily informed the crew of their existence. I had vivid recollections of Amazonian fierceness, but hopefully, if they were stricken with the disease, and saw we had women in our party, would be willing to negotiate.

We changed teams: Argon, Helena and Jenny began to pedal. Ideally, we would have liked to have landed to rest: but it was not feasible, for none of the terrain presented itself as solid or flat enough. We hoped when we eventually reached The Forest of Life that there would be a grassy margin adequate for a safe descent (I had taken little heed the last time I was there, for I had no idea I would be returning, let alone like this, and I self-castigated myself at the inability to recall): if none, we would have to reluctantly take our chances landing on the sand and hope to come to a undamaged halt. We would then have to hew trees from the forest in order to create a solid strip of land for taking off again. In our cargo we had axes for hewing wood: so, although officially we were unarmed and a peaceful mission, I had been secretly practising fighting with an axe. There were many unknown dangers out here. I had not candidly spoken about my reservations to the others: I did not want to make them overly nervous with my fertile imagination: but there were weird noises emanating from The Forest of Life, noises that had re-manifested in my dreams when I returned to my village, noises I had naively not adequately discerned whilst I was there.

As Helena pedalled, I massaged her neck and gently kissed her nape. Sometimes I pedalled with her: but if she knew, she would have earnestly remonstrated. The desert had taken on a completely different aspect in the company of my lady: before it was a vicious snarling monster breathing fire onto my acutely sensitive nerve entangled skin; now it was a shining gold resplendent jewel, magnificent in its beauty, awesome in its splendour, twinkling and glimmering: dashes of brilliant sparkling light shot into the blue ethereal hood of the sky. I transcended into Helena's swirling hair, kaleidoscope patterns were my soul, absolute love was my heart, surfeit and complete: I danced with every shape her hair made. I encompassed her, absorbed into her, and pumped through her veins. I became her lungs and heart: each breath she took imbued my being with pure life; each heartbeat of her gorgeous soul infused me with vitality. I rushed through her body absorbing every molecule of her existence. I was her essence. It was a home I never wanted to relinquish…

'Gorky!' Barney rudely awoke me. I jumped back into my own body, but instinctively kissed Helena's head. I went to put my arms around her, but snapped into complete waking when Barney said, 'Gorky, we've been flying for some time.' I gazed around me: we were surrounded by the desert. The warm air zipped past. The sun, brilliant yellow orb, hung above us. I looked at Helena's shoulders and kissed them. 'Gorky!' Barney impatiently erupted, 'it's your turn to pedal.'

'Er, mmm, yes, of, er, course,' I stammered, slowly emerging from the deep slumber. So, me, Barney and Kelly, did our stint. Helena turned and smiled at me.

'I am tired,' she yawned, 'I need to rest.' She placed a folded coat on the side of the cockpit to support her head: soon, she was drifting into sleep. Argon and Jenny also looked exhausted.

'How long have they been pedalling?' I inquired.

'I do not know. I woke not long before you. All I know is, they allowed us to wake on our own accord.'

'They allowed *you* to awake on *your* own accord,' I corrected.

'They have done a longer stint than what is good for them: I am most annoyed,' he glared at me as he wrestled with the pedals. The metallic wings beat against the arid air, and the bulk of the craft thrust forward…

It was not long before Helena was awake and wanted to take over with the toils. 'Helena, self-sacrifice will not do: we need to do this in equal measure: please rest,' I earnestly advised. She made tired protestations, but I managed to cajole her back to sleep. Barney solicitously stared at Jenny: she was completely lost in sleep: then, with grim determination pressed deep into his lineaments, he pushed on….

The hot desert air whizzed past us. The horizon never seemed to change, though I could see the dunes racing by below. 'Are you okay, Kelly?' I asked.

'Yes,' was all she would say. I gently squeezed her shoulder for morale comfort. The women demonstrated determination that inspired the men: they silently went about their business of propelling the aluminium craft through the scolding air. The men felt compelled to match their endeavours: so, as a team, the alloy wings flapped indomitably forward…

I began to grow concerned. It seemed as if we had been in the desert as long as the last time I had been on foot. We had been flying in a straight line, the same line, so I thought, that had previously taken me to The Forest of Life. The other crew members began to grow a trifle restless. Food and water rations were becoming critically low. I had bargained on reaching The Forest of Life long before now. Incremental fear slowly began to pervade me, a sense of hopelessness, dire loss, images of aimlessly flying around the infinite desert for eternity assailed my mind: I had selfishly led these innocent people into a hellish existence. With concerted volition I held my demeanour together and tried to look composed and calm: though inside, the black abyss of The Dead Forest increasingly grew. It took much effort to hold back the tears of desperation and to profusely apologize for putting everyone in such a predicament: but I knew to get out of the scolding desert alive, I had to remain calm. 'Is it much longer before we reach The Forest of Life, Gorky?' Argon asked.

'Er, it shouldn't be,' I unconvincingly claimed.

'Shouldn't be… mmm, could you be a little more precise?' demanded Barney, with subtle consternation spread over his physiognomy. 'We have drunk all the normal water, and there is little food.'

'Yes, I am aware of our situation, Barney. I can only hope we are soon there,' I tried to assure.

'Hope! That's not good enough. Where the hell are we going? Aimlessly pedalling like lunatics in this bleeding scorching air.' With that, after a few attempts to muster sputum, he expectorated on the fuselage: the spit bubbled and boiled and vanished into steam. 'We are like baking bread in an oven,' he angrily announced: and Barney should have known, used to working in high temperatures. All my compatriots had most florid complexions and were looking quite jaded.

'I propose we drink a little of Sacradia,' I advised. 'It will instil in us adequate vigour to complete the next phase of our journey.'

'Good idea,' agreed Argon. 'What do you think, ladies?'

'We have no option,' shrugged Helena. 'Our energy levels are fading fast: it is the common sense thing to do.'

'Agreed,' said Kelly and Jenny. So we administered, in measured doses, some of the healing water: immediately, I felt cooler, more vital, and, more optimistic. Helena's eyes twinkled, and the plane surged on...

For time interminable we pedalled, the wings wafting great scoops of hot desert air downwards, pushing us along, then gliding over the smooth sands. We flew onwards into the desert sun, and, as the effects of the water wore off, scorching anxiety increased. I was about to suggest another quaff of our precious cargo, when Kelly shouted, 'What's that ahead?' Argon stood up out of the cockpit, craned his head and squinted in desperation.

'I think we're here!' he cried. I looked over Helena's shoulder: there was definitely a change of scenery up ahead, but it did not look like The Forest of Life. It appeared to be a large flat expanse of grassy terrain.

4.

Dystopia

Soon we were flying over marsh land, a large flat area of grass with a smooth glassy covering of water. Mercifully, the temperature cooled, and a great relief imbued the crew as the craft became more bearable to sit in. It was difficult to discern how tall the grass was, and, hence, how deep the water. 'Water!' Jenny yelled. 'We have to land: we all need to stretch our legs and rest properly.'

'How?' Kelly inquired, 'we cannot land on this.'

'We could take the frame from the makeshift shelter and attach slats to the under carriage, thus acting as a type of, er, ski,' Jenny replied.

'Let's do it,' Barney enthused. And so, while me and Barney dismantled the shelter and clambered around the machine, and then hanging from the side attaching long wooden slats to the wheels of the plane with twine, Argon, Jenny, Helena and Kelly, pedalled on and held the machine steady. It was not an easy task, but necessity dictated that it had to be done.

'Okay,' I cried, when it had been completed.

'Right, let's land this thing,' Argon rejoined. And so, in careful gradations, we lowered, until the slats were skimming over the surface of the marsh: they hissed along the frothy water: suddenly, the water gripped them, and flipped the craft vertical, its nose buried into the muddy marsh water. We all were catapulted, sailing into the air, my stomach was left in the plane while my head waited for a painful landing, and, SPLASH! We all were unceremoniously dumped into the cold marsh water. Luckily, though shaken, none of us were hurt. The water was only knee deep. It was cool and fresh, and we eagerly bathed in it, washing away the desert sand and heat. We felt quite jubilant, splashed and frolicked: though I had concerns we were lost. We then set about hauling the plane upright: holding onto its irreplaceable aluminium skin, we gently pulled: it would not budge: then, we pulled a little harder, still no movement. 'Heave!' Argon shouted, and we pulled with all our might: the plane uprooted from the mud and crashed and splashed back to its dignified and wonted position. Apart from superficial damage, it was intact. The urn that contained Sacradia, thankfully, was securely fixed, with a tight lid, and was undamaged without a drop lost.

It was a good feeling to be out of the plane and stood upright: even though we were wading through marshy water up to our knees. 'Are we near The Forest of Life?' Jenny asked.

'It was not the way I originally came,' I said with regret. 'I have not seen this place before.'

'I just felt something slither past me!' Barney exclaimed, his eyes widened in horror, and he hurriedly scrambled back into the plane. He quickly raked through the bags and picked up an axe. His erratic nature and alarmed mien indicated that the 'something' was sizeable. His actions and expressions compelled us to all quickly board the plane. I precariously perched on the wing's edge as he passed an axe to me and Argon.

'How big was it?' Argon inquired, raising the axe above his head, and peering into the watery landscape.

'It felt strong, muscly, lithe... slimy. It zipped past me, and it curled around my leg as it did.' Barney gazed, trying to penetrate the water's surface. A gargling noise was heard, and a swishing through the grass.

'There! There!' Kelly pointed to where the grass was distinctively moving.

'Steady!' cried Argon. 'S-t-e-a-d-y.' The whole area surrounding the craft became alive with swirling grass and bubbling water. We stared on, dumb with stupefaction. Then, pop-pop-pop-pop, hairy rat like creatures stood erect around us, 5, 10, 15, 30, 100, 300... gulp... lots! They looked like humanoid rats, but had a third eye in their forehead, which blinked, and seemed more alive and animate than the other two.

'You are lost,' one said, who stood nearest the craft, sniffing and examining it, then peering deep at us. The whole surrounding group stood motionless, scrutinizing us with their tripartite vision, their raised whiskers and noses twitching as they sniffed the air.

'Forgive us for startling you. It is how we traverse the marsh lands. We sensed you near, but needed to come in close to ascertain your intent... You are afraid, and anxious to know your bearings,' another said.

'We are not afraid!' Argon growled. 'And if you come any closer... we will show you how afraid we are.'

'Yes, you are willing to defend yourself... understandable, and admirable: but I assure you such measures are unnecessary,' another said. The creature held out its sinewy arms to convey they had no weapons. The water dripped from its oily hair. They surveyed each one of us in turn.

'We are The Monads, and mean you no harm. However, you are not safe. There is a war here between the Asuras and Ophions, two fierce tribes who are vying to dominate this demesne. We are nomadic, and in continual flight of either, even though we have specifically proclaimed our peaceful intention to each... You are becoming calmer now,' another said. I lowered my axe. I felt a strange empathy with these creatures, a strong link, a flow, as if we felt exactly the same way, rather like I would for Helena, but less sensual. My compatriots' expressions indicated tacit concurrence with my own mood.

Suddenly, a hail of arrows fell all around us, and, with a blink, the Monads disappeared into the marsh: the grass's rapid wavering could be traced rippling outward as they escaped the falling arrows.

'Underneath the wings!' Argon yelled, and so we leapt from the plane to shelter under the metal wings as arrows rained down. One or two pierced the aluminium hull, a couple lodged through the wings, but most bounced off harmlessly.

In the distance could be heard splashing water: it grew louder, until we could see frothing waves fast approaching. The magnitude of the area covered by the tumultuous frothy waves rendered us with no doubt... we were in trouble. Me, Argon and Barney, stared at each other, tightly grasping our axes. I looked at Helena: she reciprocated with a dignified calm, but eyed my weapon with distaste. Seeing her vividly before me infused me with a profound determination, an electric zeal: no one was going to harm you, Helena, no one!

The splashing became louder, and soon we could descry men wearing dull habergeons and greaves, carrying soiled shields and lances, riding large dishevelled lizards, galloping towards us, yelling hellishly. They fast approached, and on getting closer lowered and pointed their lances at our midriffs. The lizards skimmed over the water, splashing in rapid explosions as they pitter-pattered over the marsh. They were charging us, and all we could hope for was to get a single swing of an axe in before being run through. The ground thundered, and the water vibrated under our feet: soon they would be upon us. I focused on the warrior I believed was heading my way. They grew larger and larger as they thundered closer. Suddenly, someone cried, 'Halt!' The reigns of the giant lizards were yanked back, reptilian roars of protestation vibrated in the air as their heads were pulled upwards, and the mighty phalanx stopped before us. 'They have women,' one stated.

'Women!' someone else yelled, and they all began raising their lances, whooping and cheering, as they gazed licentiously at our lady folk.

'It's been a long time!' one jeered, covered in grimy body armour.

'Aye, too long!' his neighbour replied, slapping him on the back, lasciviously looking Helena up and down. Me, Barney and Argon, nervously held our axes, poised to chop into their armour: I had a vision of decapitating this foul intruder effortlessly. I stared at him with malignant hate: he gormlessly smirked at my Helena.

'Take the women,' one commanded, the froth of the marsh dribbling down his unkempt beard. 'And you!' he imperiously pointed to the men of our crew, 'know that, in the short time you have left, you are to be killed by the mighty Ophions.'

'No!' Jenny screamed, to which The Ophions burst into derisive laughter.

'No!' one mimicked, which caused further guffaws. Four lizard warriors dismounted, their exophthalmic eyes like drills chilling our souls; six on lizards came nearer, rusty lances trained on our torsos. The four waded through the muddy water, unsheathed their swords, momentarily paused, and examined us over raised shields. Their leader, sat high on a lizard's scaled back, looked down at us, smug, enjoying the prospect of the kill, and the taking of our fair women. I set my sights on an assailant: I would beat him to the swing and cleft his head in two. My heart thumped against my chest as my mind emptied of thought. Do not freeze, Gorky, you are no longer battling trees and imaginary foe, or lightly sparring with friends: this is a real fight to the death: do not hold back.

'Stop!' Jenny desperately cried. She handed a dried bean to Helena and Kelly. 'See this?' She held the bean between her teeth. The four warriors on foot stopped. The leader's smirk dropped. 'This is poison… yes… poison: do not come any closer or we will swallow them.' She nudged Helena: Helena and Jenny put the beans in their mouths. 'If we swallow them… we will die… and… and.. you'll never be able to have us.'

The leader began to smile again,' *Never* be able to have you… alive,' he cackled. The warriors began to laugh again. The four who stood before us displayed their rotten teeth as they sneered.

'Believe me,' Helena seductively said, 'we will be a lot more fun alive.' She slowly lifted her skirt, and ran her finger tips up and down her thigh, and then placed her hand inside her knickers and began to seductively moan: we all stared transfixed. I could not believe my Helena was capable of such brazen behaviour. Then she stopped and displayed the bean between her teeth.

'Er, wait,' the leader ordered to the four grubby assailants: they stood motionless, beginning to look perplexed. Their devil may care attitude had dramatically disappeared. Helena's display had seemed to subdue them.

'Now this is what you're going to do,' Jenny confidently stated, 'You're going to tie a line to our plane… and fasten it to those things,' she pointed at the lizards. 'Then you're going to tow us along so that we can be lifted into the air.' The four warriors began to unthinkingly take ropes from their saddles.

'Wait!' the leader shouted, 'What's in it for us?'

'Er…' Jenny looked around at the rest of us.

'Okay, what she meant,' Kelly said, 'is that…mmm… you… can take us to your… er… where ever it is… but we will still have the beans… er… poison in our mouths… so *do not* harm our men… then you can… well… you know.' She looked around at the rest of us with bewilderment, wanting assistance for what to say next.

'Then,' interjected Helena, 'when you've done…you can bring us back here, and, er, let us all go.'

'All of us,' Kelly reiterated. The girls were buying time: when faced with death, anything to delay the *coup de grace*. I felt an unquenchable fire burn in the pit of my stomach: I was about to punch a hole in the leader's chest with the keen edged axe. Helena must have sensed it for she raised her hand to my cheek to check my intentions.

The leader thought for a moment, then broke into a broad evil sneer, 'S-u-r-e! Whatever you say!' he eventually smirked, displaying his decayed teeth and running his grubby hand through long greasy hair.

'I'll be back soon,' Helena assured, gently kissed my lips, gazed deep into my eyes, then turned and stepped forward, the bean gritted between her teeth. She walked to where the leader was perched: from his reptilian transportation he lowered his arm, she raised hers, repulsion written all over her face, and he violently pulled her onboard. Jenny and Kelly reluctantly followed, each mounted on an Ophian warrior's saddle.

The Ophians suddenly began whooping in triumph, harshly turned their lizards, and were soon skimming over the marsh, leaving a wake of churned water. I watched my beautiful Helena gradually disappear, bouncing and jerking upon the saddle, clinging to a disgusting uncivilized bloodthirsty warrior. I seethed, became blank with elementary fury, and tried to push forward: I was going to pursue and cut through the bastards like gossamer: Argon and Barney held me back.

'Let me go!' I screamed. I wrestled with them: they fell on top of me: I kicked and punched. 'Get off me!' And there we were, rolling in the marsh water, me coughing water through my nose, half drowning, furiously fighting, as The Ophions rode away with our women.

Acute anger eventually turns to acute torpor, and I lay there exhausted, but with hate and envy still surging through my mind. Argon and Barney relinquished their grip: I switched on again, jumped up, grabbed the axe and screamed, swinging it around, 'Aaaarrggghhh! Arrrggghhh! Arrrggghhh!' I flailed the glinting axe around my head, until at last I sunk the blade deep into the tail of the plane. 'Aaaarrggghhh!' I tried to pull it out to get another swing at the craft: I wanted to chop it into pieces. 'Aaaarrggghhh!' Barney and Argon looked on, bemused, as I tried to pull the axe out: try as I might, I could not free it, and my fury eventually subsided a tincture. I turned to them, still yanking at the axe, 'Why didn't we fight!? Why didn't we f-i-g-h-t?!'

'We're still alive, Gorky,' Barney calmly stated.

'Alive!? Our women have just been taken by barbaric bastards. They've, aaarrggghhh! H-e-l-e-n-a! H-E-L-E-N-A!!! A-A-A-R-R-R-G-G-H-H-H-H!!!' I punched a dent in the plane: I hit it again and again. 'A-A-A-R-R-R-G-G-G-H-H-H!!!' I kept hitting the hard metallic surface with my fists until blood flowed from my knuckles. Barney and Argon just stared. They felt the same, but realized my gestures were futile, and the energy was best reserved to do something productive...

'Have you finished yet, Gorky?' Barney eventually asked, after I had spent all my fury pounding the hull of the aeroplane with bloody fists. I looked at him, vacant, unsure where I was. 'Because if you have,' he said, then grabbed my tunic and violently shook me, and began shouting in rage, 'because if you have, you can fix the fucking plane.' Argon quickly intervened, trying to pull him away: Barney turned away in disgust.

'Come on, chaps, the fight isn't between ourselves,' Argon said, looking in the direction where the Ophians had gone. My perceptions began to focus again: Argon was imbued with an acute melancholic state: it calmed me right down, but made me want to cry: for how could such sadness be borne by one person. I held his shoulders in brotherhood.

'What are we going to do, Argon?' I implored.

'Well,' he responded, trying to sound his usual enthusiastic self, 'we can start by straightening out the plane... so when they... return, we can get out of here.'

'We go after them!' Barney powerfully yelled, squeezing my shoulder and almost breaking my collar bone: I felt an intense energy surge through me which made my hair stand on end. With the mighty Argon and Barney on my side we could defeat anyone.

'Yes!' I declared, punching the air.

With intense purpose, we made repairs to the plane, and rendered it ready for flight. It was not an easy task: in my blind fury I had done some damage to the structure. In my now rational state, I was surprised to see how much. But the desperate need to get away from this awful place propelled us onward.

Then, almost telepathically, without a word, we simultaneously picked the axes up, and went trudging through the marsh towards where we saw our ladies had been carried away by the Ophions. The underlying ground was uneven: sometimes we would submerge to our chests; sometimes the water was below the soles of our feet: but it never once deterred us. We marched with grim determination and silent fury. Every now and again I had to check my rage as I thought of Helena clambering onto a lizard, and that vile sneering man carrying her away. I tried not to contemplate what could be happening to our lovely ladies and the anguish they must be experiencing: it was more than I could bear: I had to extirpate such a fowl sight from my mind, or I would have ceased to function…

The marsh spread as far as the eyes could see: it was like a watery graveyard, gloomy and drear; tall grass hung limp. 'This is the way, isn't it?' Argon eventually inquired. I kept marching: Helena was up ahead: I had to keep going: nothing was going to stop me… NOTHING! 'Gorky, old man, stop a minute: let's think this through,' he called. I heard a vague voice, but did not assimilate. Must save Helena. Kill all Ophions.

'Gorky!' Barney grabbed me by the shoulder: it concentrated my rage.

'Get off me!' I screamed.

'Gorky, for God's sake, calm down.' He ran in front of me and held out his arms to my chest. My eyes lit: I was going to strike any obstacle: but then I saw it was Barney, my old friend: I came to my senses. 'Let's just stop and think,' he urged.

'I did not want to stop and think: I want to move,' I pleaded.

'Gorky, we are all upset,' Argon said with a deep frown, 'but there is little point in marching in the wrong direction... Let's see if we can find any clues.' He looked about him: but water and grass was all that could be seen. I recalled the lizards skimming over the water like smooth stones. I knew Helena was straight ahead... I just knew it.

'Come on,' I peremptorily commanded, 'they've got our women. What do you suppose they are going to do to them... AYE!? Come on!' I went surging ahead, wading against the resistance of the water. My Helena was in abject danger: consequently, so were those who had taken her: onwards, onwards, to do the bloody deed. I was an unyielding killing machine. Barney and Argon stared at me as I stubbornly waded away, looked all around them seeing nothing but bleak marsh, knew they had no idea where the Ophions had gone, and in unison, decided to follow me. So, on we strode in silence. All that could be heard was the rippling marsh water as we pushed on through. We headed towards the watery horizon in blind faith that our profound love would be rewarded by pointing us in the right direction.

The water around us began to seethe. We froze, feeling helpless at the frenetic underwater activity that circumscribed us. Together we lifted the razor axes above our heads, ready to strike as soon as discerned a viable target.

Pop-pop-pop, around us, suddenly, The Monads rapidly emerged, pop-pop-pop, hundreds of them. We felt overwhelmed by their sudden manifestation. We were surrounded by half-man-half-rat type creatures, their noses bristling in the air and three eyes blinking at us. There was a palpable silence as, me, Barney and Argon waited for the creatures' next move. We gripped our axes tightly anticipating rapid movement. 'What do you want, aye?' I eventually yelled as I raised my axe further above my head. 'Get out of the way!' I commanded.

'You are angry,' one calmly said.

'Aaarrrggghhh!' I screamed, and charged them: they easily evaded my attack, darting this way and that, as I fell head first into the water. I stood up and wildly glared at them. Their countenances indicated intense pain, reflecting my own profound anguish. If I was not mistaken, an acute pity was shining through each of their three eyes.

'You are sad. You have a sense of a great loss. You worry for your ladies,' another said. My anger partially abated. I fell to the floor and wept. I was a conduit, and the world's sorrow flowed through me, emptying into the sky: I satiated the universe with anguish.

'He is not well,' one said to Argon.

'Leave him for a while,' Argon advised.

'You wish to locate your females?' one said.

'Yes,' Barney said with alacrity, 'are we...'

'No, you should be going in that direction,' he pointed at least 45 degrees from the course we were on.

'Is it...' Barney tried to continue.

'No it is not far, but it is unwise to enter The Ophions' city: they will kill you instantly,' another Monad replied.

'Our women compel us onwards. We must save them,' Barney declared.

'We understand, but you stand little chance of success,' one admonished.

'So what should we do, wait by the plane for their return?' Argon asked.

'Your women will not return,' another one said.

'Not return! But we made an agreement with them,' Barney cried. (This could be seen as gullibility, but when you have a magnanimous heart like Barneys, you can tend to judge some people more favourably than they deserve.)

'You do not make "agreements" with The Ophions; and, besides, your women will be too valuable to them,' one said.

'Why will our women be so valuable to them?' Argon asked.

'During the wars with The Asuras, both sides have raped and murdered each other's women, until there were none left,' one informed.

'No women left?!' Barney exclaimed.

'We must go,' Argon urgently proclaimed.

'You prefer to die trying to save them,' one said.

'They are our women!' I proclaimed.

'Gorky! These, er, creatures said that way,' Barney pointed in the direction where The Ophions' city was. I stared at the vast tract of watery land, peering to the horizon, thinking of my sweet Helena, trying to stave off vile images, and how I must reach her. 'Gorky! It's that way,' he reiterated. I snapped from my reverie, turned round, to see the stern lineaments of Argon and Barney descrying my manic obsession, and, surrounded by the inquisitive Monads. 'It's that way,' he said once again. I glared at Barney's pointing finger, for in that direction was where I ardently wanted to be.

'Let's go,' I commanded, and began marching in the new direction.

'Er, thank you for your help,' Argon nodded to the Monads, but I was too monomaniacal to acknowledge them.

'The pleasure is ours,' one said, bowing: and they vanished as soon as they appeared.

I then heard Barney and Argon splashing after me. The rage in my veins meant that the water offered little resistance: I felt an irksome impatience, an obsessed restlessness, an overriding compulsion to save Helena, the love of my life. I indefatigably marched onwards, with my frowning compatriots trying to keep up. I waded through the water, sometimes disappearing up to my neck, sometimes tramping in the mud, but no obstacle would impede me: I was to wreak havoc amongst those loathsome Ophions who had had the temerity to take my lady...

Eventually, the land became less inundated, and, gradually, we were constantly stepping on soggy mud, pushing through swathes of waist high grass: the terrain was slippery, but we propelled forward with vigour: our clothes were soaked, our footwear squelched, but our ardour had not mitigated and we moved much swifter now...

Then, there, in the distance, was a discernible saliency: it stretched the length of the horizon, long and grey: the imposing lugubriousness of The Ophions' city. It made me shudder. It must have contained an area ten times that of our own village. Beyond the wall, I could see high buildings, towers, matrixes of rectangular stone. We walked forward more cautious now: the sheer size of the man-made phenomenon, in the middle of the marshy terrain, exuded power, and we were all awe struck, intimidated. 'Now what?' Barney whispered, as we realized how ineffectual and puny we were. We moved with caution towards the outer city walls, stooping in a vain bid to avoid detection. As we approached, the walls grew in size, towering above us. Not far ahead was a massive wooden gate: it began to lower, and a huge splash could be heard as it crashed to the ground. A large troop of warriors came rushing from the aperture. At first I thought they had not seen us, for we were relatively obscure amongst the grasses: but they made directly for us.

'It's a fight you wanted, Gorky?' Argon asked.

'Let's see what they want,' Barney said.

'I know what I want,' I growled, 'and they have her.' I boldly walked forward to meet the charging lizard warriors. I yelled in defiance swinging my glinting axe in circles through the air. Argon and Barney nervously looked on. This was chance to wreak some revenge, to vent my wrath on the culprits. The flip-flap of the lizard's webbed feet grew louder as the phalanx rode on a pace. I set my sights on the one who was riding ahead. Flip-flap-flip-flap, splash-splash-splash-splash, in unison they lowered their lances and lifted their shields, their visors dropped, and on they charged. I envisaged Helena beyond that dismal grey wall: and had no doubt in my mind that I would cut them to pieces and eventually find my lady. The closer they came, the quicker and bigger I realized they were. The splashing changed to crashing, and great frothy plumes of water shot into the air. The lizards eyes were glowing fierce and demonic, the lances long and keen, and the men began to roar guttural cries of death. They were upon me: the lance exploded into my sternum, splitting my heart and crashing through my spine, and, skewered, suddenly I was racing from whence I came. I slid off the lance and slumped head first into the mud, blood ebbing profusely, dyeing the ground in dark coagulate red…

Onwards they charged: Barney and Argon looked at each other, then at The Ophions, and knew what they had to do. There was no place to take cover and the charging warriors were soon upon them. Both raised their razor axes ready to swing. Argon managed to slip the oncoming lance and bury his axe into a rider's thigh: but the next line of attackers meant he was soon impaled and dropped to the ground, lifeless. Barney, with his blacksmith's strength, decapitated a lizard: it went sprawling across the ground, ejecting its rider: he then ran to the prostrate warrior and took a mighty swing of his axe: the blade came crashing down cutting through the armour and burying into the warrior's shoulder: but as he did, a lance exploded into Barney's back, exiting his chest: and he fell into the mud, motionless. The Ophions circled to check if there was any life in us: we lay prostrate, bloody, and still, floating in the water, with the horrors of war etched on our faces. They picked up their wounded, and rode away to do battle with their foe, The Asuras.

When the riders could no longer be heard, a silence entombed us. A slight wind blew through the grasses. The clouds swam silently by... Our bloody corpses lay still in the mud...

5.

The City of Ophions

Riding on the back of a lizard with a hoard of lascivious males intent on uncompromisingly encroaching upon us at the end of the journey, was not a prospect I relished. I gripped the bean tightly between my teeth, always making it visible, a desperate bid to fool myself, and them, it was my protector: Jenny and Kelly did the same. We often lost sight of each other in the splashing water as the riders jostled around: but we were always vigilant to try and keep each other in view. I did not want to hold onto the disgusting rider: he smelt of decay and his skin was greasy: but it was the only means to ensure not falling off (and what was the point in falling off? He would have only forcibly remounted me): so I reluctantly grasped his cold metal armour. The Ophions frantically raced towards their city. Every now and again, one would whoop in wild ecstasy at the prospect of indulging in female flesh. The splashing water soaked our thin cotton tunics and displayed the contours of our bouncing bodies. They would jockey for a privileged position beside us, ogling, transfixed, nearly touching us, forgetting to look where they were going.

Soon the water diminished and the lizards were flip-flapping over mud. Dollops of mud were thrown up, and we became covered in the marshy terrain. Up ahead, I saw a great wall: I knew our journey would soon be at an end. My stomach churned and I nearly bit the bean in half. Kelly and Jenny stared in dumb shock, not knowing what fate awaited them. Each of us, as a symbol of fidelity to my Gorky, Barney and Argon, intransigently gripped the beans between our gleaming white teeth in a face mask of mud. I thought of the anguish Gorky would be feeling. I feared he would follow us and inevitably be killed. Thoughts of escape pervaded me: at the slightest opportunity, we would be away: maybe we could commandeer lizards and skim away to safety. I would not lose hope: but a sense of dread filled me as we approached the massive wooden gates of the city.

The walls were built with massive cubes of cold grey stone. The enormous gate towered above us. It slowly swung open as we approached. I felt acute travail in the pit of my stomach as we breached the threshold, a plain wooden lintel above us, size of which no tree in Firkin could have matched. Before me were rows of dismal grey buildings, uniform: a heavy oppressiveness hung in the air. I shuddered at the starkness. Two men sat by the road were drinking a red substance from a grimy bottle: their vacillating eyelids fought to stay open, and their wits had seemed to desert them. They argued over the bottle, snatching it from each other, fighting to quaff it while the other harassed. One, in his stupor, with sore red eyes dull and unfocused, noticed the returning warriors: but then he noticed Kelly! His eyes widened and he quickly stood up: a broad decayed smile etched on his besmirched face. Then he saw me and Jenny, his exophthlamic eyes nearly popped out of his head. He began violently shaking his friend to alert him that women were entering the city. The argument with the bottle ceased: their drunken eyes followed us as we rode deeper into hostile territory. I felt a chill, for everything was drear, lifeless and austere. I tried to peer into the buildings but the casements were semi-transparent with scum. The inebriated whooping alerted other men: and they gradually emerged from these grey monotonous buildings, blinking in the sunlight, dirty, unkempt, wearing soiled body armour, and brandishing tarnished swords. Lizards were tied outside each building, and would occasionally hiss in disapprobation at the nearby men. The silence of the city turned into a murmuring, the murmuring turned into a chattering, and the chattering into tumultuousness, as on we rode. The men fiercely gazed at us with their long pent up libidinous passions, as we bounced upon the lizards' backs. I was conscious of my nipples protruding through the thin cotton tunic and felt most uneasy. I tried to turn around to see my sisters, but they were obscured in the line of galloping lizard warriors. I gripped my teeth so hard, I nearly cleft the bean in two.

Then we stopped outside a building, no more remarkable than the others. The leader jumped from his reptile, and walked towards me. 'Get down!' he commanded. I was loath to dismount. I felt safer with my thighs gripping the scaly back of the lizard. I looked down at him with great aversion and reluctance to budge. 'Get down, now!' The 'now!' was vehemently shouted with such emphasis, that I jumped, but tried not to show fear. He angrily gripped my waist and yanked me to the ground. I sprawled across the floor, grovelling in the dirt. 'In there!' he pointed. I defiantly sneered at him, displaying the bean through my teeth. He grabbed my hair: a pain shot through my head, as I found myself being pushed through a door. The walls on the inside were the same as the outside, grey blocks cemented together; the floor was dried mud; and there were stone blocks placed in the corners. 'Sit!' he ordered, and swung me onto a block of stone, which I fell on, and sat there, glum. In followed Kelly and Jenny, grim in countenance, concerned with what was to become of us. 'Sit!' he growled at them, and they sat by me on the cold hard stone. He then walked outside and barked some commands at his men: and we heard them galloping away. I thought he may have gone: I began to have hope for escape. With tears welling up in my eyes I looked at Kelly and Jenny: they looked so pitiful desperately biting onto the beans and covered in marsh mud.

In Selphus walked, grimy sword in one hand, two filthy bottles of the red liquid in the other. He handed one to me, sat in the corner, opened the other, and began drinking. 'Drink!' he aggressively admonished. I looked at the bottle: it was sticky in my hands: I smelt the top: it made me nauseated and I intensely shuddered. I held the vile bottle at arm's length, my face contorted in horror. 'Drink!' he angrily repeated and raised his tarnished sword.

'What is it?' I reluctantly asked.

'Drink it… it will, er, relax you.' He smiled a sickly and self-satisfied grin.

'Will it "relax" us like the two men we saw?' I inquired. His smile instantly dropped, and his eyes became wild: he pointed his menacing sword at me.

'Drink it, or I will kill you,' he matter-of-factly stated. I looked at Jenny and Kelly cowering in the corner: I felt a profound responsibility for their precious lives: but I really did not want to quaff this vile liquid.

'Kill us, and you won't be able to…' I defiantly declared.

'It won't stop me. You'll still be fresh. Drink it now!' Selphus had a manic lust in his exophthalmic eyes, a lust that seemed absolutely irrepressible, a lust that possessed and controlled him. He calmed for a moment, 'Or would you prefer to be sober? It may be to your advantage to be drunk… I have many men.' He took a violent swig from the bottle, while never taking his red caked eyes away from us.

'We would prefer,' said Kelly calmly, belying her emotional state, 'for you to allow us safe passage back to our men, so we can continue our journey.' He emitted a deep lamentable groan.

'I am becoming bored with your voices,' Selphus yawned.

He stood up, still heavily drinking, while casually swinging his sword around the room: his imposing nefariousness pervaded the atmosphere. He then violently crashed the blade down next to Jenny's leg: great sparks flew from the stone making Jenny jump up from her seat: he leaped to her, and violently pushed her back down onto the hard stone. 'I am losing my patience. If you do not drink, I *will* kill you, take you, string you up in the square, and leave your carcasses to the lust of my men: and there you will be left, rotting, bird food: and your bones will adorn our walls... now... DRINK!' He snatched the bottle from me and thrust it into Jenny's chest. Jenny needed no further persuasion: she grasped the bottle, and gulped the contents down: in her eagerness to numb herself, she nearly spewed the liquid up, and began choking on the potent brew. Selphus swaggered around the room, laughing, swinging his sword above his head. 'Ha ha!' he yelled, raised his head back, and filled his mouth with more of the obnoxious liquid. Jenny then took a more tentative swig, grimaced, and passed the bottle to Kelly: she refused it, but Jenny pushed it into her lap. I felt my hope sink as the inevitable began to dawn on me: I took a deep inhalation of air, inadvertently swallowed the bean and began choking. Kelly, fighting back the tears, lifted the bottle to her mouth. I gazed at her, vicariously experiencing her disgust: but, as the bottle touched Kelly's lips, she flung it to the ground and the red liquid oozed all over the floor.

'I will not!' she proclaimed. Her intense emotion suddenly filled me with resolve: I sprang up. He had his back turned on us: I leapt towards him, grabbed his head into a lock like my beloved Gorky had taught me, and with all my strength began twisting his sinewy neck: he was terribly strong. Selphus violently span round: my feet flew from the ground and I could barely keep hold. Jenny instinctively jumped up and hit the bottle over his head: the glass was so thick that the bottle did not smash but a dull thud could be heard on impact with his grimy head. Kelly quickly ceased the initiative, grasping the muscly arm that held the sword. As Selphus flailed around, we held on for dear life: I had no desire to be strung up in the square and be the victim of vile necrophilic lust! I desperately sank my teeth into his sinewy neck, biting into his jugular, and ripping the vein clean out: blood spurted like a fountain: he fell to his knees, letting go of the sword. I spat the bitter metallic taste of blood from my mouth. Kelly picked the sword up, and sank it deep into his chest, pulled it out, was going to make another incision, but he emitted a ghastly groan that made us all stare in horror: another jet of blood shot across the room from his wounded chest. He lifted his arms up, made an attempt to stand, but fell back and solidly hit the ground. He lay there twitching, then, deathly still. We gazed at the motionless body, numb with the abhorrent violence, not fully comprehending what we had done...

6.

The Monads

'*Monads... actions and perceptions harmonize
with each other*'

G.W.Leibniz.

We glided through the water, reeds and rushes zipping by our
slithery bodies, swimming like arrows submerged through the
marshy waters, streamline and quick, fast and furtive, always
moving so The Asuras and The Ophions could not locate us.
We began thinking of the strange travellers and what may be
their fate. We were certain that their lives would soon be over.
We decided to approach the vicinity of the city to see if we could
obtain any news. We slid through the shallow waters, zipping
through the grasses. We very rarely came this way, and we laid
extra low when approaching the city's parameters. We suddenly
sensed acute consternation: it hung in the air like plasma. Then
we smelt blood. We rushed to the source of the scent cognizant
the men travellers had been killed. Grimacing in horror as we
zipped through incarnadine water, we swam to the source of
the carnage. We raised our heads just above the water level,
and found their bodies floating in the water. We felt acute
lamentation: our sorrow vibrated in the air: we bemoaned the
barbarism and needless destruction. After a while, we decided
it would be best to transport them to their winged contraption,
staunch the flow of their internals, and clean them: they could
lay to rest in that vehicle which had brought them: we deemed it

would be a monument to their valour. We conveyed them over the surface of the water and soon reached their peculiar craft. We prepared the corpses and sat each one inside. Our grief was barely containable, for we felt ashamed that visitors would be welcomed in such a needless manner. As we manipulated them into dignified sitting positions, placing their feet on the foot devices, and their hands on the levers, we sensed an incredible benign presence. What was this incredible divine energy? We felt a powerful attraction to an urn in the back of the plane. To allay curiosity, the lid was unscrewed: a powerful benevolent force radiated outwards in concentric circles: our senses tingled, and our remorse was metamorphosed into a profound feeling of well-being. We were nearly overcome with euphoria, and it took all our rational faculties to contain it. Without thought, we sprinkled the alchemical water on each of the travellers. As the bodies began to glow, we became rapt in uncontrollable laughter: great waves of merriment swam over us and our bodies convulsed in helpless ecstasy...

7.

Re-animated

I opened my lids and the sun stung my eyes. At first, I did not know who I was, but, eventually, as my senses re-grouped, my memory gradually began to crystallize: I saw that I was sat in the cockpit of the plane, surrounded by marshland: I remembered Firkin, and the arduous journey it took to arrive here: then, I recalled who I was: I then remembered Helena being carried away by The Ophions: a pang of hate and sorrow assailed my viscera: I then pictured us marching to the city in pursuit: the lizard riders poured out through the huge gate, charging towards us… then… nothing…

I looked round to see Argon and Barney, blinking in the sunlight, and looking most bewildered. 'How did we get here?' I asked. Argon stared blankly around, still not fully to his senses.

'Hey?' he absently blurted.

'How did we get here?' Barney repeated, not hearing me.

'I do not know,' I replied. I looked around the craft: the lid of the urn was unscrewed. At first I thought the women had returned and saved us: a wave of excitement washed over me as I eagerly looked around for Helena: there was no sign of her, or anybody else for that matter: we were sat in the plane surrounded by the vast tract of marshy land. I checked the contents of the urn: the water was still intact. I screwed the lid down tightly.

'How did we get here?' Argon inquired, gaining his faculties.

'I don't know: but we still have to find our women,' I declared, feeling a surge of urgency re-flow through my veins. 'They've been taken, remember? By those lizard riders.' I stood up, scanned the area for any signs of life. 'We've got to save them.' I jumped from the aeroplane splashing into the marsh below. I looked around for the axes, but could not find them. 'Come on,' I enjoined, 'we've got to go to the Ophions' city.'

Barney sat in the plane, espying me with disapproval.

'I'm not leaving this cockpit,' he announced, folding his huge forearms in defiance.

'What?! Are you mad?! Are you going to just sit there?!' I went to grab his arm to pull him out of the plane: but he angrily snatched it away from me.

'It's you who's mad!' he snapped, and slapped me over the head.

'You idiot!' I growled, and jumped up to grab his collar: I pulled him from the plane: he landed heavy into the water sending a great splashing wave into the air: I then began dragging him through the water towards the city. He managed to struggle to his feet, and delivered a well timed blow to my head: I reeled, my legs buckled, and bright lights flashed across my eyes. I spat the blood from my mouth, and was about to retaliate.

'Stop it you two!' Argon shouted. 'Have you lost your wits? The enemy is out there.' He vehemently pointed towards the city of The Ophions. My anger simmered: and Barney glared at me, willing to continue the altercation. 'Oy, I'm over here!' Argon called. 'Oy, here!' I half looked at Argon while still keeping Barney in my vision: I was furious I had allowed him to hit me, and I wanted my revenge: Barney glared back, looking like a coiled spring, ready to explode at the slightest provocation. 'I'm waiting!' Argon shouted, equal to our intensity. 'Calm down, both of you.' Barney took deep breaths, as, very slowly, he began to calm down; my anger gradually turned to nerves, for I scared myself at what I might do to my friend in such fury. 'I say,'

Argon continued, 'that we get this contraption in the air, and make a reconnoitre of the city... Let's at least acquire familiarity with the topography before we encroach.'

'How shall we take off?' Barney snarled.

'Maybe the thrust of the wings will pull us out,' Argon retorted. 'It's worth a try, is it not?'

'We're stuck in the mud,' I yelled. 'Why waste energy?' It was true enough, the plane had gradually sank into the mire: with only three of us pedalling, the thrust of the wings would not have been enough to pull us clear.

'We can at least try,' Argon implored.

I looked at Barney: he reciprocated with lineaments of disgust, then said, 'Well... madman... are we going to try?' I waded back to the plane, and sat in my wonted seat. Barney put his hand in the water, and rummaged around, searching for the undercarriage wheels, until his head submerged into the marsh: he eventually re-emerged, grass hanging about his head, let out an ominous groan, then jumped into the cockpit. He gave Argon a look of despair.

'This is futile,' he remarked. Argon frowned at his apparent defeatism.

'Ready? Go!' Argon determinedly shouted. We then pushed down hard on the pedals: the wheels skidded around in the mud, and the plane jerked forward: it gave us a vestige of hope.

'Keep pedalling!' Argon urged. The wheels skidded, the wings furiously beat up and down: but, we did not move. 'Keep trying!' Argon enthusiastically yelled: but the plane remained firmly rooted in the sub-soil: and, after a while, we became exhausted: I could see it was a waste of time, and gradually decreased my efforts.

'It's no use,' I said, 'we're not getting anywhere. Let's assail the city from the ground.'

'Yeah, let's go and attack them with our bare hands,' Barney sarcastically rejoined.

Suddenly, I saw black fury, and was ready to start fighting with him again, but Argon began crying, 'Oh, bother! Botherations! Bother-bother-bother! Oh, Kelly! Oh dam! Dam-dam-dam!' He pounded the hull of the plane with his fists, and angrily sobbed. I watched Argon as he exuded despair, and forgot my own feelings. I put my hand on his broad shoulder.

'There, there, Argon, we will get them back,' I assured, as his tears fell onto the hull.

'How? We have no way of breaching the city walls. The plane won't budge!' he exclaimed, while imbued in passionate thoughts of Kelly.

'Okay, so we can't fly,' I commented, 'so let's get walking. We will think of a plan on the way. I can't sit here wallowing in misery. Let's move.' I gave Argon a gentle push to try and shake him from morbid despair.

'Gorky, we haven't even got the axes, now. What chance do we have?' Barney grumbled.

'Maybe we can find them on the way,' I replied, as I fiercely stared at him to try and rouse his ardour.

'Oh come on,' Argon determinedly enjoined, and sprang from his seat. He took a rope from the hold, and found a metal implement that he fashioned into a hook, and attached the rope to it. Me and Barney watched his dexterity in fascination. The air was dense with anticipation as we slowly realized his intentions. He went about the business with grim determination. 'We're going to scale the wall,' he matter-of-factly said, while dangling the hook in front of our faces.

'That's if we can get close enough,' Barney solemnly interjected. I nudged Barney with my shoulder, and glared at him again.

'No more pessimism, let's get busy,' I said. With the imposing figure of Argon towering over us with a coil of thick rope around his massive shoulders, I felt a surge of optimism: we were a powerful and indomitable team: we would instil confidence and strength in each other with our common purpose: the love for our ladies engendered instincts to retrieve them.

'Right, let's go,' I proclaimed. And so we departed from the plane- aware of its vulnerability partially submerged in the marsh- and trudged towards the city again, no less angry and eager than before, but a little more cautious, for we recalled the ferocity of the Ophions' previous merciless attack.

8.

The Breach

The wall first manifesting on the horizon precipitated a massive adrenalin surge. We all instinctively lowered onto our haunches, peering at the foreboding edifice between the tall grasses. 'The axes should be around here,' I claimed.

'The longer we hang around, searching for them, the more chance of being seen,' Barney advised.

'I do not fancy breaching the wall unarmed,' I replied.

'Let's wait till night fall, and go by stealth,' Argon added.

'How long will that be?' I impatiently asked.

'We can wait to find out,' Argon shrugged.

'We could be waiting for ages: we have no idea how long their days are. I think this is the place where we were slain. Wait here, I am going to scour the area for the axes: keep watching for the Ophions,' I admonished, and went off, crawling around the mud, searching through the grasses.

'I'll help you look,' Barney said. Argon nodded in concurrence: so me and Barney combed the surrounding marshland for our valuable weapons. I ran my fingers through the water, clothes soaked and covered in fronds, thinking, to encroach the city without weapons would be unmitigated suicide: at least with the axes, we had a chance, at the very least, we would die fighting. I inadvertently crawled into a pool of blood: it dyed my clothes and skin claret: I stared in utter distaste at the floating incarnadine, recoiled in horror at the realization it was our own blood, and then hit a hard object with my heel: an axe.

'I've found one!' I triumphantly declared. Barney hurriedly splashed to my side, and stared determinedly at the cutting edge. He then looked down at the blood floating on the water's surface, and his brow furrowed. He stared sternly at me, then waded into the life fluid that once pumped through our bodies. He became quite frenetic for his search for another axe, repudiating all caution, splashing around and coating himself from head to toe in gore. His large white eyes manically gazed through a mask of coagulate red, scouring the area, until he submerged into the gruesome admixture of liquid: accept for a few bubbles, the surface became still, and I waited for him to re-emerge; I waited, and stared out to the large grey facade of the city wall, then looked around the surface of the marsh: suddenly he rose, wildly staring at me, and lifted the axe above his head in silent exhultation. I felt fear at his demonic fierceness: he looked like war incarnate: a match for any Ophion: I was glad to have him as an ally. Together we searched for the remaining axe. I hoped to find a sword or a shield left by The Ophions: but our endeavours bore no fruition. We waded out of the blood, back to our sentinel, Argon. We did not want to inform him of the grim news, that he would be entering the city unarmed. We slid through the high grass, and met Argon, who was stood upright, smirking, casually spinning a mace around and around: he looked intense, but relaxed. 'A present from The Ophions,' he grinned, 'I hope to show them my gratitude.'

'What happened to the caution?' I inquired.

'My dear boy,' he said, 'after consideration, I deem it is not fit for an elder to be seen crawling in the dirt.'

'Nevertheless,' I urged, 'we should be furtive, or we will not reach the outer-perimeter of the city wall.'

'Oh, how the mighty have fallen,' Barney gibed, 'but he's right, Argon: and, although I do not like crawling around, it is an expedient strategy for the success of our objective, so, get down!' Argon looked down at us both: his smirk turned to thoughtful earnest: and then he lowered himself into the water.

And so we crawled through the marsh the remaining distance, never taking our eyes from the citadel, anticipating The Ophions to suddenly come spewing forth and attack. The watery ground became soggy mud, and so we slid, lathering ourselves for camouflage. We must have looked a weird sight, covered from head to toe in blood and mud, slithering along the ground, clinging hold of our axes and mace, burning for revenge, like hellish monsters emerging from the marsh. Ahead of us, we saw the foreboding entrance, and so eagerly steered away from that huge portal; we directed ourselves well away from there, towards the towering wall that encircled the city. As we came closer, the grey stone wall increased in size, looming above us: we craned our heads upward and stared in awe and intimidation. Our gory and muddy bodies crawled, slithered and gurgled over the marsh, nearer to the massive wall. I did not recognize my compatriots: they were like creatures from a nightmare. We eventually reached the base. My allies' large white eyes bulged at me from out of their oozy masks, their senses keen and alert. I looked up at the top of the wall, and a similar sinking feeling imbued me as when I approached Ice Mountain. Without ado, Argon stood up, the mire dripping from his large frame, took the coiled rope from his shoulder and placed it on the floor, holding the hook in his hand. He spun the hook round, sludge streaks flying in all directions, and let it go: it went flying off into the marsh land, hooking onto the grass. 'Ooops,' he feebly said, as he pulled a great tuft of grass towards him.

'Give me it!' Barney impatiently exclaimed, holding out a besmirched hand.

'No, let me have another go,' Argon asserted.

'Shush!' I nervously said, for just beyond the wall were the keen ears of the violent Ophions. Argon cleared the mud and grass from the hook, and began to spin it round again, letting it go at the optimum moment it would fly perpendicularly upwards: it zipped into the sky, parallel to the wall, went as high as the wall, but went crashing downwards, making us all jump out of the way as it splashed into the mud.

'Give me it!' Barney whisper-shouted, more urgently this time.

'Shush!' I urged.

'I am shushed! You shush!' Barney angrily remonstrated, scarcely constraining himself.

'No, you shush!' I glared back.

'Give me the rope!' Barney peremptorily commanded Argon, trying to snatch it from his muddy grasp.

'Let go!' Argon implored.

'Shush!' I admonished.

'We are shushed!' they angrily shouted in unison. Argon and Barney began wrestling with the rope like a tug-of-war; a little scuffle broke out.

'Let... me... have... one... more... go!' Argon cried, pulling it from Barney's grip. I began to be certain we would die. How no one heard us, I do not know. I listened out for anything beyond the wall: nothing. Argon, while attempting to hold Barney off with one hand, span the hook round again, making a slightly wider circle this time, and developing a better rhythm. His face was the picture of focus. He let it go... up it flew... over the wall and down the other side. 'Y-e-s!' he whispered, and Barney automatically ceased his struggle, as they peered through caked sludge at each other in jubilation. Argon, very carefully, pulled on the rope, in order to hook onto the wall's edge. I had visions of it plummeting back to earth... but, miraculously, it took hold... He gently gave it a tug... then a little harder... then swung from it, taking his feet from the ground. 'We're in!' he declared. He clambered up the rope, his huge biceps flexing, and was soon sat on the top of the wall. He peered inside, then looked down with intense focus, and gave the thumbs up. Barney was next: he pushed the axe down the front of his tunic, and climbed up to meet Argon. They then gestured for me to follow. I took one last look at the marsh, then attempted to haul myself upwards: I tightly grabbed the muddy rope, but try as I might, I could not get a grip: every time I tried to support my own weight, my aching hands and feet slipped off the slimy rope, and I landed back on the ground: I tried and tried, and the increasing anxiety meant my concentration began to mitigate: I fought back the tears as I tried in vain.

'I can't do it!' I sobbed. The demonic visages of Argon and Barney glared down at me, their crazy eyes bulging out of the mud with emotional intensity. I pathetically stared up at them. I could sense it was useless to try further, my hands and arms burnt with aching. I tried to muster all the energy I possessed, but I just could not get a grip. 'I am sorry, you will have to go on without me,' I whimpered. Barney's eyes began to illuminate as if possessed by a hurricane.

'Yeah, you wait here, while the Ophions fuck Helena,' he sneered. It was like a bolt of lightning into my soul. I grimaced and gritted my teeth: I wanted to knock Barney clean off the wall. He then proceeded to make the grunting noises of a copulating animal, while Argon's teeth shone framed by mud.

'You bastard!' I shouted at him.

'What are you going to do about it, weakling?' he taunted. I felt my body swell with anger, and a renewed vigour surge through my body: it was not long before I was climbing up the rope. Barney and Argon smiled down at me, sniggering and tormenting me, fuelling my desire to reach the top and hit them both. I began to slip as I approached them: they both stretched down their hands, grabbed my arms, and I felt myself suddenly hurtling upwards: and then, I was sat on the wall. I was too exhausted to dispute their methods of motivation: instead, I looked into the grim city.

Many rows of monotonous grey cubical buildings stretched out before us. I could hear distant cheering and yelling, but espied no life in the immediate area. Argon pulled the rope up, and lowered it down the other side. It was not long before all three of us were standing within The Ophions' dreaded city. Every moment was electric: my soul glowed like a dew drop shining in the morning sun: for I deemed any moment I would be no more. 'Which way?' I urgently asked, earnestly looking around, anticipating imminent danger.

'This way,' Argon replied, pointing towards an extensive lattice of lanes. We were desperate to get moving for we felt so exposed stationary. We foolishly left the rope conspicuously hanging were we left it, for we became fatalistic: it was like a suicide mission: I do not think any of us believed we would be leaving the city alive: we just wanted some type of revenge. We walked and trotted along the road side, exposed and vulnerable: my heart furiously pumped, nerves a jangle, high on the need to survive. I held the razor axe in front of me. My companions seemed to move with more aplomb, fluid and relaxed; every movement, for me, was stiff, and took great effort: it was like I was moving in slow motion. I felt despair at my inability to move effectively: what energy remained from the rope climb was quickly dissipating: I burnt up nervous energy and began to pant, take large inhalations of air, and lag behind. 'Come on!' Argon whisper-shouted, 'what's wrong?'

'I'm exhausted!' I tried to say, through the desperate attempts to fill my starving lungs with air. 'Our ladies could be anywhere... Where is everybody anyway?' I added.

'Do you hear that?' Barney held a mud caked hand to his ear. We stood, and anxiously listened.

'Yes!' I exclaimed, for I could hear the tumultuous gathering of excited men in the distance.

'What do you suppose is causing such exuberance?' Argon asked, as he looked fixedly at me. Suddenly, Helena imprinted herself on my heart: I imagined her being molested by hordes of sex-starved men: once again I was pervaded by an angry jealousy, instantly sloughed the despondency and debilitation as tremor cordis imbued.

'Aaarrrggghhh!' I screamed, and began to run towards where the noise was coming from.

'Oh no, not again!' Argon said to Barney.

'After him!' Barney hastily replied. And so they went chasing after me, towards the noise of frenetic Ophions.

9.

Asura' Abduction

Me, Jenny and Kelly stared down at our handy work: the Ophions' mighty leader, Selphus, stared back at us, marble eyes bulging and ghastly, so very very still: how weird to see such big eyes with no life in them, the menace no more. 'What are we going to do now?' Jenny asked.

'Get out of here,' I urgently proclaimed, pulling the cadaver's dagger from its sheath, and examining the serrated blade: then looked at the grimy sword Kelly was holding. 'I am not going to pacifically allow these animals to violate my body,' I determinedly stated. We heard the men outside growing quite exuberant: it made us feel most vulnerable. I ran to the door, and firmly bolted it. 'Right, that should buy us a little more time,' I said with grim purpose. Jenny became hypnotized by the corpse's ghastly stare, her eyes expanded in mortified horror: she was transfixed in petrifaction. 'Jenny!' I grabbed her shoulders and gave her a sudden shake, ' Wipe the window and take a look outside.'

'Jenny! See if anyone is around the back,' Kelly reiterated, realizing, like me, that Jenny needed to be wrenched from the deathly stare of the Ophion leader. Jenny absently walked to the window, then came to her senses, extricated the morbid trance, and remembered what she was doing: she jumped onto the rock furniture, with her hand wiped away some grime from the casement and created a transparent aperture, and took a cautious look outside.

'Anyone there?' Kelly exigently asked.

'Er, no, there's no one out the back,' Jenny nervously claimed.

'Any lizards?' I asked.

'Er, no, I can't see any,' she cautiously added. Outside, I could hear the men gathering. Then, much to our consternation, one loudly knocked on the door. We stared at each other in horror as lusty Ophions crowded outside.

'Hey, come on, Selphus, it's our turn now,' one said, laughing with his buddies. 'Come on, I can't wait any longer.' The banging on the door became louder and more urgent.

Suddenly, we heard the sound of charging animals, the clashing of steel, and blood curdling cries. There was scuffling and the sound of people thudding to the ground: all pandemonium had broken loose outside: it sounded as if thousands of men were locked in violent battle. Kelly wasted no time: she picked up a large stone and threw it towards the windows, smashing it in fragments. Instinctively, with the knife, I cleared the shards from the frame. Jenny ran to the window, then leaped out: me and Kelly quickly followed. I anxiously peered up and down the street: it all looked eerily uniform. I was unsure which way to go, but as my friends were too, and we were desperate to escape, I imperiously stated, 'This way.' We tentatively ran along the path until we encountered a group of lizards tied to a post. I ran to them: I went to untie one: but they opened there large ferocious blood red maws and violently hissed and spat at us. I took a step back as they strained on their tethers, snapping dagger teeth, and trying to take a bite out of us. I momentarily flinched in fear, but ultimately was in no mood to baulk: these creatures were the quickest means to get the hell out of here. 'There, there, nice lizard,' I gently said, in my most soothing feminine voice: surprisingly, the lizard stopped hissing, blinked, and cocked its head. I gently held out my hand and slowly walked towards it speaking quietly as I went: it began sighing through its nostrils, and, much to my astonishment and relief, got down on its haunches, and lowered its head.

'What do we have here?' a throaty diabolical voice lacking any humanity suddenly bellowed from hell. The lizards snapped from their docility and began spitting and hissing at the fiendishly discordant noise. I turned round: we were surrounded by demonic men with tattooed faces and shaven heads clad in unburnished leather armour. They were prognathic with short tusks protruding from their cheeks. They were mounted upon giant cats, which also hissed and spat at us, straining at the reigns, which these evil looking men were pulling back with arms like tree trunks. Seeing such formidable foe made my spirit fade to nothing: I stood there, a shadow, an empty shell forlorn of hope: we were at their total mercy. Kelly rallied, and lifted the sword above her head: I gripped her shoulder, and with my other hand, lowered the wielded blade.

'Thought we had taken all their women,' one growled.

'Y-e-a-h,' another salaciously replied.

'More sport for The Asuras, hey, Baliccan?' one laughed, turning to a fire-eyed warrior who looked most unhinged.

'Bind them. Gag them. Load them up. Come on. Let's go,' barked a particularly large man-at-arms, who, I deemed, by his supercilious demeanour, was their leader. Three Asuras sprang from the cat's back. Such was their powerful presence, we knew resistance was futile: but, as they approached, fear induced me to hold the dagger in front of me; Kelly, seeing my show of defiance, became manic, and with wild eyes, held the sword in front of her, prepared to die fighting; even Jenny appeared determined to strike at any opportunity. Baliccan, like evil personified, smirking at the sport, on a giant cat swaggered forward, growling and ready to pounce: the cat leapt forward and took a swipe so fast I never saw it: the sword went flying across the ground: the speed of the strike shocked Kelly, and she stood motionless, quivering:

but she managed to promptly rekindle her courage, and was going to attack with her bare hands: I quickly stood in front of her nervously holding the serrated dagger's point towards the oncoming assailants: but in a flash I found myself laying prostrate with a crazy drooling cat stood over me. I dare not move for it incited the ire of the giant snarling feline: so I lay helpless as my hands and feet were bound. Baliccan gleefully stared at his men's handiwork. 'Come on, hurry, The Ophions' main forces could return at any time.' The three of us were unceremoniously dumped onto the back of cats: and soon we were bounding through the city as the fighting continued around us. Gradually, all The Asuras disengaged from the conflict, and retreated into the marshes. The cats gracefully bounded over the mud: and I was painfully jostled around as they speedily ran. I was briefly relieved when they reached the watery marsh, for the big cats baulked at the prospect of entering the icy water. The riders had to kick and whip them in order to coax them forward: the cats vehemently roared protestations: I felt its whole body shake, and I trembled at the power. The cats were faster than the lizards on dry land; but they were slower through the water: the cats had to be cajoled every step of the way: and, although I was slumped over the saddle, with my head sometimes splashing into the water, I managed to raise my eyes to see that The Asuras were anxiously staring about them: for, as the lizards were far more mobile on the watery terrain, it meant that the Asuras were vulnerable to attack. Mostly, all I could see, were the paws wading through the water: and my abdomen began to ache as I had to perpetually raise my head so I would not be drowned: and, as my backside pointed into the sky, every now and again, a nearby rider would slap my bottom. I felt like a lifeless piece of meat, utterly imbued in anguish and despair.

We interminably waded through the marsh land: we rode on night and day. As we moved on, I was beginning to lose my wits: the whole ordeal was taking its toll. I had to maintain my faculties if I was to have any chance of emancipating myself from these animalistic men. I thought of Gorky: I did not want him to find me an emotional wreck; I did not want to be lost in madness: I needed to be *compos mentis*, so when me and my love were re-united I could communicate with him, and bridge the gap of isolation. As we waded through the mire, I became extremely tired: and so, (between slaps) I fell asleep…

I dreamt I was flying high and free, without wings, just me, my soul, unlimited, boundless, over the clouds, over the trees of Firkin, back to my dear little hut: I entered through an open window, and sat by the hearth: Gorky was kindling a fire: he smiled lovingly, and offered me a hot drink…

I woke violently bouncing up and down: the cats were bounding over dry land. We had reached a rocky escarpment: the cats climbed higher with consummate ease: the one I was slung over, leapt over rocks, onwards: I jostled around like a rag doll and began to feel nauseous: my emotions became overwhelming and tears fell on the cat's fur. 'Kelly! Jenny!' I shouted trying to stifle a sob.

'Shut it!' the rider growled, and struck me on the thighs with a whip: a sharp stinging pain zipped across my legs, and sadness metamorphosed into anger: I seethed in silence. The cats were running up a steep mountain side: such was the vertical incline that I thought I would fall off. Upwards we leapt, and my head rocked uncontrollably from side to side: how my neck did not snap I do not know. Then, to my partial relief, we reached level ground. The cats slowed down. We walked through a narrow fissure in the cliff. I craned my neck upwards: the cave opened up like a massive hall; the ceiling towered above us. Water loudly dropped from stalactites and eerily echoed. As we strolled further into the huge cavern, the day light gradually faded, until it became pitch dark. The cats did not slow down, but confidently moved onwards through the blackness. The atmosphere was oppressive, and smelt of death: it stimulated primal fear in my being: I shuddered: this is where I would end my existence: hell!

As the cats, with an uncanny sixth sense, silently negotiated themselves amongst the rocks, a strange flickering dim orange lambent gradually became apparent: then, I detected weird shadows frenetically dancing on the cave walls: they resembled double-jointed goblins swirling and leaping around in wild ecstasy: I became entranced in their strange movements: and I danced in savage motions over the rocky surface: I cackled as my limbs loosely swayed like grass in a storm: an atavistic spirit had taken my soul and I screamed in hideous delight as my naked body danced unhindered...

But, as the cats strolled into a large ante-chamber, my euphoria quickly subsided: body, once again, contained spirit, and eyes widely opened. The line of Asuras circled around a large fire in the centre of the cave, and gradually came to a halt. Simultaneously they dismounted the cats. The cats laid down, curled around each other next to the fire, and began purring loudly, glad their arduous journey was over: the cave resonated with their soothing rattly throats, and assuaged the morbid air. I was dragged from the cat, and heavily ushered to where Jenny and Kelly sat. We were stunned in silence: but I was pleased to see them, real human beings. They were alive, relatively unscathed: and we huddled together for morale support.

Asura warriors were gathered in groups around the fire, eating raw meat, voraciously chewing, blood and gore dribbling down their chins. We had heard of it in our myths, but were numb with shock, for never had we seen meat eaten. They noticed our disgust, took glee, and made even more of a show of chomping and slavering: we huddled tighter.

Baliccan stood before us, manic eyes bulging, chaotic flames from the fire light swirling in his dilated pupils: he thrust a piece of bloody meat in front our faces: I nearly wretched. 'Can I interest you with a piece of Ophion? Their brains are particularly delicious, though you never get a full meal.' His men began laughing, as they expectorated the gristle from their food. I stared dumbfounded, incredulous and horrified: I shrank from the dripping flesh. He smirked at my revulsion, then his demeanour turned lustful, as he repeatedly slapped the whip he was holding into his palm. 'I will enjoy you three,' he said, 'but first, I will savour the moment... I will eat... then sleep... then, maybe, go out, and kill... then maybe... eat again...and then...' Baliccan began lasciviously gyrating his groin: his men began to laugh as he sneered at me, stared at my breasts, then, defiantly gazing into my eyes, said, 'I will have you... very... very... s-l-o-w-l-y.' He then ran his tongue up and down the flesh he was devouring and began to cackle, a vicious cruel laugh, and I totally averted from his demented gaze, and stared into the orange flames of the fire trying to think myself elsewhere, anywhere!

Some fierce Asuras on cats suddenly entered, and Baliccan instantly diverted his attention onto the new arrivals. 'What news of the war?' he demanded.

'The most successful breach of their city yet,' one replied, leaping from a cat, and knocking dried blood and marsh mud from his sullied armoured breastplate.

'Aye, I thought so. We left with many of them strewn lifeless along the streets. We hit them hard,' Baliccan cheerfully proclaimed.

'Selphus is dead,' one of his warriors suddenly said as he

opened a hessian bag from around his shoulder: and, in his gripped fist, pulled out some hair, and, attached to the hair, was the distorted and hardly recognizable lineaments of Selphus. The Asura carelessly slung the decapitated head onto the ground: Baliccan's face slowly turned to jubilation as he stared down at the ghoul that gazed up at him with crazy exophthalmic blood filled eyes.

'Selphus, dead? Who killed him?' his own eyes widening in surprise.

'We do not know. He was found in a room mutilated… his jugular hanging out of his neck… It was quite vicious, worthy of an Asura,' another said, as, from a large leather sack, he pulled out a gory collection of gruesome body parts, and threw them by the fire.

'Ha, ha, my men, so strong and ruthless… yes!' Baliccan proclaimed, kicking Selphus' head across the cave: his men ruthlessly cheered at the sight. 'With Selphus dead, we will win the war yet! After the rest of The Ophions return from wasting their time hunting The Monads, and The Ophions now in disarray, we will attack again: victory will be ours! I will rule the marshes, and the mountains!' He then slowly turned to me, crouched on his haunches, so his putrid face was level with mine, and said, 'I will own everything.' I turned away in disgust: to which he stood up dementedly laughing, walked away, and left us wondering what our fate would be.

10.

Thwarted

So I surged forward, towards the multitude's vehement cacophony: in that bitter throng, was my sweet Helena, a gem amongst dirt. Oh lamentable woe to envisage her sorrowful state. I had resolved to die fighting: but, before I did, I had a supernatural urge to see her again, to be in paradise. Suddenly, I heard an explosion: I span around to see the great gates fragment into splinters: pouring in was a long procession of despicable looking demons riding on fiendish cats. My senses honed; I focused on their visages: they had violence and hate etched deep into their maniacal eyes. Their faces, tattooed in ink, were adorned in the iconography of war: skulls, swords, spears, knives and axes. Their hair was closely shaven though some had long dishevelled beards. They emitted the most blood curdling war cry, and I thought hell had verily been unleashed. How I saw them with such acuity from the distance I was stood was not feasible: but the sudden presence of these fierce warriors induced a catalyst for focusing my attention: I zoomed into their grim and hate filled countenances of war. They galloped into the city yelling guttural cries, their big cats roaring, and all pandemonium broke loose. 'This must be Asuras!' I exclaimed.

'Where are the Ophions?' Barney anxiously asked, and his nervous tone brought me back to my wonted senses. I stood petrified, unable to think of what to do next.

'When the Ophions appear, all mayhem is going to be upon us,' Argon peremptorily claimed.

'Maybe if we stay calm, we can use the distraction to our advantage,' Barney added.

I peered at him with acute doubt, for it seemed to only add to our problem.

'Maybe…' I shrugged. Helena flashed before my eyes: images of her despair overwhelmed me to action: I quickly regrouped my faculties. 'Let's keep moving, towards where these interlopers are heading: I am certain the ladies are to be found there,' I said, but did not wait for a response: I marched onwards, towards strife and certain death. We stealthily moved along a side street parallel to where The Asuras were streaming in. Every now and again, we could see them in the vistas between buildings: they charged on relentlessly, and our concern increased lest they spied us. We came to a place where we could see a large open square: we stared in dumbstruck horror: the carnage was horrifying. The people of Firkin had lived in sedate isolation: we had only experienced war vicariously in fables: which, as a child, filled me with such dread, that I practiced with a stick lest our village ever became under siege: but the fables, in comparison to this, were acutely euphemistic. The ferocity of these men was like no natural predator: they cut through each other like paper; limbs were confetti; blood poured like rivers: and the more gore there was, it only served to inspire the lust of these men to kill. I began to feel myself shrink: my axe became very heavy. We cowered behind the corner of a building trying to discern any sign of our women: amongst the chaos, I still hoped Helena would be alive.

Some Ophions, in the melee, managed to mount lizards: The Asuras cats swiped them with their steel claws; the lizards roared with pin point teeth. It was madness epitomized, utter anarchy, profound anger and violence, unadulterated lunacy. 'What shall we do?' I finally managed to choke, partially in shock at such efficient carnage.

'Let's wait,' Argon earnestly advised, instinctively putting his hand on my shoulder to re-assure himself and me that humanity still existed.

'I'm for that,' Barney concurred with strained lineaments. 'Perhaps they will all kill each other, and we can walk amongst the aftermath, and hope our ladies managed to find a place to hide.' So we gripped our weapons and hid behind a wall, every now and again, very tentatively, peering around the corner, grimacing and wincing at the violence, and promptly re-concealing ourselves...

The war waged for some time, gradually spreading outwards from the square: we felt incredibly vulnerable, and held our heavy axes in numb hands, dreading having to face one of these crazy voracious demons that had minds inculcated with the deepest pits of hell's nightmares. We huddled together, hearing maniac screams and laughter, mad pleasure in torture, butchering, and killing: the human body desecrated with steel and hate...

But soon, the noise of uncompromising war gradually abated, and The Asuras began to make their retreat. I heard one say, 'That's enough. Let's go before their re-enforcements return.' And so they vanished as soon as they appeared. Suddenly the city, but for the odd anguished groan of a slain Ophion and Asura, was deathly silent. We plucked up enough courage to carefully make our way to where the main scene of the battle had been. I will spare you, dear readers, the graphic details of carnage, for it was such a sight that could not be repeated. It made me desirous to throw my axe away, and never hold another weapon again: but I needed it for protection. We picked our way amongst corpses, and, clinging to our axes, expecting to be ambushed at any moment, fretfully peered into buildings. The interiors were as austere as the facades, and I wondered why these men existed at all. We systematically searched where we could, but dare not call our ladies' names for fear of drawing attention.

Then we heard a familiar and horrifying sound: flapping lizard feet. The floor vibrated with the main Ophions' forces return. I wanted to continue the search, for I felt a great travail in the pit of my stomach at not being able to locate Helena: but Argon and Barney started to drag me away, intense supplications of dread carved deep into their countenances. 'I must find Helena!' I blurted.

'They could have escaped,' Barney spat in my face.

'Come on! Come on! It's no one's benefit to be captured. They're not here! They're not here!' Argon implored. We ran down a side street towards where we breached the city. The incoming warriors were totally distracted by the carnage. They rode along to where the bulk of the action had taken place, giving us an opportunity to slink away. We eventually came to our rope, still hanging there, unseen: it was like the ladder to paradise. Up ahead, we could see Ophions pouring through the gate. I gripped the rope, profoundly sorry I had not located Helena, but most glad to be away from that chilling city. 'Hurry!' Argon earnestly cried. I needed no second invitation, for soon the whole city would be satiated with angry revenge seekers.

The climb up the rope seemed interminable: my limbs ached: never had I realized the weight of my body. Tears streamed down my cheeks as I hauled my heavy carcass up the rope. The top of the wall seemed unattainable, always out of reach: I was about to relinquish effort, let go, and fall onto Argon and Barney, who were eagerly lifting themselves to safety behind me. The thought of falling in a heap, exposed to the crazy butchers who lived for killing, spurred me on; in a flash, an incredible feeling satiated my soul, an ineffable phenomenon induced me to believe that Helena was alive and wanted me to live: with renewed vigour I clambered onto the top of the wall, then laid prostrate, panting. Argon and Barney, with relative ease, quickly followed: then, we hurriedly pulled the rope up after us. A line of lizard troops poured from the marsh as if the water itself was propagating them. An endless stream of Ophions poured into the city, angry and eager for revenge as the word circulated the Asuras had attacked. We waited for the last of them to enter the city gates: then we sharply descended down the wall, and was soon away, trudging through the mud.

I was stunned, amazed, and blank of thought: after the starkness of preceding events, I had become uncomfortably numb. But then I thought of the aluminium craft defiantly standing solitary amongst the grass, affirmation that our dear village existed, and felt it compelling us onwards...

As we made the long and laborious haul back to our plane, my mind became pre-occupied with my dear lady's fate. I was certain she was still alive and extirpated any notion that she had come to any significant harm; it was highly probable that our women would be safely waiting for us at the craft. I dragged myself through the mire, and that supposition, fired by intense need, transmogrified and became ascertained: of course my lady would be there: I yearned for her so much, she could not be anywhere else. We would re-unite at the aeroplane and embrace sedate. I pulled myself through the combined resistance of mud and water, and the desire to hold and feel her sweet body pressed against mine grew unsupportable.

The craft, at last, came into view on the horizon: my eyes strained to see Helena: I willed myself to believe that a silhouette of a long sward of grass was her; yes, she was standing by; she was safe, waiting for me with alacrity; my Helena, my beautiful Helena, I would soon be in her arms again, hearing her soft voice, watching her perfect lips form sweet words, looking in her heavenly eyes: I quickened my pace: my heart raced: but… as I approached… reality dawned…my spirit began to sink… the mud became thick… I dragged my legs through the viscous terrain… and, while being swallowed by the unforgiving marsh… I knew it was futile to deceive myself: she was not there!

Wet, cold, hungry and weary, we climbed into the cockpit: it felt good to be in my seat, something familiar, a part of Firkin. Exhausted, but restless, I stared at the marsh's two moons: I wondered if Helena was staring at them right now. Barney fought back the tears, which increased the lump in my tumescent heart. 'Where are they?' he began to weep. Argon consoled him.

'There, there, old boy, no news is…erm…well, at least we got in and out of the city unscathed. We did a fairly comprehensive search of that dreadful place. They *may* have escaped,' he said. I ignored the 'may', Helena was not dead: she *had* escaped, somewhere safe: I just knew it.

'What are we going to do?' Barney inquired. In truth, we were at a loss at what to do next: to go back was futile, especially as the main Ophions' forces had returned, and, after the surprise attack, would have sentinels posted everywhere. I stared at Barney's sorrow, then gazed at the moons, and ardently hoped Helena was looking at them too. Oh Helena, send me an unambiguous sign…

There was a rapid rustling of grass, and a sudden bubbling sound all around; the water scintillated with moon light, danced and sparkled. This experience always left one feeling vulnerable and perturbed: it was the perfect ambush: but The Monads were a serene race, and would have never used their incredible attributes to harm: with majestic calm, they rose from the water. All that could be discerned of these marvellous creatures, were many sets of tripartite glowing red eyes which formed an equilateral triangular shape, and brightly shone by the mystic light of the moons: their preter-natural orbs, occasionally blinking, remained stationary, dotted around the craft, and a dense energy saturated the air.

'So you entered the city, and lived?' a Monad said.

'Lived, but did n...' I tried to say.

'They were abducted from their abductors,' a Monad rejoined.

'What do you mean?' Barney inquired.

'The Asuras have taken your women from The Ophions,' another said.

'They are alive!' Argon jubilantly exclaimed.

'Yes.' The Monads' eyes blinked in the darkness and a little smile issued from their rat like mouths: we were surrounded by intermittent flashing red lights. I could feel their jubilance at us receiving such incredible news, which augmented our own; but then their faces dropped when we realized Helena, Jenny and Kelly were still captive. I assumed, in all probability, our ladies had been taken under our noses, possibly as we were cowering behind the city wall: it made me feel profound shame: I would not let pusillanimity over-power me again.

'Where do these, these *Asuras* dwell?' I shouted into the night, raising from my seat, and picking up the axe.

'The Mountains,' one said, pointing in a certain direction.

'To the mountains!' I yelled.

'You are very tired, and emotionally drained: you are in no fit state to make the journey now. Your women will be still alive tomorrow,' a Monad soothingly whispered. Suddenly, an overwhelming soporific state swept over me: I battled to keep my eyes open: but the torpor dramatically increased, like no sleepy state I had ever experienced. As I drifted, I saw Barney and Argon's head loll. I tried to call them, to move my arm to shake them...

We woke simultaneously, rubbing our eyes and re-orientating ourselves. It had been the deepest dreamless sleep I had ever recalled. Judging by the orange sunset spreading its golden fingers, it was early morning. I wasted no time. 'To the mountains!' I exclaimed.

'Wait, old boy,' Argon advised. 'Let's have some breakfast first. No use marching on an empty stomach.' So I built a fire with bracken I diligently gathered, then added some twigs and branches from a nearby shrub: soon, the makeshift hearth was crackling with heat and light: I placed the shiny brass kettle on top: it was not long before water was steaming from the spout: I placed bright verdant herbs in vivid coloured mugs, and poured boiling water in: I became part of the swirling steam: Helena danced in the steam, and sat beside me, a smile gleaming from her eyes: the flames danced in our souls: our love fused and intensified… I hurriedly drank the hot beverage whilst scolding my mouth. We munched on dry biscuits, half mine spilling down my front in haste. I almost choked on the dry crumbs as I eagerly swallowed.

'Slow down,' Barney frowned. But it was too late, I had finished my repast. I then paced up and down in the icy marsh water, impatiently waiting for Argon and Barney to finish eating theirs. I was a little annoyed at the apparent lack of urgency. I stared at them as I began tapping my glinting axe. They must have taken the hint.

'We're as desirous as you,' Argon eventually said.

'Right… Are you ready?' I demanded.

Barney leaped over the side of the cockpit, and began swinging the huge axe around his head to warm himself up. Then he suddenly stopped.

'I'm still hungry,' he complained. 'Nothing to eat around here. I feel lethargic through lack of nourishment.' He pulled at some grass, chewed it, then spat it out in disgust. I clambered back on board the plane and pointed to the urn which contained the alchemical waters of Sacradia.

'Yes,' was all Argon said. I opened the urn- I felt a surge of preternatural energy emanate from the receptacle- and, with a ladle, offered my compatriots Sacradia: we each took a eager single quaff: it felt so much more than a hearty meal: all despondency sloughed away: my muscles throbbed with pulsating energy. We smirked at each other in mutual satisfaction. Then, we began indomitably marching towards the mountains, where we believed The Asuras resided.

11.

Another Rescue Expedition

As we trudged through the muddy water, an inveterate sense of dread assailed me as I recalled the crazy cat-warrior Asuras: they were blood thirsty lunatics, utterly ruthless, dirty fighters, without a scrap of remorse: it was obvious that the word 'mercy' did not exist in their vocabulary. Although I felt vigorous because of the magic water, I did not relish the prospect of going into combat: I knew I would have to change my personality so I could indiscriminately kill, become savage, void of any emotion other than hate and anger like a starved predator. For Asuras, killing was a way of life, their *raison d'être*, efficiently, without question. I had to get myself in the right frame of mind: I imagined Helena... I did not want to... but I imagined her in the hands of The Asuras... I imagined her being raped... It fuelled my disdain, my thirst for revenge: I could feel the lust for violence pump through my veins. It bothered me, turning nasty, and I fought with my conscience: but if I was to save her, and escape alive, I had to temporarily disavow benevolence. I tried to metamorphose my ferocity to emulate the cat-warriors. My commitment had to be absolute: I was a battle hardened veteran, a man who could switch on and off his mind like a machine: no contrition. In the heart of battle I would function effectively. I was war personified, a bringer of chaos and death. Images of me carrying water and talking to the chirping birds while listening to the gentle breeze in the trees and tenderly loving my woman pervaded my soul with an heavy compunction, and a tear slid down my cheek as I knew I was about to change my life forever. I tried to prepare myself with the notion that, if I survived, I may have to live the rest of my life knowing I had killed people: it was the antithesis of the purpose of this whole mission.

Argon and Barney looked vacant as they trudged through the mire: the prospect of clashing with The Asuras had rendered them deeply introspective. In our dumb shock, we had seen Asuras and Ophions fight, no rules, no principles: they gouged, cut and thrust for pleasure, as if it was their only desire: and they did it with such aplomb and dexterity, it made our play fighting in Firkin woods look positively puerile: we were always controlled, with an element of fun: they were intense, serious, demons incarnate. It was like marching to our execution: and yet we could not deny the desire to march on, for to leave our women meant abandoning our lives, our *raison d'être*; and we would have lived the rest of our lives in ignominy and shame. I just hoped, when the time came, that I would fight bravely, not be hindered by stultifying fear, and give a good account of myself.

On we trudged. We remained fairly silent, senses keen, continually surveying the area, listening for any anomalous sounds. Then, just over the horizon, we espied a rocky escarpment. The water below our feet gradually began to allay, and, soon we were walking on arid ground. The mountain grew in stature: but I was confident we could ascend it with little difficulty. As we approached, the rocky surface became more foreboding: ugly visages seemed to be carved in the stone: they induced one's psyche diminutive: but, as I focused on one of these grimacing countenances, it dissipated into the rock, and seemed to reappear in the periphery of my vision. Barney and Argon stared at the rock in profound amazement, their lineaments mirroring my own.

Then, for a moment, my soul violently convulsed, and drastic change pervaded the whole environment: the mountain became Helena; the mountain symbolized Helena; the whole environment was Helena; the place was imbued with her presence; I became satiated with her essence: I had to reach the source. Those diabolical excuses for men filled me with acute indignation. They had the gall to steal my woman. Who were they?! How dare they?! They were nothing but idiots who wasted their whole lives killing each other, with little intelligence for anything else. I felt the wrath of divinity within me. I suddenly felt more than a match for these savages. The potency of love, the ferocity of love, the desire to live, peaceably, as was our irrevocable right, would soon be upon their unsuspecting heads. I felt an ineluctable responsibility to uphold justice: and they were an aberration of the sacred and universal law. We will show them a war they will never forget: we will leave them permanently psychologically marred. The bullies will be bullied. Our contempt will crash down on their shallow and pitiless souls. My spirit is immutable: it will remain restless until ethics are restored.

As I walked towards the mountain, I scrutinized it for fissures, or a visible aperture that may be an opening to a cave... I diligently scoured the area, the weird and unwholesome visages in the rock's surface always evading focus, but it did not deter me. I realized that the more fear I felt, the more the rocky countenances grinned in glee: these uncanny gruesome faces devoured the energy of our innate insecurities. I must find a substantial crevice, the entrance to the Asuras' cave. Yes! Up there... about half way up... a gaping black hole. 'Up there!' I pointed. Barney quickly lifted his axe ready to strike: this made me instinctively snap into a battle stance. 'There!' I reiterated, less vehemently, overcoming my reflex reaction, and relaxing a little.

'A cave!' Argon exclaimed.

'Yes, and I have a feeling,' I said, as my stomach twisted and turned, 'that's where they are.' Argon and Barney gazed at the cave, peering deep into its eerie black abyss.

'Let's go,' Barney imperiously commanded, and began charging towards the mountain. We quickly followed. Soon we were scrambling up its craggy surface. My mind cleared of all things. As we climbed, the sun synchronously descended: the higher we climbed, the darker it became, until we climbed by touch alone.

12.

Coerced Erotica

We sat huddled together, bound tightly, with gags cutting into our mouths: it was restricting our circulation. We frequently stared at each other for morale support. I would sometimes gaze into the fire and transmigrate into the swirling flames forgetting where my body was and the awful fate that awaited it. The big cats slept around the fire, and were quite docile now, occasionally gregariously preening each other, and nuzzling tenderly. I noticed they became decidedly restless when an Asura passed near them; but, I verily believed I had managed to befriend one of these potentially fierce big cats: I had tentatively poked out my foot, cautiously stroked it under the chin, which, to my delight, it contentedly purred, and, requited by licking my toes with its bristly tongue. Some warriors threw dry bracken on the fire, and it hissed and crackled, as the flames danced in Kelly's and Jenny's perturbed eyes. Asuras, in groups, were pointing to us, whispering, and occasionally emitting a loud guffaw: it was apparent we were the main topic of conversation, and I dreaded to think what they were saying. Baliccan swaggered in, as if the ground was rocking beneath his feet: he spoke slurred to his men. Whatever he said induced zeal into his men, and they began to stagger towards us with daft grins. They surrounded us, followed by Baliccan, who zig-zagged forward, and stood defiantly over us, swaying with the fire. 'I have deeeessssided,' he eventually managed to say, for vocalization seemed to take great effort, 'you will stand before my, hic, men...' the men began sniggering, their miens shone in eagerness, transfixed on me, Jenny, and Kelly, 'and ssslowwwly, hic...' the men buzzed with excitement, Balicaan's eyes oscillated between bright and wide, then narrow detached slits, 'veeerrry, hic, slooowwwllly...' the men could not contain themselves, and burst into uncontrolled laughing: he turned to them, and joined in with the merriment, then, put his grimy finger to his decaying mouth, and went, 'Shshush!' To which his men, still sniggering, became quiet in eager anticipation; Baliccan then turned round to me, stroking his tusk and eyes burning with intense lust, 'Very slowly take off all your clothes.' His vacillating bloodshot eyes tried to focus on mine: I gazed at him, my eyes imbued with fury, for we were to be humiliated in front of this drunken horde. 'If you refuse,' he said, drawing out a dagger, and slid it across his throat while his black tongue contorted from his mouth: then his physiognomy grimaced into hideous viciousness to leave me in no doubt: he would slit our throats without hesitation. 'Do you understand, hic?' Jenny and Kelly stared dumb as our bonds were cut and the gags removed.

'I am not...' I feebly tried to say.

'Shut up!' and with lightning speed he grasped me by the hair, violently jerked his powerful arm upwards: and in an instant I found myself dangling in the air, my feet kicking desperately to find the ground: a knife point rested against my abdomen: his swiftness surprised me: for, before this sudden explosion of movement, he appeared most uncoordinated. He motioned for the other two girls to join me. 'Move over there!' he growled: and then, with his wild eyes like a traction ray, he ushered us to where the main group of men were sitting, drinking heartily with eager glares. Without struggle, we succumbed to the animalistic ferocity emanating from this phenomenon. We stood before the large group of drunken warriors, vulnerable, exposed and numb: I felt my spirit shrink in its frame; my whole being was frail, innocent, afraid and lost. Tears welled in my eyes as the men ridiculed us with lewd remarks: and it seemed as though I was outside my body watching myself as the men lustily cheered. 'Strip!' he ordered, 'nice and sl, slow, hic.' I looked at my friends: tears were streaming down their cheeks. We stood there, pathetic, and uncertain what to do. A sharp pain in my head brought me to my senses: he had grabbed my hair again, and with a swift slicing action, cut a lump of it off. 'Strip you bitches, or I will fucking kill you, now!'

At that moment, time seemed to freeze: I recalled my entire life in Firkin: from a child collecting daisies in the fields with my friends; when I first met Gorky, our courting, falling in love, and our happy life together: the complete concatenation of my entire existence unfolded before me in rapid motion, as I began to unbutton my tunic...

13.

Re-United

We fumbled our way up the rock face, sharp igneous rock cutting our hands and knees: I felt no pain as I scrambled onwards: our minds were set on pushing forward to confront The Asuras. Nervous anticipation grew as we climbed upwards; we gritted our teeth and pulled ourselves over the jagged surface. The cuts and abrasions invoked a battle fury readiness; I scorned the superficial damage to my body and pumped myself up for war. Then, I sensed the mouth of the cave nearby: I could feel the dark chasmic void; but I could also detect my sweet Helena, the light within the dark. Helena, I will follow you into the darkness, for where ever you are, there is only light. We reached the opening, our hearts pounding, and waited… I had expected sentinels, but could only assume the advent of females distracted the Asuras. We hung on the cliff face, surrounded by dark sky, the two moons obscured by black clouds. From the cave, barely audible, carried by echo, was the sound of revelry: faint it was, but apparent there were many Asuras. I knew the tumult was caused by our women: I could discern the salaciousness of the tones. 'Shall we go in?' I asked. We hung onto the cliff face surrounded by the night's silence.

'What are we waiting for?' Argon exclaimed.

I said nothing more, but breached the entrance. It was pitch dark, but I had had experience at moving around in the dark, and walked forward, deeper into the bleak cavern. If I had received the slightest alien touch, or heard the most barely audible movement: my axe would have buried deep into that which disturbed. We carefully made our way along the rocky souterrain, our senses on high alert, feeling like we were making a great din as we went, though we crept with upmost stealth. Eventually, up ahead, I perceived an orange light dancing on the cave walls: shadows gyrated like frenzied demons. Argon and Barney carefully followed me, their weapons poised, sensitive to strike at the slightest provocation. It felt good to have such solid back up, for I knew the determination and strength of these two men. As for myself, I would not die easy; it would take a mighty effort to kill me. Something in my heart told me this venture was futile, that we were going to die: but I had to be with Helena when I did. I then felt in my head, a feeling, from Helena, 'The humanitarian mission': the sensation throbbed in my brain: my heart pounded even more: I saw all the ailing tribes in dire torment: and it was all because of me! I had disseminated a virulent disease across many lands: I could not bow out leaving such an awful legacy: I must retrieve our ladies and save those people: my resolve strengthened, and any fatalistic proclivity extirpated. We would leave this cave alive: all six of us would escape uninjured into the night back to our plane and fly away to safety. The orange light shone brighter: and the shadows danced more frenzied as we approached the source of the light.

A great open space suddenly presented itself before us, in the centre, a large wood fire blazed. Circumscribing the margins were dozing big-cats, occasionally lifting their sleepy heads. Asuras were sat around the fire, wildly cheering, and drinking profusely. Helena! I stood petrified to the spot, my stomach swirling in white hot fury and intolerable indignation. Helena, Kelly and Jenny were dancing before these licentious men, visibly distressed, as they slowly unbuttoned their habiliments. Helena's wretched lineaments infused into me the might of a leviathan: I began to uncontrollably shake: something came over me, an ineffable something: divine wrath. I had never experienced such exaltedness: it was like lightning from the sky had exploded into my veins: the awesome elements empowered me: any doubt transmogrified into an elemental and profound force of positive action: temporal space slowed as I rushed into the antechamber with incredible speed: I ran to Helena, my beloved, sweet lady, who was being harassed by a vulgar drunken horde. I ran to Helena, my light, my life, my love, and put my arm around her waist, as I held my axe above my head, and dared any man to impinge. I stared at the disgusting crowd with an atavistic fury, a primeval readiness, and defied any fool to attack.

14.

Cat

I lifted my head, and saw a peculiar looking man running towards soft foot with a metal claw: at first, I thought his intention was to attack her, and I was ready to strike, but it soon became apparent he wanted to protect her. I had grown fond of soft foot: I had never known such kindness from humans: I was sad that she and her friends were being treated with the same disrespect we were. As odd as he looked, this gallant man inspired my desire for insurrection: on his face was cat fierceness: but I knew he was in terrible danger. Then, two other men walked from the shadows with equal tiger like expression as soft foot's protector. I felt it was a crucial moment: if I did not act now, soft foot and her people would soon be dead. My heart elevated within me, and I knew what I had to do: my friends sensed it too. We all raised, and stretched our long sinewy feline bodies: none of the warriors or soft foot and her people took any notice of us. I casually strolled up to her, and rubbed my body against her curves. Get on, soft foot, we will take you away.

15.

Escape

I felt Helena breaking loose from my embrace: she began clambering on board the back of a big cat: I was distracted from my hypnotic reverie, and everything began moving as accustomed. The Asuras began recovering from my sudden appearance, and started to stir: this induced the cats to spit and swear: the Asuras, in their stupor, watched, for a moment, amazed. 'Jump on!' Helena cried: Jenny and Kelly wasted no time in climbing on board the big cat with Helena. 'Come on!' she shouted at me. There was no more room on her cat and I wanted her out of this situation immediately.

'Get out of here!' I peremptorily yelled, so the women could not object, I slapped the big cat on its haunches: it growled, and quickly bound towards the exit of the cave: leaving me standing in front of the disgruntled Asuras, who were rapidly gaining their composure, and fumbling around for their weapons. A large man suddenly manifested in front of me from nowhere: my eyes widened in horror at the epiphany of this animal force: his bulging mad eyes were blood red: it was like staring into the deepest pits of hell: his yellow teeth snarled like a big cats.

'I am Baliccan, leader of The Asuras, and you are dead!' he demonically proclaimed. In a flash, he was bowled over by a large cat: they both loudly roared rolling around the ground in a most violent display of wrestling. Other cats were soon upon the Asuras: their massive claws cleft the men in two with a single swipe: they mauled and chewed and cut them to pieces: the cats pounced with such vital speed, that it was verily an awesome sight: it made the Asuras ferocity pale in comparison. One bounded towards me, I tried to lift my axe, but before I could, it ran straight by me to aid its fellow cat brawling around the ground with the giant Asura who had just introduced himself as Baliccan. This particular Asura, the mighty Baliccan, so far, had been doing better than the others: for, despite the cat's massive size, he equalled it in strength and speed: large clouds of dust had been thrown up while they were locked in bloody combat. However, two giant cats were too much even for this tenacious warrior: in the frenzied lightning speed of battle, one, with its great sabre fangs, managed to get a tight grip of his neck: the ferocious cat did not let go, but, with its powerful vice like jaws, bit hard into the soft flesh of Baliccan's nape: his head was ripped clean off, and rolled into the fire: the flames howled a ghastly moan as if he had gone direct to the infernal regions. Argon and Barney, like me, were motionless onlookers in the affray: the fight went on, erratic, around us: we looked at each other, and tacitly decided to make our egress: we ran towards the exit, following our ladies. I stopped to take one last look at the carnage: big cats chased the remainder of the men around the cave, and played with them, swiping, causing ugly lacerations, before mercilessly finishing them off: I will never forget the look of fear in the Asuras' eyes, as if they had suddenly become aware that judgement day awaited in the big cats' *coup de grace*: each death caused the fire to roar in dire anguish.

We quickly made our way through the dark tunnel towards the cave entrance. The weird shadows on the craggy surfaces danced in a wild and frenzied ecstasy more than ever: for, interspersed with these bizarre creatures of the gloom, were smaller shadowy Asura figures, contorted and struggling in the shadow creatures' dark limbs: these distressed figures slowly sank and faded into the penumbra of the shadow creatures' all encompassing dark grasp:

it was the most awful array of silhouettes imaginable: and I did not stop running for fear I would also become entangled in the strange nether-scene on the wall. I ran as fast as it was expedient to do so in the pitch dark: and then, suddenly, intuitively stopped before the exit. I nearly lost my balance as my toes hung over the ledge, and a wave of fear shook my body as I prepared to tumble down the cliff: I managed to lurch backwards, fell onto the rocky floor, and there, sat, glad of solid ground. I took a couple of deep breaths and regained my composure. Echoing through the tunnel was the guttural and deathly screams of the damned, mingled with the loud and victorious roars of the big-cats. Those magnificent felines had spent their lives in continual duress: their interminable subjugation had meant increasing pent up anger: and it was now being uncompromisingly unleashed on their brutal captors. Hearing Barney and Argon scrambling downwards projected my mind outwards: I had a sudden urge to join them: I jumped up and quickly followed. The descent was steep and precipitous and I slid and grabbed the rock as I continually nearly lost control. I was glad to be out of that vile cave: and the further away I got, the better it felt. As I descended, the black clouds began to sweep away, and the brilliant light of the two moons shone their penetrating rays: I was glad to see their natural refulgence shining down.

When I had landed on horizontal ground, there waiting, sat upon the big cat, was our ladies: guarding them, Argon and Barney, axes poised at the ready. My heart satiated with elation at viewing my civilized friends. To espy their human demeanours in the moon light was a mystical experience: and I nearly sobbed for pleasure. I ran to them with tears in my eyes. My beautiful Helena was gracefully sat upon a wild cat. Her physiognomy evinced the adverse experiences she had encountered: and a new depth of expression shone in her eyes. 'I see you've made a new friend,' I smiled at her.

'Yes, he's cute, isn't he?' She bewilderedly smiled, and stroked the big creature behind his ear: and he closed his eyes in wistful appreciation.

'Are you okay?' Barney tentatively asked Jenny, unsure if she wanted him to approach her.

'Yes, we're fine,' she replied, wanting to dismount to hug her man. He walked towards her: but an anguished yell emanating from the cave made him suddenly stop and stare upwards at the dark entrance to hell.

'Let's get out of here,' he said with exigency, for was not convinced the danger was over. I for one deemed this an apt move: there could have been some diabolical fiends that had managed to escape the cats' clutches about to suddenly appear from the darkness of the cave, or some of those bellicose Asura monsters arriving from battle at any time.

'Yes, come on,' Argon concurred, smiling at Kelly, his anxiety notably mitigating; being able to rest his eyes on her once again had instantly changed his stern countenance. So the ladies remained on the big cat, as, with alacrity, we made our way from the imposing craggy mountains of The Asuras. We were most glad to feel the dun rocky precipices recede into the darkness, as we looked forward to treading through the marsh waters towards our shiny plane. Me, Barney and Argon, surrounded the cat, guarding the precious cargo, as on we marched. Our ears were keen to hear any type of noise beyond our own; and we strained our eyes, scouring the area, to penetrate the night for any intruder. It was with great relief that we gradually began to feel the mud below our feet become soggy. Then, in the semi-darkness of a moon lit night, we could hear and feel the marsh water splash around our legs: it was cold and clammy, but most welcoming. Soon, we were wading through the watery marsh land again. As we made our way, the two moons began to shine more brightly, illuminating the watery surface with a silver sheen; the water glittered as if gems had been strewn over the surface. Me and Helena occasionally exchanged loving glances: my stride became buoyant, and my heart lifted: we strode onwards towards the refuge of the gleaming plane, reunited, complete, imbued with inner contentment.

We continued to determinedly wade through the mire: then, in the distance, was a discernible bright glow on the surface of the marshland: the plane! Our paces quickened; we hurriedly splashed through the water towards the brilliant metallic reflection of two moons. Sometimes we sank to our necks; sometimes the water was around our knees: but it did not deter our purpose: we were drawn to the mystical glowing phenomenon in the night. Until, there, boldly shining in the moons' light, majestic and proud, defying the natural elements, was our saviour, the aluminium craft. We all stared in wonder at its sleek lines: and soon, we were standing by our faithful transport. The women jumped from the big cat, and it instinctively pressed itself against their bodies as it walked around them, purring. Helena had a divine smile: now we were at the plane, I had the chance to scrutinize my lady properly: she appeared unharmed and looked lovely in the moons' light, shimmering like a refulgent angel: I stood in the marsh, gazing, in awe at her beauty: her eyes were keen and alert, like two gleaming suns; her face was so alive: she inspired my soul with vital energy. I scanned her delectable body: I became totally absorbed in her: with my fertile imagination I was every air molecule contiguous to her delicious skin, caressing her sensuous femininity. I could still not fully believe she was before me: and so I stood there, motionless, voraciously absorbing her with my acute senses.

'We've got to get out of here, before we are pursued by those maniacs,' Argon stated. I dumbly stared at Helena: my beautiful and precious female surfeits my soul with elementary life force: nothing else mattered now. I felt myself drifting towards her:

the big cat mewed its approval: I gathered my lovely Helena into my yearning arms, and felt her womanhood press against my hunger. I kissed her comely face, then her soft warm moist open mouth: she reciprocated with a heavenly sigh, and eagerly fed from my yearning lips: this stimulated my need further, tumescent instinctual urge overcame me, and the kisses became more passionate.

'How are we going to raise this thing from the ground?' Barney inquired, in between tenderly kissing Jenny on the nose, her forehead, her eyes, finally, her lips, with tears streaming down both their faces. Argon, likewise, was in a passionate cuddle with Kelly, totally absorbed in their long awaited re-union. The cat continually encircled us all, rubbing the fur of its lithesome body against us, and purring approbation. Barney managed to tear himself away from the warm embraces of his woman: and while holding her hand, stared with profound consternation at the craft, which, while we had been away, had sunk further into the mire.

Encompassing the seven of us, the grass began to ripple; the water began to bubble and froth: and the sanctuary of our auras was intensified by the sudden emergence of The Monads, who rose from the water in a large ring around us. They eyed the cat a little dubiously at first, but quickly sensed its serenity. 'You are safe!' one said, with such joy, I had to fight back the tears. 'And now you wish to leave.'

'No disrespect to you, ' I said, 'but there is little to keep us here.'

'We understand: the war would drive any civilized being away, but the terrain is suitable for our needs… However, we sense a new epoch is upon us: the cats,' the Monads then smiled at the big-feline, to which it smiled back, 'have rebelled against their "masters"; and, the lizards have also turned on their captors: The Asuras and Ophions have scattered and fled, and now are critically depleted. Your arrival has precipitated strange events, but favourable to us: for we can now live without so much fear of persecution.'

'Good: you are undeserving of such torment,' I respectfully announced.

'This is all very well,' Barney interjected, looking reverently at The Monads, 'but we have a little matter of dislodging the plane, and getting it into the air, without a runway.' He woefully turned to the sunken plane, which had firmly rooted in the mire.

'A runway?' a Monad said, who was now stroking the big-cat under its chin, which increased The Monad's grin as the feline responded with a heavy staccato purr.

'Yes, a length of solid flat ground,' Kelly stated, stroking a bruise on Argon's face he had collected on his quick descent of the mountain as he simultaneously checked her over for any damage.

'We will soon be back,' said a Monad, and quickly they were submerged and gone, zooming through the rushes, speeding under the water like sleek fish.

The cat let out a loud roar that echoed over the marsh, turned to the ladies, mewed and purred, and went walking in the direction of the mountain, to join its pack. 'Goodbye cat,' the ladies called after it.

'Goodbye,' I yelled.

'Let's get ready to go,' Argon determinedly said, for we all knew that The Monads would return to administer aid in our take-off. We checked the craft over: it was relatively unscathed, other than superficial scars suffered from my previous outburst. After we had done all the preliminary checks, I huddled in the cockpit with Helena, and we relayed our stories to each other...

Helena eventually fell into a profound sleep against my body. I felt a profound peace: but remained alert for any sudden intrusion of the remaining warring tribes. I felt solace that only The Monads could be suddenly upon us with complete silence: for it was impossible for humans to traverse the marshes without noise. I listened to my woman's sacred breathing as the marsh wind softly sighed in the grasses: my spirit pervaded with her breath...

I awoke... All was calm. I smiled at Helena, who was still in a deep slumber and like a helix had coiled herself around me. I gently lifted her head from my chest, slowly untangled her limbs and carefully placed her on a folded garment against the craft. I panoramically scanned the area: the sun was just beginning to appear above the horizon, benevolently greeting me with a delicate orange light, which suffused over the surface of the twinkling marsh water. There was no sign of The Monads: but as I looked ahead of the plane, I saw a long track of wooden planks floating on top of the water: amazed, I looked directly below the craft: the wheels were resting on a wooden take-off strip.

'Er, I think they've been in the night,' I said to the others, trying to contain my joy. They began to stir, and were soon seeing the handiwork for themselves. A sudden phlegmatic excitement imbued the crew, and an increasing alacrity evinced our readiness to be away.

'How is everyone feeling?' Argon inquired: everyone responded positively. 'Good. No need to get out the plane,' he said, craning his neck downwards to see the wheels on firm ground. He checked the gears were in the right position; had another perfunctory scan of the drive system; pushed and pulled the levers for the rudder and flaps: with certitude, they swung up and down, left and right. With intense emotion we stirred at the wings, and then at each other. 'Right then, ready for takeoff?' he asked.

'Should we wait to say thank you?' Jenny inquired.

'If it's all the same to you, I've had enough of this place.

Let's get out of here!' Argon said. We were all in agreement, other than the spiritual Monads, this wretched place held no attraction.

'I shall leave this to show our gratitude,' I said, and left a small container of Sacradia on the runway as a gift for those extra-sensory beings.

'I think we should all take some before takeoff,' Kelly claimed. We all agreed, and took a quaff of the preternatural elixir: vigour pulsated through our muscles leaving us in no doubt that we would soon be in the air again.

'Okay. Let's go!' Argon cheerfully shouted. We all pushed down on the pedals, and the craft easily surged forward, trundling over the makeshift runway: the great aluminium wings flapped faster as we gained speed: the end of the runway was approaching: but I sanguinely felt we would be in the air before that: the wings gave a mighty flap: we came to the edge of the wooden runway, then the wheels left it behind, and skimmed over the surface of the water: for a short while the wheels trailed in the water and grass: but as we pedalled harder, the craft lifted into the air: suddenly we were soaring higher and higher: and we managed to acquire enough altitude to level off, and begin cruising in a straight line. As we flew onwards, there, below us, in the water, appeared a brown mass, and we espied tiny hands erratically waving upwards at us: the Monads! We reciprocated their valedictions with cheerful waving of our own. I tried shouting to them in order to thank them for their gift of the runway, but I was uncertain if they heard. We soon left the watery throng behind: and it was not long before we were flying over the mundane grid system of the grey Ophion city: we could see the occasional lizard casually strolling along the street, but not a single Ophion could be seen: we lifted higher and away, and we flew towards, we hoped, The Forest of Life.

Soon we were flying high over the vast tract of marsh land the other side of the grey city. It felt good to be in the air making headway again. The utter relief of having Helena sat in front of me spurred me on to new efforts: my heart suffused with warmth and jubilation as we soared through the air. I would occasionally gently kiss her hair as the clouds floated by: sometimes we were enveloped in misty vapour, which soon passed to reveal the marsh far below us. Water and grass was all that could be seen to the horizon: and it was to the horizon the craft boldly flew. It was a little disconcerting having no navigable method, relying on chance, the purple lodestar nowhere in sight.

On we pushed, believing if we flew in a straight line long enough we would eventually encounter a change of terrain. To our joy, the interminable marsh land began to dissipate: water and grassland slowly turned to yellow sand: the heat of the sun intensified. Soon we were flying over The Desert of No-Night again. I had an intuitive feeling that I had passed this way before: I became satisfied that we were heading in the right direction towards The Forest of Life…

Onwards we flew, over the scorching desert. My memories of the heat belied vivid reality: for never could I recall the sun being this fierce. Luckily, Argon had filled the canteens with marsh water, for this had completely escaped my attention: I was glad to be surrounded by solid, rational and dependable people: I felt secure that my own inadequacies could be compensated for in such trustworthy company. It was a blessed relief to leave that diabolical war torn land behind: for I had no desire to live in such a way. The whole point of the journey began flooding back in my mind: the need to rectify my past errors became more urgent: everything gained renewed perspective: I was overcome with guilt… My stint of pedalling eventually passed, and the three others took over. I rested my aching calves and thighs. The heat was so stifling, that I squirmed uncomfortably: I began to feel acutely lethargic and restless, and I impatiently shuffled in my seat as I thought about the dangers I had put innocent people in: and, though I was actually vexed with weird imaginings of their possible sufferings, I slowly drifted into a heat oppressed sleep...

16.

Memento Mori

*'Through the gross and murky air I spied a shape
come swimming up, that might have quelled the
stoutest heart with wonder.'*

Dante Alighieri

I was reluctantly entering The Asuras' cave again: the tunnel
was longer and darker than before: and I was aware of something
profoundly more sinister lurking within. As I blindly felt along
the sides, sliding my palms over the rocky surface, carefully
feeling my way forward... or backwards, a warm fluid began
pouring down my arms. I gently dabbed my finger in the ooze,
smelt it, then took a tentative taste: blood! The razor sharp rocks
had slit my palms to ribbons: as I opened and closed my hands,
I felt the lacerations gaping and pursing. A morbid compulsion
urged me onwards... Ahead, I saw a dim lurid light. I cautiously
walked towards it... There, in the rock face, appeared a great
yew-wood door with a large brass knocker: it was drenched in
ichor, long coagulated stripes like prison bars ran down it. I had
to breach the threshold, so I boldly banged the knocker, then
winced at the loud sonorous noise I made. My warm blood
covered the cold brass and slowly dribbled down the gory door.
I waited... nothing. I knocked even louder, this time prepared
for the ominous clamour, and brass on wood echoed along the
subterranean cavern... Then, I heard the shuffling of feet the
other side of the door, and the jangling of keys. The big brass

lock turned, and the door slowly creaked open. As the door slowly opened, a vile miasmic air came rushing out: the stench was incredible, and I gagged and convulsed. Standing there, silent and still, was a tall imposing figure, garbed in a long grey robe, with a hood that hung to obscure the face: I tried to look into the shadowy hood, but all I saw was darkness. The creature ponderously turned around, and slowly raised its arm, as it did, from out the robe, a skeletal hand appeared, and, with its long bony forefinger, pointed into the pitch black: I knew I must follow. It ushered me down a dimly lit corridor with lurid green flambeaux hanging from the walls. Behind me, I heard the massive door ineluctably slam shut: the sound eerily echoed along the passageway: I felt my hope drain away and replaced by infernal despair. We solemnly walked along a gloomy corridor, deep into darkness. It was deathly silent, and I felt my soul shudder as on we went. Something inside screamed and pleaded for me to turn around: but an overriding feeling that fate, indelibly carved into the eternal stones of time, could not be eluded: a powerful feeling of inevitability coerced me onwards. We came to a dreary spiral stair case carved into the rock that tightly spiralled down-down-down into the pitch dark. The grim usher glided downwards, round and round, down and down, deeper, darker, deeper, darker, into the abyss: I could do nothing but follow. I became deeply entranced by the monotonous circular motion downwards: temporal-space abandoned me as downwards we went, round and round and down and down the dreary rock spiral stair case. Every step, my fear and reluctance to go downwards increased; every step, I felt an insidious force gaining control of my wits; every step, I felt the ownership of my soul abate. After an ineffable time, we came to the end of the spiral staircase. There were torches of flame reaching out of the rock walls offering a dim lurid light. Before me, was a labyrinth of tunnels, ramifying in all directions, all identical in appearance, still, silent, and very dark. The usher began walking down one of them: and I had to follow. The tunnel had a slight gradient downwards, and we walked and walked deeper into the gloom. I felt I had left all life behind, irretrievably lost forever: indeed, I eschewed all recollections of my former life. Then, as we continued to walk downwards, along the interminable tunnel, deeper into the tenebrous dark, I saw shadows of groaning figures against the jagged cave walls. Suddenly, out of the darkness, came the most hideously contorted creatures one could ever have the misfortune of seeing. At first, I was concerned for my safety: but these pitiable creatures stooped and sluggishly limped along and seemed the epitome of feebleness. Their arms and legs were roughly sewn onto their torsos with coarse thread, and deep scars could be seen were the limbs had previously been sliced. The various skin tones on each creature indicated they had been constructed by different dismembered bodies. Legs were of differing length, and they hobbled as they wailed. Their necks had a necklace like stitch around the throat: and their faces evinced eternal absence. I thought I recognized Asuras and Ophions, but they were so violated, it was hard to tell. We easily pushed by these wretched creatures, deeper, through murky corridors… Eventually, we arrived at a dreary ante-chamber, which was roughly carved into the antediluvian rock. Inside, was a gathering of sinister creatures similar to the usher, garbed in long grey robes, all sat along a long stone table. The usher slowly raised its long gnarled forefinger, and pointed to a dark recess: I obediently went and sat on the small rocky seat provided, and watched the gloomy proceedings. The usher disappeared as I silently waited, curious to know what was happening. Then, in an unrecognizable language, the council began quoting and discussing the parchments that lay in front of them. They treated me as if I was not there; it was quite disconcerting to be treated as an unwanted interloper. Eventually, they ceased locution: and the usher returned. The council quietly spoke to the creature, and, every now and again, it solemnly nodded. When they had finished, it sauntered to me, stopped at my side for a moment, then began slowly walking into the darkness of another passageway. I followed as it led me along more lugubrious corridors. We sauntered through labyrinths of murky tunnels, deeper into the dark. I had no clue where it was leading: all I knew was that I had to follow. Then, we came to a large opening in the caverns. There, in the infernal gloom, I could just descry more long tables. The figure in grey slowly raised its bony hand and pointed to an empty seat: without question, I went to sit down. I was surrounded by direful creatures with sunken eyes and shrivelled visages, mouths permanently and emphatically turned downwards; their stinking hair was matted with a viscous substance; they wore rotting hessian sacks that hung from their emaciated frames; not one made a noise, so deathly was their silence: and each exuded a festering air of ineffable despair. I looked downwards, on the table in front of me, was a sullied tin plate, and, on it, contained the most vile and despicable 'nutriment': weird insects, with many tiny hairy legs, crawled and slithered around, and gnawed on each other. The glum creatures at the table picked up the 'victuals', then, very slowly, began to mournfully eat. My face twisted in horror as I incredulously stared at them chewing this muck. Loud crunching noises ensued, as the insects' shells cracked between their rotting teeth. I began to feel nauseous, and could not refrain from vomiting across the table: to which I heard a demented cackling from somewhere. Suddenly, there was a long stream of yellow steaming liquid flowing from the ceiling that splashed onto the table, splattering over the plates. I gazed upwards to see an iron grate: and, stood on that grate, peering down at us, with the most scornful, distorted, and hideous physiognomies imaginable, was hate personified: mocking demons, glowering with malevolent satisfaction. They sneered, and began hocking up viscous phlegm, and expectorated large globules, which rained down, splattering all over: one hit my eye with such force that I was sure my eyeball had burst. Another defecated, which hit my plate, sending the contents all over my lap: a long-slimy-worm-thing wriggled from the faeces, squirmed around my waist, and began struggling to gain entry into my tunic: I leapt up, knocking the mess away with my lacerated hand: the hideous worm lodged itself into an open cut on my palm, and began sucking my life fluids: I tried to pull it out, for it was burying deeper: eventually, as it stretched ,and screamed disapproval, I managed to tear it free. I slung it as far away as possible. The demons, all the while, cackled with unabated and perverted pleasure. My unmitigated disgust induced profound introversion: I focused deep into my soul trying to mentally emancipate from this foul situation: but I was violently jolted back: for, inconspicuously resting on the plates, were barbed hooks attached to lines, which ran along the floor and up through the grate: the poor unsuspecting creatures at the table had swallowed the hooks, which then lodged deep into their entrails: the demons began gleefully pulling on the lines: and, in silent agony, the glum creatures were raised from their seats: eyes popped out of heads, legs erratically kicked, as they became suspended in the air: then, the demons gave the lines a sharp tug: the hooks ripped from the victims' insides, and, still attached to the barbs, were, remains of viscera. The glum damned creatures slumped on the floor, writhing in mute horror, as blood poured from their mouths … When 'meal time' was over, the creature in long grey robes appeared, and slowly walked over to me. It lifted its long gnarled finger to one of the many dreary apertures in the rock: then, walked towards it: I was compelled to follow. It ushered me through more dreary corridors. We walked deeper into the darkness: and the wailings of eternally tormented and lost souls satiated my heart with despair as we made our way along the dark subterranean passages. Then, the creature suddenly stopped in the darkness, and, so did I… It slowly raised its bony finger: and with severe attentiveness my gazing eyes followed the gnarled digits: it pointed into a most hideously lugubrious corridor which contained rows upon rows of thick solid iron bars that stretched into the depths of pitch black. I tried to see further down the passage way: but all I could see was a dolorous darkness stretching far into the stomach of the earth. I shuddered at the drab silence of that grim place: there was no end! An inveterate fear surfeited my soul. Far down the tunnel, in the drear stillness, I heard a murmur; the murmur turned into a hum; the hum turned into a drone: and, then, the drone turned into a buzzing, a buzzing which steadily increased in loudness until the whole cavern vibrated. It became intolerable: I had to put my hands over my ears: but still my head reverberated with the intense buzzing. Suddenly, we were engulfed in a dense black mist: a swarm of massive bluebottles. They attacked my eyes, intent on sucking the fluids dry: and so I had to close them tightly shut. I tried to swat them away, but when I did, my ears hurt with the reverberating noise: and so they landed all over my body, crawling, searching for sustenance. I stood like a statue, mortified. Then, beyond the manic buzzing from the thick cloud of stout flies, I distinctly heard a cell door clanking open: coming towards me, was the sound of ponderous footsteps dragging a heavy iron chain. I smelt the increasing foul putrescent stench of decay. My fear augmented. I squinted my insect assailed eyes, and tried to peer down the corridor to see what awful aberration was approaching. Out of the gloom, slowly dragging its iron fetters, appeared the silhouette of a colossal being, around 7ft tall, whose broad shoulders indicated immense strength. As it slowly approached, its figure became more distinct: the clanking iron chain was connected to a solid ring pierced through its cheek bone: and the two sockets in its cranium, where eyes should have been, were empty. The already foul atmosphere became increasingly oppressive: the ghastly convict exuded a profoundly dislodged psyche, bitter, twisted, angry, remorseless, wild, extremely dangerous, hate incarnate. I suddenly became overwhelmed with a powerful notion that its *raison d'être* was to kill me… Mortified, I stood motionless, fearfully anticipating its evil presence. It cumbersomely hauled itself to where we stood. As this creature of eternal perdition advanced, the flies nervously began retreating a little further down the corridor: and there, the large buzzing insect cloud, anxiously waited. I apprehensively lowered my hands from my ears, and cautiously opened my eyes to the full. From its grey robe, the usher produced a razor blade, and, carefully handed it to the homicidal prisoner who eagerly snatched the nasty weapon. The giant monster issued a distorted grin and rapidly lurched towards me. I stood petrified as it greedily sliced my face and chest. I could do nothing while it flayed my flesh with the razor sharp instrument. I felt no pain, only the horrifying awareness that my precious skin was being violated. Then, the chain connected to my remorseless assailant's cheek bone began to shorten and pull its cadaverous skull back towards the cell. In shock, I looked down to see gaping lacerations in my chest: then, I felt my face slowly peel open: a teeming stream of red fluid poured forth: I was standing in a large bloody puddle. The flies, with voracious rapidity, returned, and in a wild frenzy, tried to feed on vital fluids oozing from the open wounds, and the pool of gore on the floor. Some of the avaricious insects became trapped in the bloody puddle, their bloated bodies floating on the surface, kicking their tiny legs in a vain bid to extricate, and, finally, drowning. The grey robed creature, satisfied, then led me away, leaving the foul insects swarming around the blood that remained. My blood continued to pump from my wounds, which expunged some of the flies lodged in the cuts, and I plucked the others out, disgustedly flicking them away, plastering them on the catacomb walls. I slipped on my blood as I followed the usher down the dreary corridor, my mind engulfed in frenetic fear contemplating the next horror that awaited me. The moans and groans of the tormented and lost souls became more urgent now, and I felt my skin prickle as the ghoulish cries penetrated into my psyche. We eventually came to a ledge. Once again, the usher slowly raised its bony finger, pointed at me, then pointed downwards into the darkness of the pit. In profound trepidation, I stared over the side: there was a direct drop into an infinite black void. Absolute despair pervaded me, annihilating any vestiges of hope that could have possibly remained within. The creature then gave me a sharp push: I stumbled, and then fell, down-down-down, forever-down; I plummeted headlong into a pitch black abyss whilst simultaneously feeling my way once again through the gloomy subterranean tunnels I had before traversed; I was mortified by the sheer drop... falling rapidly downwards into the infernal darkness... suddenly stark fear induced acute awareness that somewhere below me was solid ground, and I was going to hit it with fatal force at any moment; I felt my way along the dark tunnel, for I knew, at the end of the tunnel, in the core of darkness, was my soul, fettered and assailed: I had to retrieve it in order to regain my humanity: I had to re-acquire my sensibility, or be cast in perpetual isolation and numbness, falling forever, and always profoundly anticipating the solid smack of ground: for, as I made my way along the dank dark tunnel, I was aware of my lack of empathy: I walked onwards, towards the dark core of the cave, for, there, was, my soul: in my emptiness, I pushed on forward, and blood gurgling primeval screams of the eternally tormented intensified, overwhelming me with shock waves of fear which oscillated through my marrow as I plummeted deeper and deeper into the pitch dark abyss... then, the tunnel opened into an antechamber... there... I saw... the most odious aberration... my head, with the most abysmal and woebegone expression roughly sewn onto an ashen cadaver, mournfully dragging along, with other forgotten souls: and, on my forehead, was scorched the word, 'DISEASE'!

17.

The Volant

I tempestuously awoke, and alarmingly heard the distinctive sound of a bluebottle buzzing out of my ear: but when I searched around, the odious little creature was gone...

I nervously gazed around: mercifully, I was in the cockpit! The vast bright cobalt ether above was shining on my beautiful Helena! Then, in an instant, I eidetically recalled every moment of the dream and panic pervaded; severe abreaction ensued: I felt the blood rush from my face, and my soul began to drain through my feet: I instinctively clung to Helena. 'Gorky! What's wrong? You gave me such a start!' she protested. Barney laughed, as I kissed her sweet head over and over again. 'Gorky! I'm trying to keep the plane in the air. Let me pedal!' I could not stop. I clung to her, kissing her passionately, making Barney laugh even more. 'Gorky! For God's sake! What's wrong with you!?' Helena stood up in the cockpit, and with one less pedalling, and the sudden alteration in aerodynamics, the plane veered and plummeted. My stomach suddenly exited my mouth, and quickly brought me to my senses. I began to furiously pedal in order to compensate for the sudden lack of power. Helena sat back in her seat. The plane levelled and began to fly parallel to the ground. Helena stared at me reproachfully. 'What got into you, Gorky?' she demanded.

'I've just had a dreadful nightmare, lucid, real,' I blurted.

'It was just a dream, Gorky!' she scolded.

'Some dream!' Barney sniggered.

'We've *got* to get to The Forest of Life,' I manically urged.

'That's where we're heading, old boy,' Argon merrily replied.

'Do we have Sacradia?' I earnestly asked. The others looked quizzically at each other. I anxiously turned round to check the urn, unscrewed the lid, there was the miraculous water glistening in the sunlight.

'Are you okay?' Helena inquired.

'Are you?' I replied. She looked at me accusingly again, turned round, and began to resume pedalling. So I sat still, staring at her heavenly silky hair that tumbled and flew in the sky breeze, allowing tresses to stroke my finger tips: but not daring to let her feel my touch, for fear of repulsion. Yes, I gazed at sweet Helena, innocuous, gentle, sensitive, friendly, moral, and divine.

We flew onwards. I perceived the desert differently now. I breathed the warm fresh air deep into my lungs, and it was an elixir for my soul; the wind sang a celestial tune, and the blissful harmonies exalted my spirit; the sunlight, bright golden yellow, suffused my mind with the pleasant fragrances of life: I stared outwards with wide eyes, eagerly drinking in the natural environment, utterly relieved that it still existed. Below, the sand glistened golden in the bright sunlight. I had an overwhelming feeling of gratitude that its beauty was permanent.

'What is that, ahead, there, hovering in the sky?' Jenny pointed forwards, towards a violet amorphous fleck in the distance that was moving independent of the wind. It veered casually from side to side, and seemed to be imbued with sentient life. At first, I was unsure if it was coming towards us, or moving away: but, as we flew onwards, the nebula discernibly grew. The violet nebulous haze slowly metamorphosed into a more distinctive shape. It had wings, for I could see them flapping. The violet transformed into multi-colours, yes, iridescent feathers shimmered in the sun light and totally covered its bulk. As it came closer, the sheer size became more apparent: and I felt a distinct pang of fear in my stomach, for this air-borne creature far exceeded the size of our craft. We became transfixed on this peculiar phenomenon approaching us: but could not descry a face, and so could not ascertain if it was belligerent: but its size suggested we would be completely at its mercy if it was hostile.

'What is that thing?' I asked to anyone.

'I don't know, but I don't think we should take any chances,' Kelly replied.

'I agree. I think we should take evasive manoeuvres, try circumvent it,' I quickly decided.

'Good idea,' Kelly concurred. So we did, we altered our course to avoid this un-identified volant: but it altered its course in accordance: we veered to the left; it veered to the left: we veered to the right; it veered to the right: interception seemed imminent.

'It seems to be tracking us,' Jenny said. Suddenly it sped towards us at such speed that it made our own craft pedestrian in comparison: it was on us before we could blink. It hovered above us, blotting out the sky: we feebly craned our heads upwards in its shade, trying to discern a face. Our craft was buffeted about from the back draft of its wings: Argon wrestled with the controls to hold us steady. Its iridescent feathers glistened, and if it had not been for its intimidating presence eliciting anxiety, I would have admired the creature's splendour. I scanned its bulk in order to make eye contact. Barney had other ideas, and reached for an axe: he lifted it above his head, and slung it at the great mass of rainbow feathers: it harmlessly bounced off, recoiled back into the cockpit, and sliced into Barney's instep: he yelled in dire agony. I quickly looked at his severed foot: it lay lifeless on the cockpit floor: it had cleanly detached from his leg, which was now oozing blood all over the plane. Jenny quickly ripped a strip from her skirt and tightly wrapped the stump in order to staunch the flow. The creature emitted a loud 'SQUAWK!' and I fearfully stared upwards: I then saw a refulgent yellow beak: either side of this, two large shinning black orbs encrusted in the multi-coloured feathers; two gleaming penetrating eyes were gazing down at us.

'My, my, 'tis strange, to say the least, aye, strange, a flying creature with six heads and twelve beady little eyes, aye, and no feathers, nay. Aye, most strange. Does it speak? Aye, does it? Ask it, aye, ask then. Does it speak then?' the peculiar creature said in dialogue with itself. We all looked on mortified: but I knew one of us must speak lest it take any more offence.

'We are people,' I said. 'We are flying to The Forest of Life… to help the tribes.' I thought, by adding the latter part, we would show our peaceful intent.

'People? It just said, people. Aye, I heard it, aye, people right enough. It's going to The Forest of Life. Aye, I heard that also. Ask it where it has been from. Should I? Aye, ask it then. Where has it been from?'

'We have travelled from Firkin Forest, and lost our way: we had to land in a marsh: but we managed to rally ourselves, and make our way onwards,' I shouted upwards to its towering head above.

'It said people, aye, people is what it said, people, people… People! I know people! Aye, I know people as well, bloody, violent, and strange, aye, that's people, so it is. Ask it why it threw an object at us. No. Go on, ask it, aye, go on… Why did you throw an object at us?' Its massive wings moved through the air with ease, hovering before us: it was obvious the sky was its home, so ensconced in the air it sat. We nervously pedalled onwards, completely at its mercy.

'We thought you were going to attack us. You moved towards us so rapidly without warning,' I said. Jenny had finished binding Barney's leg: and there she sat, gazing in turn, at the bloody stump, then the motionless foot on the floor of the cockpit. The rest of us were staring upwards at the awesome sight of this imposing creature.

'It said it thought we were going to attack it. Aye, it did. I was not going to hurt it. Nay, nor me. Tell it that we were not going to hurt it, aye, tell it then. You tell it, I told it last time. Should I? Aye, and tell it… What? Tell it, it should not have tried to hurt us. Should I? Aye, go on. I was not going to hurt it. And it should not have tried to hurt us.'

'We are sorry. It was a terrible mistake,' I shouted.

'It said it was a terrible mistake. Aye, I heard it. Shall we hurt it back? I don't know. Should I ask it. What? Ask it if it wants to be hurt back. Shall I? Aye, go on. Does it want us to hurt it back?'

'No!' I implored. I looked at Barney, who was visibly growing more pallid and faint. 'We have already been hurt back.'

'Did you hear that? Aye, I did. It said it has already been hurt back. What shall I say? Say, it was not you that hurt it, but it that hurt itself. Shall I. Aye, go on. It was *people* that hurt itself.'

'Er, yes, and we wish not to be hurt anymore,' I shouted.

'It said. I know what it said. Aye. It does not like being hurt, but it does not mind hurting us. What shall I say? Play a game with it. A game? Aye, a game. Why? So that if it loses, you can hurt it back, and if it wins, you can go far away from it, into the big sky. You win either way. What type of game? It said it's been to the marsh. Aye, it did. Ask it, if it gives you some marsh grass, it can pass. Shall I? Aye, go on. If it gives me some marsh grass, it can pass.'

We desperately searched around the cockpit for marsh grass but none could be found.

'Can anyone see marsh grass?' I turned to the others, and they looked blankly at me while searching about their person (apart from Barney and Jenny, who were totally involved in their plight). I fumbled around my clothing, and looked at the soles of my shoes. Argon, leaped up, and began search through the blood on the floor of the cockpit for a single blade of grass that would allow us to freely pass. Despair mounted as we scoured the plane.

'There!' Helena exclaimed, and pointed to the tale of the craft: attached to the rudder, was a single blade of marsh grass. 'There!' she shouted at the creature. The creature flew around to the rear of the craft, and just as it located the blade, the grass detached, fluttered in the air, hovered for a short while, and then descended to the hot desert sand. With incredible dexterity and effortless speed it flew in front of the slow plodding plane as we furiously pedalled to keep it steady. The creature deeply scrutinized us, as we returned its penetrating gaze with deference.

'What shall we do? What do you think? I don't know...' it said.

'You said, if we had some marsh grass, we could go free,' Helena boldly but courteously reminded.

'Did we? Yes we did.' It hovered for a moment more, blinked at us, then accelerated like light. Whoosh! Gone.

'Get some of Sacradia on that foot. Now!' Argon shouted at Jenny, who was overcome with despair. His bellowing voice snapped her out of it, and she went diving towards the urn. She returned with a ladle full of the magic healing water, and stared down at the injury. She then picked up the gory foot, unwrapped the leg, and pushed the foot against the stump. She then poured Sacradia over the wound: it began to hiss, and suddenly the cockpit became engulfed in a tremendous orange cloud of smoke which totally obscured our view: but, in a little while, the rushing wind cleared the cockpit. We all eagerly stared down at Barney's foot: it was perfectly knitted back on to his leg without the slightest scar. He smiled and wriggled his toes.

'Onwards, then, to The Forest of Life,' he cheerfully said.

18.

Hot Under the Collar

Our plane boldly pushed on through the xeric desert air. The craft was notably more manageable and easier to propel when the imposing presence of that giant creature vanished. Once it had gone, I realized I could have asked it if we were going in the right direction: but, on second thoughts, I deemed we were lucky to escape unscathed.

On we flew, and the heat increasingly became more stifling. Barney, who was sat next to me in the cockpit, spread his elbows out like a bird in flight squashing me against the hull: my elbows were pushed into my ribs as I tried to make myself as small as possible: the smaller I made myself, the more space he took up, until I felt hemmed in, unable to move my upper body. As the sun burnt down, I became more irritable. 'For God's sake, Barney, give me some room!'

'It's you that's taking up all the room!' he vehemently retorted, flexing his blacksmith's arms outwards and invading my space.

'Me?! I can't move. I'm squashed in. Look at your elbows,' I rejoined, glaring at him, trying to push back.

'Look at your elbows,' he angrily replied, pushing his arms out further, and crushing me against the hot aluminium hull. I felt a surge of fury, and, pushed my elbows out with all my might. So, there we were, in a test of strength, pushing our arms against each other, both gradually becoming increasingly irked.

He had the powerful arms of a blacksmith, and it took me all my strength and guile to counter his shove: I felt my strength begin to wane, and became frustrated and furious: I jumped up, and leapt upon him, pinning his shoulders into the seat with my full body weight.

'You ignoramus!' I yelled.

'Aaarrrggghhh!' Barney became wild eyed fury: with a swift forward thrust of his arms, he pushed me up and out of the cockpit: against all my instincts, I found myself being lifted from the safety of the plane and hanging over the side: then, he let go: I fell downwards, and thought I was going to ascend to my doom: adrenalin surged through my body as I resigned to the imminent drop: my hands desperately flailed for anything solid to grasp as I plummeted: I found myself clung to the side of the cockpit by my aching finger tips: in his blind rage, he started to unhook my urgent clasp, and, in stark fear, I prepared to descend rapidly to my death: but Argon grabbed Barney's broad shoulders: both went flailing backwards landing heavily onto Helena, who had to stop pedalling with the impact. Kelly and Jenny, with every ounce of energy, pedalled amidst the wrestling, as the plane veered from side to side. I tried to haul myself back, but every time I managed to hook my leg over, the plane violently swung, and I lost my footing. The craft was quickly losing altitude, and soon the under carriage skimmed over the sand dunes. My fingers burnt, and so excruciating was the pain in my stretching and strained digits, that I began to consider relinquishing my grasp: although we were flying along quite fast, I deemed, as I was close to the ground, landing in the sand and surviving with minimum damage was possible.

'Calm down, Barney!' Argon cried. I had been quickly brought to my senses: but Barney and Argon still wrestled. Helena was lost somewhere underneath them, as Argon held onto the writhing bull-bulk of a blacksmith's ire. Barney slowly regained his senses as he realized the impending doom if he did not sit down and steady the craft: which he eventually did, and began furiously pedalling, ignoring me hanging on next to him. Argon hauled me on board, and I quickly resumed my position, a little shaken by the debacle. Before long we were all frenetically pedalling. The plane began to ascend again and steady its course. Barney still took up more room than I would have liked: but it was preferable to crashing in the desert. I sulkily sat there, impatient to reach The Forest of Life, so I could alight the cockpit and acquire my own space. I took my frustration out on the pedals, pushing and pulling hard in a cyclic motion, as the wings pushed and pulled against the hot desert air.

We flew deeper into the desert, and the heat steadily increased. The only consolation was that we did not encounter the marsh or The Dead Forest again, which gave us a pseudo-feeling of progression. However, when the last of the marsh water had been drunk, a tincture of despair crept in: the desert seemed to exponentially expand. I became uncertain that we could reach The Forest of Life before our condition became critical. Nevertheless, I did not want to waste any more of Sacradia: it was imperative that I ensured there would be enough for the stricken tribes: but Barney was eager to drink some more. 'We need to drink,' Barney asseverated. 'We need to prevent sickness: this blasted heat can imperceptibly affect you… before it's too late… you're enervated and terribly ill.'

'How is everybody feeling?' I asked. Nobody answered. 'Kelly, do you need any water?' She looked at Argon, and did not say a word. 'Jenny, how are you?' I inquired. She ignored me, and continued to peddle. 'Helena?' She stared straight ahead, apparently oblivious to my question. I turned to the scowling Barney, and said, 'We are always dipping into the water: there will be none left for the tribes.'

'There will be none left for the tribes if we crash into the desert through heat exhaustion,' Barney angrily replied, flexing his biceps, and pinning me to the side once more: my fury switched on, for I hated his body squashing me, and was going to elbow him in the face, but quickly remembered the consequences of last time.

'I feel okay,' I said, containing my anger. 'Helena, how are you?' She sighed, and began to pedal all the more harder. 'Helena, how are you?!' She took a deep breath, hesitated, then braced herself.

'How do I feel?' She replied.

'Yes,' I answered.

'Like I wish I had never set foot out of Firkin! We are lost in the desert, aimlessly pushing onwards without sign of end. The heat is unbearable, and I'm beginning to feel sick.'

'Me too,' said Kelly.

'Er, mmm, I don't feel too good either,' said Argon.

'See?!' Barney victoriously exclaimed. With that, he leapt up, turned to the urn, unscrewed the lid, dipped in a ladle, and fed some water to each of the crew: but, tantalizingly, allowed it to pass my head: then, he threw the ladle in the back of the plane, screwed down the lid, without offering any of the magical alchemical water to me. My eyes, burning with indignation, nearly popped out of my head: I silently fumed, while he smirked. My heart thumped against my chest. I wanted to resume our fight: and even though everyone had visibly perked up, there was no way I was going to demean myself by drinking some of the water. Helena tutted, pushed past me, retrieved the ladle, dipped it into the urn, and held it in front of my mouth. Barney continued to smirk, waiting for the triumphant moment when I took a sip. I malevolently glared at him, and then looked innocently at Helena.

'Oh drink some, you big baby,' Helena impatiently declared, and pushed the ladle to my mouth. Barney raised his eyebrows, enjoying every moment: I sulkily gazed at my woman. She tried tipping it into my mouth, but I sealed it shut, so the cool delicious water dripped down my chin: it hissed and bubbled on the cockpit's floor: and Barney laughed hysterically. Helena emitted a sigh of exasperation, and resumed her seat.

'Mmm, how soothing the water was, how sweet. Did you notice how magically cold it stays?' Barney asked, to no one in particular. 'I have a sudden incredible feeling of well-being: indeed, the magic water acts as a shield against the heat: yes, the cockpit is discernibly cooler, and I feel s-o g-o-o-d! I did not realize how effected I was with the intense desert heat, the heat, that is so... very... very... hot.' With that, I leapt up, manically searched for the ladle, and took my share of the liquid.

The craft pushed forward with added vigour, sliding through the aridity with renewed purpose. Despite the wondrous effects of the mystical water, it was still insufferably hot sat in that small cockpit, and, after a while, the repetitive and monotonous thrumming of the wings began to have an hypnotic effect: I gradually and imperceptibly fell into a self-induced trance: I detached from heart-beat and lungs. I soared above the plane as if I had wings: I tracked it, following the crew, peering at the tops of their heads. I saw myself sat in the cockpit: I was bewildered to see myself looking so forlorn and vulnerable: I was sat there wistfully gazing at Helena's long shining beautiful hair that was dancing with a hot desert zephyr. In comparison to the vast desert, we all looked so small and insignificant; I was surprised to see how puny we were. The small aluminium craft shone like a tiny mirror, and I descried, in its reflection, a spiralling swirling black and white disc, like cream poured in stirred coffee, which was spinning around a central axis: my psyche! The shock at seeing my entity in its fundamental state jolted me back into the plane. My eyes burst open, and I clung to the hull, fearful, lest I transmigrated again. I gazed at the back of Helena's head, as her flying glossy hair lightly brushed tears away from my cheeks.

I sat there, patiently waiting for my turn to pedal, concentrating on maintaining my attention in the stifling aluminium cockpit. There was nothing to do but stare out at the desert, and I began reminiscing about the long arduous journey I had previously encountered on foot. I recalled each footstep, the yielding sand, how it got in every crevice; the heat, how it mercilessly burnt my frail skin: I starkly recollected the sheer vulnerability of a human body... There was no escape... I wanted so much for it to end... My soul grovelled and begged: but the desert ignored my supplications... I am dying.

The desert is a lonely place.
You can travel for miles and miles
And never see a friendly face,
Never see a smile.
All you can see is a sea of sand,
And no one will lend you a helping hand.

Crawl over the sand,
Take a long hike,
There's nothing you can do to deter
The sun's piercing rays of hot spikes.

You desperately gaze around,
But there's nothing in the desert,
And your gasping breath is the only sound.

And you walk and walk and talk to yourself,
And only yourself answers back,
I am lonely,
This is crazy,
Where is the beaten track?

And you walk and walk,
And your body aches,
And you start to feel unwell,
And your feeble body talks
To you,
Why have you brought me to this hell?

And you know if you stop,
It's certain you'll die,
And your blistered skin pops,
And your body complains when you try
To walk.
And you're surprised at the meagre strength flesh has got,
But your spirit cries, never baulk from the effort,
Or you will lay prostrate in the scorching desert,
And your carcass will rot.

And the desert is big…
And the desert is wide…
And it takes all the determination you have inside
To pull your heavy limbs along,
And to maintain morale,
And to keep you strong.
So you sing a song,
But the words fry in the desert heat,
And the skin peels from your feet,
And you yearn to see a friendly greeting,
Or something of that kind.

Nothing but sand in front…
Nothing but sand behind…
Nothing but the scorching sun,
Upon your head it dines.

Walking, walking, into the shimmering heat,
And your body oscillates
In accordance with the waves that rise from the sand,
And your spirit dissipates,
And your faculties lose command.
Walking, walking, through the desert sand,
You're delirious, you laugh,
And believe you see an oasis,
Where you can have a cool bath.
And you walk and walk to find it,
The place where it appeared,
But as you drag your body along,
You realize it's not there.

And you ask yourself, why
Did you come into the desert to die,
Traipsing all alone,
When instead of hearing your gasping breath,
You could be hearing your woman's heavenly sigh, her sweet moan,
Wrapped around her, safe at home.

But you have committed yourself
To face the challenge,
And now there is no turning back,
But still you wish you hadn't,
As you sink into the sand,
And leave no tracks...

The desert is unforgiving,
So anyone who tries
To defeat the expansive tract,
You'll realise what you lack,
For the desert's magnificent beauty belies
The harshness,

And once you step inside,
No matter how much you ask the desert for mercy,
You fry…

'Gorky, it's your turn to pedal,' Helena entreated. My glazed eyes began to focus: Helena was looking quite fatigued. She was in urgent need of a rest, so I eagerly took over. I was pleased to be alive: and on my stint I worked with much exuberance: until Argon advised, 'Steady old boy, pace yourself.' I tried to curb my effort, but my soul was so replete with the relief that the hellish dream had been extricated, that it took continual conscious control to hold back. I began to feel optimistic. 'The Forest of Life is up ahead,' I proclaimed. 'We will be there soon. You will smell the verdure, and taste the sweet thirst-quenching citrus fruits. You will relax in the cool shade of the beautiful trees. Your life forces will be replenished. You will acquire new resolve and depth of experience.' Barney bit his lip, and looked most irked, and scowled at Jenny, who returned his glare with mild eyes in order to appease him; Kelly gave a sheepish smile to Argon, and he shrugged his shoulders; and Helena, stared trance-like, far into the desert sky, imbued with profound life, but elsewhere. I was aware that I had not impressed them with my speech intending to encourage: so I decided to maintain diffidence, and concentrate only on pedalling: I focused on the task at hand. I wanted so badly to reach the life giving forest, so this terrible phase of the journey could be over for all of us, and so we could start the humanitarian operation…

We pedalled onwards, into the hot desert sun, all the time anticipating some sort of sign on the horizon. Barney became increasingly fidgety, until he could refrain no longer. 'I think we should make a 180 degree turn and make for home.'

'We could be nearly there,' I said.

'"Could be"? We *are* in the middle of nowhere,' he replied, 'and the more we pedal, the more in the middle of nowhere we go.'

'It can't be long now,' I affirmed. 'Just hang on.' There was no question of me turning back: my conscience was simmering, and the only palliative was to actively seek the tribes. 'Take some more of Sacradia if you want,' I nonchalantly said.

'That bleedin' water is not going to change our position: and the position is this, we are pedalling like lunatics in a little metallic vessel, slowly cooking, and getting nowhere.'

'The "little metallic vessel",' I replied, 'was your pride and joy before we left the village.'

'It's going to be our tin coffin!' he scowled. 'And I'm sick of sat in it listening to your silly optimism, and while you take up all the room: move up!'

'It's you who takes up all the room,' I fulminated.

'Listen you two,' Jenny interjected, 'bickering is not going to change a thing: and I am too hot to listen to your whiny voices piercing through me.'

'I don't whine!' Barney remonstrated.

'Let's all be quiet,' Argon requested.

'I was being quiet,' I replied, 'until he started.'

'I did not start,' Barney complained.

'You did,' I rejoined. 'You're always moaning. "We should go back. We should go back."'

'It's the common sense thing to do,' Barney growled, beginning to inflate his chest.

'After we've come all this way?' I scorned. 'You call that common sense?'

'Oh, give it a rest!' Barney yelled, restraining himself in his seat.

'No! You give it a rest!' I screamed.

'Both of you give it a rest!' Kelly impatiently said. 'Jenny's right, it's too hot to argue. We have a simple choice, go on, or turn back: let's have a vote.'

'A vote?!' I shouted, wanting to argue, but quickly realizing that the suggestion rendered nothing to argue about: and so we took a vote… and it was three against three: and I could feel a heated debate about to erupt, when I smelt the most amazing and welcoming thing: blossom! 'Can you smell that?' I jubilantly asked.

'That's it, I'm going to hit him,' Barney roared, jumping from his seat.

'No! Look ahead!' I desperately screamed, in order to evade a massive blacksmith crashing down on me. Barney's eyes were roaring fire: but a cawing crow compelled him to look into the firmament: and, it instantly defused him. The air became pervaded with the fresh smell of flowers and lush vegetation: the aroma of citrus enlivened our palettes. Barney, appeased, sat down. Suddenly, a long line of green appeared on the horizon, a grand, imposing, majestic sylvan impressed on the welkin. My heart swelled in exultation: I triumphantly and lovingly kissed Helena's hair: she did not turn round, but quietly kept on pedalling… There was a distinctive sense of relief in the cockpit: tenseness dissipated; the crew began to smile, relax, and speak of what they would do when on the ground. Then, we began to discuss landing procedures…

We circled around the margin of The Forest of Life, and descried a strip of grass: it meant bringing the wing tips perilously close to the crown of trees: and, once descending past them, bringing the wing tips ominously contiguous with the trunks, as the under carriage searched for the ground. Argon dextrously manoeuvred the craft over the grassy margin, and then said, 'Okay, stop pedalling.' The three team members immediately ceased their efforts: and the aluminium wings ceased their flapping and stretched outwards, still. We could hear the wind zipping past more plainly now as we began steadily gliding downwards towards the ground. We smoothly descended until we could distinctively make out individual leaves on the trees: then, the hard aluminium wing tip brushed through them, and leaves bristled with verdant vigour. As the wing disappeared further into the crowns, small twigs and branches began violently cracking and snapping. The plane began jerking about, and a sudden look of consternation swept over the crew as the cockpit became filled with various types of citrus fruits and nuts. We continued to descend, and there was a sigh of relief once lowered past the threatening branches. With eyes earnestly fixed on the wing tip nearest the trunks, Argon slightly trimmed the rudder, and, carefully edged the plane inwards. Then, his head began erratically oscillating between the trees and up ahead. He slightly trimmed the flaps in order to lower the wheels onto terra-firma.

Suddenly, we hit the ground with a startling, BUMP! We continued to uncontrollably zip forward, buffeting around, bouncing out of our seats, and heavily landing back into them. The plane wiggled and squirmed, as if protesting it had been pulled out of the air and unceremoniously dumped onto the ground: but Argon would have none of it, and firmly held the craft in a straight line. We fought to stay in our seats, waiting for friction to abate inertia. Up ahead, the grassy margin stretched as far as the eyes could see, so there was no danger of colliding with anything.

The plane eventually mitigated its struggle, and came to a safe halt. Its aluminium hull ceased vibrating, and we sat motionless on the ground. The stillness was an awesome religious experience. We sat quietly for a few moments, savouring the silence, assimilating the change of atmosphere, beginning to realize we had safely landed... Then, Argon turned to hug Kelly; Barney turned to embrace Jenny: and I gazed at the back of Helena's head... As I watched the two couples feed on each other's love, I squirmed in my seat, not knowing what to do. Helena sat still, staring at the forest, totally detached.

After the tender displays were over, we realized that the cockpit was now like a basket full of nature's harvest: so, I joined in with the others, and we stripped the branches of the edibles. It was a relief to alight the stifling cockpit and stand on the soft grass stretching our aching legs. Then, courtesy of The Forest of Life's providence, we sat there, picnicking, eating the ripe delicious fruits, and cracking nuts with the blunt side of the axes, replenishing ourselves. It was indeed a wholesome repast. The mood of the crew had totally transformed, and we avidly discussed the preceding journey. There were many congratulations and hardy handshakes: but gradually the realization that the journey was far from over began to dawn.

I had a strong compulsion to go ahead and find the tribes: but, it was eventually agreed we should spread out, and spend a little time with our partners, relaxing in the cool shade of the trees. The desert crossing had been a most arduous ordeal and it was expedient to make a good recovery. I vividly remembered certain ordeals of the first quest on my own, and earnestly informed my comrades- not entirely truthfully- that, although I did not encounter any real dangers, it was necessary that no one strayed too deep into the forest, and that it was paramount to remain near the margin, with the plane well in view. I still baulked from mentioning The Rubber Clad Dryads, or my recollections of the weird sounds mysteriously emanating from deep in the forest. I did not want to cause anxiety, or reluctance from my companions to seek the stricken tribes: and I figured we would all be safe if we took these precautions. We decided that when we had rested, to meet back at the plane to plan our next move.

19.

Paranoia

Helena walked purposefully towards the shade at the edge of the forest; I sauntered behind her. She then stopped, and looked up at the branches of the nearest tree: it was a large citrus tree decked in glowing mandarins: she emitted a little hum of approval. Although I felt frustrated that she was not acknowledging me, I had a glowing pride, like I had grown the forest myself, as she perused the prolific fructuous fertility of The Forest of Life. She looked up at large golden orbs, which were tantalizingly shining in the benign sun: she reached up on tip toes, stretching her voluptuous body upwards, and casually plucked a large nectariferous apricot: she closely examined it trying to conceal a little smile. She then looked at her feet, pulled a large water melon from the ground, and began peeling the rind: as she ripped the pith away, the juices sprayed over her cleavage. She voraciously gazed down at the fruit, totally absorbed in the process. Then, with glowing eyes, she licked her lips, and zestfully bit into the shinning flesh: the sweet juices dribbled down her chin, as her eyes shone with pleasure. By this time, I had walked to the foot of the tree, laid down, waiting for her to finish eating, and ensconce her curvaceous body next to mine: but, much to my disappointment, she settled under a neighbouring tree, and peered out to the desert: my heart burnt with despair. 'Are you angry with me?' I eventually asked, as she gazed out to the hot shimmering horizon in a trance. She seemed to be lost in her musings, and I was reluctant to disturb her: so, I just watched her, realizing how wretched I had been on my previous lone venture. Even though Helena was seemingly absent in mind, her beautiful body was indubitably nearby: and her glorious presence augmented The Forest of Life's splendour: the trees seemed a more vivid green than before, and the air was filled with magic. I stared out to the vast desert plain, trying to share with her what she saw: her presence rendered the desert less foreboding, less forlorn: everything shone a refulgent gold. But, it was no use, though she was in my constant view, a pang in my heart told me my lady was distant: and, try as I may, the verdure of the forest began to fade, and the desert became an inhospitable fire breathing monster again. I recalled how forsaken I had been in the desert on my own, and how it was my love for Helena that drove me onwards. I tried to surmise that which was possibly ailing her: maybe the ordeals during our journey had taken their toll, and she needed a little space to recuperate: so, I decided not to impose myself, but waited to see how she would eventually respond: but, frustratingly, she did not, she just stared into the desert, never saying anything, or even moving. After a while, despair welled in the pit of my stomach, for I could acutely feel her apathy: she had shut herself off from me, retreated into her shell, and extirpated all emotions: my zeal sank as the desert became even more barren. 'Helena, are you okay?' I solicitously inquired.

'Yes,' she replied in monotone: and I felt my loneliness increase. I wanted to say something else, to make conversation, to bridge the gap: but I could not think of anything, for it would have been artificial and forced. I was worried my voice irked her: I shrank inside my frame. I felt greatly troubled as I closed my eyes and tried to rest...

I was an atom in a void, a minute particle floating in vast space: the space was surfeit with destitution, and I was sensitive to it all: I was overwhelmed with the pain of isolation: I was so very tiny, and yet aware of a great desolation: I aimlessly floated in this void aware of eternal solitude: the pain became insupportable, and I emitted a massive primordial scream of anguish…

I awoke to find Helena not there! I manically stared at where she had been resting: an empty space. The air was redolent with her potent vibes. Glum and pathetic, I gazed at the consecrated place she had visited. It was unlike her to vanish while I was asleep, without either, prior informing were she would be going, or, leaving me a message. Total recollection of my previous lone journey flooded back: and gnawing anxiety that she may have died of the disease assailed my spirit. Pain and fear irrevocably lodged in my heart: the notion of losing my lady induced my soul to contort in horror; I felt my soul contract in its frame, and an enervation take over my body. Pull yourself together, Gorky: for, if she saw you grow weak and so obviously dependent on her, it would further repulse her. In desperation, I gazed towards the aircraft: she was there! My despair assuaged as I saw Helena animatedly chatting with the other women: but then, envy mocked me: why was she looking so at ease with them, relaxed and obviously enjoying their company, but behaved so awkwardly with me? I was so looking forward to our first tete-a-tete in the forest, that I was overcome with disappointment. Her aloofness meant it had been a complete disaster. I walked up to the craft, trying to be composed and insouciant: but, inside, I felt feeble: I was unwanted, vile, and imposing. I took quick glances at Helena: but knew my profound supplicatory gaze repelled her more. 'Enjoy the rest?' I asked to know one in particular: and my voice sounded alien to me, weak and pathetic.

'What's the plan?' Kelly inquired, very confidently. I was being rebuked as a nuisance. I looked at Kelly sheepishly, and was reluctant to reply lest my voice offended her: but then I deemed if I did not speak, I would also offend her. I apologetically stared at Helena, though I could not figure out what I had done. They all looked expectantly at me: I stared at the ground and nervously shuffled my toes over the grass.

'Gorky,' Jenny said, 'where do we go from here?' Her voice sounded piercing, and by the tone, I felt castigated. I slowly looked up, conveyed a conciliatory sickly smile, and began to gently rock my shoulders.

'Gorky, where are the tribes?' Argon impatiently inquired. I was an outcast, exiled from my own people, banished onto the margins of society: it would take a long time to once more become integrated. I had to speak, and fast: I had to sound normal: I had to portray myself like a person would. Take a chance, speak, Gorky.

'Er, I think I have an idea where I first saw them... mmm... let's locate them first... then we can, er... bring them to the plane... for, mmm... er... treatment.' I thought I pulled it off: I sounded convincing, like there was nothing wrong: yes, it was coherent: it made sense. I stood there; they waited: and there ensued a long embarrassing silence... Barney looked quizzically at Jenny, she gave a faint smile and shrugged her shoulders in return; Kelly imploringly stared at Argon to say something.

'So, er, Gorky old boy, do you think you could lead the way?' he finally asked. Was this a trap? I would be in front, so they could make disparaging gestures behind my back. I looked at him, as if to say, why are you doing this to me.

'Gorky,' Barney imperiously said, and I quickly turned to him, on my guard against his sudden voice, 'today would help.' Sarcasm, I knew it, that confirmed it, but I had to remain calm.

'Er, right... well... mmm... er... this way,' I said with false aplomb. I slowly walked forward, not taking my eyes from any of them, my guts filled with rocks. I looked at Helena, but not too long, for when I did, I felt about to die. I ambled onwards: and then, a hefty blow: someone tutted; my eyes burst open in stark horror: I *was* the carbuncle of the crew.

'Gorky!' Barney growled: I quickly span round, my eyes alert, ready for anything. 'Aren't you forgetting something?' He threw an axe to me: I leapt out the way, tripping and falling, as the axe head stuck in the ground next to me. There I laid, sprawled on my back: they all stared down at me: but I did not return their glare: I focused on the axe. Had Barney tried to cut me with it? Then, I thought of the whole point of our journey, and my motivation returned: thus, deemed it inappropriate to carry this intimidating implement whilst searching for the tribes.

'This is a humanitarian mission: I will not be needing that,' I stated, my indignation offering ephemeral confidence: but quickly feeling the despair of ostracism creep back. I picked myself up, and continued walking into the forest.

'Speak for yourself,' Barney replied, 'for you were most unconvincing when trying to assure us this forest is safe: and, considering our conflicts in the marsh, I will feel unprotected without the axe.' He picked up the axe lying on the floor, and handed it to Jenny, who, initially, was unsure whether to take it: but Barney forced the thing into her hands.

And so we cautiously walked into the forest, the crew behind me: Argon holding his appropriated mace, Barney and Kelly (Jenny had hurriedly handed it to her, and Barney could not be bothered to protest) holding the axes. The radiant sun shone through the dappled translucent leaves: the air was humid, but comfortable. As we walked deeper into the forest, I cogitated over what could be bothering Helena. Although her eyes shone an incredible intensity after her ordeals at the marsh, on the whole, she seemed okay, and directly after our escape from the Ophions and Asuras she was most tender towards me: but, that may have been because of the initial relief at being re-united. She could now be suffering the aftermath, a post-traumatic stress. Then, a horrific thought prevailed: she may have only told me a version of her plight: what if she had deliberately omitted crucial details: for instance, that her body had been vulgarly molested. The notion was too horrible to contemplate: and yet, the increasing worry grew like a canker in my mind. How was I to ask her? Should I ask her? No, it could wait. Let us concentrate on the task at hand. I was here to cure the tribes. They were here somewhere, and most likely suffering terribly from the iniquitous disease, in desperate need of a remedy. We continued to walk further into the verdant forest: but, it was no use, Helena was keeping a dark secret from me, something that alienated her from me; something that created a gulf between us: something, Helena, that had hurt you so much, you were unable to speak of it. My mind raced, trying to imagine the vile ordeals she had endured with those despicable barbarians, wracking my brain in order to re-live her conceivable encounter. I deemed, if I could envisage what she had gone through, I could share it, and alleviate her misery: but, although I re-played possibilities over and over again, I knew I could never experience what it would have really been like. I walked on, deep in reverie, oblivious to my surroundings, but managing to automatically negotiate any physical obstacle.

Suddenly, we came into a clearing, and the change of terrain brought me into the present. It was familiar: it was where I had seen the Pooh-Poohs chanting in a circle. Yes, definitely: this was the place. I recalled my first encounter with them, the repetitive noise of the ceremony, which made me increasingly irked: and how I had been further annoyed when they so disdainfully rebuffed me. Now, because of the passage of time, I regarded them differently: I surmised that their uncooperative behaviour could have been because of the manner of my address, for, although I chose the appropriate words, my facial expression and tone of voice suggested irritability at having to wait so long for them to complete their ritual: and, hence, they reciprocated by treating me as if I was nuisance. I stood in the middle of the coppice. 'Here,' I said, 'here was the place where I met the first tribe, the Pooh-Pooh: they were sat in a circle chanting. Yes, definitely, I approached them from over there.' I looked beyond the clearing for any sign of them: but they were nowhere to be seen.

'So where are they?' Barney incredulously inquired, mooching around the bushes, pushing foliage aside with his axe.

'Er, I don't know. Maybe they only come here for ceremonies, and they live elsewhere.' I shrugged, trying not to envisage they could be all dead. 'Pooh-Pooh!' I yelled. ' Pooh-Pooh!' I cried in desperation, as the idea that I was guilty of genocide increased. I stared aghast at the ground, and quietly said to myself, 'Pooh-Pooh.' Barney tried not to smirk, and Jenny began sniggering. 'What's so funny?!' I indignantly exclaimed.

'Nothing!' Jenny replied, trying her up most to fight back the chuckles. With that, Argon and Kelly began to grin: and even Helena had a wry smile.

'It's not funny!' I cried. 'They maybe dead: and I did it!'

'I'm sorry, old-man,' Argon replied, recomposing himself, 'the journey has been a little stressful.'

'Heeey, it's that doood who we had a smoke with.' Suddenly, from the clearing, came the corpulent smokers, but so much thinner, gaunt, and pale now.

'Yeah... Hey, maaan, where did y' go?' said another one, holding out a lit cone as way of an offering. I took a step back, for I remembered the heady effect of this substance before.

'No thanks,' I said. With that, he offered it to my comrades, who, though curious, had seen my reactions, and so vigorously shook their heads in disapproval.

'Come on, maaan,' he urged, 'have a toke. Y' know y' wanna... It's goood.' He held it to Argon, who absently took it from him and looked at the glowing substance inquisitively. He began to raise it to his mouth.

'No!' I shouted, and carefully took it from him. The cone

was in my hands, and the delicious smelling smoke rose up to my nostrils: I greedily stared at it. I found myself drawing it to my mouth. No! I said to myself, and gave it back to the tribesperson. I examined the two: they had lost so much weight, I could hardly recognize them: their skins were pallid, and eyes sunken in red sockets, with stringy hair limply hanging down. They did not particularly look the picture of health the last time I had encountered them: but now, there was a distinct dullness in their eyes, and it was apparent they were most unwell. 'What's happened to you?' I despairingly asked, having, of course, a strong inkling.

'Maaan, it's weird. Everyone in the forest is dying of a strange disease. We just can't figure it out.' He put the lit object in his mouth, and took a long deep draw: I vicariously shared the experience. 'Sure y' don't want any?' he asked. I intensely stared at it, momentarily forgetting the line of conversation: then, by sheer volition, reluctantly continued.

'Listen,' I said, 'we have, at our plane, a remedy for the disease, a magical recuperative water. Gather all the tribes and bring them here: we will lead you there.' He took another deep draw, passed it to his companion, who did the same, and they casually sauntered away. I was unsure if they had heard me: their eyes were so glazed and detached. When they had gone, contrition drove deep into my marrow: those men had so drastically altered since our last meeting: they were like sticks, on death's door. The air, by now, was pervaded by a thick heady smoke, and, we, the travellers, unaccustomed to such ambience, began choking on the fumes.

Jenny, Kelly, Helena, Argon and Barney, had big daft grins on their faces, with eye lids slowly oscillating. 'A tribe's person,' Kelly casually said, with a deep rooted care free propensity, then let out a little giggle.

'Yeah,' Barney replied, and put his arm around her.

'Hey,' Argon said, with a broad smile, 'don't get any ideas with ma missus.' His eyes shone, and his face evinced he had not a care in the world.

I began to feel a familiar sensation, an influence I had encountered on my previous journey: I could feel myself becoming immersed in soporific inebriation: but this time, I had no desire to repeat the experience, and, consequently, it filled me with dread. I tried to battle against the effect which was creeping through my veins: but it was too strong, and I was helpless to extirpate it. I felt acute fear and anticipated doom. I was surrounded by danger; the forest contained imminent death. My eyes bulged with stark horror. My crew became alien. They were my accusers and tormentors. I became acutely anxious that they were about to say something derogatory. They were in league with each other, conspiring my down fall. They hated me, and had nothing but contempt for me. There was no love in the universe. Love was an illusion which only I mistakenly believed in. The tribes were gathering to kill me: in the vistas I could hear them taunting me and coming near: the bushes rustled all around me. Every noise filled me with horror. My crew eagerly waited to witness my brutal slaughter. The crew had somehow contacted the tribes before we had arrived: this was a set up: the crew had led me here so I would be at the mercy of the tribes, the tribes who sought revenge, the crew who wanted revenge: everyone that ever existed wanted me dead. I knew they knew I knew, and I stood hopeless, and helpless, waiting for the inevitable. I tried to petition Helena with an earnest gaze of contrition: but she recoiled at my stare… I was alone… I was to die… Soon, yes, a horrible death, a slow death, a most painful death: and everyone would celebrate and enjoy each moment. Petrified in bewilderment, I watched as they smiled at each other, a cruel smile, a callous smile, a smile of indifference, a foreboding smile, a smile that looked forward to my demise… I ran from them. I ran into the forest. I ran into the waiting tribes. I wanted it over with. I kept running, but no one was there. I ran and ran, broad leaves slapping in my face. I had to get away from my tormentors. I had to distance myself from the people who wanted to destroy me. I ran and ran in blind panic, mad fear, insane despair. I ran and ran towards the nerve centre of insanity and chaos…

I ran straight into the stream I had previously encountered. I fell face first into it. The cool water revived me; my faculties gradually came back; everything slowly came back into perspective; my pulse slowed, my wits returned, and the forest threatened no more. I bathed in the cool invigourating water, submerging myself, feeling blessed relief. I washed away my despondency. It felt good to have a clear head. I could relax once more…

As I recovered my faculties, I began to feel lonely, and my urge to socialize returned: and so I made my way back to the clearing…

On my return, I was most surprised to see all the tribes of the forest had began to congregate, integrating freely, and chatting most amicably: Pooh-Poohs were debating with Dryads, Muldari convened with Smokers, I was pleased to see the amazing Lacertilia: all permutations of the tribes in debate indicated an unprecedented community: they spoke quietly and controlled; there was not a hint of animosity between them. As I approached, I expected a derisive comment from a Pooh-Pooh, or to be grabbed by the throat by a Dryad, but they barely stirred. Most of them looked in thrall of the vicious malady: and a familiar stench of the disease engendered reminiscences of the day I returned to my own village. I saw the grandeur of The Lizard King's sheen had noticeably waned. I eagerly approached him. 'Hi King. How y' doing? What brings you to the forest?' He looked at me with faded eyes. 'Having the disease made the desert heat unbearable. We sought the shade... I really wanted to cure my people,' he sheepishly smiled, 'but it turned out, I couldn't do anything.' I issued a consoling pat on his once august back, which was noticeably stooped now.

From the forest, more of the tribes slowly appeared; and so, as we waited, the tribes gradually sauntered into the clearing in dribs and drabs. I stood by my compatriots, but felt isolated; I was no closer to my own people than to the people of this forest. After a while, the influx of tribes ceased: and they all expectantly turned to us: there was a intense silence indicating an earnest anticipation. Never had I seen such an orderly gathering: and I instantaneously felt compelled to address the bedraggled audience: but I stared at them, not knowing how to begin. My fellow travellers turned their heads to me, so it was apparent they wished me to speak. Jenny gave me a small nudge to prompt me. I had not prepared to say anything: and I was feeling guilty and vulnerable, and wanted to curl up in a small ball and hide somewhere: but I felt an ineluctable incumbency to speak: so I spontaneously orated. 'Er... people of Firkin... mmm... people of The Forest of Life,' the tribes then looked quizzically at each other, ' er, what we refer to as The Forest of Life, for I never did inquire what you call your own forest... mmm... anyway... people of The... people... I have some, er, bad... news, and, er, some good news.' I had to tell them it was me who brought the malady so as to shrive my soul. The audience listened attentively. Shame tore at my spirit: seeing firsthand the extent of the malady confirmed my imaginative dread: they stared with gaunt faces and sunken eyes; strips of flesh hung from them: and they leant against each other, such was the enervation. I wanted to runaway: but conscience urged me to face my responsibility. I could detain no longer. 'The bad news is... it was me that brought the disease.' I waited for a response: I expected anger... a missile! I waited for an attack...

Surely the fierce Dryads would not contain themselves... but they all stood silent, waiting for me to continue. 'But, this is why I have returned, to try and make amends for my, er, thoughtlessness. We have brought a panacea, a magical libation that will cure your malady.' Again, I waited for a response. They stared at me: the group gaze was relentless: I could not ascertain if it was malevolent or indifferent.

'All the tribes of the forest have lost many of their people,' a Dryad then called out. With that, the intensity of the glares increased: large eyeballs bulged from shrivelled sockets, like death had come to accuse: I felt the indictment burn in my heart.

'This water,' I said with acute alacrity, 'can reanimate the dead.' The ensuing silence indicated the incredulousness at such a fantastic claim: and I turned to my compatriots for corroboration: they looked at me in a similar fashion to the stricken tribes: everyone knew everyone else, except me, who knew no one. 'We will lead you to the plane,' I said, using the word *we* in hope I could persuade my people I belonged with them. 'Then,' I continued, 'if you lead us to where your people are buried, we can take measures to restore them back to life.' Before a stony silence engulfed me, I quickly added, 'Come, follow me, this way. Everything is going to be okay.'

And so I led everybody back to the symbol of liberty: the aeroplane. The tribes, without prompting, queued in an orderly fashion, as, one by one, were administered the alchemical and incredible Sacradia. Each was soon restored back to health; and me and my crew also took a quaff as a precautionary measure.

Without ado, we were led to the burial grounds. To my surprise, the different tribes had been buried alongside each other. I also saw acts of affection between The Dryads and men of the other tribes. I discerned through adversity that these people had created a society: for, no matter whom it was that crawled from the ground, everyone, without exception, demonstrated joy and relief. It was a deeply moving scene: and, although the tribes remained aloof from me, I felt profound happiness that the disease had been quashed, and life and health had been restored. There seemed little else for us to do, and so we decided, unnoticed, to return to the plane. As I turned to leave, I was approached by a Pooh-Pooh, he held out his hand: I shook it heartily: he smiled, and said, 'Thank you.' It was a much appreciated gesture, and went some way to ease my conscience. We then departed from the re-union, back to our flying machine, in order to make preparations for the next part of the journey. We would have to fly over Ice Mountain, and visit Nubile's tribe, a tribe I had never met, a tribe I hoped would receive us favourably, a tribe I hoped would receive us as calm and stolid as The Forest of Life's people.

And so the tribes, or should I say tribe, for it now appeared they were one, dispersed into the forest, leaving us to sit and ponder over the next phase of our journey. I vividly recalled the daunting height of Ice Mountain, and the extreme weather: but we had a tested and proven flying machine, and I was confident we would not be experiencing the horrific physical trials of yore. We split into three parties to retrieve water and provisions, which, of course, are abundant in The Forest of Life: I ambled into the hinterland of the forest with Helena. I was still feeling uncomfortable, not knowing how to start a conversation. I bashfully looked at her as she insouciantly sallied around the great girths of the trees. I went about the business of acquiring victuals, while all the time monitoring her whereabouts. My petitioning expression must have conveyed urgency: for, eventually, she casually said, to one of the large ripe peaches she had just plucked and was inspecting, 'When the women were restored, they were all beautiful.'

'Er, I didn't really notice,' was my feeble reply.

'Yes you did,' she retorted, imparting an indifferent gaze towards me.

'Did I?' I embarrassingly rejoined.

'You know you did,' she calmly interjected, filling her basket with delicious golden pomegranates, 'your eyes lingered, and only concerted volition could allay intensity and draw them away.' She nonchalantly sat in the shade of a fig tree, and waited for me to finish filling my basket. Although I detected a distance in her voice, at least she was talking to me. It was always easier when she led the conversation: but I was unsure if it was bringing us any closer together. 'I noticed a young boy who looked remarkably like you,' she continued. 'Did you see him?'

'No!' I blurted in panic. She lazily stretched her lithe female limbs, and all her contours pressed against her clothes. She emitted a little yawn, and closed her eyes. I squirmed in the unsupportable silence, on the verge of confessing my exploits.

'I'm only joking: no need to get so flustered,' she sighed. 'I'm going to take a nap until you have finished collecting your provisions. Wake me when you have done.' I stared at her as she lay under a large pear tree. Her body looked so inviting, and it took great control to detain the powerful urge of wanting to wrap my aching body around her delicious curves. To distract myself, I hastily plucked some walnuts, ripping and breaking the branches, which then fell on top of me. I fought with trees, and became scratched and bruised: one plum tree got me in a strangle hold, and it took all my strength to break free. I was most pleased when I had finished filling my basket: and I was anxious to return to the margin of the forest, lest I became a permanent captive of an apple tree.

'I've finished,' I eventually said. She stirred, stretched her long sensuous arms, emitted a small endearing sigh, and gracefully stood up to reveal her perfect female form.

'Oh good. Let's go then.' Her calm aloofness was disturbing

me: but I had no idea how to thaw it. I wanted to confront her, but feared it would repel her further: so I solemnly traipsed back to the plane, where everyone was waiting...

We wasted no time in loading the provisions. When we had prepared the craft for takeoff, I felt the need to warn the crew about the hostile mountain: but I did not want to demoralize them, so I decided to make it brief and euphemistic.

'The next stage of our journey,' I declared, ' entails, as you know, surmounting Ice Mountain: it's... er... quite high... and... mmm... it gets a bit nippy: so I suggest you put on as many clothes as you can.' I fumbled around for words, and was painfully aware that my description and advice fell well short of what was required; but I surmised, by sheer effort, we could overcome the massive ice obstacle, and soon be gliding down the other side.

'Gorky,' Barney said, and I could tell by the tone of his voice it was not good news, 'we have been talking it over... and... we are unsure if we want to continue.' My insecurity and hesitancy suddenly dispelled at their lack of intrepidness.

'What?! Again?! You had the same attitude in the desert, you wanted to turn back: and, look, we got here, and saved all these people. We can't return doing only half the job... Who doesn't want to continue anyway?'

'We never said we do not want to continue: we said we do not know if we want to continue... It seems the further away we get, the more difficult it will be to return home,' Jenny forthrightly stated.

'But there are still tribes to save... I climbed Ice Mountain on my hands and knees... Six of us will easy fly over it,' I propounded.

'Then there is The Sea of Leviathans, old man,' Argon interjected. 'It seems the further we go, the more chance of... well... something going, wrong.'

'Nothing's going to go wrong!' I exclaimed. 'We're on our

way now. I can't return doing only half the journey. I won't be able to. You saw the state of this tribe. You remember how our tribe was affected. You remember the misery, don't you?!' I glared at them all. 'Out there,' I pointed, 'I'm responsible for that misery to others. We have the opportunity to rectify it. We can't turn our backs on this chance. If we turn back now… it's all over. Do you understand?! It's all over!' I was almost in tears as my emotions reached a crescendo: my eyes bulged and nose flared: I felt myself inflate with earnest supplication: my heart and soul cried out to aid the inflicted: I could not relinquish the task. The strain of the journey was taking its toll, but there was nothing in my mind that even hinted at giving up. I waited for their decision.

'Gorky, we know how you feel,' Argon assured, 'and the thought of travelling to new places fills me with relish: but you cannot refuse a democratic decision: you have to consider the wishes of the crew.'

'Yes, you have to consider *their* wishes,' Kelly concurred.

'*Their* wishes?' Argon queried.

'Yes, I for one have no qualms about continuing,' she confidently enjoined.

'I thought you were dubious,' Argon replied. Kelly scrutinized my wretched state with pity.

'I was a little: but Gorky's right, we have come this far…' she replied.

'Okay, then I want to go on too,' Argon confidently said.

'Helena?' I asked. She absently shrugged, and as I was obsessed with the need to continue, I did not petition her further. 'Jenny?'

'Barney, what do you want to do?' Jenny asked.

'You said you were missing home,' Barney replied.

'I know… but those poor people,' she retorted while staring at me. He carefully ruminated, creating eidetic images of the suffering in his mind, becoming one of the inflicted.

'Yes, those poor people,' he slowly and deliberately

mumbled. 'Let's go on, and get this thing over with.' So, it was finally decided, that we should continue. A large pot of vegetable stew was cooked under the cool shade of a banana tree. We all mentally prepared for the ensuing flight. We were to fly over Ice Mountain, to seek Nubile's tribe in the forest by the sea to administer aid if need be.

20.

Approach

We made a reconnoitre of the outskirts of the forest: we walked along the grassy margin, carefully inspecting for any potholes, or salient points, like bumps or stones. There was a long strip of fairly smooth firm ground ahead for the plane.

I urged my crew members to put on as many layers of clothes they comfortably could. At first, because of the clement climate of The Forest of Life contiguous to the desert, they were most reluctant. But at my insistence, they unwillingly complied. Wearing such bulky clothes piqued their imaginations to what lay ahead.

We confidently took off without incident. As soon as the undercarriage left the ground, Argon adjusted the rudder and flaps so as to quickly veer away from the nearby trees. We soared into the air, and steered towards the imposing Ice Mountain…

The craft was soon flying over The Forest of Life, a verdant expanse before us. Lush vegetation zoomed past below. The flourishing carpet of verdure rustled and whispered: and, initially, the innumerable trees' intense buzz sounded like they were discussing the feasibility of the small craft's potential for surmounting Ice Mountain. I could not ascertain whether the forest believed we could do it or not. I made myself believe that it was advocating our success…

As we flew on, we became completely enveloped in the most amazing scene: the panoramic view of lush green was most uplifting. The air smelt fresh and the trees radiated a primordial energy that positively vibrated profoundly into the enlivened soul. There is a magnificent spirit on Zugra, a living breathing entity: and the trees, deeply rooted into its being are one of its emissaries...

Onwards we boldly flew, and the magnificent sea of rustling trees seemed to speedily propel the plane along: the craft was suspended in the air by a natural force as we effortlessly moved forward. We were awed by the pure energy emanating from the forest: vibrant rurality poured into our voracious psyches: our perceptions were purged, and the nature of being became elucidated...

We flew on... Conditions were uncannily perfect, everything was in order: the crew worked together in inordinate efficiency. I felt my companion's divine presence inspire me: the goodness in their souls emanated forth, soothing doubts about existence: any isolation was summarily dissipated and an unprecedented unity prevailed. We were calm, controlled, and preter-naturally focused...

As we flew, I began to feel reluctant to leave The Forest of Life- this verdant sanctuary- behind: and it was with a pang of regret when I finally saw ahead, in the far distance, a mist, smoky and grey, the precursor of the next phase. Then, I felt a subtle drop in the temperature: suddenly, my marrow induced a memory of the bitter cold that was, Ice Mountain...

We flew onwards, and each beat of the wings meant the temperature slightly lowered...

After a while, we were upon the margin of the forest on the other side: and soon we were leaving The Forest of Life behind...

The cold hit us like a wall of ice: even though I had been this way before, I was shocked at the sudden violent drop of temperature. Barney uttered execrations as the icy air assailed our exposed skin. For extra thrust, so as to ensure we would surmount the peak, we all pedalled in unison; and, also, deemed it was the only way to maintain circulation and keep warm: any inactivity would have meant frozen blood...

Then, we hit dense mist: our sight was totally obscured. This meant further colourful language from our blacksmith friend: to which I inwardly concurred. We had an unforeseen problem: the mist meant that, up ahead, somewhere, undetectable, was the real wall of ice, that foreboding presence: Ice Mountain. We were flying at a constant altitude parallel to the ground: I deemed it expedient that we ascend immediately. Argon altered the flaps, and, slowly, we began to rise. However, the cold weather meant that we were limping along and not gaining as much height as we expected...

As we flew on, the increasing fear that we would hit the mountain head on at any moment became intolerable. All that we could see was the ice vapour that clung around the ferocious precipice: our vision was nil. We were hurtling forward into unknown and unseen space: and, there, somewhere, waiting for us, was a massive solid wall of ice and snow. I desperately tried to envision the height of the mountain, and compare it to our current altitude: although we were gradually increasing our height, it did not feel enough to clear the peak. The impending doom of crashing harassed my senses; I was wracking my brain in tortuous contemplation, when, I could bare it no longer: I was convinced that we were going to smash into the side. 'Stop! Turn back!' I yelled.

'What?!' Barney exclaimed.

'We're going to crash into the mountain! We are not high

enough. We should turn back, rest at the forest, and start again, utilizing the hot desert air to gain altitude a lot sooner,' I admonished.

Argon did not need a second invitation: he promptly turned the craft round, and headed back to the forest. It was a big relief to be flying towards open air again…

As we flew, the weather became more clement…

Soon, the sound of swishing leaves were welcoming our return. The trees seemed to be whispering their agreements between each other that they had expected this to happen. We flew back to a similar area where we first took off from, and landed with aplomb…

The crew disconsolately alighted the cockpit, and mooched around: a deep sense of failure pervaded the atmosphere. To eliminate any incipient doubt that could grow into inveterate despondency, I knew I had to address them now. 'If we start by flying over the desert, we can utilize the warm thermals so as to gain as much height as possible: and then we should continue to ascend from there, so that by the time we reach the mountain, we should be able to, er, we will be able to, clear the peak.'

'How high is this bleeding mountain?' Barney inquired.

'Er, quite high,' I sheepishly replied.

'Quite high?! What kind of height is that?' he remarked.

'I did not realize visibility would be so bad,' I said.

'Bad visibility? You mean *no* visibility!' Barney impatiently marched around, looking ready to rip a tree from its roots. It was apparent he was most frustrated, partially because he, and the others, had never seen a mountain before, and had no idea what they were up against, other than the abstract descriptions I had imparted. Also, when I had vehemently yelled 'Stop!' they obviously detected in my tone the magnitude of the obstacle concealed in the mist. Moreover, the shocking introduction to an unknown climate meant the crew had notably changed in demeanour. They were now pale and lack lustre, becoming deeply introspective.

'Let us rest, then try again… Consider the previous attempt a practice run: you now have an idea what we are to encounter: and, I am sure, if we begin our ascent in the desert, we will scale the mountain with little difficulty.' The crew exchanged glances evincing their uncertainty: and began doffing their protective clothing. The weather was becoming rather oppressive wrapped in the multi layers of garments: so, reluctantly, I did likewise. I immediately made a fire, brought out the cooking pot, and stewed some tea. We sat in silence, as we drank our beverages.

When I had deemed we had sojourned long enough, I packed everything away. The crew was sprawled out by the edge of shady trees, looking upwards with squinting eyes, soaking in some of the desert sun. I donned my extra clothes again, and climbed back into the cockpit. I patiently sat there, staring at the sun worshipers. No one stirred. 'Come on,' I urged. 'We've rested long enough.'

'Go on then, we'll catch up' Barney said, accompanied by a stifled snigger from somebody.

'Are you giving in?' I asked.

'Oh, for heaven's sake,' Barney groaned, standing up, and began to put on the essential protective attire. The others followed, occasionally muttering denunciations to themselves, as they slowly put on their extra clothes, which apparently weighed like lead. Then, they dragged themselves to the plane, climbed back in, and sat there. I waited for Argon to cry out 'Ready?': but it was conspicuously not forthcoming.

'Ready?' I confidently shouted with inner reservations: but no one replied. I pushed down on the pedals: but received no assistance, and so, consequently, the craft remained stationary. 'What is a matter with you?!' I cried in exasperation.

'You may be enthusiastic at the prospect of flying into an icy hell: but we find the whole idea abhorrent,' Jenny replied.

'Do you think I enjoy flying into that cold?' I indignantly rejoined.

'Do you?' Kelly interjected.

'Of course not!' I blurted, pausing for a moment to consider, but blocking the notion out of my mind. 'I have to get to…'

'Yes, yes, those tribes, old boy. And I relish a challenge, but one that is feasible,' Argon said.

'Challenge? Feasible? Look, Argon, if you turn back now that mountain will haunt you for the rest of your life; but if we face it, conquer it, return a success, think how much easier that would be to live with yourself,' I exhorted.

'I have already learnt to live with myself, Gorky,' Argon calmly stated.

'But to return to our village, a complete success!' I reiterated.

'We have already proven "successful". We've got this far relatively unscathed.' Jenny claimed.

'And we will continue to do so,' I retorted.

'Do you admit this attempt is risking our lives?' Barney asked.

'Life is unavoidably a risk' I whispered. Then, I felt a tumescent urge begin to grow in my heart. Tears welled as the primeval energy started taking over my body. As the crucial force pulsated through my blood, I could not detain it any longer, and in a state of profound ecstasy, I screamed, 'I won't be able to live with myself if I do not save those tribes!!!' My voice gushed outwards, shaking the crew, vibrating the plane, and piercing the sky. The group's eyes widened in horror: and suddenly they became alert. Barney and Jenny, Argon and Kelly, exchanged glances: then, Barney nodded at Argon.

'Okay, Gorky, we acknowledge how important this mission is for you. But you can understand our reservations,' Barney asked.

'Yes, of course,' I answered.

'It's just that we don't share your conviction... or... er... guilt,' he continued.

'I understand,' I said.

'But we are a team. I have known you from childhood. I could not stand you moping around the village for the rest of your life, relentless conscience sapping your spirits,' he smiled, and gave me a pat on my back. I looked around at the crew, their expressions indicated that they concurred with Barney.

'Okay. Is everybody ready?' Argon asked.

'Let's go,' Kelly responded. And we all simultaneously pushed on the pedals as the craft surged forward.

We headed into the desert, gaining rapid altitude as we went. The sky was clear, and we could descry the shrinking ground below us; as we rose, the ripples in the sand began to recede. The rising thermals pushed the sleek aluminium craft vertically upwards, and we soared high like a bird, lifting further into the sky. The air grew thinner: breathing became discernibly more erratic as we began to work harder to maintain oxygen levels. As the craft rose, a fearful travail grew in my stomach: the ground was quickly disappearing far below: and the higher we rose, the more insignificant I felt...

On we flew, vertically spiralling upwards over the hot desert sands: and the higher we got, the wider my eyes became... 'I think we are high enough,' I eventually informed Argon, when I could abide it no longer.

'Are you sure, old boy?' he inquired, with a possible hint of sarcasm.

'Yes, are you sure, Gorky. We can keep on going upwards if you like,' Barney added, smirking at Jenny. I felt a pang of annoyance at being ridiculed, but deemed if I vehemently indicated it, I would lose my credibility: so I ignored their derision.

'Yes, I am sure. We should level off, and start heading towards the mountain now,' I calmly announced, gazing downwards, incredulous at the altitude. Argon trimmed the flaps, and turned towards the forest: and so we headed towards the formidable obstacle: Ice Mountain.

Soon we were flying over the forest: it could not be heard or smelt: just a hazy green could be seen far below, though its vibe was still subtly apparent. It seemed strange to think that there were actually people down there in that mini forest…

As we flew on, the height began to torment me. Was it not unnatural for a frail little mortal to be up so high? What if the craft malfunctioned? I would plummet to my death; I would fall and fall, and then my tiny body would explode against solid ground. All that was holding us up was a piece of tin. How could that be? Was it possible that a lump of metal could support the incredible nature of my being? A vacillating giddiness induced seminal panic: my hands tightly clasped the side of the craft. 'We've, we've got to keep pedalling,' I absently said.

'What? More height?' Barney answered.

'Don't tease him, Barney. I don't think he is well,' Jenny earnestly interjected.

'Keep pedalling,' I reiterated.

'That's what we are doing, old boy,' Argon rejoined.

'Keeep perrr…ddling,' I slurred, as my head began spinning out of control, faster and faster, round and round. Then, I rose from my seat. 'I've, I've got to get out,' I absently muttered, ready to jump over the side.

'Sit down, fool,' Barney shouted, grabbing my shoulder, and violently pulling me down: with one swift motion, I crashed back into my seat…

I found myself hunched in a little ball shivering with cold. Where was I? It was completely dark. My faculties gradually began returning: my body remonstrated against the bitter drop in temperature. I then realized that someone had thrown a blanket over me: I peered from my cover: there were the pedalling feet of the crew. I was huddled on the floor of the cockpit. I knew I had to resume pedalling fast, or freeze. I sat up, and my heart sank as I saw we were once again engulfed in the grey mist; a great mass of vaporous ice particles enveloped us. I stared in a trance at the swirling amorphous garment that clothed Ice Mountain: visibility was zero again. 'Ah, the intrepid explorer as graced us with his presence... Now get pedalling,' Barney ordered. Ordinarily, I would have rebelled against Barney's peremptory tone: but embarrassment compelled me to comply.

'I'm sorry,' I feebly announced: but my apologies were met with silence, so I concentrated on physical exertion...

It became increasingly difficult the colder it got. Icicles hung from the fuselage, and our upper clothes became frozen solid. I began to feel guilty at leading the crew into such a horrific situation: but, another 'Sorry' would have sounded feckless and pathetic. I was over-wrought with ambivalence: I thought it was only fair that we should turn back, and save my friends from such an awful ordeal: after all, it had not been them that proliferated the contagion; nevertheless, an indomitable force within my soul would not allow me to retreat: I had to undo what I had done...

We all pedalled intrepidly onwards, battling against the elements. Suddenly, great wads of snow came pouring down, large lumps of fluffy ice, flumping everywhere, filling the cockpit, and weighing the craft down. 'Keep pedalling!' I shouted, as I raised myself out my seat in order to bail out the snow. The grim crew, reticently, and resolutely, pushed forwards... My hands throbbed with cold, scooping large dollops of snow from around them. Flakes as large as our heads relentlessly pelted downwards. The wings raised and lowered, batting more snow and ice into the cockpit... As we pushed towards Ice Mountain, the snow began falling faster than I could bail it out: the craft became inundated... It began to feel as though we were steadily descending. The crew, like automatons, pumped on the pedals, defiantly pushing on. I recalled the height we had previously attained, spiralling upwards into the desert sky: and put any idea of hurtling headlong into the cliff face firmly out of my mind. As we pushed on, we became concealed in a pile of snow: but the only thing that mattered was surmounting the peak...

Suffused in hyperthermia, my mind became vague: we had already flown over the mountain, it was behind us, and soon we would be feeling the warm sea breeze. Yes, we were flying away from the maelstrom, heading towards the clement climes of fair Nubile's tribes. We would soon be effortlessly gliding on warm thermals towards the beach... 'KERBANG!'

21.

Kimtiv

Through bloody eyes, ice pelted down on crumpled heaps of bones and aluminium. I was not fully engaged in temporal-space as I espied the remains of my friends, and so the complete starkness did not immediately assail me. Fading into soothing darkness, willingly leaving pain behind, transcending to another realm: alarm! Struggling against compelling tide. Battling as to not leave familiar world behind. Reaching for body. Must inhabit corporeal frame. Regaining consciousness. Incarnadine orbs open: so did conduit to pain. I groaned at intolerable discomfort. In panic, I tried to move: but I was jammed in the cockpit, pressed into the metal, and it had sealed itself around me. I tried to wriggle and squeeze out of it, but could not move at all. I looked down at my torso: I stared in horror at a lever that had entered deep into my stomach and was pinning me to the seat. The sight of the horrid intrusion induced faintness. I began to think it better to die. My head lolled, and I waited to extricate the bonds of misery. Salt tears welled to fuse with the blood, cleansed my eyes and rolled down my stained cheeks. I waited... I would soon be far from this tortuous place: but as I waited, my indomitable spirit refused to budge from flesh... I lifted my head, and there, in front of me, undamaged, was the urn! I moved my arms: but one lay limp by my side. My free arm stretched outwards towards the lid: and I grimaced as the embedded lever searched for internal organs. My stretching finger tips, eventually, found the lid: but I could not adequately grip it. Pushing my body forward meant pushing the lever further into me: and I was about to relinquish the struggle, when I saw my beautiful Kelly. Her image began to assimilate: and it invoked extra volition. I surged my torso forward, and the lever slid through my soft viscera and hit my spine. I choked in surprise at the peculiar sensation. Blood streamed from the apertures of my head, and my body began to fail. Instinctively, my bloody hand grasped the lid, and I managed to screw it off. My hand groped inside the urn: I knew as soon as I touched the water, the restorative powers would pervade my body. My fingers desperately searched around the inside of the container, but I could not push my hand deep enough in. I pulled at the urn: it was stuck fast. I clung to the lip of the urn with my straining fingers, not knowing what to do next. My head began to sag; my soul began to dwindle. A voice inside my head kept saying, 'The water, Argon! The water!' but I knew it was in vain. The blood from my nails trickled down the inside of the receptacle until it suffused with the magic alchemical water. The clear pure water became dyed bright red as my life fluids flowed into it. The celestial liquid began bubbling and steaming. The long dribble of blood was like a conductor: and the pulsating water crept up its stem. Sacradia entered the incisions on my hands, and imbued into what blood was left inside of me. My body began tingling with a pleasant warm sensation. I felt bones fusing, and ripped flesh and ligaments sealing smoothly together. My stomach spewed out the control lever: it effortlessly slid from my body as the slit that remained sealed shut in an instant. The blood from my eyes, nose, ears, and mouth, began flowing back into my head: and all signs of traumas completely vanished. I was sat bolt upright in the wreckage of the plane, perfectly healthy and strong, as the cockpit pursed its mouth and gave me room to move. I had one dominating urge: save my friends...

As my eyes began to focus, I discerned someone resembling Argon stood over me: in my perplexity, I managed to surmise that he must have just been finishing administering some of Sacradia: I also assumed the urn was luckily still intact. I scanned around, stretching my curious hands outwards: I was laid on ice; then my fingers came to a ledge, and a sheer drop. I had been thrown clear of the aeroplane. A stark recollection of my long and arduous climb pervaded me: I was on one of Ice Mountain's plateaux. My senses were further jolted when I saw limply laying next to me, the mangled body of Barney. I stared in dismay at the disfigured corpse twisted around the wreckage of the plane. Argon poured some of the precious water onto Barney: his body began to emit sparks and begin to thaw, then, bubble and fuse together. It was not long before he was recovering, and imparting imprecations of incredulousness. Helena! My fuzzy head scanned around: I saw some shadowy figures pressed against a startling white backdrop: and, as my eyes focused, I saw the ladies, already huddled together, safe, but disconsolate, as the snow fell heavily around. 'I was the only survivor,' Argon said, smiling, trying to sound enthusiastic: but his eyes still reliving the horror.

'The plane's had it,' Jenny stated, helping Barney onto his feet, and giving him a hug in the howling wind. 'Pity the water cannot repair inanimate objects,' she mused. I gazed at Helena: she was hugging herself and stamping her feet against the bitter cold. I tried to catch her eyes, but she was lost in herself. I slowly pulled myself up, and shook the ice and snow away. I turned to inspect the twisted wreckage that had been our transport: damaged beyond repair. We were stranded on a small plateau, with no means to ascend, or descend. We all stood dumb in the pelting ice and snow knowing this could be our final destination. I walked over to Helena: I thought this was an appropriate time for a rapprochement: besides, cuddling each other would keep us warm. I went to put my arms around her: she recoiled from me, and backed towards the cold stony ice cliff face.

'What's wrong?!' I cried in disbelief and exasperation. She stood there, silent, slowly becoming concealed in snow. I positioned my head in front of her, in hope that her beautiful eyes may rest upon mine. My lineaments supplicated for her to look at me and speak. Please, see me, Helena, for I am only alive in your sight; please, talk to me, Helena, I am dying of despair. It was with great joy that she focused on me: my gaze penetrated deep into her soul in order to demonstrate my love. Her eyes widened, and I waited in nervous anticipation, for I knew she was at last to speak.

'Do you want to know?' she quietly asked.

'Yes, of course!' I implored.

'In the desert,' she continued, 'in your fit of temper, when you got up to attack Barney, you elbowed me in the ribs: I would show you the bruises, but it is too cold; you used my face as an object to push against as you jumped on him; and, as you wrestled him, you hit me again; then, when Argon and Barney were struggling, they fell upon me with their full weight: I was in great pain: but when you got back in the cockpit, you never once apologized, or asked me how I was: all you kept doing, you idiot, was inanely stroking my hair as if I was your pet dog.'

'But I had nearly fallen out of the plane: I was too shocked to realize,' I complained, quickly assessing the information, and beginning to inwardly chastise myself.

'If it had not been for your awful temper, you would not have been hanging out of the plane in the first place. Can you not remember what you did?' she demanded. I could not remember anything during the initial surge of anger; it was blind rage: and now I felt utterly deflated at my thoughtless actions. My woman did not approve of me: I stood there ashamed, lost and lonely. I was to die with her being so near me: but she did not care anymore, which was insufferable torment.

'I am sorry, Helena: it was the heat, and…' I thought it best to shut up: I was only making excuses for inexcusable behaviour. I stood there like a scolded child: my head dropped and bottom lip protruded. I did not want us to end in such a forlorn way.

'Come here,' she then whispered: her voice instantly soothed me. I looked up to her face: her eyes had a sheen of tears over them. I took one step, put my hungry arms around her, and hugged her. We both began to sob, and great sorrow welled inside me.

'Sorry,' was all I could say, as the snow fell heavily about us. I continued to chide myself for lack of control regarding my previous anger: the stupidity of allowing my temper to disavow commonsense nearly lost me my woman. She had silently bore the memory ever since: and, quite possibly, if it was not for our dire predicament, she may never have forgiven me. As I held her in my arms, I felt so privileged to have a second chance.

There were earnest attempts to extricate from the ledge: the rope we had on board the craft was no where long enough to reach the next plateau; the stirrups Mountain Monk had put in were gone: but Barney and Argon tried desperately to descend and ascend the defiant faces of the mountain. They toiled for hours, then resting, wracking their brains to find ways to emancipate from the austere plateau. As time went on, their motivation began to wane. The mountain seemed more insurmountable than ever: its aspect had seemed to change from last time, as if it had resented someone scaling it, and took measures to ensure that it would never happen again. Anyway, I knew from experience, without having the correct equipment, all attempts were futile. It was terribly frustrating: Barney was reduced to stalking around the small ledge, angrily looking down at the sheer drop, furiously peering up at the gargantuan ice wall, and continually cursing these insurmountable obstacles. At intervals, we drank Sacradia (of course, being magic, it never froze), which instilled our body with heat and vigour: but this only delayed the inevitable. In time, as our hope decreased, so did Barney's cursing: but, also, so did the contents of the urn, until, there were none left. We then knew, as defeatist and pessimistic as it sounded, the only thing to do was wait and freeze into oblivion. The snow and ice deleteriously pelted down with blatant rage. The mountain was like a famished beast, and it was desperate to have its quarry: we were irrevocably ensnared in its icy maw. The sensations of my body imperceptibly assuaged into numbness. My arms froze around Helena. 'Are you awake?' I whispered to her as my lips froze onto her icy cheek. She stood ominously still and silent, like one of Mountain Monk's ice carvings. My care and anxiety melted away as I became drowsy: I felt a profound contentedness and far reaching happiness: I issued a daft grin at the pelting snow and ice which seemed like celestial jewels glittering in the winter sky.

Then, before me, in the haze, hovering in front of the plateau, garbed in long diaphanous saffron and a crimson silk veil, which gently floated in the air incongruous with the wild swirling mountain wind, was an old woman. She examined us all in turn as we huddled frozen together in a cadaverous mass. I am uncertain, but I think I felt my feet lift away from the plateau and begin to float towards the ledge...

On awakening, the six of us were in an iron wrought cage suspended by a chain. I examined my crew members: each seemed relatively unscathed, but rather disorientated. I looked out, beyond the thick iron bars: the surrounding walls were made of logs; and, on one of the walls, was a familiar looking goat's head. There was a large stone hearth with a great orange fire dancing, not unlike the old woman's veil; and in front of the fire was a long table laden with delicious looking victuals. At the head of the table, there was a single chair, very grand, like a throne. It perplexed me why so much food had been set for one. We were all suddenly painfully aware of our hunger, which had accrued during the frozen sojourn on the plateau. We gazed at the food, hypnotized as the appetizing smells tantalized our taste buds. My stomach felt like a massive void filled with yearning and desire to be satiated with repast. 'Is everybody okay?' I eventually asked when I had disengaged from my hypnotic reverie.

'Where are we?' Kelly inquired, gazing around the room, which, apart from the hearth and table, was quite sparse.

'So you are awake at last!' a raucous voice screamed, which seemed to emanate from the fire.

'Yes,' I cautiously said to the air. 'Why are we incarcerated?'

'Because,' said the old woman, as the flames roared and rose as she nonchalantly stepped from out of the fire, 'you are my prisoners.'

She casually sat down at the table, poured herself a chilled fresh orange juice into a tall glass, which soon glistened with condensation from the frosty liquid.

'Er, I do believe that this is, er, wrong, I mean, the wrong thing to do,' Argon said, frowning at his own cumbersome speech, while staring at the delicious libation. The old woman raised an eyebrow, smiled a little, tore off a large piece of fresh smelling bread, lathered it in a thick layer of creamy butter, and began to tuck in. 'Taking prisoners, is er…' he tried to continue.

'Wrong?' she interrupted. 'Was it wrong to save you from the ledge?' We did not answer, but watched her enjoying the feast. 'Are you not warmer, and safer, now?'

'But, you have taken our liberty,' Kelly admonished.

'Would you rather be back on the plateau?' The old woman smiled sardonically, smeared butter on some steaming potatoes, watched it melt, sprinkled a little salt, put a portion in her mouth, and, slowly, chewed. We gazed in dismay as she self-contentedly fed herself, taking immense pleasure in each moment. She then sliced herself a large slab of chocolate cake, and walked to the cage. 'Would you like to be back there?' she smirked, opened her mouth wide, and took a large bite of cake, chocolate cream oozing from the slice. Her glee was short lived: for, when she had finished gorging, she turned and stared into the fire, illuminating a most profound melancholy in her eyes: such was the acute woe, I shuddered inside: but, when she turned to face us again, she tried to disguise her anguish. 'You will be my pets... until I get bored with you... then I will dispose of you, in ice, or, perhaps, fire.... What do you prefer?' We diffidently stared, incredulous at the old woman's behaviour.

'Why did you bother saving us?' Jenny inquired.

'How miserable do you feel?' the old woman retorted. 'Tell me, describe what it feels like powerless trapped in a cage. Does my food look delicious? Are you hungry?' She scrutinized each one of us up and down, eager to descry misery.

'Personally,' Barney said, 'I love it in here. I am so very... very... happy.' He malevolently and defiantly glared at her.

'Happy? HAPPY?!' the old woman screamed, 'then I may get bored with you sooner than I thought!'

'We are all miserable!' Kelly suddenly interjected.

'Arrr! Miserable!' said the old woman. 'Tell me more about your unbearable misery.'

'It's unbearable,' Jenny said.

'Yes, it is terrible, isn't it?' the old woman triumphantly proclaimed.

'Very terrible,' Kelly answered.

'Very very very er, terrible,' Argon said. The old woman glared at him, beginning to be annoyed again, to which Kelly gave him a small nudge to shut him up.

'And we are s-o hungry,' Kelly said, rubbing her stomach and trying to appear woebegone in order to assuage the old woman further (which was not too difficult, because the food had incited great yearning). The old woman waited, thought a little, and scrutinized us some more.

'Very hungry?' the old woman cautiously inquired with inveterate hope.

'Very,' Kelly replied.

'How hungry?' she retorted.

'It's terrible,' Kelly said

'Terrible?' the old woman queried, relishing every word.

'It makes us miserable,' Kelly said.

'You are so hungry, it makes you miserable?' the old woman confirmed.

'Yes,' Jenny said.

'Do you want something to eat?' the old woman asked.

'Oooh, yes please,' Kelly said, obviously expecting nothing.

'How much do you want something to eat?' the old woman said, beginning to walk around the table to proudly display the wares.

'Very much,' Kelly said.

'Oh this is ridiculous!' Barney impatiently exclaimed. 'Let us out, you silly old hag. We're tired of these daft games.' The old woman's contented expression suddenly ceased. She slowly walked to the cage, and, as she approached, though she did not discernibly increase in size, something about her became immense: her eyes intensely gleamed, and her expression indicated ferocity akin to Ice Mountain's storms.

'What did you just call me?' she calmly inquired with a subtle under tone of the most manic rage.

'I said,' spoke Barney, trying to stand up to his full height, but stooping in the cage, 'let us go… you… s-i-l-l-y… o-l-d… h-a-g.' The fire in the hearth began to crackle a sickly green: and we began to breathe condensation as the room's temperature dramatically dropped. She pointed her long wrinkled finger at Barney: an electric charge zipped from it, enveloping him in a fierce blue light. We all had to back against the cage and protect our eyes from the concentrated energy that engulfed him. Suddenly, he was gone. Vanished… All that remained of him was a charred patch on the cage floor. The old woman waited a few seconds for the shock to set in.

'Anyone else think I'm "s-i-l-l-y"?' she calmly asked.

'Where has he gone?' Jenny choked.

'Yes, he's gone,' was all the old woman said. She then sat back down to continue her meal. The lurid green flames changed back to orange, and the room instantly warmed. Jenny was about to issue a diatribe: but I muzzled her mouth with my hand and hugged her anguished body: she silently sobbed into my chest.

'Now, tell me again, how hungry are you?' the old woman nonchalantly inquired...

And so we watched her eat, as we reluctantly kept reminding her how delicious the food looked, and how very hungry we all were, which seemed to assist her appetite: and, although we were extremely irked at having to pacify this harridan, we figured, for now, it was expedient if we were to stand a chance of extricating from her evil clutches...

After she had finished her meal, she sat back in her chair, and dabbed her chin with a very ornate napkin. 'Mmmm, that *was*... d-e-l-i-c-i-o-u-s,' she slowly enunciated, smiling to herself. 'And now a little after-dinner entertainment.' She casually looked up towards the cage: but she focused on none of us. We stared at her, wondering what was in store. I wanted to make a vociferous protest, but knew it was futile: besides, it may have only added to her warped pleasure. I found the situation increasingly humiliating: and I did not know which was worse, the freezing plateau, or this old woman's antagonisms. 'Would you like some dancing?' the old woman asked.

'Er, you dance?' Kelly replied.

'No, you do,' came the quick and venomous retort. 'Dance!' she imperiously commanded.

'We need room,' I said, looking around the cramped confines of the cage.

'And we would dance much better out of the cage and if we were fed,' Helena added. The old woman imparted a sly smile, and uttered some strange words under her breath. At first, nothing happened: but, very slowly, the iron cage of the floor began to heat: I felt the soles of my feet begin to warm: at first it felt quite comfortable: however, the comfort gradually turned into a notable discomfort: and we were all forced to stand on one foot, to relieve the other, then, change feet. Before long, we were all hopping around in pain: and the old woman chuckled in glee, clapping her hands.

'Dance! Dance!' she yelled, as we jumped around in excruciating agony, the soles of our shoes burning away, and blisters developing on our feet. Soon, she was dancing around the room in manic joy. 'La-la-la-la-la,' she unharmoniously sang.

'Stop this!' Argon shouted. 'Stop it now!'

'Dance! Dance! Dance!' the old woman screamed, leaping about the room, twirling around, as a weird discordant 'music' began to fill the air, which seemed to keep time with our painful staccato hobbling. The pain was increasing, and I was reaching the threshold of my endurance: I thought I was going to pass out.

'Enough,' I whimpered. But the crazy old woman swirled around in an ecstatic mesmeric state, heedless to her surroundings.

'E-N-O-U-G-H!' Argon bellowed. This awoke the old woman from her trance: she suddenly stood still, and fastidiously watched us. She was fascinated at us hobbling around in dire agony. She issued a little self-satisfied smile, and then uttered some more strange words. The temperature of the cage's iron floor began to cool: and we were gradually able to put our sore feet on solid ground.

'Did you enjoy that?' the old woman asked.

'Y-O-U!' Argon shouted, about to issue potent execrations: but Kelly muffled his outburst with her hands.

'Yes, we did,' Jenny said, fighting back the tears, and examining her injured feet.

'No, we did not!' Argon furiously rejoined, freeing himself from Kelly, and looking in anger at his and her scorched feet. 'You know full well we did not, you silly old shrew.' Argon was the heaviest of us all and had the largest feet: the skin on his souls had bubbled and blistered red raw: he was now bleeding quite profusely. 'Who enjoys being caged and burnt? You termagant!' The old woman's smile quickly turned to a malevolent glare: her eyes shone a fierce ray of hatred, and it struck Argon full on: he recoiled across the cage, banging his back against the iron bars. He lay there in a crumpled heap, dazed and confused. Then, the old woman lifted her wizened finger, and pointed it at him.

'NO!' Kelly exclaimed. It was too late: an electric charge leapt from her finger engulfing Argon in a refulgent blue light; there was an intense crackling: and then, he was gone.

'Now you won't need so much room,' the old woman said, and clapped her hands: the volume of the cage reduced by half, cramping us all together, leaving us no room to stand or move. My female crew members were dumb with horror and rage: they glared at the old woman: and, if they had been un-caged, no magic in the world would have saved this cantankerous sorceress from their wrath.

'Let's not waste time,' I said to her, 'what is our ultimate fate?' She walked over to the fire, which began to wildly swirl and crackle with preternatural energy: she walked into its intense glow, and disappeared: leaving us hanging in the cage to nurse our wounds.

'We have to escape,' Kelly asserted, examining Helena's feet.

'She can probably hear us,' Helena replied, as we all watched the fire dance and crackle.

'What shall we do, then, just sit here, mute?' Kelly sarcastically retorted, glaring at Helena, battling against the notion that she had just lost her husband.

'The bars are very solid,' Jenny said, grasping and shaking and trying to loosen them. I sat there, tired and weak, scrutinizing the weeping blisters on the soles of Helena's feet. I could barely contain the fury at my woman being hurt. Her delicate body had been callously violated: and I had a powerful urge to wreak revenge. I examined my own feet, the soles of my shoes had completely burnt away, and charred pieces of rubber lay embedded in my glutinous skin. It would be a long time before any of us could walk again. The old woman's magic was powerful: we were at her mercy.

As we wretchedly waited for her next appearance, we began to feel drowsy. The snowstorm raged outside: but the flames in the hearth suffused the cabin with warmth. It was not particularly comfortable huddled up in a small iron cage, the floor was hard, and leaning against the bars became painful: but, in time, sleep will have its dominion…

I met Helena on a ridge, below us a steep precipice. Love glowed in our eyes as we took each other's hand. We danced nimbly around the mountain, swirling with the snow flakes, skipping over the peak, and rushing along with the howling wind; we leapt over plateaux, skipping over the ice wall surfaces, at one with each individual flake, suffusing into the intricate patterns, the divine symmetry, the beauty and majesty of the elements…

When we awoke, we found the old woman pointing her craggy finger at Kelly's forehead. 'Want to escape?' she malevolently asked, emitted an electric bolt, and Kelly was gone. 'There, you have escaped.' The old woman then sat down to a sumptuously laid table of food. At first her misery made her face sag: she moved with effort and looked vacant: but then she noticed our fixation with the food, and began to perk up. 'Mmmmm, d-e-l-i-c-i-o-u-s,' she said, as she took a mouthful of steaming treacle pudding and warm custard. 'I suppose your hunger has increased?' she demanded, as she continued to gorge herself. We glared at her, unsure if we could maintain the polite charade. Watching our friends so nonchalantly murdered, the indignities and discomfort of being cooped up in a caged, the searing pain of our feet, and the old woman's scorn, became intolerable: but I controlled myself, for always believed where there was life, there was a way.

'Oh, I'm not going to play your silly game anymore,' Jenny blurted. 'Kill me now!'

'Okay,' the old woman casually said, absorbed in her food: while continuing to eat with one hand, she lifted her zapping finger, and, Jenny disappeared in a flash. Only me and Helena was left. I wanted to bestow physical affection on my lady, to reassure her: but I was afraid that this would incite contempt from the old woman, and zap us both. 'And then there was two,' the old woman smirked, biting into a crisp red apple. I then noticed a change in Helena's expression: she was losing patience and growing angry: I knew she was about to say something derogatory. I placed my hand on her lap in order to try and subdue her: I could feel her heart beat thumping in preparation. I gently squeezed her thigh: no, please, do not say anything while in an emotional state, Helena. I put my hand to her mouth, but with unwonted strength, she moved it away.

'You know...' Helena said, I tried to re-locate her mouth with my palm, but she skilfully evaded me, ' watching you pig that food does not make me feel hungry.' The old woman suddenly stopped eating, and became attentive to what might be said next. 'No... watching you, you grunter, makes me want to vomit.' Then Helena began to imitate the grunting sound of a pig. I sat in front of Helena, attempting to shield her from what would happen next. The old woman's eyes glared a furious red: the flames in the fire roared and belched from the hearth scorching the table and its contents. The old woman then screamed an ear splitting yell that drowned the noise of the wild storm outside. A massive refulgent cloud of sparks burst from her hand, so bright, the skin on my eye balls shrivelled: then a ray of intense blue light leapt from her hand and flew past me: I reeled backward, my clothes on fire, hair singed, and skin peeling. The energy hit Helena full on: she was gone in an instant.

I slumped in a heap, blind, burnt, aware of consciousness, but emotionally void. Then, my body felt a burning pain: my clothes were on fire. I began spontaneously rolling around to extinguish the flames from my garments. When my skin was satisfied the molesting heat had been extirpated, I found myself laying there, motionless, panting. A pungent smell, burnt cloth, charred skin, and the aftermath of the electric energy, hung in the air: and I inhaled a sickly reminder of the old woman's irrefutable power. I heard her chuckling as she stepped back into the fire: it welcomed her with violent crackling. Then, the flames subdued as the old woman became ensconced in the hearth.

I sat in the corner of the cage, numb and lifeless. I could not properly absorb what I had just witnessed. A strong compulsion induced me to believe Helena was still by my side. I began talking to her. 'Are you all right sweet? It's okay, the old woman's gone now my darling. There, there, don't worry love, I'm here.' I rocked back and forth, speaking sentimentally to my woman as I hugged myself...

As time went on, I became more bewildered. Was she with me? Had she gone? I blindly groped around the cage. 'Helena! Helena!' I searched every corner; my blistered hands moved along floor and ceiling; I grasped each bar in turn. 'Helena, where are you?' She will be here soon, yes. She will be here soon. I interminably sat in the cage, waiting for her... waiting for her... waiting for her...

She will be here again,
Then we will be united:
When that time comes,
All will be well with the world.

She is bound to come;
We are bound by love:
It is decreed above
That we are one.

One, not two,
The perfect fit,
Like hemispheres conjoined,
Masculine-Feminine,
Attracted,
Selected for alchemy,
Together a paradise,
Never parting in spirit,
Always joined by love.

If I have to wait forever,
Finally she will arrive,
For we are only alive
In each other's sight.
One without the other
Is desolation and frustration,
And a mere precursor
To our meeting.

We will greet sweetly.
We fit into each other neatly.
Absence is fleeting
Compared to our need.
We'd rather be nothing

Than something without
Each other.

I will wait for you, Helena,
As I know you wait for me.
Only together are we
Truly free.
Our love is meant to be.
It is obvious to see
That this, without effort,
Occurs naturally.

I feel you in my heart.
I feel you in my soul.
You are my goal.
Together, we are whole;
Apart, we wait
For union.

Me and you on a cloud
In our bed,
The promises said before God,
The holy path we have trod,
Living and growing together,
Whether the weather was rough or smooth,
Our love always saw us through.

There is nothing we cannot overcome.
Two hemispheres conjoined
Make the sun look pale.
We will not fail.
Death, with its armoured mail,
Is no more than a shell of a snail,
A feeble barrier easily surmounted by our attraction.

We are carriers of the divine wish.
I am yours;
You are mine.
Love knows no time,
For we have a direct line
To heaven
Evinced in our actions.

Evil will quake before love's majesty.
It will realize its own tragedy
When it witnesses
Our happiness.
It will slink away,
Withered and worn,
Torn apart.
The love it has seen
Will mend its heart,
The start of the end of chaos.

I feel loss, Helena,
And the frustrated anticipation of your return.
We have learnt love together.
We have earned each other's trust.
Death must realize that
It cannot co-exist
With such power.

And though every second,
Every minute,
Every hour,
Every day away from you
Fills me with consternation,
The anticipation of
Facing you,

Staring in your nonpareil eyes,
Why, the sky will be aware
That its light and size
Is incomparable to our love.

So I wait, Helena,
I wait for you.
There is nothing else I can do.
My indomitable hope will help me through.
I know you are where people are as true.
Let your beacon shine bright,
Dispelling night
With the radiance you bring.

With you, I am a king,
A bird on the wing,
And everything that is good.

We will amble in the woods again,
Listening to the silver rain.
We will generate love and happiness.
We will be at peace once more:
For where you are serenity reigns:
And, oh, rapture,
Your eyes tell me you feel the same…

Helena, where are you?
Where have you gone?
I am now only half of one.
What as this old woman done?
I do not know if I can carry on.
She has taken away my sun,
My moon,
My rain.

Helena, I cannot refrain from misery.
I am wretched, dying inside.
I recede to where the darkness hides.
No matter how I try,
I cannot stop the weakness in me.
I am fading.
I hate my life.
Without you there is too much strife.

You are not here...
Soon, you will be here...
You are not here...
Soon, you will be here...

The flames soothingly sang... I thought I heard benevolent voices persuading me to rest... My misery fought against the balsamic rhythms... but... they oscillated in harmony with my entity... I became attached to them... and... drifted into slumber...

I wandered over Ice Mountain, lost and weary, vividly remembering the painful ascent of my first endeavours with Mountain Monk: every muscular effort was recorded in my soul and poured forth to augment my current wretchedness. Everywhere was cold and grey: I was acutely aware that there was no life on this miserable mountain other than my waning self. I located the wreckage of our craft, and hovered over it: now, an ice tumulus. The pile of twisted metal encased in solid frost once blithely soared amongst the clouds. I seemed to hang over the snowy grave forever, watching it gradually become entombed in thick ice. A wing tip, all that was left visible, finally disappeared as a large snow flake sealed its fate. I stared at the ice mound, all my hopes and aspirations gradually sinking deeper into the ice depths. I broke from my melancholy reverie to take advantage of my incorporeal state, and search for my friends in the storm. I cried Helena's name: but my voice was swallowed by the howling wind…

In sleep, shock gradually mitigated…

I awakened. My eyelids opened, the sand filled orbs shot electric shocks deep into the sockets: I was blind! I manically searched around the room, desperately eager for light, but only wretched darkness engulfed my soul. Panic pervaded me: I was blind! Would I never see the beautiful world again? Would Helena only ever be a fuzzy memory? Would I live the rest of life in abject tenebrous gloom? The prospect of perpetual blindness instilled wretchedness in my heart. As feelings seeped back into my sore skin, reality hit: Helena was really gone! Materializing back into the small iron cage with acute physiological and psychological discomfort filled my heart with dismay: I would have rather wandered over the barren waste land of ice as a spirit eternally searching for Helena, than caged, encased in nerve tormented skin. Love informed me we would be united; despair told me to be uncertain. I dared myself to re-live the despicable incident: the old woman killed Helena! I forgot my blindness and a manic urge for revenge thumped in my head. I did not know how I would exact it… I felt anger surge: I was about to pound on the bars and issue demented screams; when, I was overcome with a strange calm, as if sent by divinities. I sat there ruminating, reaching deep into the well of my guile… Wait, Gorky, wait for the right moment… You must punish this wickedness… And so I sat waiting, my soul quietly burning with an unprecedented energy, fearless and furious to attack the evil. Perfectly focused, I waited, my whole being now a vessel for revenge… I waited… and waited…

'You are in a pickle,' said a calm voice from the corner of the room, startlingly familiar… then realization.

'Mountain Monk?' I croaked, hardly daring to believe my ears.

'Er, yes, whatever… Listen, cannot stay, she is rather hot on the ball: though, if I'm brief, I have the power to elude her… and, this goat's head is rather demeaning,' he said.

'Is it really you?' I incredulously asked.

'Would you p-l-e-a-s-e listen…' He waited for a moment, then continued, 'she never used to be misanthropic, remember?'

'Er, yes, is…'

'P-L-E-A-S-E! It was a rhetorical question…'

'Oh, I…'

'P-L-E-A-S-E, SHUT UP!' He waited another moment, then resumed again, ' She loved a man once, but he rejected her: it filled her heart with hate; she allowed resentment to take control: but, if you can incite her to remember the love she once felt, to reach her…'

'I think she is too far gone,' I outwardly mused.

'She has surrounded herself with ice: but she dwells in flames of fire: see you later old chap: good luck.' Then I sensed emptiness: he had gone, leaving me alone with the harridan.

After a while, the fire roared, and I sensed her emanation. 'Ah, the blind boy is still here,' she sarcastically cackled. I listened attentively, like a wild cat locating its quarry: every minute rustle of her gown, every breath, the smallest movement of her shoes against the floor. I heard her sit at the table. 'Can you smell the food, blind boy?'

'Er, yes,' I replied, my soul dilating with eagerness: all my faculties screamed, Helena's killer is in the room.

'Smells delicious… does it not?' she said. I could hear the slicing of food and chewing.

'Er, yes,' I replied. I am waiting old woman. You have murdered Helena, and you display the remorse of a stone.

'How delicious, blind boy?' she continued.

'Er, very,' I said. But not as delicious as when I lay my hands on you.

'Do you want some?' she asked.

'Er, yes,' I muttered. You will not want some of this, but you are going to get it.

'How much do you want some?' she queried.

'A lot,' I said. Oh, I want it so much.

'A lot?' she said.

'Yes, a lot,' I said.

'Beg,' she ordered. My head exploded with indignation and hate: calm now, Gorky... cunning... patience.

'Er, please, can I have some food,' I half heartily asked as I ground my teeth.

'Beg, as though you really mean it, as if your life depends on it,' she commanded. Come on, Gorky... guile.

'Oh, p-l-e-a-s-e give me some food: I am dying of starvation: I cannot stand it any longer: I need food: please give me food: please give some, please: I'll do anything,' I ostensibly pleaded, in the most woebegone pitiful voice I could muster. I sat and waited, my soul animated with the urge to attack. She sighed with pleasure as she chewed her food, making exaggerated eating noises, and saying, 'Mmmmm,' after each slow and deliberate mouthful. I sat in silence, keen and alert, listening to every sound. 'All finished,' she eventually said, with a deep tone of satisfaction. 'How is the blind boy?' I did not reply, but brooded, considering the purport of what Mountain Monk had said: maybe, beyond that hard exterior was vulnerability I could exploit; I had to win her trust so I could expose her weakness. 'Is he lonely?' I continued to sit in silence, still not knowing if I would hurl a paroxysm of abuse at any moment; remain calm, Gorky: become angered, and you have lost. 'Was she your... l-o-v-e-r?' My expression momentarily turned to fury, but I quickly checked it, as I keenly waited for what she would say next. 'How does it feel to lose the one you love?' I sat there, becoming immune to her taunting, the pain of losing Helena could not be increased. I momentarily lost focus of my objective, as an eidetic image of Helena illuminated my dark lids. 'She *is* gone for good... blind boy,' the old woman said and her taunting voice quickly erased the heavenly image: and there was further silence as she waited for some kind of emotional display: but none was forthcoming. 'Oh, the sadness, the misery,' she cackled in exaggerated dramatic fashion. I could hear her walking to the cage. 'Boo hoo,' she said, emitting more cruel laughter. Although I was immersed in taciturn lamentations, a strong feeling that I must somehow befriend this old woman channelled my drives. 'Little baby,' she jeered, 'are you going to cry?' Be patient, Gorky, in the course of time, anything may arise. 'You need cheering up.' If you can remain calm, in time, she may lower her defences, reveal weakness and you can exploit her vulnerability. 'A little after dinner entertainment.' And the longer you can wait, the longer you can dissemble, the more you will learn: and the more unaware she will be when you eventually strike. She spoke the same incantation as before, and the heating of the floor started to distract me from my musings... Oh, no, the coming of the scolding floor! Oh, no, the pain! Oh, *no*... the... pain! I know: I will exaggeratedly dance for her delight; I will yell and cry and plead for mercy: I will give her what she wants, a pitiful display of despair, and maybe she will prematurely curtail the torture and think I am weak: this could possibly induce the beginning of complacency, which could eventually lead to her revealing personal details and lure her to the cage: and then... then...

But, a sudden stark picture: the anguished lineaments of my beloved lady, of dear friends, the horrors they endured: uncompromising fury flashed into my soul; the indignation of injustice overcame me: I was overwrought with uncontrollable emotion: this time, I would not suffer the humiliation of hopping around in agony for her delight. I would stoically bear the pain until I swooned!

I crouched in the corner of the cage waiting for the imminent arrival of pain… The iron floor began to steadily heat… And then… it began to burn my already sore feet. I gritted my teeth and thought of Helena. 'Dance!' the old woman cried: but I remained stationary, as the floor rapidly became hot. Soon, the searing heat was shooting up my legs. 'Dance!' she yelled. I held Helena tenderly in my arms, and made love to her, gently kissing her soft lips as she made sweet moan. 'DANCE!' the old woman screamed: my soles hissed and bubbled: I felt light headed: and I knew it would not be long before I would fall flat onto the red hot floor and die. The excruciating pain was encroaching upon my senses, seeping into the image of Helena, and claiming dominion. 'D-A-N-C-E!' the old woman raucously yelled in anguish. Helena vanished, and the horrors of hell were upon me: I languished in wretched agony, willing to relinquish life to stop the awful pain.

'I hope… you feel… pleased… now,' I managed to mumble, preparing to fall to my death. Then, the old woman let out a guttural cry of torment, 'AAAAARRRRGGGGHHHH!!!' The floor's temperature began to drop: and I slumped down, taking deep gasps of air, unsure if I would remain conscious. As I lay there, I was sure I heard a stifled sobbing from the old woman as she disappeared back into the flames of the hearth: and, through my anguish, I felt satisfaction that I had penetrated beyond her hard exterior.

So you do have feelings other than hate and anger, old woman. I heard you whimper, yes, like a little child. Emotions I can prey on… You are not so ruthless then, are you? Now I have a way into your weakness. You are mine old woman, mine for the taking. My resentment makes me strong. My pain makes me strong. My hate makes me strong. My wrath makes me strong. Your weakness makes me strong. My hunger for revenge makes me lethal. You are nothing compared to my urge for revenge. I have waited a long time. I have been patient for a long time. Beware the anger of those with forbearance. The longer I suffer at your diabolical hands, the need to kill you increases. I am hungry for your death. I will reach into your soft under-belly. I will grasp your delicate insides and squeeze so that the blood oozes between my fingers. I will twist your entrails round and round, until they snap.

To further my chagrin, the feeling in my soles slowly came back: I gently dabbed them with my finger tips: the skin was fluid and mushy. I sat suspended in the cage, the chain creaking, and the fire crackling. I tried to contact Helena with my yearning love: but my psyche only projected into the darkness of my eyes, realizing the empty void therein. I hoped Mountain Monk would return: but intuitively knew he would not. I grasped the iron bars, and shook in a vain attempt to budge them: but they were solid. All I could do was wait for the old woman to re-emerge for more ritual taunting... But... I *did* hear her sob. There must be the passionate fire of humanity beyond that icy surface. That little evocation evinced another facet of her character, although deeply buried: compassion. In that small sob was my hope for freedom. That subtle display of emotion encouraged the notion there was something to be exploited. I could now instigate the process of winning her trust. I will patiently appeal to her loneliness and natural desire for human comforting. She would not escape with impunity for murdering my people.

After a while, the fire began to roar: the harbinger of her return. The room imbued with the smells of all manner of delicacies. 'Do you like peach pie?' she asked. I felt my stomach curdle in hunger. I had an impulse to blurt out what a cruel old witch she was: but I did not want to excite her anger and drive down further any magnanimous feelings she may harbour.

'Yes, I do,' I said.

'And fresh cream?' she asked.

'Yes,' I replied.

'Oh, g-o-o-d… Guess what I'm eating,' she said.

'Peach pie and fresh cream?' I said.

'Yes! How did you guess?' she cackled, as she made deliberate sounds of gorging. 'Can you hear me eating it?'

'Yes.'

'Can you smell it?'

'Yes.'

'What does it smell like?' she asked, and I could hear her sarcastic smile.

'Er, d-e-l-i-c-i-u-o-s,' I exaggeratedly stated. She stopped eating, and listened attentively to me.

'Are you making fun of me?' she queried. The fire began to crackle a tincture more intensely, and, steadily increased to the verge of a wild roar: it seemed to incite my own anger.

'Are you making fun of me?' I suddenly retorted. This was not the reply that I had intended, but my contempt for the old woman was most difficult to contain, and I found myself speaking inadvertently, as if possessed by a demon. I expected repercussions for my impudence: and it seemed like aeons as I waited for the reply…

The fire eventually mitigated its roar, but continued to blaze. I listened to the flames crackle… and the powerful ominous silence of the old woman. Then I heard myself speak again, in an impatient attempt to reach out to the old woman's vulnerability. 'Are you lonely?' I asked, hoping I could elicit sadness, as she had in me. I felt her scrutinizing me with her supernatural penetrating gaze. I was growing most annoyed at being stared at… 'Well, are you? It appears you spend all your time on this barren mountain without any company whatsoever. What has induced you to live in such an anchoretic manner?' I waited for her response. I deemed I had said sufficient to be zapped: in despair, I anticipated my demise: but it did not come. Had I sensed a change in her, as if maintaining callousness was becoming a strain? She quietly moved towards the cage: I could hear her saffron gown rustling as she approached. I faced her, subtly assuaging my defiant mien as she drew near, in hope that I could draw her closer and invoke sentiment: and during her emotional confession I would throttle her. She stood there, I sensed just out of reach, staring intently at me.

'Continue,' she supplicated, which *sounded* as if she was eager to hear an honest opinion: but it could have been pseudo-intrigue: for, although I did hear a sob, this old woman was not to be underestimated. Anyhow, she was drifting nearer the cage, and if I could lure her within arms' length, I could get my hands around her scrawny neck.

'You are incredibly cruel,' I blurted out, again disregarding any contingency, frustrated that pure emotion was dictating my speech and over riding the strategy: I had meant to slowly break her down, gradually building to an epiphany: but indignation would have its say.

'Cruel?' she said, moving a little nearer.

'Have you always been like that?' I asked, knowing, of course, that Mountain Monk had told me that once she had loved. She quietly stood before me for a short while, then emitted a small wistful sigh. 'What has made you become like this?' I continued, aware she was in a subdued mood, but still anxious that any moment could be my last. The fire continued to gently crackle as I heard her pull a chair up to the cage. That's it, closer... She sat down and silently watched me. Although I was waiting for an opportunity to attack, I thought it could have been another one of her cruel games, taking her time before she inflicted some sort of torture: and yet, I *did* sense a change in her demeanour...

'Would you have always been together?' she eventually asked.

'Me and Helena?' I replied. Saying, *me and Helena*, increased the density of the rock in my stomach, and also awareness that the vile instigator of our unwanted parting was before me: but I had to be patient, the old woman was now mild, I had to maintain this unwonted mood.

'Helena?' she spoke the name as if it was connected to a living breathing person: the old woman's voice did not sound harsh. 'Yes, you and… *Helena*,' she said, her tones much softer now, as if revealing an inner tenderness: either that, or it was her subtle way of mocking.

'I cannot think of life without her,' I answered. I wanted to reveal my sensibilities, so that the old woman would come closer, and be all the more unsuspecting when I struck.

'What is life like without her?' she replied.

'Empty,' I ingenuously asseverated.

'Empty…' she repeated, fully understanding, and dwelling on it, before continuing. 'What if she suddenly started treating you very cruelly?' she inquired. I nearly blurted, no one could be as cruel as you, you old hag: but engaging in unprecedented active dialogue assisted my patience, for I now felt as if I was making some progress towards my revenge.

'It depends what you mean by cruel: there are different levels of cruelty: she is not capable of the worst kind: but if she was aloof, which is cruel as she could be, there would be good reason,' I stated.

'What if there was no reason?' the old woman continued.

'There would be a reason,' I rejoined.

'But what *if*?' the old woman urgently asked as her voice wavered with emotion. It was difficult to envisage such a scenario: Helena never acted unfriendly without cause: but I could tell the old woman needed an answer.

'Then I would be deeply hurt,' I said.

'Deeply hurt…' she again lingered on these words, before asking, 'Would you continue to love her?' I was being presented with hypothetical situations which were, to me, unlikely. I had recently, for the first time, experienced Helena's aloofness, but she later explained why: during this awkward period between us, I had loved her as ardently as ever.

'I suppose love never really dies… if it is real love,' I finally answered.

'Do you know what it is like to be duped into loving unrequitedly?' she inquired. I had an idea where this was leading: and I thought if I kept her talking long enough, I may be able to cajole her to the cage bars: and then, she would be no more… I decided to recall a memory from my early life so she would feel more familiar with me.

'Well, when I was a boy, I duped myself, I suppose… There was this woman… she was beautiful… and I would always make a point of watching her whenever I could. At night, to help me sleep, I would imagine us being together. I fell in love with her. Then, one day, as I was walking in our village, wondering if I would see her, I saw her with a man: they had just performed the wedding ritual: I was devastated.'

'Marriage… MARRIAGE!' her voice reached to a crescendo, and I thought she would begin ranting, and finally put me out my misery with her potent magic: but she then calmed down again, and exhaled a long wistful sigh. 'I loved a man,' she said: and, I thought, yes, another break through. Keep talking old woman. Then, much to my annoyance, she leapt from the chair, and began marching around the room, trying to fight back what she wanted to say, but, suddenly, 'However, I was not a child.' Her voice became erratic as she punched her fist into her palm. 'But I was not a child, not a child.'

'Tell me,' I entreated, trying to take advantage of the moment, 'what happened?' To my delight, she instantly replied.

'I used to live far from here, a beautiful place… warm, and lush with green… I was happy there. I was a milkmaid…' She waited for me to make comment, but none was forth coming: I wanted her to continue. 'I was a milkmaid,' she repeated, and halted… She remained motionless… and silent… Outside, the storm eerily blew… Inside, the fire crackled in anticipation… I could not stand the suspense any longer.

'Yes,' I said, 'and…'

'And… and… ' she baulked.

'And… go on,' I urged.

'And… and… I milked the king's cows… I brought the milk to his kitchens every day…' She hesitated again. Her voice was indicating intense suppressed emotion, as if she would burst into tears at any moment.

'Yes, I'm listening,' I said. 'Please, go on.'

'Well… well… unbeknown to me… I was being observed… by a very interesting young man…' I heard her sit back down. Yes, that's it old woman, closer. I crawled to the bars, and pressed my chest up against them so I could get as near as possible to her. Judging by her sigh, she was still just out of arms' length: I poised myself ready to pounce at the first opportunity. The fire gently murmured. The old woman was most relaxed now as she commenced, 'One day, while I was milking the king's cows, he came into the sheds. He covertly watched me as I worked, until I realized he was there: with a start, I looked up, spurting milk all over the floor. It was the king's son, the prince. He told me I was lovely. I was very embarrassed, and did not know whether to curtsey or bow my head. I did neither, but stood up from my stool, inwardly wishing him to leave, for I deemed he was mocking me. He then informed me he had been surreptitiously watching me for a long time. He asked me my name: which, as he was the prince, I assumed it only proper to impart: he then told me his. He advised me to never mention this meeting: flattered that I was receiving such attention from nobility, I assured him I would not. He began to regularly visit me in the cow sheds: and, well, our conversations gradually became more intimate... and... amorous. One day, he became rather, er, persistent: his eyes evinced frenzied passion had taken control: I could detain him no longer... After, when he had, er, finished... I wept: my virginity was gone... He did not seem to understand the significance: but I ascribed this to his inexperience. He now visited more frequently, always insisting I stop milking the cows, and tend to him. On many occasions, I asked him where this was all going to lead: he said he was going to petition his father for permission to... to... marry me: but, in the mean time, I must remain silent... One momentous day, I notified him I was to have his child: to which he became very pallid, and chided me. He told me he knew of an apothecary that could deal with the situation. I was stunned, for I really believed he cared for me. He became very strange after that, and kept well away. I understood his dilemma, for, conventionally, it was a misalliance: but, I did expect him to send me a message of some sort. Not long after, two henchmen appeared, and became very threatening, asking me if I had been to the apothecary yet. I told them I had no intentions of doing such a thing: they warned me, that, if I did not, it would be the worse for me. I thought little of this, because I was sure that when I informed the prince, he would apprehend the ruffians (love can be naive): however, there was no way of contacting him. Eventually, the two thugs returned, and asked me again, if I had taken care of "the problem". I reiterated what I had told them before: I intended on keeping the child: so, they beat me... badly... repeatedly striking me in the stomach, until, I passed out... I awoke... with a pool of... blood... between my legs... News circulated that I had been trampled by the cows: and, although I tried to tell people what had really happened, I was unheeded: but sacked from my job for negligence. Unable to support myself, I found myself begging on the streets...

I became destitute: but my morale was maintained by the belief that the prince would soon publicly declare his love for me, and we would be joyfully re-united. Then, one day, while I was sat on the curb, an old lady walked by. I asked her if she could spare some loose change. She stopped, and looked down at me: for an instant, her eyes flashed, evincing inordinate power, piercing deep into my being, and rendering me defenceless: but it was transient, and I was unsure if it was a trick of the light. Anyway, she took pity, and invited me back to her dwelling place. I told her of my plight: she slowly nodded, listening attentively: for the first time in my life I felt that I was communicating. She introduced herself as Zeeta, and said I could live with her, providing I did the house work: so she fed and clothed me. She warned me to never enter a specific room: though she never imparted the reason: and, as time went on, my curiosity grew. Only she would ever enter: and though I would often listen outside, I could never hear a thing. Then, one day, I could abide it no longer: I had to know what lay beyond the door. I waited for her to take one of her long walks: then, I prepared to go in. I anticipated it being locked, but much to my surprise it swung open. As I entered, a strange ambivalent energy pervaded me, an elemental force: I could not ascertain if it was good or bad. On the dusty shelves, there were many tomes on ancient lore in most peculiar hieroglyphs: and, as I perused her impressive library, it was most apparent she was more than a frail old woman. Suddenly, she stepped out from nowhere with a broad grin on her face, and said, "Ah, she could not stand the suspense any longer... I must say, you controlled your desire to pry for an extraordinarily long time." Then, she revealed all: she descended from a long line of powerful witches: but, due to the existing ideologies of the milieu, to evade persecution, she now had to maintain an absolute covert identity... Well, I was amazed, for, as I said, this old woman appeared so innocuous: but, I felt more secure knowing I had come under the auspices of a sorceress... All this time, I was still convinced my prince would come: until, one incredible day, I learnt of the most unbelievable news: he was to be married to a princess from the neighbouring country... I was incredulous; I was still certain we would eventually be together... On the morning of the supposed wedding day, I was up early, impatient to prove the rumour wrong. Eventually, people started congregating, which was the first sign it may be true: I went to stand with them, my heart over wrought with anxiety. Then, I heard in the distance, a clip-clop of horses, which preceded a long line of regal pomp: this induced my stomach to churn. Soon, the procession appeared, and my nerves increased, for the dreaded moment of truth was nigh. Suddenly, I espied the prince in a gold filigree coach with his new wife: she was very pretty, and they looked so blissfully happy. They rode by, waving to the cheering crowds: and, as he past me, he looked straight through. I stood dumbfounded: and, as the crowds dispersed, I remained, and relived over and over again what I had just seen, and recalled how he had sworn his undying love for me. Now, he was with a beautiful princess, with the prospect of a contented future: and me... I was a social outcast, with solitude to look forward to. I began to feel a lurid green jealousy grow inside me. I ran back to the hovel and howled an irrevocable lament. Zeeta, of course, knew what was ailing me. After my initial paroxysm, I begged her to teach me witchcraft: she was very dubious, for I was not emotionally stable, and she feared I would use the magic for a most abominable revenge. I assured her I would not: though, surreptitiously, I intended on walking into the king's court, and, in front of all the retinue, expose and ridicule the prince: then, wreak on him the most foulest of spells. Daily, I systematically subjected Zeeta to calculated entreaties: one time, I threatened to expose her identity: but quickly realized it unwise to attempt coercing a powerful enchantress in such a manner: her eyes flamed, and she demonstrated, thankfully, on a piece of furniture, what would happen to me if I carried out that particular ploy. I became more cautious in my supplicating after that: but was still determined to persuade her. Eventually, after much pleading, and though she expressed deep reservations, she took me into her full trust: and revealed her darkest secrets of atavistic magic… I practised obsessively. Zeeta's doubts gradually decreased, and she became most pleased to be passing her heritage onto such a fine student. She told me I was a natural: and, after much diligence, I exceeded all my expectations. The day was not far away when I would feel confident enough to carry out my revenge. However, I never had the chance: for, one night, some of the king's men made silent entry to our dwelling and decapitated Zeeta in her sleep. I am sure I heard her voice as I slept, urging me to wake and quickly evacuate the premises. I awoke to hear them ransacking everything. I fled before they had chance to detect my whereabouts: and I managed to take with me some of her most esoteric books. Later, I heard through the grapevine that those who had killed Zeeta went crazy and committed suicide. This did not surprise me. And, I cannot help but think that she willingly let them murder her: for, as she had now transferred her powers to me, it was her time to depart to the incorporeal realm. She was too other-worldly to be so easy caught off-guard. I became an unmitigated pariah, hunted from country to country, with a price on my head any self respecting witch would have been proud of. I tried to settle down: but every time I thought I found some where safe, I was pursued by zealous folk eager to burn or banish me: so, I lived in exile, until I found this mountain. A little magic ensured it unapproachable and inhospitable: and, finally, I acquired sanctuary. You may wonder why I did not use magic against the people who persecuted me: I could have done, easily: but, initially, I only wanted to punish the prince… However, as time elapsed, in the prolonged solitude of an icy existence, I have unwittingly let the pain and canker grow… and… I have turned… wicked.'

The old woman, at hearing her own avowal, burst in to tears: she wept and wept: and, as she wept, she leaned towards the cage within grabbing distance: but, I could not do it. Instead, I found myself saying, 'There, there,' and gently patting her head through the bars... As I did, my feet began to grow new skin... and... then... I felt light begin to push into my orbs... and... soon... my sight was restored. I squinted in the bright yellow sunlight as birds began singing in the sky, and the air became sweet. Yes, the snow had stopped falling: sun shone through the window. As she continued to weep, the cage melted away, and I floated to the ground. Then, to my profound joy, Argon materialized before me... then Jenny... Kelly... Barney... and Helena! At first, they stood there bemused: but soon became orientated and began greeting me, and each other, with merriment... Helena poured into my arms and I became enveloped in gracious femininity: I smiled, thankful that the cosmic decree of love was ineluctable: Gorky and Helena were born to be together. We lovingly caressed assuaging pain of involuntary parting...

After a while, our attention turned to the old woman, who looked discernibly younger now, and milder, as a pool of silver tears shimmered on the floor. 'I am sorry,' she wept, 'for the pain I have caused you... It made me no happier... only worse!' And she cried some more, a woeful misery that struck the core of my being: a tear trickled down my cheek as she uncontrollably sobbed. We waited for her to stop: and as her pain abated, the tears fell less: until she was able to regain her composure. She looked at us a tincture embarrassed, and waited for a derisive comment.

'Are you feeling a little better?' I asked.

'Er, yes, I think so... I did not realize I had harboured such grief: I had forced it deep inside: it quite overwhelmed me as it came gushing forth: I feel a poison inside me has dissipated.' She issued a little smile: and she seemed to grow even younger: Helena nudged me, for I must have been staring too long. I walked to the window and peered outside: I took a deep breath at the dramatic transformation.

'It appears that Ice Mountain has turned green,' I said. 'The sky is... blue... The mountain is strewn with verdure and flowers... and... there are airborne song birds melodiously warbling... Not a sign of ice or snow anywhere!' The old woman... I mean, the young woman's smiled broadened.

'I have detained you long enough,' she softly said. 'You will want to be on your way now, I suppose.'

'Yes, if you do not mind... We are on a mission,' I eagerly explained, 'but our craft...'

'You will find your aircraft is repaired... most fine craftsmanship... Everything is intact,' she said.

'The water?' Helena asked.

'The water? Ar, you must mean... Sacradia... I was surprised to see vestiges of *that* within your vessel... You are most intrepid people... Yes, your urn is full...' This was a boon indeed, and the thought of renewing the mission with everything intact lifted my spirits even further. We eagerly made for the door... 'One other thing,' she remarked, 'while you fly over the mountain... the wings will work themselves, but once the other side, you must use your own strength again.'

'Thank you,' Argon grinned.

'It is the least I can do. You may leave now. Your plane is outside,' she smiled and nodded to the door: the anticipation of flying freely in the open sky after being cramped and caged induced jubilation. Argon was about to egress, but hesitated, and turned to the woman.

'Woman, what is your name?' he asked.

'Kimtiv,' she replied.

'Kimtiv, what do you propose to do with your life now?' he continued.

'I yearn to make people happy, to put my magic to good use,' she said.

'Have you pen and paper?' he asked. With that, fitting for a witch, pen and paper materialized on the table. Argon began writing.

'Here is a map that will lead you to Firkin Forest. Also, here is written permission from me, an elder of Firkin, to live there unmolested if you so choose: providing, of course, you do not make a nuisance of yourself.' He stared at her, and she reciprocated with an expression that suggested this would be unlikely. 'Hand this to Boswald,' he continued, 'and tell him I sent you: my name is Argon.' He held out his hand: Kimtiv did not know what to do, but beamed and nodded her approval.

22.

Clones

The cabin door opened inviting us to exit. We stepped outside, and sure enough, our noble chromium aeroplane glinted proudly in the sunlight. We looked around in wonder: it seemed a different place. The mountain, still grand and majestic, was carpeted in flora and pine trees that swept out towards The Forest of Life, awe inspiring to see the two forests contiguous. It was warm: and a pleasant smell of fresh pines filled the air…

Our plane, gleaming like a mirror in the refulgent sun, reflected the hues of green from the mountain. We stood for a moment, staring at the noble contraption, restored to its original grandeur, contentedly waiting for its passengers. One by one, we stepped back into the plane, sitting in our accustomed seats. I felt a nervous excitement as I settled into the cockpit, placing my palm on the immaculately polished aluminium hull, staring out at the beautiful rurality. I exhaled an anticipatory breath at the awesome prospect of flight over the mountain. It was good to feel a part of the aeroplane again. I looked for Kimtiv to bid farewell: but she was nowhere to be seen.

Suddenly, the wings began flapping powerfully back and forth: and the craft surged vertically upwards. We sat amazed, and felt quite powerless at the unwonted take off. The g-force pushed us down into our seats and distorted our faces, dragging the loose flesh downwards, displaying the bottom of our eye balls. All we could do was hold on and try admire the view as the pedals whirred round faster than anyone could ever have pushed them: on any other occasion I would have been concerned that the mechanisms would have fractured with the stress and the wings break against the force of the air: but I had faith in Kimtiv's magic, and the structure held sturdy and strong, wings oscillating with incredible rapidity, like a dragonfly's. Upwards we flew, parallel to the mountain's face, watching the pines zip past. We were rising with such velocity I wondered if we would ever stop: I had visions of us rising forever, up, up, into the ether, upwards, beyond our atmosphere, into space, forever flying onwards, to the outer regions of the universe, and into infinity…

Soon we reached the summit of the mountain: my eyes eagerly glared at the peak, hoping the plane would recognize it no longer needed to ascend: sure enough, the wings suddenly stopped, and spread aloft like a cruising bird of prey. We then began gracefully gliding down the other side. The sudden change from ascension to descent induced my stomach to perform all sorts of acrobatics, and it felt as though my brain was being turned inside out. However, I quickly adjusted, for I was determined to enjoy this effortless flight and incredible scenery. The pellucid sky above, the verdant hues below, rendered a sublime view, humble sentience satiated, profound pleasures didactic nature bountifully bestows on the discerning. The wings, akimbo, held steady, cutting through the temperate air as downwards we rushed away from the green mountain towards the region where Nubile's tribe should be. My heart began to beat faster as I recalled her stunning beauty and how I was so utterly enchanted: to visit the place where she lived held a profound fascination for me. We swooped downwards…Argon assiduously took charge of the controls, expertly trimming the flaps and tail rudder, holding us on a steady descent.

'We want to be down there,' I shouted in the rushing air, pointing to a tributary that ran through the forest. Either side of the water vein was flat even ground: and, although I did not know the exact location of her tribe, I surmised it would not be far from there.

'Okay,' Argon replied, as he aimed the nose towards the margin of the stream. We rapidly descended towards the heart of the forest. The lush green trees gently swayed in the breeze, and each fluttering leaf symbolized the memory of that extraordinary woman. Soon, the crown of trees that had been below us, were towering above us, as we ran alongside the winding stream, waiting for a straight stretch so we could land. As soon as there was opportunity, Argon quickly placed the undercarriage on the smooth margin: and we landed safely alongside the running water, and came to a halt.

I leapt out, rather nervous, as I scanned the trees that fair Nubile must have frequently looked upon with her enigmatic eyes. She may have been stood in the exact same place I was now: I inwardly smiled thinking of her voluptuous body.

'Are you okay?' Helena inquired.

'Er, yes, I'm fine,' I replied.

'You're looking rather wistful,' she rejoined, 'like a cat who's just had the cream.'

'Am I? I am not!' I shook myself out of my cogitations, and took action to digress the conversation. 'Helena.'

'Yes,' she said, carefully alighting the craft, and examining the melodious stream.

'When Kimtiv zapped you...' she looked at me, the light of the rippling water twinkling in her eyes, 'where did you go?' The other crew looked knowingly at each other, smiling.

'Go?' she eventually answered.

'Yes, can you remember?' I asked.

'Let's just say, you never told me about your first love.'

She then climbed into the stream: and it gurgled with pleasure as it swirled around her ankles. I looked at her feeling myself culpable, until I affirmed it was a time before I knew her, and so I was exonerated from that particular fascination. She smiled, and became absorbed in the glistening patterns of the stream: I could tell she was going to add nothing further so it was pointless to supplicate her. I surmised she had heard the conversation between me and Kimtiv, that my vanished comrades had been present all along.

'Er, I do not think that the tribe will be far from here,' I rambled, voraciously drinking in the magnificent scenery.

'Are you okay, Gorky?' Helena enquired. 'You are acting rather peculiar.'

'Stop saying that! Or I *will* start behaving... Aaarrggghhh!' With that, I saw Nubile appear from the bushes, carrying a bundle of clothes, which, I inferred, she was to wash in the stream: then, she appeared again... and again... and... again... until, there were, at least twenty Nubiles, heading this way, each delectable... I mean identical, carrying pots, pans and piles of clothes. My mouth dropped and I stood petrified. I felt the blood rush from my face and I began to feel quite dizzy: I staggered a little, tripped over a rock, and fell backwards into the stream. The water quickly revived me: and I allowed it to flow over my head, not daring to raise myself to confirm what I had just seen: but soon, of course, I needed air: and so, I anxiously raised my head out of the water: and, sure enough, twenty women, all looking like Nubile, were stood on the margin peering down at me.

'Is this the tribe you seek?' Helena ostensibly asked.

'Er, no, no, definitely not, never seen her before, er, them before,' and I lowered my head back into the water again, hoping when I re-submerged, she would be... they would be, gone. When I could hold my breath no longer, I leapt up, gasping for air, inhaling large quaffs, panting with all my might. No one took any notice: the crew was in active dialogue with the girls: there was some gesticulation from both sides, then Argon approached me.

'Are you getting out of there?' he asked.

'Er, I like it in here,' I replied.

'What is wrong with you?' he inquired.

'Stop asking what is wrong with me: I'm fine.' I took a deep breath, then boldly marched out of the stream, slipped, and nearly fell back in... 'Hello,' I feebly said, and waved at the girls... 'Er... How are you?' They looked quizzically at each other for a moment, then went on speaking to the crew.

'Gorky!' Argon shouted, prodding me into awareness that he was there.

'What!' I irritably retorted.

'They do have a section of their people dying of an unknown disease: they have quarantined them in a separate part of the forest. They are totally baffled at what caused it... Gorky, are you listening?' Argon demanded.

'Yes, yes... what?' I said, as I stared at Nubile, then looked at Nubile, then ogled at Nubile... and recalled past times...

'We have explained to them we have a cure for the malady. They are going to take us to the infected people... If you wish, you can guard the plane.... Gorky! Guard the plane!' he scolded.

'Yes... I'll guard the plane... I'll... I'll stand here... guarding... guarding the plane...' I said. So the urn of Sacradia was carried into the forest, while I was left staring at the stream as it rushed by. The trees gently soughed, and white fluffy clouds slowly glided along a cobalt sky. I tried to refrain from reminiscing: but an eidetic image of Nubile with the sea breeze blowing in her hair dominated my mind.

'Hi,' a voice suddenly said by my side. It was her!

'Hello,' I impulsively replied, trying to ignore her loveliness: as I stared into the water, I saw a vivid reflection of her smiling up at me.

'You did not want to go with the others?' she asked.

'Nubile! I thought you were dead!' I said, gazing right into her big shining eyes.

'Nubile? I am not Nubile. I am Fairmoan...' She stopped to think for a moment, then proceeded, 'Nubile? I have heard of her... It is said she defiantly ventured into a forbidden part of the forest, and was eaten by the pit monster... Nobody likes to speak of it... accept our leaders, who use the story to remind us of why we should not leave the confines of our marked territories.' She became glum: and I could not tolerate seeing her sad pout.

'Nubile! It is you!' I earnestly held her naked arms: she screamed, struggled free, and ran back into the forest. 'Nubile!' I shouted after her, 'Nubile!' But she was gone... It was not long before a group of angry male tribe members appeared, all identical: and all very annoyed as she led the way.

'Him! It was him!' she shouted, inciting the tribe's further ire. I did not know whether to run: but where would I have gone? Besides, I could explain to them that I was with those who had come to help... They stopped in front of me.

'You have laid hands on one of our women!' one angrily declared.

'What? Er, I only held her arms... like this.' I went to demonstrate: but he took swift manoeuvres to stand in front of her, as she stepped back and became enveloped in protective bodies. 'Nubile!' I beseeched.

'You will not say that name,' he vehemently proclaimed.

'Nubile, tell them we know each other,' I implored, trying to catch her eye.

'I do not know you!' she screamed, 'and you attacked me!'

'Nubile, tell them, please!' I supplicated.

'You will leave our lands,' a tribe member said. 'Go now!'

'I can't go yet, my friends have not returned,' I complained. He thought about this, and I could tell the mention of my comrades had partially pacified him. He examined me up and down, closely, looking disgusted.

'We do not like you,' he eventually stated. 'Make sure you do not move… and… behave yourself.' He turned to face the others, and they nodded their approval of how he had handled the situation: and soon they were walking back into the forest…

To appease my disappointment, I raided our supplies: Kimtiv had bestowed our hold with victuals similar to those that had adorned her table. I felt great satisfaction as I tucked into the appetizing food… Afterwards, I felt drowsy, so I laid my head against a turf mound, and listened to the babbling stream: there is emollient for a weary soul in talking waters: the silver tinkle chimes lulled me in to a profound soporific state: my cares melted away, and my soul imbued with divine insouciance: a protracted and dreamless sleep overwhelmed me, until, at a specific moment, I awoke…

My companions appeared from the forest in animated discussion with some of the tribe: they were laughing and chattering as they carried the urn containing Sacradia between them. Kelly said something: and the whole group chortled and nodded in agreement. Then 'Nubile' caught a glimpse of me: and the tribe went sullen. I shuffled around, my heart aching for a rapprochement with her; I wanted it to be how when we first met. As they approached, I became quite frigid. They congregated around the plane: and one of the tribe began to talk, 'Well, thank you, you who have miraculously fallen from the sky to cure our people. This is truly a remarkable occasion: and, although it has caused a commotion amongst some of our leaders, the people have been alerted to new possibilities beyond our wonted purlieu.' He shook Argon heartily by the hand. I looked Nubile over, then looked Nubile over, then scoured Nubile's beautiful body: and remembered the time she had given me permission to physically explore her smooth curves.

'We were pleased to be of assistance, old boy,' declared Argon, as he and Barney loaded the precious urn back on board. I stared accusingly at Nubile, then at Nubile, then frowned at Nubile. Argon addressed the crew, 'Well, I do not know about you, but after that fine meal, and that comfortable rest, I feel fit and ready for the next phase.' What fine meal? What comfortable rest? And would you not wish to hear what the next phase entails? The crew nodded and averred to Argon's proposal: and they all clambered on board the plane, as the tribe stood smiling and waving.

'Gorky!' Kelly cried.

'Yes?' I absently replied.

'Are you coming?' she asked.

'Yes,' I bitterly retorted, reluctant to depart, for unwilling to leave the delicious Nubile behind. My heart transmogrified to lead, and I became apathetic and dour. I tried to send an urgent message to her through my yearning eyes.

'Well, come on then!' Jenny exclaimed. I exuded a deep sigh, and, against all my instincts, and, with great determination, I climbed on board the craft. I stared straight ahead, along the flat ground we would soon be speeding along.

'We will visit again,' Argon declared...'Ready? Go!' We all started pushing down on the pedals. The plane gave a gentle lurch forward: soon, the craft moved assuredly along the margin of the stream, bumping and veering slightly gathering apace until the wheels left the ground and the plane swung into the air. We soared over Nubile's forest...

'How peculiar,' Barney mused.

'What,' Jenny replied.

'That those people had no notion that they all looked the same,' he continued...

Although I left my heart behind, I knew I had to look forward: I kept myself busy, pumping the pedals, and mentally preparing for the challenging crossing of the expansive The Sea of Leviathans.

Suddenly, salt air filled our lungs: a pang of excitement ensued...

Soon, far up ahead, I could just detect the coast line that was the precursor to The Sea of Leviathans: my stomach churned at descrying the imposing presence. 'That way!' I confirmed with emotional anticipation. Before us, was the incredible glittering aquamarine carpet which was the sea: the vast expanse before us stimulated an acute awareness of what we were about to embark upon. My crew members stared in shock at the incredible scene: they had never seen the sea, and their souls expanded as they mentally ingested it. Unified adrenalin made the craft feel more powerful than ever before...

Then, my spirit surfeited with awe, because, I could just descry a faint glimmer in the sky... the geosynchronous Purple Star. 'You see there?!' I yelled, triumphantly pointing deep into the sky.

'Where?' Argon asked.

'There, the tiny purple glittering... just there!' They all strained their eyes to see in the direction I was indicating.

'Yes!' Argon eventually exclaimed, and trimmed the rudder: for, below that lodestar, was our final destination: The Masked Tribe.

23.

That Sinking Feeling

We flew on, the ocean instantly upon us: the sounds of the sea sailing over the salty air sending a salient reminder of its size; the air was satiated with the sounds of the sea as suddenly we were over the prodigious blue-green. I became profoundly aware of being suspended in a flimsy flying machine, the sea below like a gaping hungry throat eagerly anticipating our fall. Now, even if we wanted to, we could not land: below us, was a heaving turquoise mass, breathing and restlessly rolling, stretching out beyond the horizon, mirroring the sky: The Sea of Leviathans. We anxiously stared out to the horizon, and with no land in sight, we knew that our lives would depend on our bodies' finite strength, and this little craft, that could have been swallowed by one of the voracious waves in the ocean's vast array of armaments. Yes, I remembered the innocuous glass surface suddenly erupting into chaos, one moment the sea was still and sedate, and then, without warning, dramatically changing its psyche into something startlingly fierce. But we were above it this time, surely we were immune from its influence, safely ensconced in the sky.

On we intrepidly flew: and the wind began to strengthen. We could hear the shifting brine roar and crash. The plane buffeted about, being tossed around like a feather, zigzagging to the left and right, up and down. At one point, the craft dropped so violently, that we all sat above the cockpit, almost out of the plane, as we held onto thin air; then, the craft rose so quickly, we slammed back into our seats: I thought I had broken my pelvis...

Night came: cosmic curtains descended shrouding the luminous sky in eerie matt black. We were flying in a dark void, a tiny capsule enveloped by infinity. We were most grateful that the Purple Star glittered in the dun night like a benevolent eye, winking and encouraging us to take heart, and fly to its protection...

The rain began to pour down like buckets of falling pebbles. It relentlessly crashed into the plane: great globules splashed mini explosions, making the aluminium ring in consternation. The plane furiously rocked from side to side: and I was extremely anxious we would be tipped out. The wind ruthlessly howled, the storm raging in my ears, screaming in lunacy. We grimly pedalled on, at the mercy of the wild and untamed elements. Argon fought with the controls, his face contorted and eyes rolling with the sheer strain. We were drenched through as the plane became inundated. Our faces were covered in a stormy sheet of water, dripping like faucets down our necks, clothes heavy with ice cold rain. Suddenly, the plane went plummeting, our inertia parting us from the seats. I waited for the wonted rise: but the craft kept falling, falling, falling, and my stomach informed me the plane was oddly limp, falling like a lifeless lump of metal through dark space towards the stomach of the sea. Kelly frantically grabbed the controls alongside Argon, and both pulled upwards on the levers, the wind and rain zipping past at lightning speed, stinging our faces as it belted us. The wind howled like a ghoul in my sensitive ears, screaming like a harbinger of death. My eyes closed tight with the sheer pain: for it felt as if my nerve replete orbs were being assailed by a million needles. With great relief, I felt the plane begin to correct itself; wings took hold of the air once again: and the heroic craft levelled off just above the leaping froth of the waves. We were smashed in the face by a great salty wave: I quaffed a large mouthful and choked it out my nostrils: my eyes watered in anguish. I manically glared out at the night, supplicating for mercy, wanting to extricate the aluminium fetter.

There, in front of us, was a silhouette. I ardently squinted in the pouring rain trying to discern what it could be. Faintly showing in the dark, was that land? I could just see it through my streaming vision of sea and rain. 'Land!' I shouted. 'Look!' The plane must have seen it before us: for it swooped ungainly, hitting the sand, and catapulting us across the shore. Luckily, the sand made for a soft landing, and no one was hurt: though we were all shaken.

We quickly organized ourselves, our predicament now making us oblivious to the harsh weather. It was agreed that I would make a reconnoitre of the vicinity, while the others pulled the plane upright and checked it over. I scanned the area, walking along the shore line in a night storm, keeping the mad sea to the right of me. Out to sea the waves were crashing like thunder: I felt diminutive to hear such rage. As I pushed into the wall of wind, I wondered how the craft had managed to fly for so long in such tempestuous conditions. I walked in a straight line, and soon found myself back with the others, who were making minor repairs to the craft. 'Did you not leave in that direction?' Barney asked, pointing to where I had walked into the dense night.

'Yes, I have done a full circuit. We are on a small island,' I stated.

'So this is not where The Masked Tribe resides?' he further inquired.

'No... I have never encountered this place before,' I replied.

Tiny island,
Encrusted
In vast black night,
Circumscribed
By imposing raging ocean,
Foaming waves
Bashing along shore,
Intimidating,
Diminishing us,
Hemmed in
By giant wild sea;
Rain belted
In relentless wind:
All was noise
And movement
By nature's decree.

'The plane is not seriously damaged,' Argon shouted through the howling rain. 'We should wait for day light, and the storm to subside: and, hopefully, we can take off again.' We retired under some scant palm trees that were dotted in the centre of the island, it was hardly adequate shelter in such a torrent, but at least we eventually began to feel a little warmer when a fire was lit. There was still an abundance of stores in the craft's hold, so we roasted bananas, heated up some raspberry pie, and drank the cool and sweet juices of grapefruits. Helena ensconced herself into my body: and we lay listening to the raging sea. Although it felt safe to be on terra firma, I shuddered as it sounded like the ocean was directing its anger at us: it seemed to be protesting with crazy frustration because we had escaped its voracious maws, and taunted us as poltroons, not daring to take flight. As we huddled around the fire, steam rose from our clothes: I began to feel its benign heat seep through my body. I concentrated my being on Helena's salubrious vibrations: soon, mine were in sympathy and accord with hers: we became one, impenetrable against the storm: but the sheer effort against the untamed sea had at last taken its toll: I felt my whole body ache as I drifted into sleep…

Skimming over the flat sea like smooth round stones, laughing cheerily and long, spray splashing against shining skin, me and Helena racing over the aquamarine mirror, salt sea air rushing deep into our bodies, water hissing at our feet, fast and fleet, sweet Helena's curves glimmering wet, naked we zipped over the sea's surface, faster and faster to the elusive horizon as the ocean speedily rolled by…

I was rudely awoken by the lapping of ice cold sea in my ear. I quickly gained consciousness to find the whole island had become immersed in the ocean: the tide had sneaked up in the night, intending to claim its quarry by stealth. In dismay, I quickly stood up. The sea, which was much calmer now, danced around my ankles. 'Wake up!' I shouted, gently kicking the others who had drifted into a profound slumber after the night's efforts. They began to stir, and were soon shocked to find the island had disappeared under the sea's surface. The only indication of the island ever being there was the few palm trees stretching out of the sea reaching for the morning sky. We were circumscribed by the vast sea, no discernible land. How intimidating to be in the clutches of a merciless mass of heaving water. We stared at each other in consternation, trying to subdue terror. I instinctively searched for our aeroplane to acquire some security. The plane! It had gone! In panic, I gazed out to sea: in the distance, glimmering on the clear blue sea, bobbing up and down on the waves, was the aluminium craft. 'The plane!' I shouted. 'Look!'

'Oh dear,' Jenny said, as the others stared in amazement.

'We've got to swim to it!' I anxiously cried.

'I... I... I can't swim,' Barney stammered... 'The... the sea... where's the l, l, land?... it's all... oh heck.'

'Who can swim?' I urgently inquired. All the others had swam in our creeks, and indicated thus. Argon tightly grabbed me by the arm, volunteering me and him to retrieve the machine: I nodded and turned to the rest of the crew, 'We have to swim to the plane, and paddle it back here... You four wait here... Don't worry, Barney: the palms are still way above sea level: if the sea rises any further, you can all climb up them: maybe the sea won't get any higher.'

And so, without further ado, me and Argon forcefully waded into the sea, kicking through the resistance of the water, to reclaim what the sea had stolen. It was not long before the ground disappeared from underneath our feet, and we were swimming towards the plane. With every stroke we made, I expected the craft to sink below the waves: and, although we swam frantically, the plane did not seem to get any closer... Occasionally, I turned around to view my stranded companions: and, each time I did, the water had risen a little further up their bodies: until, I saw them helping each other shun up palm trees. Manically, we swam towards the plane: without it, we would not be able to extricate from the island... an island, I mentioned to Argon when we started swimming, that would hopefully start to re-appear as soon as the tide had started changing direction. Argon was a stronger swimmer than I: and, even though he was considerably older, never ceased to be an inspiration at how one could, if one looked after oneself, maintain physical puissance into old age. He was soon holding onto the fuselage, then positioned himself around the tail: and, though the plane sat low in the water, he was able to start paddling with his feet pushing it towards me. When I had reached the craft, we both positioned ourselves behind each wing, and proceeded to paddle the plane back to our stranded crew members. The plane was slowly taking on water: and, as we swam, the craft sank lower and lower, making propulsion more laborious. We wanted to bring our aircraft as near to the island as possible before it totally submerged: if it did sink, it would be easier to retrieve once the tide had gone out. We arduously paddled on, pushing the heavy metallic object through the dense water as small oscillating waves slurped around the hull...

Eventually, with much effort, we managed to reach the palm trees. By the time we had returned, our companions were clinging to the top most leaves, and the water lapped around their necks. Argon grabbed a bunch of leaves, and slowly pulled the plane towards the palm trees. Barney was looking most horrified, as, occasionally, a small wave slapped against his face. 'All we can do now,' Argon said, 'is wait for the tide to go down.' So we waited, and watched, as the palm trees were gradually covered by the ocean: and, although there was little we could do to stop the plane from slowly sinking, we held on so it would not drift away. The ever submerging trees were now far below us, completely swallowed by the tide: and so, most reluctantly, all six of us had to let go. Barney desperately lunged for the fuselage to aid his heavy frame. We clung onto the hull, violently thrashing our legs, our metallic companion hardly buoyant enough to support us.

Hearts sank as our craft was sucked in by the voracious sea: for whatever reason, we all decided to sit back into our wonted positions in the cockpit. As the plane had been reliable, maybe we deemed it only proper to stay with it till the end; or maybe we felt it a fitting and dignified way to die: at any rate, I do not think we would have lasted long aimlessly floating in the sea: for, the island sank further and further below us, and would be some time before re-appearing: also, without the plane, it would have taken at least three of us to support the dead weight of the increasingly panicky Barney. As we sat there, the fuselage sank below the surface: then the brine filled the interior of the craft: the sea came rushing in around us: until all that could be seen was our heads poking above the gentle waves anticipating a watery grave at any second.

It must have smelt our fear... Lurking in the depths was a famished leviathan: its great bulk swirled around the ocean bed, slithering through the seaweed: then, it rapidly rose to the surface and opened its giant maws, approaching, approaching...

As I began contemplating death, with arms tightly around my beloved Helena, I saw a disturbance on the surface of the sea up ahead: the water unnaturally frothed and foamed as a heaving black mass broke the surface. It approached with such a ferocity of speed that made everything else move in slow motion. Suddenly, before us, a giant gaping mouth full of razor teeth honed in on the target, and I knew we would all be gone in one bite.

It was like a giant cave that blotted out the sky: entering the throat all was dark, as we were enveloped in the stench and foul air from its stomach.

The recoil from the wave within its maws shot us out of its mouth again: and we violently span around, skimming through the water as it pursued us. It swam faster, its hungry mouth gaping open yearning to swallow us as we were pushed along by the wave it produced. We began to rise out of the water: and, suddenly, we were clear of the sea. 'Pedal!' I cried. No one needed a second invitation: our feet simultaneously banged onto the pedals: and the wings flapped, pushing us up into the air: suddenly we were flying! The leviathan leaped out of the water after us, driven by a voracious instinct, still determined to have its prey. We could smell the miasmic digesting acids emanating from its gut bubbling in hungry protest that food was evading it as we rose into the sky. The creature slowed its ascent, reached a zenith, then rapidly descended towards the ocean: its great bulk crashed into the sea, sending massive shock waves high into the air as it submerged back into the depths, foiled and fierce. We stared at the glassy smooth surface of the water, thoroughly relieved we had evaded certain death: but then, it rose just below the surface again! Consternation imbued us as it began tracking the plane; horrified, we watched as it followed our course. We blindly pedalled for a while, trying to gain as much height from the sea as possible, instinct and adrenalin propelling us forward, eager to survive. We tried dramatically altering our course: but soon, other leviathans joined it in the pursuit: until a great school of giant leviathans were hot on the trail below us…

After a while, when we had calmed down a little, whilst bailing out the sea water, Kelly yelled, 'The star, it's over there!' Argon altered our course accordingly, so that the nose was pointing directly towards the glorious Purple Star. We ensured vigilance was maintained and kept the sea far below us, for was surprised to witness the leap a leviathan could achieve: erstwhile during the crossing of the sea we had been unaware of being such a potential target for those snapping jaws. The air was fairly still, an occasional zephyr buffeted the craft slightly, and the sea hissed below waiting for us to come near. The leviathans were tenacious in their pursuit: but, our fate lay in the reliability of the aeroplane, and the weather was ideal for flying, so Barney became scornful of the giant monsters below us. 'Ha ha ha! Come and get us!' He shook his fist at them: and you would not think it was the same person that had so nervously clung to the palm trees. After a while, we fell into a routine again, three pedalling, three resting: and we made slow but steady progress. The wings beat against the salt air: and the regular rhythms lulled me to sleep in the knowledge that my crew members were resolute and sure...

I rose from the plane, floating above it, looking at my sagging head in the cockpit. The heart of the sea urged and compelled me into its depths: and I found myself being drawn to the vacillating waves. The frothing foam grew louder as I came nearer. I hovered over the surface of the undulating water, aware of the leviathans skimming through the vast and deep ocean: but I knew they were initially unaware of me. They were beautiful, so graceful, perfect swimming machines: and I detected a profound connection between each of them, a unity, a bond, that made my heart cry with gladness. Above, I could hear the wings of the aeroplane calmly flapping as it moved on. Via primal emotions, I communicated to the creatures that I wished them to disavow their tenacious pursuit of the craft. All at once, they began to disperse and sink into the ocean's heart... Something below the waves was calling me: and I could not deter my need to enter the liquid brine. I submerged and instantly transformed my consciousness: temporal space became uncanny. Lower I sank: the glittering sun light that danced on the surface receded as I sought the sea bed. I felt myself become a part of the ocean, a great living entity forever in flux. Lower I sank as the compulsion increased to be at the heart of the sea... What is that? There, lodged in the sand, ghostly and lifeless: a boat. Yes, a sailing ship, strangely familiar. Nubile! Are you still on board? I will save you from the wreck, and carry you to light and air. I approached the boat, which was half buried in the sand. It was adorned in barnacles and coral: seaweed danced like mermaids around it. The occasional dumb goggle-eyed fish casually glided through its apertures. Nubile, I know you are in there: I will save you. I hovered over the deck and recalled her standing there wistfully staring out to the horizon with the spray glittering in her windswept hair. The boat looked like an eerily silent sepulchre now, a shadow of its former self: I shivered recalling how it had effortlessly glided over the vivacious waves in a refulgent sky, and was now reduced to laying lifeless, entombed in the murky ocean bed. Nubile, I am here, to bring you back with me. I floated into the hold, deep and dark: there, where the hull had been breached, was a luminescent plaque: it must be a clue to where I could reunite with Nubile. I eagerly approached it. I fervently read what it said: 'Cherish Helena.'

Startled, I awoke in the cockpit. There was Helena, courageously pedalling onwards, keeping my once sleeping corporeal frame from plummeting into the sea's maws. I began to dote on this fair and patient lady: she had always stayed with me through my ever changing moods...

Then it was my turn to pedal, onwards towards the geosynchronous Purple Star, and towards The Masked Tribe. I reflected on how I had left them on less than favourable terms: but I envisaged the disease would subdue them and render them conciliatory, especially when we offered a miraculous cure. I fell into a trance like rhythm as I pumped the pedals. My muscles responded well; I felt healthy as my warm body perspired: it was envigourating working that plane towards a shore line... We performed well as a crew, effectively staggering the journey with our rota system; we tacitly became more unified, a team spirit prevailed: the sum of the whole was greater than the sum of the parts, and we derived immense strength from each other's presence and sense of common purpose.

So we cycled over the carpet ocean,
In a sure and steady motion...

The awareness of such a great expanse
Enlarges the mind and strengthens the stance
That Zugra is truly a fantastical place:
For spinning in infinite space
Is a planet with a beautiful face:
But do not be fooled by the beauty,
For to the unsuspecting it can be unkind,
Because if you are not properly prepared,
It will ensure a perished rind:
And what then the journey for extricated mind?

One has to be strong; one has to be cool:
To succeed is not the journey of fools.
One has to be patient; one has to learn,
If the sea's respect you wish to earn.

And so on we flew, over the sea:
And to my friends it revealed its mystery:
For they had never seen such a thing,

And how the waves dance and sing
The ancient song of Zugra:
And everything that is heard
Enlightens the spirit, ameliorates the soul,
If you know how to listen to the atavistic call.
There is wisdom in a crashing wave:
The lost soul can be duly saved.
There is magic in the hissing foam:
Listen, and you will find a home.
The spirits of the sea will sing you a song
And make you believe that you belong
On the planet on which you stand.
And Zugra will take your hand
And lead you in your life

Away from loneliness, and all that strife.
Believe in the wisdom of the world,
For it is your home:
Each boy and girl belongs to it.
We all should live
Together,
And the past forgive.

On we flew, over the waves,
For the stricken tribe to save,
To make amends for what is wrong:
And the sea rewarded us with a song.

Our aluminium wings beat on the updraft,
Our lives suspended in the aircraft…

And I recalled my time on the boat,
And how my hope stayed afloat,
And when facing death,
One seldom gloats…

On we flew, sure and strong,
Straight as a bird along
The quickest line to the shore
To a place where I'd been before.

My valiant crew by my side,
Tried and trusted by the ride,
Flying high above the waves,
To a tribe we had to save.

No land in sight, only sea,
The sky above, my friends and me,
Cycling with all our strength

Along the immense length
Of the sea.
Onwards we flew,
A determined crew,
From within deep we drew,
And never knew defeat.

The metallic wings beat;
The drive chain whirred:
We sat in the seats of our silver bird,
Its nose pointed towards The Purple Star.

Onwards we flew, and we flew far:
Over the sea, over the waves,
Leaving behind all the close shaves.
Through the blue sky, through the floating clouds,
Never thinking we would die,
Or that it was allowed.
We had spirit; we were a team:
And this was better than any dream.

Onwards we flew:
Straight and direct, straight and true,
The ocean and sky a perfect blue.
We grew very tired,
Unsure we'd get through,
But giving our best was all we could do…

Then, oh marvellous comforting sound! I heard a distant and welcome scream, the raucous cry of hardy seagulls… Soon, circumscribing the aluminium craft, was a hovering mass of white and grey birds with bright yellow beaks, curious to see what the unusual flying object was: they flew along side, escorting us towards the eagerly anticipated terra firma. The craft discordantly squeaked: the pedals were stiffening: and I could hear salt grinding in the wings' hinges as they beat up and down: the battered and weather beaten plane was in desperate need of lubrication.

And then: land ahoy! Nothing filled our hearts with joy more than when we saw the long line of palm trees along the sun kissed white sandy shore. We could not land on the softer dry sand: but where the tide had regressed, it was firm and flat: there was a large unmissable landing area... We became excited as the dishevelled craft descended towards the beach, for it had seemed that land was going to remain a distant memory. It was strange-familiarity as the undercarriage smoothly skimmed along the gentle wave dimpled sandy surface, and came to a placid halt without incident. Barney cried out in elation at our best touchdown yet.

Everyone smiled and laughed in relief as we remained seated and taxied the craft to the looser sand where the sea did not encroach. We then alighted and heaved the craft further on to the hinterland: it was difficult after such a long physical exertion, the wheels buried themselves in the soft sand, and we slipped many times, pushing the heavy metal craft piecemeal: but necessity compelled us, for the idea of our craft floating out to sea and sinking in the depths of the ocean was a most abhorrent thought. When we were satisfied the craft was safe, we slumped onto the sand, staring out at the sea's horizon, caressing grains with our hands and feet, in a semi-state of shock and elation at what we had just achieved...

24.

Disarray

We remained sat on the beach to re-group. There was a sense of profound unity emanating from us. It is only when you rest that you experience the true extent of your tiredness. 'Is this the place?' Barney eventually asked.

I looked around: the beach did seem familiar. 'I think so,' I replied.

'I just love your method of navigation, Gorky, the optimistic guess work is to be commended,' he smiled at me; I smiled back, for the relief at traversing the mighty sea was palpable. Suddenly, there was a rustling in the long grasses. From the sand dunes came a horde of Masked Tribe, who were no longer wearing their masks (so I guess they would now be more appropriately called The Un-Masked Tribe): but were still brandishing their barbed spears. Our relaxed attitudes meant that the tribe were soon upon us. 'Don't move,' one said, as the tribe aimed their spears at various parts of our bodies: we remained seated. They then looked at each other, not knowing what to do or say next. I espied that they were indicating clear signs of the disease: their long ears were sagging; fur was coming away in tufts; some of their large protruding teeth were missing, or loosely dangling, flapping in the mild sea breeze: one or two held on to their teeth, pushing them up into the gums in a vain bid not to lose them; their little beady red eye was clouded over with an opaque grey; and their smell evinced the malady.

'We have come to...' I said, but was promptly interrupted.

'No talk,' one said: then they continued to look perplexed. It was about this time that I expected their imperious leader to appear: but he was nowhere to be seen.

'Sit,' one said.

'Er, we are sat,' Helena replied.

'Stand,' another said: we remained seated, for we had just been ordered to sit: but a prod in the leg with a spear coerced us to stand, so we all tiredly stood up.

'Sit,' another said: we remained stood, looking at the little peering eye, trying to elicit some sort of common sense: but, the obligatory prod with the spear ensured we sat again, so we sighed and sat down.

'Stand,' another said.

'Hold on,' I abruptly snapped.

'No talk,' one said.

'Now wait a minute,' I admonished, 'where is your leader?' They looked dumb at each other for a while.

'Stand,' one eventually said. Barney contemptuously guffawed: a swift thwack with the butt of a spear against his jaw demonstrated that these creatures were not to be taken lightly: he soon shut up, spitting blood. My comrades began to reluctantly stand: but I intervened.

'No, we are not standing up,' I peremptorily declared. 'You have a disease, do you not?' Again, they looked at each other for a while, their small festering eye blinking.

'No talk,' one said

'No talk? But we have means to cure your ailment,' I urged.

'A-i-l-m-i-n?' one said.

'Your illness: look, your fur, your teeth... your eyes! You have a disease; and we have a cure,' I said, cautiously viewing a spear head that was uncomfortably near my face. There was a hiatus, as again, they dumbly stared at each other.

'Stand,' one said.

'Do you want to be cured?!' I yelled in exasperation, hoping increased volume would induce comprehension. Confounded, they looked at each other yet again: then, to our relief, walked away, though nearby. An animated argument ensued: they were all talking at once, and nothing could be heard amongst them: then two began pushing each other: it was not long before they were all yelling and pushing: some started wrestling, rolling along the ground issuing execrations, angry shouts and curses: sand was thrown everywhere in the fracas: and soon it was a free for all, as punches and kicks flew from all directions. Thankfully, they had slung their weapons to the side: and, as we slowly stood up, could have easily appropriated their spears and apprehended the tribe: but, instead, we incredulously watched the scene unwind. This bizarre scene continued until they all became exhausted. Then they started debating again. There was some shoving and I thought at one point a fight may break out again, but, wearied and panting, they eventually approached our group.

'Yes,' one said.
'Yes, you want to be cured?' Jenny tried to confirm.
'No,' he said.
'He mean yes,' another said.
'You want to be cured?' Jenny reiterated.
'Yes,' he said.
'You want to be cured?' Jenny re-reiterated.
'Nnnn… yes,' he said.
'Right,' I promptly said, 'let's get the urn out.' The Un-Masked Tribe expectantly gathered around the aeroplane: then, there was more rustling in the long grass, and the women came from out of the sand dunes, integrating with the men: there was a noticeable improvement of accord between males and females, for, as they waited, were engrossed in active dialogue between each other, and it even appeared there was an element

of deference from the males. We gladly began administering Sacradia: but the first few of the tribe we gave the healing waters to spat it out.

'What's wrong with them?' Kelly asked.

'I do not know,' I shrugged, and carefully tasted the water myself. 'Sea water!' I exclaimed, grimacing at the unpleasant taste. I thought for a moment, then said, 'When our plane submerged, the sea must have seeped into the urn, displacing our precious cargo.'

'You make fun!' an Un-Masked Tribe's creature angrily shouted, picking up his spear and shaking it at me.

'No,' I appealed, 'we had a mishap...'

'Sit!' he bellowed.

'Wait,' I said, 'I can explain.'

'No talk!' he snapped, and thrust the spear so fiercely into my abdomen, that I had to recoil with the impact to save myself from a nasty incision. So we all sat down again, flummoxed at what to do next...

I gazed out to the crystal sea: it seemed incredible that we had devised a flying contraption that had taken us over the prodigious expanse of water, to a new land: I scanned around, descrying the large palm trees that were strewn along the margin of the sun bright white sand: beyond them, I could just see, in the distance, the craggy mountain, in which dwelt... 'The dragons!' I whispered with excitement.

'What?' Helena replied.

'The dragons will have some of the magic water: it's not far from here,' I said.

'Ask them if we can go there,' Helena admonished.

'I know how to acquire some healing water,' I called out.

'No talk,' one said, shaking his spear. The expectation of being cured from the malady had temporarily appeased them: but now, the disappointment had made them as hostile as ever.

'I can go alone, and soon return. I *can* make you better. What do you have to lose?' I rhetorically asked. They really were in a desperate situation: for, I could see that, despite their truculence, the disease was causing great suffering. A furious debate ensued, with further pushing and shoving: then, the tribe pushed one surprised and reluctant member forward. He turned round and tried to push himself back into the group: but with a mighty shove, he came hurtling before us: he tried to turn back again, but a row of fierce little eyes deterred him: so, he had no choice, but to speak.

'Er... er... er... why you know where cure... er... er... we don't?' he said, half talking to his own people for security: they nodded at him for support and approbation at his effective communication. At this, I felt a pulse of indignation well in my heart.

'Because, you have spent your existence persecuting without ever inquiring,' I blurted. They perplexedly looked at each other, and had no notion what so ever what I was referring to. 'The dragons,' I said, 'have the cure.' With the mention of *the dragons*, the one before us leapt back to his comrades. Their mouths dropped in anguish: and they all took a backward step in horror. Suddenly, one was ejected from the group again: he knew he had to talk, or he would not have been permitted back.

'You go to dragons?!' he nervously said, then promptly resumed his place in the throng of the tribe.

'Yes... the dragons have the cure for your people,' I advised. Another, against his will, was pushed forward.

'You go to dragons?!' he nervously said, then leapt back to his group. I stared at them, disbelieving that they could be so obtuse. They all suddenly burst out laughing, pointing, and saying, 'He go to dragons!' We sat there, waiting for the hysterics to subside. Another squabble ensued: one reached to another and pulled out his front teeth: this seemed to exacerbate the dispute, and it went on for a while: although, this time, physical abuse was kept to a minimum: eventually, the debate concluded. One more, without warning, was then thrown forward.

'Go to dragons!' he said. With that, they all began laughing again.

'Go to dragons!" the tribe said, inducing more mirth. My friends began to rise with me: but it was made known with spears that it was to be me only that went.

'I will be back soon,' I assured my companions.

25.

Noog

So, I marched into the forest, unhappy that I was leaving my fellow travellers with the hostile tribe, but knowing it was the only way to extricate from the predicament. An unpleasant thought crossed my mind: what if the dragons had fled their lair: there was no other way of retrieving the precious water, our plane could never fly to the Purple Star; what if they were there but had used all the magical water, or refused to give me some this time. I put these obstacles out of my mind, and concentrated on endeavouring to meet them. I could not allow myself to be vexed by the idea of coming this far only to fail. I could see glimpses of the rocky mountain between the vistas of the trees: and within that mountain contained the dragons' cave. Seeing the craggy precipice silently towering over the trees induced hope. I quickened my step, looking forward with alacrity to encountering the marvelous mystical beasts. As I walked, I heard a man chattering to himself.

'I don't care, no, I don't care. They won't last long without me. They're, they're idiots, yes, that's what they are, utter buffoons, ha ha, mad they are. Ha ha ha… Yes, this is much better… Yes, just me.' It was the leader of The Masked Tribe: or should I say ex-leader of The Un-Masked Tribe: although, he was still wearing his haughty looking mask… He was bounding up and down in a most irate state: then, he saw me. 'You!' he bellowed fiercely: then his body's gestures conveyed horror. 'You! Are you here for revenge? Well, well, I'm not in charge any more. No. Ha ha. You want them. Yes, that's who you want, them… those, those nincompoops, yes, them, them!'

'I have not come for revenge,' I calmly said. 'What has happened?'

'What? Those, those clots, that's what they are… clots. Clots! Ha ha, clots,' he said.

'Yes, what about them?' I asked.

'Those, those…' he said, fighting frustration to find words.

'Clots?' I said.

'Yes, clots,' he concurred.

'What about them?' I repeated.

'They decided I was of no use anymore… Those nincompoops, those foolish imbecilic… idiots!' he shouted: and the vehement words disappeared into the dense foliage. 'Me! Their great and omnipotent leader… ostracized! Me! The perfect one, the fabulous… er… ha ha, fantastic… well, they got rid of me.' His voice trailed away into a rather sorrowful and pathetic tone: I could discern, beyond his ire, he felt most dejected.

'Could you initiate a rapprochement?' I inquired.

'What?! Me, the glorious one… grovel to them… those fools! Ha ha,' he imperiously shouted.

'But, you are alone in the forest, talking to yourself. Maybe you can go back and compromise, perhaps work alongside them?' I proposed.

'Me!? Along side… *them*?! Ha, ha, never!' he cried.

'Then you will always be on your own,' I matter-of-factly stated.

'Good! GOOD!' he exclaimed. 'I would rather be on my own, than with… those… those…'

'Idiots?' I said.

'Yes! Idiots!' he proclaimed.

'Then, why are you so angry?' I inquired.

'Angry! I'm not angry!' he bawled. 'I like it here. Yes, ha ha. I'm… I'm glad I'm away from… them…' His head dropped on the word *them*: it was difficult for him to perpetuate his anger with such underlying melancholy.

'Maybe you could teach them to be clever, like you... not in a condescending way, of course,' I admonished.

'Teach them to be... like me? But, I am their leader,' he proudly announced.

'Not anymore,' I quietly advised. 'And, maybe, you would derive satisfaction in assisting them... They are in a state of disarray,' I informed. He examined the floor, and sulkily kicked a pebble.

'I do not think they want me back,' he said.

'I am going to obtain some magical healing water which can cure your people's disease... Maybe you would like to help me bring it to them, as a way of propitiation,' I urged.

'Magical healing water? Is there such a thing?' he wondrously asked.

'Yes... Will you help?' I inquired. He paused for a minute to consider the implications of this.

'Well... alright... but, ha ha, do not forget who you are talking to,' he reminded.

'The leader?' I asked.

'Yes... *The* leader,' he peremptorily claimed while heaving his chest and lifting his head to the sky in rather a dramatic fashion. I sighed: to which he quickly looked at me with, I assume, suspicion. I smiled, and began walking: he followed: and we made our way to Dragon Mountain...

On traversing, I appreciated how difficult it was for this diminutive figure with such a large and cumbersome mask marching through the dense foliage: he would walk into low hanging branches, trip over roots, and generally struggle all the way. I wanted to tell him as his tribe had disowned their masks, would it not, for the sake of pragmatism and acceptance, be advisable to do the same: but I deemed one step at a time.

We eventually reached the base of the mountain: him trailing behind muttering grievances: but, at last, he caught up. He stared at the mountain in sudden recognition: his mask began trembling slightly. 'This... this is D... Dragon M... Mountain,' he quaked, wrestling with the words as they rolled around his tongue.

'I know. It is from the dragons that I am hoping to procure the magic water,' I said.

'The, the, the, d, d, d, d, dragons?!' He began fidgeting as his mask violently shook. 'Out of the question. I'm not going up there!' he exclaimed.

'Do you want to wait here... *leader*?' I nonchalantly asked.

'Are you patronizing me?' he indignantly replied.

'I think so,' I smiled. 'Is the great leader afraid?'

'Follow me!' he snapped, and began scurrying up the side of the cliff. I calmly followed, well versed with this terrain. The ex-leader, in his fear and ardour, rapidly climbed upwards. I carefully picked my way amongst the boulders, fully aware that if I hurried, it could cause me to slip; he sent dust and stones flying downwards upon me as he erratically clambered over the rocks. I called for him to slow down: but he manically stumbled over the terrain, his adrenalin hurling him onwards. It was most awkward climbing with him above, for I had to negotiate the stony shower that relentlessly fell upon me: but I thought, at least he was participating in the bid to cure his tribe... Through the falling debris, I could see that he had past the lair's entrance: it was an inconspicuous fissure for such sizeable creatures: however, such was the eerie moaning wind that emanated from within, I could not help think he may have conveniently overlooked it. I climbed further up, until I was level with the entrance of the dragons' abode: but the ex-leader was heading towards the peak, monomaniacally climbing in blind panic.

'It's here!' I called, standing at the cave's mouth. The falling dust and stones were turning into a hail of rocks: and I wondered how a small creature could cause such a disturbance. 'It's here!' I shouted upwards into the falling missiles. Luckily for me, I could shelter in the cave's mouth.

'Oh, oh, g, g, g, good… good… good,' he shouted back, as he kept on climbing… quicker than ever!

'Er… leader… It's here,' I reiterated, my voice echoing along the tunnel. It was not the way I wanted to introduce myself to the, if treated apt, congenial reptiles.

'Yes, yes, it's here, ha ha, yes, good, good,' he ranted, as he reluctantly stopped, and peered through his haughty mask down at me, his claws tightly gnawing at the stone in consternation. Such was his alarmed state, I thought I would try and calm him.

'What is your name?' I inquired.

'Er, er, ha ha, L, L, L, leader,' he nervously blurted.

'Is that your real name?' I asked.

'Er, y-e-s,' he unassuredly replied.

'Oh, you were born with that name?' I affirmed.

'Ye… s,' he said, forcing the word while fidgeting on the escarpment, looking most agitated… 'No, my name is… Noog,' he feebly and solemnly declared, as if he was revealing something discreditable.

'Well, Noog, the dragons' entrance is here… Do you want to wait up there?' I asked.

'Yes,' he answered.

'You do not want to be integrated with the tribe? Just think if you went back to them and claimed you had confronted the dragons?' I waited as he fought with his fear. I felt pity for him ranting alone in the forest, and was eager for him to be re-united with his people. I felt, if he improved his attitude, he had a lot to offer them. If he could say he had parleyed with the dragons, and bestow upon his tribe the curative waters, I was sure they would be appeased. Also, I deemed it a good opportunity to dispel the ignorance concerning the fire-breathing creatures.

He gradually loosened his grip on the rock, and, very slowly, began to descend. He came to the lair's entrance, nervously gazed inside the dark labyrinth: and began to shake some more. 'Follow me,' I admonished, and stepped inside...

26.

Nothing

'*Nothing is more real than nothing.*'

Samuel Beckett

So I gingerly tiptoed into the cave. Noog, at first, was most reluctant, his knees vigorously knocking together. I impatiently waved him to follow, and, hesitatingly, he ventured forth... Only a few steps at first, then he stopped, about to turn back. 'Come on!' I whispered. One's senses were acutely awakened by dripping water loudly plopping, echoing from within. We nervously crept further into the dark stomach of the mountain. We looked back to where we had been: a dim light from outside reached deep into the tunnel, which facilitated traversing. A steamy vapour swirled and danced along the rays: and the sun's energy seemed mystically transformed inside the confines of the rocky mountain: I sensed an ancient force undulating through the antediluvian stone.

'Is... is... th... that the water?' Noog inquired, pointing to the water dripping from the ceiling of the cave. His bearing had noticeably petrified.

'No, we have to ask the dragons for that,' I said: with that, he span around in an attempt to make a quick getaway back to the forest: I had to grasp his arm to detain him. He began struggling and whimpering: but, after a while, calmed down... slightly! I walked further in: but soon stopped when I realized he had not moved. Because of my desire for the water, and the tension of entering a dragons' lair, my patience was wearing thin: with frustrated gestures, I flailed my arms beckoning him to get a move on. He stood there, motionless... So, in exasperation, I marched to him, and forcefully pushed his furry shoulder blades: his little legs reluctantly plodded one in front of the other, until they gained enough momentum to move on their own: and so we walked further into the cave.... The tunnel, for a short while, became pitch black as we left the light of the entrance behind: and we had to walk forth unaware what lay directly ahead: but I knew continuing we would reach the dragons' antechamber. I felt Noog hold my arm. I was surprised and impressed he raised no objection, but determinedly followed. Sure enough, the dreariness soon dispelled, as we became surrounded by glowing green stalactites and stalagmites radiating a refulgent glow: I stared in awe at their natural beauty. Then, I turned around, Noog's nerves had returned and was cowering behind a rock, helplessly shaking. 'Noog, come on... It's okay,' I whispered, though my own trepidations of yore began to creep back; I felt fear churn in my stomach: anyone who has encroached upon a dragons' lair, if had prior acquaintance with the dragons or not, will testify to increasing adrenalin while approaching to where the creatures might be. Noog continued to hide behind the rock, his trembling ears protruding like quivering leaves in the wind. 'Noog! Come on!' I whisper-shouted, although I was not entirely comfortable with the idea of confronting the dragons myself: I was accompanied by one of their main persecutors. He would not move: so again I had to march back to where he was, and pull at his arm, 'Come on!' I desperately implored, trying to curb my aggressiveness.

'Get off!' he feebly squeaked, pulling back.

'Do you want to be re-united with your people?' I firmly asked. He crouched there, violently shaking. 'Or do you want to remain in the forest for ever ranting to yourself?' I glared at the rock he was hiding behind, trying to penetrate through it and reach his courage. 'Imagine, Noog, alone, forever alone, aimlessly wandering the forest... alone!' This must have induced a mental image in his mind: he pondered it over for a while: then, very cautiously, stood up. We continued to walk through the tunnel, the large hanging stalactites and stalagmites growing from the ground, gradually growing in size, increasingly intimidated us the further we went: for they resembled the giant scales on a dragon's back... Then, instinctively, I uttered, 'Can you hear that?' We both stopped, and remained silent and motionless, until Noog began trembling, and his rattling mask drowned out any other sound: I held it steady. 'Listen!' I urged. Sure enough, a faint intermittent hissing travelled along the tunnel to where we were. Noog nervously nodded. 'That's the dragons!' I admonished. With that, he dived behind another rock, violently quaking. 'Noog, come on!' He cowered, trying to contain his need to sob. 'Noog... eternal isolation!' I emphasized. He thought a little.

'I don't care! I would rather have eternal isolation than death!' he whimpered.

'The dragons are friendly,' I rejoined, not knowing for sure.

'Friendly?' he queried.

'Sure,' I urged.

'They were always angry with our tribe,' he stated.

'That's because you did not understand them, or get to know them,' I said. He thought for a little more, then reluctantly raised himself again, manically staring down the tunnel for any sign of the large fire-breathing reptiles. 'It's okay. This way,' I assured. We continued to walk along the tunnel, Noog treading on my heels. As we walked, the cave became adorned with the many brightly coloured paintings that the dragons had so masterly executed, life like scenes of wild animals that looked ready to jump from their static positions at any moment, creatures I had never seen in the outside world, or ever wished to. 'That's the pictures they paint,' I informed him, pointing to them, eager that he would begin to see the dragons differently. He eyed the skilful cave paintings suspiciously through his mask, made no comment: but tentatively peered up ahead, as if his death was imminent. As we carefully moved on, the hissing grew louder: and I recalled how the mother dragon had always known of my approaching her mountain, let alone the impinging of her cave. The noise we had made on climbing the mountain, and entering the cave, left me in no doubt that the dragons would have been aware of our presence. We came to the entrance of a vestibule, and cautiously stepped inside: there, in the open recess, large and looming, was father dragon! He was poised... waiting... facing us... with bright red eyes glaring, apparently peeved beyond rapprochement. I stopped in my tracks, tumescent eyes bulging out my sockets. Noog continued walking, and banged right into me, knocking his mask off: his little eye, like mine, was wide with fear: his mouth dropped to his chest, and he emitted a tiny shriek of terror. I stood there, petrified, staring at the enormous beast before me: his glowing red-hot eyes scrunched in primal anger, brow deeply furrowed, and snarling through deadly fangs. 'Er, hello,' I feebly said through my dry throat. I heard a low guttural growl: a harbinger for a fierce roar and deathly strike: he slowly lowered onto his haunches, ready to leap upon us in a single motion. 'It's... it's me, G, Gorky,' I whimpered. The growl continued: his ferocious red eyes flamed in hellish anger burnt into my waning spirit. 'Y... you r... rem... ember?' I managed to say, as my words trailed away into insignificance.

'What do you want?!' the dragon growled imperiously, still coiled, and showing no sign of abating his intimidating posture.

'We need your help,' I asseverated. His low growl turned to a fierce roar, as flames gushed from his mouth hitting the wall beside us: we leapt askance of the ball of fire as it exploded in all directions. We stood cemented to the wall, incredulous we had just evaded the attack.

'Whatsss the fussss?' I heard mother dragon say from another tunnel (much to my relief!).

'Intrudersss!' father dragon roared. Suddenly, she appeared in the ante-chamber, and peered at me and Noog: we were trying to burrow our backs into the rock, pushing hard against the cave wall, not daring to move, wishing we could absorb into the rock and vanish.

'Gorky, isss that you?' she asked. (I could not help think this sagacious beast was feigning ignorance.)

'Y…y, yes,' I choked.

'Well, well, Gorky… You have met Gorky, dear… Calm down,' mother reproached. The great male reptile eyed me with contempt: it seemed he had completely forgotten our previous tete-a-tete, and had resumed his hatred for 'oomans'. 'Come here, Gorky, let me sssee you,' she said, and opened her two front claws in a welcoming gesture. I stumbled towards her, trying to ignore the vexed beast beside her, but waited to be frazzled at any moment, feeling utterly exposed as I stood in front of these two massive creatures. Much to my surprise, she grabbed me, and hugged me into her soft under belly, as if I was one of her children: my face squashed against her smooth scales, and initially was worried lest I became an instant pancake: her claw gently ruffled my hair: then a wave of comfort swept over me, and I nearly cried at feeling so safe. While this was happening, four giant dragons appeared from a tunnel, towering above the two already in the vestibule. When I saw them, I instinctively clung to the mother dragon for protection. These four large beasts made the other two dragons look innocuous in comparison: they were veritable monsters, and I surmised could raze a whole village with a single fiery breath. They stared curiously at me, then looked at the two parent dragons. 'You remember my children, Gorky?' mother dragon asked. I craned my neck upwards to look at these incredible creatures looming over me: I reluctantly peered at their countenances, and descried familiar features, but more mature now. The four baby dragons had grown into an awesome sight, leaving me feeling quite insignificant and vulnerable. Lacking any confidence, I conveyed a nervous smile and feebly waved at the four giants: and I was heartened to receive smiles of recognition in return.

'Gorky,' one said, and held out his huge paw.

'Hello,' I replied, and cordially shook it, my heart full of joy that they had grown up looking so fine.

'And what isss that, ssscuffling in the shshshadowsss?' mother inquired.

'Er, I have brought someone to meet you,' I un-assuredly said.

'Helena?!' mother dragon joyfully proclaimed.

'Mmm, no... Noog,' I replied, unable to belie my disappointment. 'Noog! It's okay!' I called. A further scuffling could be heard: then it went silent: Noog had, during my conversation with the dragons, sidled behind a rock. 'They won't hurt you,' I implored. He continued to crouch, concealing himself most dexterously: until I approached him, and unceremoniously pulled him from behind the large stone. He imparted a piercing squeal, broke from my grasp, and began grovelling around the floor, searching for his haughty looking mask: as he picked it up, father dragon noticed the wooden visage in Noog's paw.

'Y-O-U!' father dragon bellowed, and was about to spew a plume of flames: but this time with a deadly accuracy that would have engulfed the little furry body of the ex-leader and frazzled him in an instant. Noog was fumbling to put the mask on: but on hearing the dragon's roar, jumped in horror and slung it high into the air: the mask vanished into the darkness. Noog, stood there, exposed and quivering, forgetting his mask... and everything else!

'Please! Please, don't hurt me! Please, don't hurt me!' Noog blubbered, looking quite pathetic as he held his paws in front of his face, little knees knocking together. Father dragon inhaled a deep breath; his body swelled enormously, indicating the force of the flame that would follow. I prepared to witness ensuing carnage, petrified and helpless to deter it; I stared in dumb horror at the little furry body that was about to become a ball of flame.

'Father! Letsss sssee want they want. He'sss with Gorky. Pleassse refrain,' mother dragon urged. The great male dragon glared at her in disbelief, and trembled in frustration as he gradually exhaled the mass of air in his giant lungs: all his senses compelled him to reduce Noog to a furry conflagration. He stared at Noog with malignant hatred, and snarled: his giant razor fangs glittered from the lambent glow of the stalactites: he so dearly wanted to kill the scourge of his family. He looked at his beloved wife once more, eyes red hot anger: she reciprocated with a supplicating gaze urging passivity.

'I will have nothing to do with thissss,' he growled, and slinked away into the dark depths of the cave.

'What do you want, Gorky?' mother dragon sighed, gently ushering me towards Noog. I stood next to Noog, who continued to conceal his face with tiny paws, and was trembling profusely: I felt ashamed to be seen in his company.

'The Masked Tribe... The Un-Masked Tribe, they are suffering from a deadly disease: there is only one cure: Sacradia,' I apologetically intoned.

'Really?' she said. There was a silent hiatus, as she raised her brow disapprovingly at me: then looked disdainfully at Noog. 'How did the dissseasse manifessst, Gorky?'

'Er... I don't know,' I said, scratching my head and trying to look blameless. I looked at Noog, who was doing an uncannily accurate impression of a trembling statue. I could not abide the culpability of such an awful occurrence any longer; I would not confess, for I could not cope with being continually recognized as the proliferation of death.

'A dissseassse that came from nowhere?' mother dragon said, eyeing me with penetration.

'Er... apparently,' I answered, feeling uneasy, and looking around the cave in mock innocence.

'I cannot help you,' she eventually claimed.

'But, you *do* have the water?' I implored.

'I will not help you,' she reiterated.

'But, this is an opportunity to ensure you will never be persecuted by the tribe again. I am certain that if you issue them Sacradia, they will leave you alone. Won't you Noog?' I said, turning to Noog, who stood quivering motionless, starting to assimilate that he actually was in a dragons' lair... 'Noog! Tell the dragon you no longer have bad intent.'

'I no longer have bad intent,' he repeated in monotone.

'See!' I exclaimed. Mother dragon smiled at this spectacle, and casually picked her great fangs with her diamond tipped claw.

'Gorky, I cannot help you, because, *you* are lying,' she matter-of-factly said... I gulped... 'Tell, *Noog*, why hisss people have the dissseassse.' I then realized how foolish I had been to be mendacious before the dragon: after all, I had previously informed her of everything. After leaving The Forest of Life for the second time, I had attempted absolution by confession to the various tribes: the cold indifference of the tribes' response mortified me: I had not the strength to testify any longer. Nevertheless, I knew I had to redeem myself in front of this beautiful, noble and wise dragon, and inform Noog, or there would be no chance of curing his people. I turned to him, my head lowered in shame.

'Noog, it was me that brought the disease to your shores,' I asseverated.

'Oh, thanks,' he mechanically said, mesmerized by the dragon.

'That will probably regissster later,' mother dragon admonished. 'Gorky, I know you did not mean to do what you did, but you mussst own up to your errors.'

'I am sorry... I could at first: but it was not making me feel very good seeing the reaction from the tribes,' I said.

'It may not make you feel good at firssst: but, if one wantsss to improve, one needsss to be honessst with otherssss, as well as with one ssself,' she solemnly stated.

'Sometimes, that's not easy,' I answered.

'I know, Gorky… but it'sss advissssable if you do not want to go on repeating the sssame missstakesss… Now, I *maybe* in a posssition to help,' she smiled.

'Oh, really! Great!' I excitedly blurted.

'Do you like conundrums?' she inquired.

'Conundrums? What kind?' I asked.

'If you guesss right, you can have the water of SSSacradia… If you guesss wrong… I fry you both… Isss that fair?' she said, without a hint of joking.

'Fry us?' I nervously repeated, slowly mouthing the words in contemplative horror.

'SSSacradia isss one of the wondersss of the universsse… a rare and preciousss comodity, difficult to find and retrieve: it doesss not come cheap… Do you underssstand?' she hissed. What could I do? I had arduously travelled over land and sea to save The Un-Masked Tribe: and that was what I intended to do: I could not leave them in a state of gradual decay, and, finally, extinction: it would torment for the rest of my life knowing I was to blame.

'Er, yes,' I eventually said.

'Anssswer me thisss, which isss right: nothing isss nothing; or nothing isss sssometing?' I nearly impetuously answered, for it seemed obvious: nothing *is* of course nothing: but then, I thought, if it was so obvious, would she have asked such a question? Unless, she wanted to deliberately make it obvious, so I would think it was too obvious, and then opt for the wrong answer: or maybe she was making it easy because I was an old acquaintance. Is nothing nothing? Or is nothing something? My head span in numerous permutations… and got nowhere. I decided to go for the obvious: nothing *is* nothing: of course nothing is nothing: how could nothing possibly be something?

'Er... nothing *is* nothing,' I doubtfully answered, trying to sound confident.

'If nothing *isss* nothing, then nothing mussst exissst,' she said, 'for *isss* is the third perssson sssingular presssent of the verb, *to be*, and if sssomething isss *being*, then it *isss* sssomething.'

'Mmm, y-e-s,' I vacantly nodded, for she had lost me in mid explanation: but then, suddenly, I realized the purport: I had chosen the incorrect answer. I stood there dumb, realizing I was about to be frazzled.

'Ssso, you are wrong,' she smiled. My face dropped at the confirmation. I tightly closed my eyes, waiting for the flames... The quest flashed through mind: I tried to concentrate on the tender moments with Helena. There was an unbearable lacuna... 'I am teasssing, Gorky... Whatever anssswer you would have imparted, I would have proven you shshshould have picked the other.' Oh Helena, we have come so far, travelled over many lands: we have bonded with common experiences: I love you more now than ever: I will see you again someday. She issued a single nod to one of her brood, who walked away, and came back carrying an ornate urn. 'The shshshore tribe have not bothered usss for sssometime... They are no longer coerced by... *Noog*... You will never bother my family again, will you... *Noog?*'

'No,' he automatically said, peering from between his claws. She stared at him, knowing full he had never possessed the courage to venture into the lair himself, it was always his victims he bullied to do the dirty work for him: and, as he now knew what it felt like to be intimidated, and he had irrevocably lost his leadership anyway, she deemed he was no longer a threat.

'Take the water, Gorky,' she urged, as the giant dragon placed the ornate urn before me. By this time, I had caught up with events, and, embarrassed, began to compose myself. I once again attempted to move the urn containing the magical healing waters of Lake Sacradia: but once again it would not budge.

'Noog, help me with this,' I requested: to which he, in a trance, began pushing the great urn with me: it made no difference. The mother dragon sighed as a small flame flickered from her nostril.

'It sssemsss you need sssome more help,' she stated.

'Er, yes,' I answered in frustration, for I felt I had already asked enough favours from this congenial beast.

'Ssson, help transssport the urn to the coassst line of the tribe, would you, pleassse?' she asked. Her giant dragon of a son nodded his approbation. He strode across the vestibule to where me and Noog where: our heads raised further and further up as he approached, until we were directly gazing up at the enormous beast towering above us.

'Hop on,' he casually said. I raised my eyebrows at him in order to confirm, for I did not want to antagonize this creature in any way: he smiled and nodded consent: so I clambered on board the massive frame of the formidable lizard. The dragon then picked up the urn with his talons, and waited for the other passenger. Noog stood, frozen, highly reluctant to move any closer to the huge scaly creature.

'Noog, it's okay,' I assured. He remained stationary: so I had to dismount, and push him piece meal, to where the dragon patiently waited. 'Get on!' I urged. 'Noog! Climb on board!' I gave him a strong push, as mother dragon looked on bemused. She still had bitter memories of this little creature sending all and sundry up to her home in order to try and kill her family: but she had always advocated an harmonious cohabitation of the land and believed revenge only perpetuated hostilities: and so she gently coaxed Noog on to her son's back, gently pushing him astride with her muzzle. Noog, sat around the giant dragon's neck, dumb and mortified, there in body only.

The mother dragon gave a small nod to her huge son: and then we were bounding along the tunnel that led to the egress. He did not stop at the edge, but flapped his leathery wings, his great bulk suspended in the air: so smooth was the transition that it felt we were still on the ground. We soared through the sky more rapid than our plane could ever have mustered: and it made me realize just how inferior our aircraft was in comparison to this organic flying machine: graceful flesh and bone wings smoothly caress air; cumbersome metallic wings rudely scar sky... Soon, we started circling downwards in a spiral towards the beach...

27.

Resumption

The Un-Masked Tribe had spotted the colossal beast as it descended in gradations towards the sandy shore: they waited for him to get into range, then began hurling their spears. Two or three zipped past: I heard them whiz as they past my head. 'Be careful!' I admonished the dragon as I crouched low upon his back.

'Thanks for the obviousss advisssse,' he replied. Noog nearly fell off trying to dodge incoming projectiles. Then, I heard the dragon exude a woeful groan: several spears had pierced his soft under belly, deep into his viscera. Suddenly, graceful flight turned into a dead drop; we plummeted towards the sand in a headlong motion, as we clung to the scales of the beast. BANG! We hit the sand with incredible force, smashing the urn underneath. I landed heavily, and slid from the reptile onto the sand, severely concussed; Noog catapulted from the beast, gracefully summersaulted, and harmlessly landed on his feet. The Un-Masked tribe, who had retreated in order to avoid the impact, hid and watched the large bulk of the motionless dragon. The dragon remained stationary, slumped in his own blood. After a while, when they realized he was probably dead, they began to charge in order to finish him off. Noog purposefully leapt forward, 'Stop, you imb… fellow tribe's people.' He held out his hand in a gesture of halt: to which they did. 'This dragon is here… *was* here, to help us,' he proclaimed. They blankly looked at each other: then began to attack again. 'Stop!' Noog shouted, placing himself between the recumbent dragon and the tribe. They stopped again, within striking range of the prostrate beast, who was bleeding profusely, making no attempt to move, and slowly drifting into unconsciousness. The urn the dragon had been carrying, lay shattered beneath him, and the contents began seeping into his open wounds: the macabre incisions began to bubble and steam, spears lodged in belly disintegrated: and, with the mystical water as conduit, blood flowed back into flesh: the dragon's wounds perfectly sealed, leaving no indication of trauma. The magical waters continued to run along the beach, hissing as it preternaturally skated over the sand, as if drawn to disease, incumbent to cure: the sacred alchemical water swirled around the tribe's feet, bathing their skin in the mystical emollient: the liquid pervaded their pores, and they began to tremble with atavistic energy: instantaneously their dilapidated bodies began to repair: and soon they were the proud owners of strong ivory incisors, and thick shining fur. All of us were enveloped in a burgeoning refulgent orange glow. I leapt up feeling quite invigorated. The dragon raised to its full magnificent height and angrily gazed down at the recuperated tribe. Me and Noog stood alongside the ancient beast to confront the tribe, who had forgotten our presence, for were smiling and touching new fur, copiously congratulating each other on their sudden recovery. The dragon began to inhale a large quaff of air, and I knew he was about to frazzle the furry tribe in one breath. I firmly slapped him on his flank and shouted, 'Please! No!' He glared at me, holding his breath: then, with a malignant stare, turned to face the tribe, who were frolicking and laughing with glee, and most distracted with their celebrations. The large beast emitted a low guttural growl: the furnace fire in his stomach rumbled and crackled like a volcano: but, thankfully, he slowly exhaled, and only a small blue flame appeared from his flared nostrils. However, ire vie patience, meant he had to breathe heavily, as he watched the gambolling of the tiny furry creatures, who were now most ecstatic. Eventually, one Un-Masked Tribe's creature, in the corner of his single red eye, noticed and then remembered we were stood there: he began nervously shaking his neighbour, who, laughing, started shaking him in return, their heads wobbling around as if on rubber necks, one in total fear, the other in utter elation. Eventually, the one who had noticed us, managed to communicate what he meant: and gradually, as the news disseminated, the tribe turned to face the giant reptile. They prepared to hoist their spears and assail the dragon. The beast stared at them with furrowed brow low over bright red orbs: then he accusingly glared at me, began flapping his great leathery wings, and soared up into the air, pursued by a ballistic hale of spears, which he dexterously managed to evade. He disappeared into the sky, returning to his lair, and would most likely inform his family of the inhospitable welcome he had received. The tribe continued to throw their spears after him, shouting abuse, and shaking their tiny clawed fists: but it was too late, the dragon had gone.

'Why did you do that, you stup... Can you not see the dragon came to cure you?' Noog yelled at the tribe, for it was apparent that due to direct experience with the noble creatures his perspective had notably changed.

'You not leader. We not stupid. You go,' said one of the tribe, shaking a threatening spear at their ex-leader.

'But it was me who brought the dragon here with the restorative water,' Noog proclaimed.

'That why you go. We not want dragon here. You not leader. You go,' another joined in, until all were chanting the refrain crescendo. 'YOU GO! YOU GO!' Noog, with his quick mind, was not going to be easily out-witted by the people he once despotically ruled.

'If you do not accept me back in the tribe, I will make the disease re-manifest,' he declared over the din.

'We do not wear vests. You go now,' one urged, as the tribe all began checking what they were wearing.

'Oh... you id... I never said you wear vests... I said... I make d-i-s-e-a-s-e,' to which Noog made exaggerated gestures of illness, limping and groaning, then said 'come back.' He fell on his back, then rolled around in spasms, and finally lay there, still: it was quite a dramatic enactment of death, and we all engaged vicariously. Then, he leapt up, said, 'Me can do,' and started to waggle all his fingers in mock mysticism, rather like a conjuror, his little red eye growing wide, and his furry body moving up and down as if he was floating: the tribe recoiled in horror. They lowered their spears, and one was about to genuflect his knees to supplicate for clemency: but two others stopped him, though they regarded Noog with suspicion. They then began frantically gibbering amongst themselves, the usual scene of pushing and arguing ensued, until one was suddenly thrust forward. He stared at Noog, frozen in fear, for this ex-leader, though fallen, still had a lofty aura when confronted alone, and so the others began prodding the involuntary interlocutor in the back with spears to instigate his speech. He wrestled with his self-control, and eventually managed to blurt out hurried words.

'You help us?' he whispered meekly, and tried to push himself back into the throng, but his attempts were met with a line of thrusting spears to ensure he stayed put.

'Yes, it was *me*. ME! Ha, ha, I risked my n-o-b-l-e life to confront the a-w-f-u-l wrath of the very very, er, ha, ha, big, and, very very dangerous, d-r-a-g-o-n. I managed, with my great strength and bravery, ha, ha, to subdue the very very awful d-r-a-g-o-n, who, er because of my irrestible persuasive powers, is quite, er, nice now, ha, ha. *Me*, your splendiferous lea...' I could see Noog was lapsing in to his old condescending habits, with his self-aggrandizement, strutting around with his chest thrust forward and little snout in the air, and was re-electing himself as leader, so I gave him a sharp nudge accompanied with a stern glare of disapprobation. Noog looked at me and instantly understood, then continued. 'Er, yes, ha, ha, I have helped you, as, mmm, a fellow tribe member would.'

'Dragon nice?' another asked, from the crowd.

'Yes, you clow… you, ha, ha, fellow tribes people,' said Noog, 'I ordered them to be, er, *nice*, ha, ha, and they obeyed.' He folded his arms across his expanding chest, raised his head, and boldly looked out to sea, with such august histrionics, I could not refrain a wry smile. The Un-Masked Tribe stared long and hard at Noog: the memory of his leadership unpleasantly lingered, how they had been continually arbitrarily insulted and ordered. There then ensued a vigorous debate amongst them, a further examining of their new found health, and pointed at Noog while ignoring him. They eventually ceased their dispute, and turned towards Noog. One was suddenly pushed out of the phalanx as wonted: he appeared most annoyed at being volunteered: he tried to sidle his way back in as was the custom: but someone gave him such a mighty shove, that he hurtled forward in front of Noog.

'Er,' he said, turning to his companions for support as the little fellahs tended to do: they frantically waved their hands at him, urging him to continue. 'Er,' he said, then conveyed to his friends a pathetic pleading expression. The tribe reciprocated by erratically waving their arms, pretending to push their stranded tribe member towards Noog. He reluctantly turned back to face Noog. 'Er,' he submissively murmured: then it went silent, as he stared at his ex-leader in awe… The tide shushed along the shore, pervading the salt air with its ancient song, and there followed unbearable anticipation as to what the Un-Masked Tribe had decided would be the fate of their previous autocratic leader.

'Oh, for pity's sake!' shouted Noog, 'Spit it out, you foo…'

'Noog!' I interjected, and shook my head in a most disapproving manner. Noog looked at me, emitted a sigh of resignation, and continued. 'Er, ha, ha, there's a good fellow, ha, ha, you can do it. Come on, speak to your lead…' Again Noog peered at me, and I replied by shaking my head and wagging my finger, gestures that suggested he must check his attitude, and start a fresh. 'Er, ha, ha, you can speak to... er... ha, ha... er... h-a... h-a,' then Noog became silent, and the ex-leader and the tribe's person both stared at each other... The wind blew through the palm trees... Every one stood there... motionless... like a tableau vivant... I could feel myself growing impatient.

'Tell him what your name is!' I exclaimed to Noog.

'Er, ha, ha, oh yes, my name,' Noog said, giving me a rather sheepish grin. I nodded towards the tribe member, further urging Noog to tell him his name. Then Noog, in the most humble voice I had ever heard, while eyes firmly fixed on the ground shuffling his foot in the sand, mumbled, 'My name is... N... N... Noog,' he finally managed to force out, after much effort. He emitted a deep breath of relief, then lifted his head in supplicatory shame, waiting to be berated by the tribe. The tribe stood stared at him, their mouths dropped, incredulous to what they had just heard: they had always taken it for granted he was called *leader*: I verily thought they were about to assail him: but, other than the occasional muttering between themselves, nothing happened. This nomenclatural revelation from Noog gave the tribe's person unprecedented courage to address him: he inflated his chest, redolent of his ex-leader, and, in a stabbing motion towards Noog's chest, forthrightly pointed at him.

'You no leader!' The tribe's creature imperiously glared at Noog. For a moment Noog glared back, and I thought he was about to issue a vicious retaliatory diatribe: but he looked at me, and I raised my eyebrows in admonition and lowered my palm to the ground as a gesture to remain calm: then his lineaments became more benign.

'No, I am *not* your leader,' he firmly stated, though he gave a discernible shudder. The spoke's person smiled at this, and turned to look at his tribe.

'He no leader!' the tribes person exultingly declared to his comrades: they reciprocated with broad grins and erratic nods of approval. The tribe's creature then turned to continue addressing Noog.

'But, you be with us. Yes?' he said with confidence. Noog fidgeted, trying to keep up with events.

'Er, yes, I would like that,' Noog humbly replied, but it was difficult to ascertain if he was feigning obsequiousness for sounded uncertain. However, this mollified the tribe: for they moved aside so I could see my companions, who did not waste any time in walking towards the broken urn, and drinking the dregs of Sacradia as a precautionary measure.

During our preparations for the long flight back to Firkin Forest, we cautiously watched the tribe: and they, in turn, monitored our every move. With seaweed, we scoured the plane until it shone; and then lubricated all moving parts with coconut oil. We were allowed to plunder the forest for victuals and fresh water: and, although food was not as abundant as in The Forest of Life, we acquired adequate provisions. As we struggled to pull the plane from the soft sand onto the firmer sand ready for takeoff, Noog appeared: he walked towards a wing, and, without prompt, began assisting us: other tribe members saw Noog's actions and modelled his behaviour: soon there was a large group of Un-Masked Tribe pushing our beautiful aluminium aircraft, it was easy to push the light metallic bird over the sand.

'Thank you for coming to help us,' Noog said, as he pushed on the wing with all his might.

'That's okay... It was incumbent upon me to provide remedy... It was...' but then I trailed off, for I really wished not to dwell on such ignominy.

'You did not have to help. You risked your life coming here. My tribe will be eternally grateful,' Noog said, and held out his paw.

'You no leader,' a tribe's person said, and prodded Noog in the back with a claw, which made him wince and turn around.

'No, I'm not your leader, you mor… er, fellow tribe's person: but, er, ha, ha, I be with you,' he painfully grinned. This seemed to pacify the tribe's person, and on they pushed together. Once the craft was on firmer sand the craft effortlessly rolled along. 'I think that's enough,' Noog advised.

'You no leader,' another said, as the Un-Masked Tribe continued to push. Me, the crew and Noog, broke away from the plane, and together, we watched the tribe push the craft towards the sea.

'Do you think they will stop?' Jenny asked, smiling at the spectacle. The tribe then began arguing amongst themselves and prodding each other: one or two tried to break away from the plane, but others pulled them back. Then some began to push the metallic bird whilst others pulled: the aeroplane ground to a halt. A further altercation ensued until they eventually came to a reluctant agreement which way to go. We stood and watched them push the plane all the way to the ocean's edge: and then, to our relief, they halted. Small waves smacked against the under carriage, and the wheels quickly became immersed in water as the tide quickly came in. This induced me and my comrades to frantically run to the plane, as the tribe stared blankly at the sea. We quickly climbed into the cockpit and began pedalling the plane away from danger. Noog watched at a distance, his paws on his hips, shaking his furry head in disbelief.

'Keep pedalling!' Argon shouted. 'We're going home!' And so, in unison, we pushed down hard on the pedals. The spinning wheels accelerated, furiously rotating kicking salt spray up into our faces which invigourated us more as the sea air flowed through our lungs and hair. Then, our stomachs dropped at the rapid ascension as the exciting feeling of suddenly becoming airborne imbued us. Up we lifted, higher and higher: and soon we were soaring over the crystalline carpet that was the vast aquamarine ocean, our faith now resting on the durability of our physiques and the aluminium machine…

28.

The Journey Back

At first, the crossing was calm and straight forward. We kept the geostationary Purple Star directly in line with our tail as we skimmed along the clouds. The plane operated smoothly: we made good headway and began to think we would cross without incident. The sun gradually descended below the watery horizon and the Purple Star shone a refulgent mauve behind us. The swirling sky was bedighted with twinkling stars, blinking approval at our successful quest. I felt a blessed relief that all the tribes were now free of disease. All that remained was the return journey to our home, Firkin Village.

Suddenly there was a distant rumble. We naively thought nothing of it at first and boldly pedalled onwards. From out of nowhere an angry pelting storm hit us: it raged as before: and, although we were more experienced now and rode the gale instead of battling it: for a long while we lived in fear of plummeting to our deaths. The raging weather seemed interminable and implacable: but the preceding journey had exponentially increased our piloting dexterity and stamina, and the thought of home spurred us on...

Needless to say, it was with profound joy that we eventually saw Nubile's welcome coast on the horizon. It felt good to have traversed and survived the fretful sea once again; it exalted my spirit and rendered me with a fine sense of achievement. It was agreed that we would land in the clearing by the stream, as before, so we could have much needed rest for the lofty ascent of the precipitous mountain.

We were pleased to receive a friendly welcome from Nubile's tribe, and, also, from The Forest of Life's tribe, who, since the thawing of Ice Mountain (which had now metamorphosed into Green Mountain), had been freely communing with each other: now it was much easier to pass over the mountain range, a gateway had opened between the tribes. As for me, I stayed in the background: I had accrued enough opprobrium, and felt I made the tribes uncomfortable: also, it seemed there was a tacit agreement between me and Helena, that in this particular region, we stayed aloof of one another: probably due to my blatant behaviour around those tempting women who reminded me of Nubile. I was curious to understand why Nubile's tribe had never interrogated me concerning my knowledge of her: after all, she had disappeared without trace: but their censure was aimed at her for disobeying tribal laws: that was all their concern: and, annoying as it was for me, they simply had no curiosity, even though their consciousnesses had expanded to discover the domains beyond their demesne and learn of other people existing beyond the darkness: they conveniently blotted out the past, and forgot her: for, it was assumed, she had contravened former sacred customs and traditions, which, to them, displayed arrogance and disrespect. They had no inclination to honour her as an explorer: but regarded her as an individualist who thought she was above the law: hence, to them, she no longer existed, even though it was now apparent the territories beyond their village had not proven to be treacherous: and, of course, partially because of her, it was now unavoidable that they must vigourously revise all their folk lore and fable. I yearned to inform them of her intrepidness, and how new relationships for their people had transpired, and they probably would not now have access to the bountiful Forest of Life if it was not for the remarkable courage of Nubile: I yearned for her to be remembered and esteemed appropriately. She *was* the catalyst for our sudden appearance: and it meant they had no choice but to accept there *was* life outside the confines of their purlieu: they *had* to adjust accordingly. Nubile had imposed reality on them: truth is immutable. Argon made further promises that it would not be long before other people from our tribes would visit: he promised to trade our engineering skills for their raw produce: and most seemed excited at the prospect of these unprecedented transactions: although some mooched around uncomfortably, wondering what the future now held exposed to the outside world: the unfamiliar can be daunting.

Even though the mountain had now dramatically changed in aspect, surmounting it would still not be easy. The sky was clear, and the wings hung on warm thermals: but it was as usual a fairly steep ascent: although, thankfully, not the insurmountable icy mountain of yore. After great effort, we flew over the peak, and a breath taking sight lay before us: Green Mountain's lush vegetation spread outwards connecting with The Forest of Life: hardly any distinction could be made between the two. We dangled over the dingle like a dexterous dandy lion clock, gliding smoothly, descending along Green Mountain's impressive topography: it was evident that our adroitness at handling the machine had improved immeasurably: we were at one with each other and the craft, a complete unit working in perfect harmony. We confidently swooped down the mountain side over The Forest of Life speeding towards the margin were the formidable The Desert of No-Night began: we became intoxicated with speed; it was positively exhilarating utilizing the momentum of the descent and zipping over the verdant crowns of leaves that vibrantly rustled and hissed a radiant energy.

We decided before traversing The Desert of No-Night, to land on its scorching edge to acquire viands. We descended with aplomb onto the margin of The Forest of Life that was the prologue to the vast expanse of boiling sand. I leapt out of the cockpit and wasted no time in cajoling Helena into the cool leafy shade. We gathered a myriad selection of victuals in baskets: hazelnuts, almonds, Brazils, apricots, pears and pineapples etcetera. We then lay under a mango tree and casually ate some of the delicious fruits and nuts. After surfeiting on forest's providence, and now my conscience was clear, I felt most amorous. Helena detected my mood, pleased that my mind was eased, sidled up to me: we were like two billing doves wantonly courting in the verdant woods.

When our passions had been abated, we cosily slept in each other's arms: we slumbered long, deep and sweet: we became leaves, the wind, and the waters of the perpetually moving stream: we were the gentle rain that fell, and the lush grass that grew: we danced over the crown of trees, swirling with the clouds, skipping effortlessly up and down Green Mountain: we knew only love, profound and eternal...

We woke simultaneously, opening our bright shining eyes at the same time, viewing each other, gazing with deep glowing orbs: her eyes were the soul of love: she was a divine spirit, and I worshipped each sacred beat of her heart. Our psyches mutually expanded. We smiled and kissed in bliss: our souls suffused in ineluctable and ineffable pleasure: our foreheads touched, the tips of our noses: the perfect symmetry of love...

'You two, are you ready for taking off?' It was the gruff voice of Barney. He had lineaments of earnestness, as well he might, for the desert was a redoubtable obstacle. We all starkly remembered the previous arduous crossing. Reluctantly, we rose, and carried the baskets to the plane. We loaded all the provisions that the comely forest provided. The crew then exchanged unprecedented gestures of most solemn encouragement: for this time, we would not have the magic life-saving water of Sacradia to bail us out of trouble! With an intense silence, apart from the leaves eerily moaning, and the clank of our feet on the fuselage, we boarded the plane.

The desert crossing was hellish: our water supplies rapidly depleted; the heat perished a large part of our food supplies; and we all became tremendously vexed again. An argument ensued whether we should turn back to The Forest of Life, or even land in the desert, to rest in the meagre shade of the plane, and, when we had recuperated, try take off again, or resume the rest of the way on foot. Inside the hull of the craft was like a baking oven: the intense heat rendered us utterly disorientated: our bodies were pushed to the limit of endurance. I became nauseous with heat sickness, delirious, and started mindlessly ranting, 'Please, not the pit! Not the pit!' which rather disconcerted the crew, for they remarked later that, whatever 'The pit' was, it was certainly a place to be avoided: and Barney commented that I had been a most wretched soul, pervaded with the most lamentable and profound fear imaginable: my visage twisted as if some alien being was trying to extricate; my voice chillingly unrecognizable, and the words spoken... dreadful and ominous... I was shocked and dismayed the underworld had starkly manifested itself once again in my psyche, for I had deemed that my now clear conscience would have nullified its abhorrence: but its re-emergence would always ensure that I could never be complacent, that I would always be aware of the possible dualities of being, and that I must always be vigilant in order to ensure benevolence, so when I eventually die, I am not consigned to that dreadful place. Indeed, my memories of suffering in chthonic were so stark, that when I had fully regained my wonted demeanour, no one desired me to elaborate on my experience. Consequently, the atmosphere inside the cockpit, even without the searing heat, would have been most oppressive: the crew regarded me with anxiety, as if they were sharing their space with a demon of the underworld: I could feel their aloofness, their discomfort at my presence: and I brooded as I pedalled along wondering where I belonged. I derived no solace from Helena, she was a divine being: and, right then, we had nothing in common: she would not understand the horrors I had seen: I did not want her to know: and it bothered me that she could, from now, look upon me with doubt, like she had seen a side of me she was unaware of, a dark side, I had now, unwittingly, flagrantly displayed...

On we pedalled, and I made a somewhat miraculous recovery. Images of Firkin Forest compelled us forward. However, we were quickly approaching the limits of endurance. 'I think we should land in the desert,' Kelly finally uttered. It was what we were all thinking.

'Agreed,' Jenny concurred. Argon was about to trim the flaps when a violet amorphous fleck appeared on the horizon.

'Is that...?' Jenny queried. We peered at the nebulous silhouette rapidly approaching us.

'Yes, it looks like that peculiar bird,' Helena stated.

'We can ask it for a tow,' Argon claimed.

'It was not very forthcoming before,' Barney replied.

'It's worth a try, 'Argon yelled, 'We've got nothing to lose... These are desperate times!' We eagerly watched as the creature veered from side to side whilst rapidly approaching. Soon we could see iridescent feathers shining in the searing heat. Before long we were overshadowed by its massive bulk, and though we felt intimidated, we were grateful of the shade.

'It's that little flying thing again. I know. What is it doing? I

410

don't know. Ask it. What are you doing, little flying thing?' the incredible creature asked.

'We're trying to get home. We're very tired. Could you help us?' Jenny shouted.

'What did it say? It said it's trying to get home and wants us to help it. What should we do? I don't know, what do you think? Ask it why we should help. Yes, good… Why should we help?'

'Because it's the right thing to do,' Kelly shrugged.

'What did it say? It said it's the right thing to do. Do you think it's the right the thing to do? I don't know, what do you think? I asked you first. Mmmm, we could help. Are you sure? Mmmm, yes, let's help the little flying thing. Tell it we will help. No you. No you… Erm, we will help… but then we will eat you.'

'Eat us! Are you joking?!' Barney cried.

'Are you joking? Yes, I was joking. You better tell it you were joking. We are joking.'

'I'm glad to hear it,' Argon nervously laughed.

'Ask the little flying thing if it liked your joke. Did you like my joke?'

'NO!' I yelled.

'If you don't like my joke, we won't help you, will we? No we won't.'

'Ha ha ha, that was some funny joke,' Jenny exclaimed.

'Is it laughing at us? It sounds like it. Ask it if it is laughing at us. Are you laughing at us?'

'No, no, not *at* you, but *with* you,' Helena cried.

'What did it say? Not *at* but *with*. Not *at* but *with*? Yes. Oh…'

By this time we were beginning to feel conversing with this creature was futile. And though help did seem tantalizing close, I was about to inform it we would take our chances landing in the desert. But suddenly it grasped our tail with its mighty beak. At first I truly thought we were about to be eaten, but suddenly we frenetically propelled forward. The warm air incomprehensibly zipped past us. The desert below was a yellow blur. We had to tightly close our eyes at the oncoming rush of arid air. The giant creature instinctively followed our previous trajectory simply by extrapolating on our current course.

We all thrilled at the appearance of The Dead Forest up ahead. The giant creature, assuming this was our destination, without warning, suddenly extricated its tight grip and veered away, soon becoming a violet amorphous fleck in the distance. We glided unimpeded and could not believe our good fortune at receiving aid from this peculiar creature. The Dead Forest signified the near completion of our journey and the harbinger of our homely village beyond it.

29.

Regression

The Dead Forest had been waiting for me, patiently, resolutely, knowing full well I would return: it seemed to welcome me, the darkness, like a familiar friend: and yet my soul cringed at the thought of being immersed in this sombre place: my being, my nature, was at odds with itself, ambivalent, half wanting the black womb of nothingness; the other half crying for light. While the crew celebrated at the arrival of the land mark, I whimpered, my soul cleaved in two, one half pulling one way; the other half pulling the other: oblivion versus being. I desperately looked at my dear crew members, and a sudden flash of inspiration revived me: pedal for them. I bit my lip, battled against ennui and despair, and pedalled on: a strange atavistic duty compelled me, edified me: do not abandon your beloved people. The Dead Forest was fast approaching, and we all began pedalling in unison: the rest from physical exertion afforded by the peculiar creature gave us fresh impetus, our effort became more exerted, more urgent: we were only too well aware of The Dead Forest's relentless pull: and the thought of this incited us to profoundly reach within to muster every mote of exertion.

We did not baulk, but determinedly pedalled onwards, over the still lifelessness of its gaping maw. The Dead Forest unfolded its black void underneath us: and we sensed its bottomless pit. Terrified souls inflated eyeballs: we tried to resist: but The Dead Forest knew we were vulnerable, and it was hungry for lost souls: it easily drew us downwards, into the deep dark nothingness of its lifeless heart: it licked its pallid lips at the prospect of tasting human despair in its shadow lands. Our souls grieved as our bodies succumbed to its attraction: the plane sank further and further: we feebly pushed against the pedals, legs burning, satiated with anxiety: oh, the increasing despair when one is aware the dark void is near... Suddenly, the under carriage was ripping up black foliage: the dried twigs and branches cracked and snapped as the plane ran headlong into the darkness. SMASH! The craft flipped over, thrusting through the canopy, into the heart of darkness. CRASH! We heavily hit solid ground, and like rags scattered amongst the darkness.

We all lay still, separated from one another, surrounded by nothing but ominous darkness... It was deathly quiet... deep... deep in The Dead Forest...

The dark void is ancient,
Older than time itself,
Immutable, and still...
There is nothing to hark
In stark darkness.
Try and shout loud,
But the sable shroud
Will kill the sound.
The isolation of its nothingness
Will chill the most ardent of spirits.
It is uncompromising, unyielding,
And inextricable to the desperate,
The deluded and rash:
Distorted perspective here
Will lull you deeper into its cold nether world.
Virulent sable roots profoundly ramify

Into the brain of the uninitiated:
Enter, spread and pervade with despair,
And deliverance is not there:
Your wretchedness will multiply,
And you will be devoured
By your own bile.
Your guile and cunning is useless here:
Darkness is not duped:
Sham is shaven away;
No safe haven for mendacity.
No matter how stubborn
Or tenacious you adhere to duplicity,
No matter how impervious
To veracity's call,
In denial its brilliant light will startle you:
For, in the pitch darkness,
All are exposed.

I lay bruised, bloodied and battered. When I had somewhat recovered from the impact, I was acutely aware of an imposing stillness and inscrutable blackness. I called to the others, but my voice absorbed into the void: I sensed my words reached to no one. I was aware of a surrounding mockery, as if a joke was all I had ever been. A paroxysm of fear exploded in my stomach: I found myself to be a child in my father's house...

'But father, I want to be a wrestler: I have no desire to become an elder.' My father responds by angrily punching the table: I shake in intimidation.

'I am an elder, my father was, and so was his: Argon, you will not disobey tradition. You must train in the ways of the ancient council... It is your ineluctable fate,' my father peremptorily commands. I look up at his towering frame and his stern countenance admits no refusal: but, the vision of sitting in the class which trains future governors, being told what to say, and how to think, fills me with dread.

'I wish to choose my own destiny,' I defiantly say. His eyes light in silent fury.

'I can permit no such thing. Get out of my sight,' he yells. In my despair I go to the annual fair where the wrestlers are holding an exhibition. I watch the crowd cheer as two giants perform feats of guile and strength. I mimic their moves, the way they strut, the intensities of their visages, and add my own individuality. I would make a great wrestler, one all the tribes of Firkin would admire and respect. Suddenly, I feel a heavy hand over my head which sends me reeling, knocking me to the ground. Dazed, I look up, blood trickling from my nose.

'Get to the house!' my father commands. Not long after, due to my father's influence, physical pursuits are decreed illegal in Firkin. An official edict is issued: *The council, after due consideration, has decided that the practising of martial arts are a threat to the status quo of the tribes, encourage unnecessary aggression and potential injury: so, henceforth, will be summarily prohibited.* I think this hypocritical, for elders would carefully select individuals, and train them as their security guards: and security invariably makes their physical presence felt if there is any dissidence. I am coerced to attend classes and learn the ways of the elders. I bitterly sob at night in profound frustration at continually being made to repeat elder proverbs: *The elders know all. The elders are infallible. The elders are regal and eminent, exalted amongst the common people.* Any expression of opinion is met with acute scorn and rebuke: this fuels my need to vent my feelings: so I retire to the margins of the woods and practice wrestling moves with imaginary opponents. My body grows thick and strong: and I disguise my musculature by stooping and looking feeble: I inwardly battle to maintain my identity, even if it means concealing it: and I resign to reticence as a means to least conflict...

The childhood memory incited profound weeping, and, as I sobbed, my body convulsed in spasms: I felt a redolent pain gush from me that had long laid dormant: my angst spewed into the open void, leaving me deflated. Suddenly, I was aware of my carnal cage replete with physical discomfort, and... the uncanny darkness; I lay bruised and haggard in the eternal tomb of The Dead Forest: I groaned, as I felt the aches and pains of my mortal frame. I quickly prepared to die, and suffuse into the void...

The aluminium wreck of the plane glowed in the dark. It began to shimmer and vibrate, then lifted from the ground and hovered in the darkness. It started to transmogrify into a spherical blob of metal. A curvaceous torso took shape, round breasts, then elegant limbs sprouted from it... and... before long... the Silver Woman emerged. She drifted to where the weeping Argon lay, philanthropically smiled upon him, and gently took his hand: his body instantly healed, and he raised himself from the ground. She quietly led him through the darkness, to the centre of The Dead Forest...

I lay in a contorted heap on the floor, in semi-shock at my broken state. I fought to open my eyes: but when I managed to coax the lids open, it made no difference. I licked the blood that sprang from my gums. I mustered all the strength that remained and called out to the others: but the profound darkness voraciously swallowed my feeble cries. I was aware of myriads of hateful eyes sneering at my condition, pleased to witness me lying there, as if other's misery was their only joy. I had an overwhelming notion that I would never be found: a stark fear assailed me...

I am in the field working with my father and mother: we are assigned to cultivate the land. We are costermongers; it is our job to provide the tribes with vegetables. As a young child, I had enjoyed the freedom and the fresh air: but, now I am older, I also enjoy and appreciate the importance of school. As a tribe member, I am taught the rudiments of mathematics and communication skills, the importance of civility, and to never question the elders' wisdom: then, we leave school, and continue in our parents designated roles. I have shown aptitude in all lessons, and am eager to continue my education: I want access to the esoteric knowledge of our tribes: I want to be an elder.

'An elder! Jenny, love, you have learnt to till the land. It's what our parents did, and theirs... Besides, amongst other things, and, I am sure you have noticed, you are a girl! It is out of the question.'

'But, I want to assist in the progress of our tribes: and, I was top of my class, surely that qualifies me,' I say.

'To assist in... progress! Progress? Jenny, please, get the silly notion out of your head.' Father is still jovial at this stage: but, I can see my future life, stooping over cabbages, and it fills me with disconcertment.

'Mother, father, I want to go to elder school!' I plead. Mother becomes most earnest, and tightly grabs my arm as she fearfully looks around to see if anyone is listening.

'Jenny, you must get the idea out of your head... Please!' She says the *please* with such profound supplication, that it truly puzzles me what bothers her. I walk from the fields in disgust, trampling over carrots as I go. I feel cheated and it induces profound indignation, for I have worked with diligence and competence all my brief school life: I see my future life torn asunder by bigotry: and with nurtured determination, I march straight to the school where my teacher is conducting a lesson. I boldly march right into the class room, my heart beating zealously: the teacher stops in mid-sentence, and his mouth drops; the class, intrigued as to what might happen next, silently watch me walk to the front. I am, by this time, overwrought with emotion.

'I want to go to elder school!' I blurt, and glare at him defiantly: perpetual obsequiousness while being condescended to has taken its toll. The class emit sighs of incredulousness; the pedagogue's countenance burns in thunder, and he erratically rings a large brass bell from his table. Suddenly, security come rushing in: two grab my arms, another tightly clasps me around the neck: and, as I kick and scream, physically usher me back to my parents. Security drag me all the way to my room, violently push me inside, and the door uncompromisingly slams behind me. I hear my parents receive a violent reprimand; security bark orders, and hurl threats as to what would happen if such insubordination re-occurs: then security leaves. It is deathly quiet for a while, other than my mother sobbing. Now my impassioned effusion has subsided, I wait in nervous anticipation for the consequences. Startled, I watch the door of my room suddenly swing open: my father, visage pallid and aghast, eyes stone cold, intently glares at me. In his hand, he has a spade, and he slowly raises it towards me.

'Come here,' he quietly says: and the calmness and assuredness of his voice compels me to do so. I walk to him, feeling shame that I have caused such trouble for the family. He gives me the spade; I deferentially take it from him. 'Go outside, dig the field, and do not stop until I say.' Such is his unprecedented peremptory tone that I comply without question. I gloomily walk to the field with the spade, and dig all day and night, limp hair and clothes sodden in the rain, lathered in mud, tears of lament suffusing with the waters from the sky, laboriously digging... digging... digging...

I begin to sob: and I palpably feel cumbersome pain that had lain and cankered for years float from my body and dissipate into the void; woe pours from the core of my being. Suddenly, I am gazing into the preternatural darkness of The Dead Forest. Tremendous physical discomfort comes flooding in: my bones and muscles are twisted in dire agony. I choke as I weep at the unpleasant sensation of damaged corporeality...

Through the darkness came a glowing figure: she was comprised of refulgent silver light, and she floated towards the prostrate weeping Jenny. The Silver Woman hovered above her and benevolently smiled. The glittering entity gently took Jenny's arm, and her pain instantly assuaged as broken limbs healed: the Silver Woman led Jenny through the pitch shadows, to the centre of The Dead Forest...

I am sprawled on the ground, disorientated, tattered, torn and worn out. With much effort, I lifted my heavy head, and stare into the profound pitch darkness: I thought I heard distant voices emanating from the stillness, negative comments aimed at me: 'Shut up bore... Go away pest,' and other bizarre attempts at tormenting me. I blank them out, and call to my friends: but the words are swallowed by dark derision, and sniggering, evincing an unwholesome pleasure at my woeful cries. The thought of being forsaken in this dreaded gloom for eternity instigated tumescent fear in the pit of my stomach; ineffable despair swamped me...

I am a boy, holding a wooden sword, and standing before the swaggering figure of a young Gorky. 'On guard,' he arrogantly says, and thrusts his own wooden sword into my abdomen: I wince and fall to the floor.

'I was not ready!' I remonstrate, examining the welt of blood with a silent mounting anger.

'Is that what you will tell your enemy?' Gorky scoffs, smirking at my apparent discomfort.

'We have no enemies in Firkin,' I say, standing up, and brushing myself down, intensely descrying him and his sword.

'What about security?' Gorky says, thrusting the point of his sword into my ear lobe, and splitting it. I cry out in anguish, and spring backwards. I check the wound with my fingers, and feel a long and deep laceration running around the edge of my ear: then I look at the blood on my hands… and scowl at him.

'Talk like that will get you detained,' I say, momentarily hating him, as he gloats at the red rivulet pouring down my cheek. I want to complain at his rough sparring methods, and how he insists on not blunting the swords: but my pride won't let him know I am bothered.

'Barney, you are always whinging. On guard!' With lightning speed, Gorky swings his sword and it zips across my face just missing my nose. The fool is going to take my eye out: and a growing rage inside me prevails: I am determined to inflict revenge on him. I stand on my back foot, parrying the occasional attack, deliberately thrusting my sword slowly, trying to draw him in, so I can launch a lightning riposte. Sure enough, he begins to become over-confident, strutting and posing, circling me in contempt. I feign dismay: and he becomes quite cock-sure and fancy. He casually lunges forward: I anticipate his move and beat him to the thrust: he walks straight onto my sword point, square into his chest: he recoils in horror.

'Take that!' I bitterly and sarcastically retort. With surprise, he looks down at his tunic: a garnet wound opens upon his chest, dying his raiment vermilion. His horror turns to fury: for he cannot tolerate humiliation. He stares at me: his eyes illuminate in determination and focus. Although I am a tincture unnerved at his dramatic change of comportment, I return his glare with a contemptuous grin. He springs onto his toes and begins moving more urgently. Our sparring session has now turned nasty: I know I am in for a hard fight, he won't be duped by that particular ploy so readily again, and now I must really buckle down.

'What is the meaning of this!' a vehement exclamation manifests from somewhere. We both disengage from the trance of combat, and turn to the voice: and, still with the residue of fury in side of us, for a moment, defiantly glare at... an elder! Our rambunctiousness soon subdues.

I am locked in a cell... The interrogation... repetitive suggestions... manipulation... thought control... I will be a blacksmith... Blacksmith's work is good... Fighting is bad... I will not answer back... I will obey without question... I will enjoy blacksmith's work... I am lucky the elders are so kind and generous to give me another chance... The elders are good... On and on, day after day, relentless, until I scream in primeval chaos...

Aaarrrggghhh! My being opened, and a torrent of substantial anguish poured forth: the core of my soul cried out in pain as torment gushed out into the black void that was The Dead Forest. I wept and wept until I felt empty. My limp body ached, muscles drooped, bones grated against delicate nerve entangled flesh. Woe and misery had come upon me, encased in my throbbing ribs like a solitary forlorn caged bird...

Through the darkness came the refulgent glow. The resplendent Silver Woman hovered above the tattered shadow of Barney smiling with profound love. She benevolently took him by the arm: and all his angst and injury dissipated. He rose, and she quietly led him through the darkness, to the centre of The Dead Forest...

I lay with my legs folded underneath me. I verily thought I was dead: it seemed impossible that my body had survived such an impact: I had heard my limbs snap. In a daze, I peered into the darkness, and knew it was an eternal black void. Yes, I remember this place… You hold no more fear for me. I am ready this time.

I am in the market place. We have traded some garments for Jenny's vegetables. My mother is a seamstress; and my father weaves the finest fabrics. Every alternate day, I attend the market with my parents, trading clothes for other items. I dreamily look beyond the tumultuous throng of people, to the borders of Firkin village, through the vistas of the permitted woods, onwards, to the prohibited forest, and further still, to that categorically forbidden place, the so called, *Dead Forest*. My mind became obsessed with that place, the place reputed to circumscribe our habitation, a place where no one is allowed to go. Every day my curiosity grows. Why is it called The Dead Forest? If it was a forest, how can it be dead? Why will I die if I enter it? If it is so dangerous, how can we safely live circumscribed by it?

'Mother?' I say.

'Yes, Kelly?' she replies.

'Why are we so confined in Firkin Forest? Why is it not permitted to venture further afield?' I ask. My mother gazes at me with such acute disapprobation, that I feel extremely undermined; my sense of self worth mitigates under her critical eyes. She then continues to barter with customers, as if I had not spoken. Hence, I deem it apt to solicit my father concerning our immobility: he responds similar to my mother: and I feel effrontery at the slight. Do they think my curiosity will vanish just by chastising me? I decide to choose a time when they will not notice I am gone.

I venture into the permitted forest, moving closer to its outskirts, towards the perimeter fence. I hide behind a tree, and wait: then, I espy two security guards patrolling the area. I wait until they move away, and, at the optimum moment, I run to the fence. I quickly scramble over it, into the prohibited forest.

I keep running, and do not look back. I feel stark consternation: for being surrounded by unfamiliar and *apparently* hostile ground is acutely intimidating: but I do not stop: I have to go near The Dead Forest, just to take a look. I hurriedly and fearfully run towards the irksome mystery and the woods seem to reproach my audacity: strange trees leap out and warn me to turn back before it is too late; weird faces in gnarled bark sternly stare and chide me as if I am a naughty little child: the forest loudly buzzes its relentless criticism; the staccato yapping of acute cynicism is rife through the rapidly oscillating leaves; the woods are thoroughly disgusted at my impudence, and the trees erratically sway from side to side, madly waving their branches around in a bid to deter me: but my heart swells in defiance, and on I run. Then I begin to feel an uncanny dreadful vibe emanating ahead. As I approach the vibe steadily increases and it takes me all my self-control to moderate dread: but I am absolutely determined to satisfy my curiosity, so defiantly on I run, which slows to a walk, which slows to a reluctant saunter, but on I push....

I feel profound trepidation as I approach the fearful Dead Forest: to our tribes, this forest engenders the epitome of terror: those who enter ineffably die. I stare deep into its awful darkness, and it seems to go on forever... pitch black nothingness... but... I sense something else... beings... creatures... strange... diabolical. I have no intention to enter: and yet stubborn inquisitiveness compels me that I must. I try telling myself to go back to the safety of my cosy hut , and that I have at least seen The Dead Forest really exists: but I find myself involuntarily walking into the dark...

I aimlessly wander into the blackness for time incalculable. Psychosis attires me in primeval chaos. I lose my identity, find it, and then lose it again, on numerous occasions. I cackle uncontrollably, sob, scream, beg for mercy, and run wild in the pitch dark. I have horrific imaginings seemingly of an extraneous influence, for I felt incapable of such bizarre notions from my own limited experiences. Vestiges of sanity tenaciously struggle to exist. I deem the darkness inextricable, lunacy seductive: but I must cling to my wonted identity! The Dead Forest incarcerates my oppressed soul and uses the essence of my being as a play thing: my soul is worthless, except for the cruel darkness's amusement value...

Then, when all my hope has finally vanquished, and I feel myself sinking into ineluctable despair, light seeps through the gloomy vistas, and the air begins to smell fresh.

I find myself at a purling moat: beyond that, is a vast glowing desert stretching to the far horizon, like the one in our forbidden fables. I feel elation at finding our incessant propaganda ill-founded: I had entered The Dark Forest, and left, alive. My beloved equilibrium returns as the sun pours down on me: I remember who I *was*; although, who I *am*, has slightly changed. My contented contemplation soon turns to dread as I realize I have to return the way I came if I ever want to see my village again. I am uncertain if I can endure the horrific ordeal once more: The Dark Forest stretches beyond the limits of volition, leaving one vulnerable and exposed to terrifying influences: that most precious of motivators, hope, is extirpated. I stare intently into the inscrutable darkness: for some inexplicable reason, I abandon all caution and re-enter.

The journey back is far worse! What becomes of my precious wits, I cannot recall. All I know is that a young innocent girl should not experience the abject horrors contained therein. I am shocked and bewildered at confronting gruesome images of the starkest and vilest kind: they are as palpable as the hand that touches my face. Beings void of humanity. Demons manically feast on raw fear. Absolute hate glares from the crevices of shadows. But there is something in the soul, an immutable and indomitable spirit, call it love, call it what you will, but the demons could not harm my essential being, and this enabled me to traverse the tenebrous darkness... It seemed fortuitous that I stumbled out of the darkness onto the margin of Firkin Forest... a permanently changed girl...

The sun! Oh the blessed sun light! The sun shines down on me: but I view it differently now: its golden glow has preternaturally altered: I comprehend the nuclear fusion within its heart and dance with the photons. I look around the prohibited forest which is the outer most region of Firkin, a forest that previously I would have not dared venture into, a forest that had previously appeared so belligerent: and now seems most innocuous, calm, and welcoming: indeed, haunted, but imbued with uncanny benign stalwartness. I quietly glide past the sedate trees: the bustling leaves seem to express approval and congratulate me. I reach the perimeter fence. I take one last look to where I had been: I stare with heightened awareness through the vistas and emanate a profound satisfied smile.

I easily evade security, back into the village: I stealthily glide like a ghost. How my parents and friends do not notice my altered aspect is either because they dare not say, or I manage to conceal it: nevertheless, I gradually become more distant from everybody: eventually rebuffed, and, finally, isolated. Rumours circulate that I am a zombie, or a witch, which only makes me feel more awkward and aloof. I find myself continually monitored by the elders: and, it if was not for Argon displaying an amorous interest in me, I would have been permanently reviled, to the point where I would have to flee Firkin Village, re-enter The Dead Forest, and take my chances in the desert.

Argon says he could tell I was different to the others, and that is what drew him to me. Eventually, when he wins my trust, I tell him of my adventure, and how there *is* something beyond The Dead Forest: this incites his own curiosity to sally forth: and, after much tenacious wrangling with the council (although he never mentions my escapades), he finally acquires permission to venture in. He vanishes for some time, and I grow concerned he is permanently lost in The Dark Forest; and so, although reluctant, I resolve to rescue Argon. As I am preparing, he returns. I recognize in his lineaments my own experiences. He is rigorously de-briefed, and advised that he should boast of his exploits and most fortunate to cheat death: viz. the official story is maintained, and thus, ensuring the enthralment of the tribes. He receives great accolades for his 'unprecedented journey': which makes him become most humble towards me, with frequent private bashful apologies.

Here I am in the familiar darkness again… that place… yes… I remember… It's only darkness… But I wince as I attempt to move, for my body is direfully dysfunctional, and I prepare to expire in the dark…

The effulgent glow of the Silver Woman benignly envelops Kelly. The Silver Woman benevolently smiles down at her, and carefully takes her arm. Kelly's physical pain instantly assuages, and she raises Kelly to her feet. The Silver Woman safely escorts her through the darkness to the centre of The Dead Forest…

Where am I? Ugh, my body! How can something so frail elicit so much pain? I stare into the pitch darkness, trying to detect the others; I attentively listen for their congenial sound: oppressive silence. Never have I been surrounded by such stillness… I am afraid to call out lest I alert the awful creatures of the gloomy dark: and yet I must if I am to find my dear friends. 'Are you there?' My call is swallowed by Stygian darkness. The blackness, like an inscrutable wall, profoundly chills my exposed soul. I sense a demonic hatred nearby: it ridicules everything I am: it exists only to torment me, has studied me all my life, callously assessed my weaknesses, and has been plotting my destruction. Fear (potent energy) flows through by body, and induces my hair to vibrate: the demon drools and licks its wart infested lips.

I am tending my garden, secretly collecting herbs. Gorky has persuaded me to attend covert meetings where certain people of the tribes gather in order to tell forbidden tales concerning our past culture. At first, I am reluctant and nervous: but, I become enchanted by the tales of our ancient lore... especially the stories of witches, powerful women, who had the ability to destroy, or create. Unbeknown to Gorky, I become friendly with people who belong to an even more surreptitious group: I begin to attend meetings of the most abstruse knowledge of our ancient tribes... witch craft. I want to learn the art of medicine, to propagate well-being. I concoct potions that enable me to transcend the limits of my wonted consciousness. My senses sharpen: I feel so alive! But, I always practice secretly: only a few select members attend the private soirees. Of course, if the elders discover us, we would be executed, or banished into The Dead Forest. I want so much to tell Gorky, particularly when the disease mysteriously manifests: I believe I have a potent remedy: but the select members expressively forbid me to even mention magical powers. What is the use in having ability if one is afraid to use it? I cannot even administer the potion on myself, for my sudden good health would only raise suspicion. Then, Gorky says he is leaving to find a cure. No! Don't go! I can save everybody! But I do not! I let the poison spread through the tribes' veins: there is no way to covertly administer the potion, for it has to be at specific time of the night under the full moons, it means painting ancient symbols on the infected, and chanting recondite incantations: I cannot perform the cure without revealing my ancient craft: and so, in despair, I watch as my lover leaves, probably never to return: and, I slowly deteriorate, while hearing each painful groan of the village.

In the diseased delirium of fever, all manner of incubus assail me, greasy abhorrent monsters of the deep, weird and ugly 'faces' suddenly appear from nowhere, twisted snouts touching mine, grim demented sickly 'eyes' stare right into my soul: they spit in my face and issue vile abuse in an unknown tongue: they try take possession of my soul with their primordial energy: I can only lay helpless as they run amok and desecrate my equilibrium. I could never tell Gorky the horrors that I have seen, for it would only make him uncomfortable in my presence.

The bitter regret and disgust at my cowardice overwhelms me: I had the power to avert the extinction of my people, but did not use it; I did nothing. Oh, what a stupid decision I made! I sob and sob, and my wails are voraciously received by the shadow lands; I weep bitter lamentations and the darkness drinks my woe.

The silver glow that is the divine lady hovers over Helena. Like a candle flame in the darkness she came. She looks benevolently down to Helena and smiles a preternatural love. She gently touches Helena's arm, and the physical and mental anguish instantly mitigates. Helena stands, and The Silver Woman leads her through the darkness to the centre of The Dead Forest…

I open my eyes, and there is no difference: indeed, dense darkness comes flooding in and presses against my orbs like a malignant miasma: I feel the pitch dark engulf my soul and an indescribable malaise overwhelms me. An ominous silence torments the essence of my being. I am here again, a place I never wanted to return to. In dire physical torment, I stare defiantly into the thick shadows: but the darkness suddenly reaches into my head and I silently scream...

'On guard!' I lightly thrust my wooden sword, it glances past Barney's stomach: and he makes a great show of the supposed injustice. I laugh at his childish display, and am eager for him to stand up so we can resume sparring. Barney angrily rises to his feet, looks really uneasy, and fumbles around cumbersomely as I prance around just out of range. I begin to feel light on my toes as my confidence mounts. I bide my time watching his slow movements. I obviously intimidate him: and know it will not be long until I score another strike. I bully him with my superior moves. Suddenly I lurch forward and find the point of his sword jab into my midriff: excruciating agony shoots through my body.

'Take that!' Barney gloats, glaring at me, displaying scorn I cannot comprehend. Seeing his disrespectful mien incites my indignation: and I switch on, eager to wreak my revenge: I completely focus eschewing complacency and assimilate his every move: I am alert and ready. Our duel absorbs us: and we do not notice a disgruntled spectator.

'What is the meaning of this insolence?!' We both turn in annoyance, and glare straight in the eyes at who is there: but soon deflate when we see an elder with a face like thunder: Argon's father. I am unceremoniously marched to an interrogation hut...

Beatings... Torture... Torment... Cruelty... You will never practice fighting again... You are violent and a nuisance to society... You have an evil character... You will be a waterboy... A waterboy is a good job... You will thank the elders for this opportunity.... No! I am Gorky! I will choose my vocation... Pain... Torture... Torment... Cruelty... You will no longer practice martial arts...

You are the waterboy... Waterboy is good... It will help your iniquitous character... Do as we say and you will be happy... I am Gorky! I will be what I choose to be! Beatings... Torture... Torment... Cruelty... You are the waterboy... Who are you? I am G-O-R-K-Y... I... I... I... will... be... what I... c-h-o-o-s-e... t-o... b-e... Beatings... Torture... Cruelty... Torment... You are the waterboy... Who are you? I... am... Torture... Pain... Who are you? I... am... Torture... Pain... You are the waterboy... Who are you? I... I... I... Torture... Pain... You are the waterboy... Who are you? Torture... I... am... w-a-t-e-r-b-o-y... Who are you? I... am... the... water... boy...

I am an emotional void. I speak to no one. I submissively carry the water from the stream to the tanks. I quietly walk past the elders forbidden to make eye contact: so I bow my head and stare at the ground. Security monitors me. I slowly repair the psychological damage, and say inwardly, I am Gorky. My wonted spirit returns and I begin to feel a burning defiance. Eventually, after much wrangling with him, I persuade Barney to carry on practising martial arts in private. At first, he is horrified at the suggestion: but I tell him, if he is a man, he must exercise his free-will: for a person is not born in chains.

I am Gorky! I begin weeping... My soul dilates: and I satiate The Dead Forest with misery...

A silvery light imbues my consciousness. 'Gorky, you have endured much hardship. Your intransigent courage during torture took you to the brink of death. When you eventually displayed obeisance, you perpetually castigated yourself as feeble and weak. Although you decided to surreptitiously defy, you felt yourself to be a coward at your initial overt deference... Cry Gorky... Let the pain out... Let the forest swallow your misery... Exercise the anguish you have harboured so long...'

30.

Linked

I felt myself pressed up against a warm woman: her pert and ample breasts spread over my pounding chest: and I instinctually cupped my hungry hands around her firm round bottom and urgently pushed her into my aroused groin. 'Who is that?' Kelly asked, startled.

'Er, it's me, Gorky,' I feebly answered: and I felt her gently wriggle free.

'Argon?' she said, 'where are you?'

'I am here, my sweetie,' said Argon nearby: and I heard the rustle of clothes as they embraced.

'Gorky? Is that you?' It was my Helena. I held out my arms and felt her sensuous hair brush past my finger tips.

'Helena, I'm here,' I eagerly said, and like the two opposites of a polar magnet, we attracted and coalesced. I moved my eager palms over the curves of her waist and hips and pressed against her delicious femininity. My hungry mouth searched for hers, my lips passionately caressed her warm moist mouth, and like a skein, we passionately ravelled around each other.

'Are we all here?' Kelly solicitously asked, and we all affirmed our presence. 'Good… I suggest we all hold hands, and don't let go,' she admonished. So I gladly held onto Helena's hand, and felt it glow with warmth. I held out my other for somebody: I was relieved to be holding the dainty hand of a woman. 'Who is going to lead the way?' Kelly inquired.

'Whoever is at the front,' Barney replied.

'How do we know where the front is in this pitch darkness?' Helena retorted.

'Who is at the ends of the chain?' Kelly asked. Nobody replied: so, after brief dialogue, ascertained we were holding hands in a circle. 'Follow me,' Kelly confidently proclaimed, letting go of my hand: hence, I found myself at the end of the line.

We walked through the intimidating pitch darkness but derived solace from each other's presence: Kelly negotiated the trees with remarkable aplomb: I had nothing to do but be led along, striding through the empty darkness, past the lifeless trees (the presence of which one was uncannily constantly aware of).

As we trudged along it grew more and more monotonous: we blindly groped through thick darkness for ages: and, such was the urgency to extricate from this dreadful place, no one spoke...

We walked and walked, staring blankly into thick night, and I was so glad of Helena's tender hand in mine leading the way. I smiled as I felt the gentle pulse of her fingers as our hands melded into one. I listened intently for her breath, and every now and again she would issue a little sigh of frustration at being continually engulfed in darkness: on such occasion, I would squeeze her hand gently to assure her that I was with her, and would not allow, under any circumstances, anything bad to happen. She was my woman, my life, my light, she had taught me how to love when I had become cynical of human nature; she had elevated my spirit, purged my soul of baseness and wickedness; she had made me a good man: I owed her my life, for she had saved me from hell.

On we walked, through the inscrutable Stygian darkness... on... and... on... nothing but dense night and the doleful presence of dead trees reminding us of frail mortality. I began stroking Helena's hand with my thumb, and moving my hand in hers to enhance the sensation of female flesh. She was warm, alive, and I could feel balmy red blood pump through her veins; I sensed a feminine life force oozing through her pores.

We walked onwards into the maws of moribund darkness... on... and... on... and the pitch nothingness sneered at my face, thirsting for my madness, lusting for my demise: the looming presence of the sable void enveloped me, and my mind battled not to project into its awful emptiness. I ardently imagined the female form attached to the hand I was so contentedly caressing: Helena was a rare beauty: her body was flawless; her eyes were a safe haven; her demeanour, her movements, all evinced a special woman, deep and sophisticated.

In The Dead Forest the darkness is relentless... On we walked, deeper, into opaque night. I was on the threshold of fear and panic: I could sense the obtrusive coldness of lifeless trees yearning for me to become one of them: a strange parasitical deathly presence pursued us, always there, always reminding us it was watching. My hand was attached to a feminine life force: the female form before me was gracefully moving, fluid, undulating, woman's smooth flesh, sensitive to a stroke, legs, her legs, lady's long luscious legs, shapely legs attached to voluptuous female meat, fresh and tasty. My free hand, hanging flaccid in the dark, became concupiscent, bicep twitching, hungry hand need feel of woman, hungry hand want to sprawl all over bouncing female flesh, explore woman's body with free hand. Palm started at her hip, and slid over her waist, hand moved up and down, up and down, waist and hip, waist and hip, feeling her delightful curve, marvelling at sweet shape; then, hand moved under her tunic and over her exquisite stomach, palm moved in circles for a while, enjoying the warm smooth sensual sensation of bare skin on bare skin; then, it slid around to rest on her exquisite bottom, and felt the movement of her delicious buttocks as she walked, hand squeezed each cheek gently, and I became a little more excited; searching hand then moved around, eager to slide up and cup her round breasts, her comely home domes: salacious palm moved upwards, over her garment, stimulated at the prospect of cupping her perfectly shaped bosom: soon, hungry hand was there, and gleefully and carefully pushed onto the material until it could feel her soft plump mammary, fingers gently closed around the cloth so as to perceive the delectable flesh underneath: I felt her erect nipple protrude through the thin cotton like a button, impressed into my hungry palm. I was almost euphoric she was allowing my hand to roam freely around her body: and so hand became most aroused at the prospect of sliding inside her knickers. Before I knew it, hand was sliding downwards, towards panties, anticipating soft pubic mound, down below skirt hem, up onto thigh, mmm, delicious thigh, hand stroked up and down smooth warm thigh for a while, delaying entrance into knickers; hand wanted to first feel pudendum through cotton of underwear; hand moved slowly onto gusset.

'Gorky, this is not the time!' Helena finally complained, gently pushing my reluctant hand away: alarmed at hearing her voice, I broke from my sensual reverie, hand unwillingly let go, and was relegated to contiguity with the empty shadows.

On we walked, carefully picking our way through the lifeless foliage that hung limply. After a while, Jenny began a pitiable whimpering; her whimpering turned to sobbing; then she began wailing uncontrollably; which then turned to manic screaming: she tried to break free from the chain: luckily, she was holding the firm hands of Argon and Barney: and, try as she might, she could not extricate their grips.

'My, she is strong,' Argon remarked.

'Calm down love,' Barney tried to assure. 'It's okay. We'll soon be out of here.' We listened to her in the inscrutable darkness: and her lugubrious tones enhanced the doleful oppressive atmosphere: an eerie sable sadness hung in the stagnant air. Eventually, she began to calm down: but, as we continued to walk, every now and again, she would issue a little whimper.

'We're doomed,' she would say under her breath: and her calm resignation made my stomach turn: but I knew if we were to escape, we must control our fear.

On we walked, the dark silence diligently watching our every move as we traversed through its nothingness. Kelly uncannily seeming to know the right direction incited my curiosity: she evoked my admiration at how boldly she led the way. 'Is everybody okay?' she would confidently ask now and then: and, one by one, we would exhale our meagre voices into the infinite darkness, trying to gain solace that human ears were receptive to the sounds.

On we walked, and memories of my previous encounter with this immutable dark force emerged: I recalled the horrors that had induced stark insanity: but it seemed I had become, to a degree, inured to the ordeal, though my consciousness was more sensitive to the environment: and, consequently, my over-active mind became acutely aware of protracted temporal-space…

I was certain, on my previous encounter, I had not been trapped here so long. Nevertheless, I derived great consolation knowing I was linked to my lover; her beautiful presence offered monumental succour. 'Helena, I love you so much,' I earnestly said.

'I know, Gorky, and I love you,' she dutifully replied: and my soul was illumined to hear her sweet voice.

On we walked, into dense interminable darkness… We became concerned at Jenny's condition, reflected in her non-sequitur speech.

'Dig, dig, mud, mud, mud, dig, dig, dig,' she would say, then whimper some more.

'Why did you try and put my eye out?' Barney blurted into the darkness.

'Are you talking to me?' I asked.

'You know I'm talking to you!' he shouted.

'Control yourself!' Kelly demanded. 'Do not let go of each other's hands!'

'You could never control your sparring!' Barney exclaimed: and his vehement words disappeared into the pitch nothingness.

'You were always a wimp,' I ardently rejoined: and the words blunted in the void.

'A wimp, am I? You, you… Where are you? Let's settle this once and for all!' he yelled: and his anger was voraciously swallowed by the shadows.

'DON'T LET GO!' Jenny suddenly screamed: and her primal energy made my eyes widen in horror: her voice touched the pit of my soul inducing tremendous awareness of life: the purport of her words shuddered The Dead Forest's sable roots.

'You've all been great friends to me,' I said, weeping at the thought of losing my dear comrades.

'Keep walking!' Kelly urged.

'Nothing is going to happen to any of us, Gorky,' Helena said… Her voice, had I heard it till now? I swam ecstatic in her gorgeous tones; how divine her sweet sound, so soothing: I imbued into the harmonious vibrations, the corona of her delightful feminine spirit.

On we walked, into the never ending tenebrous darkness… on and on… trudging past cadaverous trees that emanated an awful morbidity, a perpetual mnemonic of what we would become if we did not emancipate from their ghastly grasp. We walked on in silent resolve, pushing onwards into relentless gloom. My instincts compelled me to shun death and move towards light: my senses became sensitive to the female life force who's hand I was so pleasurably feeling: I could hear each rustle of fibre that clothed her body; I could hear thin cotton rubbing against her; I could hear the tops of her thighs deliciously stroking each other; I could hear her breathing, more heavily now, as we had increased our effort: I helplessly fell into a state of erethism: my mind became acutely attuned to her moving shape: an overwhelming prurience excited me: I recalled roving hand, how it was detained before it reached into her panties to gain access to her gorgeous vagina, her sweet aroused moisture, where smooth soft creases unfold like a flower around her shiny pink erotic entrance, aaahhh, moistened love tube, mmm, her sweet moan when my throbbing manhood slides deep into her gorgeous girl gash: my urge became insupportable. 'Helena, if I hold onto your shoulder, could you relieve me with your free hand, and I will do the same for you?' I whispered into her ear. I was eager for my lusting fingers to sensuously suckle on her lower-love-lips and explore her silky erogenous zone; while feeling her gentle fingers caress, touch, stroke up and down my sensitive shaft, inflated bulb, and full sack.

''Gorky, are you for real?! We're in the middle of hell, and all you can think about is sex?' she exclaimed. I did not want the others to hear: but it was too late: I became the source of much amusement: they laughed at my lasciviousness: and called me such names as, animal in the dark.

On we walked, through ghoulish night... on and on... and I shuddered as a grotesquely twisted branch scratched past my face as if it was trying to ensnare me in its grim grasp. In disconcertment I rapidly recoiled, deliberately pushing my nose near Helena's long silky hair, and leaving it there for a while, breathing in her fragrance, my heart beating relief at her miraculous existence. The deathly darkness was trying to tempt me into its ostensible serenity: but I knew its ruse, for once lulled into its spurious blissfulness, the horrors of disequilibrium would ensue. I imagined Helena's breasts bouncing as she walked, the graceful movements of her firm round bottom, and her damp tender pleasure hole, as a means to distract me from the mundane darkness and its determined petitions. I considered auto-eroticism as a way to distract me and defy death: but something in my spirit admonished me that it was an inappropriate time, and that I must master my carnal desires: I heard my soul say, 'Ejaculate into this dark void, and propagate with succubus: then be forever tormented by fiendish offspring.' And so I shuddered, walked on, pride increasing, for spirit was stronger than primitive desire.

We walked through the darkness, on and on... I could feel the darkness becoming increasingly frustrated as I shunned its solicitations: it grew more intense in its manic lust to ensnare me: it concentrated all its efforts, focusing on me, glaring in fury. The miasmic air grew more stagnant, like decaying corpses: and we all began to choke in dismay. The sound of frenzied bluebottles seemed to be swarming around our heads: though not one did I feel. The Dead Forest tried to breach our brains and induce eidetic images of horror: the incipient imaginings of mangled torsos tried to enter the sanctum of my mind: grotesque death and gore tried to claw its way into my heart: the entire history of intense human suffering was crying out for attention: it verily chilled my bones, and I could not ascertain if we were walking deeper into the merciless maws of pitch darkness, or its anger was due to the fact we were slipping its grasp and approaching its perimeter. All I knew was, being perpetually aware I was inextricably attached to Helena, who was attached to my cherished friends, bestowed upon me inveterate morale, and compelled me onwards, slicing through dense wads of darkness and vile evil...

In the Dead Forest, time itself does not exist...

We walked and walked... past supplicating desiccated trees, but try as the infinite void of eternal darkness might, our irrevocable life forces could not be subdued; together we negated the sable imposition of The Dead Forest; all encompassing darkness did not permeate our psyches; the cores of our souls shone an intense glow: for the blessed love in our hearts would ever illumine the most abominable of environments...

'I thought I saw a flicker of light up ahead!' Kelly exultingly cried. Our hearts simultaneously leapt in excitement at the prospect of sunlight and the fresh wind on our faces. Our steps quickened... My brain vibrated with The Dead Forest's ghastly shriek of, 'N-O-O-O-O!!!' and I felt a diabolical force try coerce me back, pulling at my stomach, which sickened me to the core: I desperately fought against its vile influence, yearning for aureate day: the crepuscular curtain ahead became more perceptible; through the vistas I gratefully descried a glimmer of precious light, and my powers to defy the darkness increased manifold.

As we urgently walked towards the beckoning vistas of sacred light, I began to see the adumbration of my beautiful woman manifest before me; her exquisite outline became discernible: soon, her glorious colours were restored: the epiphany of an angel...

31.

Ipse dixit

'People are not capable... of not reacting to injustice, of not protesting against oppression, of not striving for the good society.'

Nelson Mandela

Then, we were on the margin of Firkin Forest! Our squinting eyes flickered, gradually letting light in as we became more accustomed to the day. The sky was a refulgent sapphire; the glorious luminescent firmament arched overhead, and streaks of brilliant white clouds shimmered and glowed. We all stared up at the effulgent ether, satiating our souls with its divine light. The sun, fiery yellow orb of intense heat, encrusted in this magnificent numinous vault, shone its glorious majesty as the most precious of existing jewels. The breeze benignly blew a welcoming song gently over our ears. Lush verdure rapidly vibrated emitting the primeval sough our souls had evolved with. Our voracious spirits sucked in the emerald forest's ancient life force, immutable nature in harmony with our psychical rhythms: we instantaneously became replenished, our starved senses feeding on the forest's beauty.

I turned to Helena, who was gazing around at the day in wonder. The sunlight ensured I could see every detail of her face: my soul warmed. Her comely countenance had matured a tincture: and, if it was possible, she was now even more endearing. Her

441

wide eyes shone deep lustre: and the life force within indicated profound sensitivity. My heart thrilled as she turned to me and smiled: it was a smile of the upmost compassion, of profound empathy, of the most pure altruistic love. Mine own eyes opened wider to drink in her essence, and her sacred soul came rushing through my orbs, replenishing my hungry spirit with sweetness and light: revitalizing energy pulsed through my veins. I smiled and gazed into her sunlit eyes in order to display my sincerest gratitude, attempting to reciprocate my own burning love for her. I took a step towards her and held out my arms; she took a step towards me: and then we were hugging each other tenderly. Joy and relief flooded over me as I held my precious woman in my welcoming arms. She buried her head into my neck and shoulder, her dainty arms coiled around my waist, and she held onto me; my arms encircled her, and I lowered my head onto her shoulder, feeling her long silk hair against my cheek: and there we stood for a while, cuddling each other, loving each other. Simultaneously, we moved slightly apart to look at each other's face: we reverently scanned each other's lineaments, and gazed into each other's eyes: we were as one. I gently kissed her soft open mouth: and we delicately stroked and touched each other's face…

We looked over to see Argon and Kelly embraced in a similar manner that evinced that they may never let go of each other; Barney and Jenny were beaming at each other as if nothing else in the world existed…

After the lover's re-union, Argon announced, 'Well, I guess it's time we walk back into the village.' We all nodded in concurrence, and began to head towards Firkin Village. I held Helena's hand, Argon held Kelly's hand, and Barney playfully piggybacked Jenny on his broad blacksmith's shoulders. It felt good to see the familiar woods of our origins, the place where we had grown from children, the place that was once our only world. We walked through the congenial trees, pleasantly contented to be amongst the ancient forest of our youth. I stroked some of the venerable oaks and helms as I past. I knew them by sight, for many times had I climbed them when younger: and it was re-assuring to know they were standing upright and strong, the same as they always had done.

On approaching Firkin village, we began to hear a faint unwonted noise which we could not explain. We walked closer to our village, and a hive of unprecedented activity from beyond the trees was sullying and drowning the sound of the breeze bathed leaves. We sensed a great change had come about the village: that's if it *was* our village. The familiar layout of the forest suggested it was: though the whole atmosphere had altered in aspect: the peace of the surrounding woods was desecrated with strange persistent noises, the hustle and bustle of perpetual and relentless motion.

As we attentively walked on, the noise grew louder: and we became greatly concerned lest some evil had manifested during our absence. We hurried our steps, and became most surprised when the woods prematurely ended: were a thick phalanx of trees had once been, there was now a clear open space, a *concrete* floor, and an unrecognizable imposing set of edifices towering before us. We stood in amazement at the scene in front of our incredulous eyes: our village was gone!

Argon sighed lamentable resignation: and we all nervously stared at each other, uncertain whether to enter this new world. Argon issued another sigh, and stepped forward: we followed, anxiously gazing around, utterly disorientated and perplexed at what lay before us. We walked straight into what had been Firkin village, daunted by the new ambience. We then saw people who were dressed in strange new clothes: they moved with more aplomb and purpose: and, though it was piquant to descry more self-assuredness, I was unsure if I approved of the urgency. We walked nervously onwards, anticipating ourselves to be apprehended at any moment: but the people seemed utterly pre-occupied with their own lives, and so they hurriedly walked by as if we were not there. The new buildings were constructed of finely hewn stone, and towered high into the sky: we craned our necks upwards, and were induced with vertigo: we could discern the tops of them rocking slightly in the wind. Now unsure of our objective, we continued to walk down a... *street...* and noticed something called... *electric lamps...* which were strewn along the... *pavement...* A little boy suddenly cried out, 'Look at those funny people, mummy!' And the woman, who was initially going to chide the child, stared to where he was pointing: and her mouth then dropped in disconcertment. She grabbed someone who was walking by, who became most agitated and flustered at this intrusion: determined to get his attention, she erratically shook his coat and stuttered out some incoherent words while pointing to the rag garbed crew. 'Unhand me madam!' the man regally proclaimed: but she continued to manically pull at his coat.

'Them! Them!' she eventually managed to shout. And so, most vexed, he turned to see where she was pointing.

'By Jove!' he exclaimed. This man then attempted to intercept someone else by standing in their path: it was another man, rather in a hurry, and apparently late for something: the oncoming man frantically tried to negotiate the obstacle before him, zigzagging this way and that along the pavement: but the other man skilfully anticipated his swerves, and successfully halted him.

'What the devil is a matter?' the accosted man finally exasperatedly exclaimed.

'Look!' the other man said, pointing at the conspicuous

crew... Soon, a little group was gathering: and, rather than address these people, we tentatively walked onwards. As we aimlessly wandered through Firkin village... *city(?)*... an increasing crowd followed, stirring at the dishevelled prodigals; they followed us, pointing and chattering, as we ambled through the streets: us, in the mean time, were still wondering if we were in the right place: for we were as lost as when we had been in the vast desert. Intimidated, we aimlessly slunk along ... *pavements*, past... *shops*... and other strange buildings. The group of following people behind us grew, and so did the volume of their speculations, muttering to each other as we limped on, beginning to think we may be assailed at any moment. We hastily turned a corner, trying to evade the crowd behind us: and, before us, much to our intense joy, was the familiar sight of Barney's workshop, which had seemed to have been preserved (later we learnt it was a *museum* in memory of the intrepid travellers): its ancient architecture looked most incongruous to its modern surroundings. We quickly walked to this familiar edifice: outside, we noticed a brass plaque with an engraving of our plane and names of the six crew members: 'Gone but not forgotten.' Alongside the workshop were three large aeroplanes standing proudly, far superior to the initial design. 'They work by petrol engines,' Kimtiv said, smiling. 'I hope you do not mind, I thought the place could do with a few changes.' A gathering crowd now stood before us, garbed in fine silks, lineaments of pleasure and amusement at the scruffy travellers in dirty rags. They then began to cautiously move forward, as each waited patiently for a turn to shake our hands in order to congratulate us.

Suddenly a loud siren sounded, echoing around the city streets. The people, as if in a trance, shuffled towards the plaza. We follow, curious to see what compels them thus. A huge throng are turned towards a balcony, all heads raised in expectation.

Then, a figure appeared on the balcony dressed in shimmering scarlet with giant epaulettes and wearing huge military headgear that covered half his face. He was wearing a beard down to his waist and his long hair dangled loosely about his head: but I instantly recognised that sneer of cold command: Gavin!

'I am president Machiavellian of Stupidia. You will cheer everything I say. Hail the president!' Gavin manically yells.

Hail the president!' the crowd dutifully reply.

'I decree from 12 o'clock tonight all Stupidians will shave every hair on their body off. Repeat after me, baldness is good!' Gavin screams.

The crowd, in enthusiastic unison, yell back, 'Baldness is good!'

'Hairiness is bad!' Gavin imperiously shouts.

'Hairiness is bad!' the people cry.

'Those found with a single hair on their body... or more... will be intensely ridiculed then summarily executed.' With this, Gavin menacingly pointed at the docile throng.

'What about you?' a tiny voice shouted within the crowd.

'Who was that?' Gavin yelled.

A group of people circumscribing a small girl nervously move away from the culprit and eagerly point accusingly at her.

Take her away!' Gavin ordered. With that four identical burly security guards- now armed with what I later learnt are machine guns- march the child away. The intrusion of the guards seemed to induce even more attentiveness in the throng.

'Hail the president!' Gavin bellowed.

'Hail the president!' they cheered.

'Those with blue eyes will not be permitted to talk with those with brown eyes. Hail the president!' Gavin roars.

'Hail the president!' they replied.

'Because of the fortuitous appearance of Vimtit, or whatever her name is, we now have the technology to easily fly to other lands: and with our newly acquired powerful weapons we can

446

encroach and colonize. We can then enlighten other tribes about our superior ways. Hail the president!'

'Hail the president!' replied the throng.

'How can we unite and invade if brown eyes can't talk to blue eyes?' one woman shouts to the president.

'Yeah, and I have brown eyes and I am married to someone with blue eyes,' another yells.

'Take them away!' Gavin barks, and eight identical burly security guards march the two dissidents away.

'You will succumb to your desire to obey. Hail the president!' he screamed.

'Hail the president!' they rejoined.

'No, no, repeat the succumb thing,' he impatiently mumbled.

'You will succumb to your desire to obey!' they shout.

'No, no, *you* will succumb to *your* desire to obey,' he bellows.

'You will...'

'STOP! When I say *you*, you will say *we*,' he angrily declared.

'Ugghhh?' they all shrugged.

'Hail the president!' he yelled, giving up on that line of brainwashing.

'Hail the president!' they obediently replied.

'I have awarded myself a medal for having lots of medals. Hail the president!' he snarled.

'Hail the president!' they yelled, but one or two were becoming slightly impatient. Gavin detects this, momentarily loses his composure, then quickly changes tact.

'I feel... I feel cake is upon us!' he manically declared.

'Hoorah!' they exuberantly cry.

'Loads!' he grins.

'Hoorah!' they ecstatically cheer with arms raised in approbation.

'Massive!' Gavin screams, his face turning purple.

'Hoorah! Hoorah!' the crowd jumps up and down.

'I will shower you with cake!' he ardently reiterates.

'Hoorah! Hooray!' The crowd is now acutely exuberant.

'Hail the president!' he screams one last time, but the crowd are dispersing at the great news. There is much dancing and celebrating in the streets. Gavin, a lone figure, clings hold of the balcony, and with baleful contempt, peers at the disappearing throng.

'Should I zap him?' Kimtiv says.

'Here we go again!' Kelly remarks.